Tomas would sometimes consider, in later years, whether there were any chance that his Fate might have been different. Yet only upon occasions of the greatest rarity would he so wonder, when gripped by a black and somber mood, perhaps, or perhaps when drifting through the gates that link wakefulness to sleep--or Elfland to other realms. For Tomas had grown to understand, far better than most mortals, that to questions about Fate there are no true answers. There are only, sometimes, reasons.

The Rhymer and the Ravens

The Book of Fate

A historical fantasy by

Jodie Forrest

Published by **Seven Paws Press**

POB 2345
Chapel Hill, NC 27515-2345 USA
919-929-4287; FAX 919-929-7092
http://www.intrex.net/alyra7paws
email: alyra@intrex.net

Printed in the United States of America.

First Edition
First printing, November 1995
Second printing, March 1996

ISBN 0-9649113-0-2

Library of Congress Catalog Card Number 95-71656

For information and orders of additional copies,
contact Seven Paws Press at the above address.

Cover art and Dragonship logo by Mike Roig.
For information contact Mike Roig at 2001 Mangum Ct.,
Chapel Hill, NC 27514, tel. 919-933-4947.

Maps drawn and lettered by Jodie Forrest.

For my husband Steven, with love.

CONTENTS

Acknowledgments

My gratitude to the following people and organizations for their assistance, encouragement and support: Joyce Allen, Antero Alli, Alpha Video, Aurora Restaurant, Baker-Johnson Book Printing & Binding, Linda Belans, Cyril Beveridge, Frederica Bishop, Moacyr Bittancourt, Thomas Brown, Jan Burger, Seth Callen, Tom Capps, Captured Live Studios, Chris and Katie Chamis, Sky Chandler, Art Chansky, Mary Charlton, Andrea Cohan, Lisa Creed, Richard Curtis, Mike Czeczot, Rebecca Dalton, Chris DeBarr, Patricia Domingo, Ben Dyer, Stephanie Erickson, Peter Estep, Sue and Tommy Field, Glenda Fletcher, Ginger Gaffney, Jean-Michel Garcia, Jose Carlos Garcia, Duffy Gilligan, Kristen Gooch, Dave and Donna Gulick, Kathryn and Scott Hammond, Paul Hansen, Julie Harris, Diana Hawes, Sam Heaton, Camille Hildebrandt, Tom and Mary Kay Hocking, Bill Janis, Catherine Jones, Prudence Jones, Steve Jordan, Gloria Karpinski, Dan Kee, Louise Kessel, Odie Kimball, Cedar Koons, Eric and Beth Kurtz, Alphee and Carol Lavoie, Rob Lehmann, Edson Lodi, Catherine Losano, Carolyn and Richard Max, A.J. Mayhew, Tom and Jan McCall, Jennifer McKee, McIntyres Bookstore, Michael's Bar and Grill, Jessica Mills, Dominic and Judy Miller, Mary Moss, the Music Loft, Rick Petty, Beth Rambo, Michael Rank, Susan Rice, Ruth and John Rocchio, Bob Roig, Sara Romweber, Savannah Scarborough, Bruce Scofield, Ken Schonwalter, Skylight Exchange, Phyllis Smith-Hansen, Marian Starnes, Sting, Trudie Styler, Sue Strassle, Sarah Walker, Callie Warner, James Weinberg, Sue Williard, Henry DaVega Wolfe, Cindy Wyatt, Rosales Wynne-Roberts, Tom Young, Donovan Zimmerman and my extended family.

My husband, Steven Forrest, wrote all the lyrics to the songs except the one in Chapter Fifty-Four, which I wrote.

Affectionate thanks: to Steven Forrest for composing our rock opera, "The Rhymer and the Ravens;" to the other members of our Dragonship band, Linda Smith, Michael Chandler and Mike Roig; and to Theresa Arico, Carol Chandler and the Valkyries Dance Troupe. More thanks to Robert Griffin for his musical inspiration; to my friends Poppy Z. Brite, Carol Cole Czeczot, Sinikka Laine and Meg Switzgable, for a multitude of reasons; and to all the kind people who've supported us by coming to Dragonship's "The Rhymer and the Ravens" shows.

Finally, I am deeply grateful to Robin Williamson, modern bard extraordinaire, for his prompt and gracious encouragement to borrow the line: "To be a poet, it is said, one needs a harp, sorrow, and a wandering road."

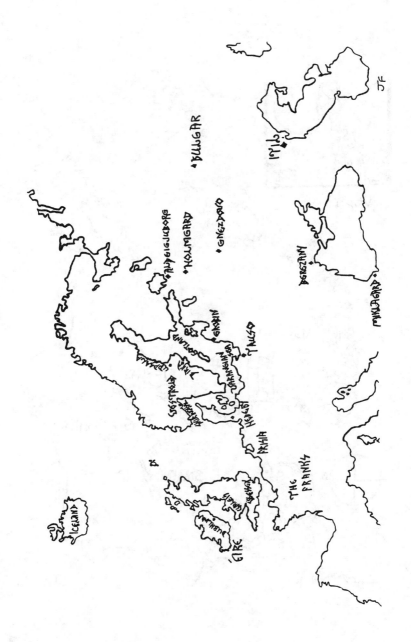

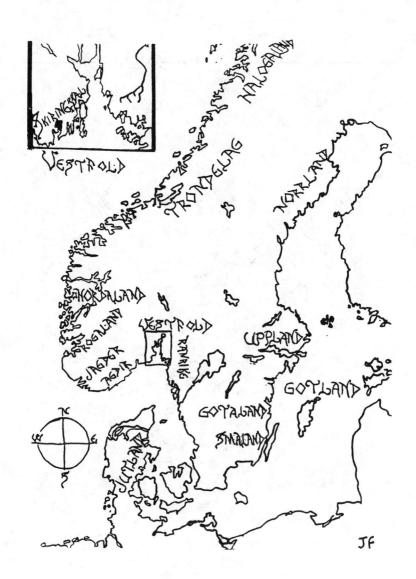

SCOTLAND

GALLOWAY

NORTHUMBRIA

EIRE

DUBHLINN

THE
IRISH
SEA

MERCIA

NORÐ

WALEIS

SÆFERN

THE RIVER

CIPPANHAMM

ALFRED'S
CAMP

WESSEX

JF

Tomas would sometimes consider, in later years, whether there were any chance that his Fate might have been different. Yet only upon occasions of the greatest rarity would he so wonder, when gripped by a black and somber mood, perhaps, or perhaps when drifting through the gates that link wakefulness to sleep--or Elfland to other realms. For Tomas had grown to understand, far better than most mortals, that to questions about Fate there are no true answers. There are only, sometimes, reasons.

PROLOGUE: TOMAS AND SIGRUN

In the kingdom of Vestfold, in what would become southern Norway, early in the month of Sowing-Tide, 871 A.D., Christian reckoning.

A jab in Tomas's ribs. Another jab, and the insistent push of a small warm hand. There was rustling, then muffled thumps, as of furs tossed from the bed-closet. Cold air struck his bare shoulders.

"Wake up, Tomas!"

Sigrun Bjornsdottir's voice. The flower of the court: Sigrun of the swaying walk and the thick amber braids that fell, when unbound, to the deep curves at her hips. Of the frozen blue eyes that had followed Tomas of late, when her husband Torbrand's attention turned elsewhere.

Ah, yes: Earl Torbrand himself was elsewhere these several days past, errand-riding for King Harald. More than Sigrun's eyes had thawed. Tomas sat up and reached for her.

She cuffed his arms away. "The bondmaid says Torbrand's home early. *Get out!*"

Tomas slid out of bed and into his clothes. Should Sigrun be found with a lover, Torbrand could kill them both without legal reprisals, most likely. And would probably kill them regardless. Tomas yanked his soft leather boots on, grabbed for his harp.

"Take this." Sigrun clapped a runestick into his hands; it was carved with verses he'd written her.

"Don't you want it?"

"You know I can't read, Tomas. Take it and go!" It was evidence. If adultery were proved, the full weight of the law would fall upon 'Sigrun.

Tomas gripped her wrist in the darkness. "Come with me."

"Where? Are you mad?" She jerked her arm free.

"Any court in the North--"

"Would welcome your poems, but that old horse of yours won't get us far." The flintiness of her tone came as a shock; he would have wagered his flute that she'd leave with him. "Torbrand would track us with all of his men. Now go! Do you want to die?"

On the following afternoon, in the main hall of his father Sigtrygg's longhouse, Tomas said carefully: "No, I don't want to die." Sigrun's refusal still smarted, but that wasn't the worst of it.

"One would think otherwise." The earl Sigtrygg's brooding blue gaze was remote. Straight-backed as always, his wheat-colored hair scarcely touched by the years that had etched grim lines about his eyes and mouth, Sigtrygg sat upon his high seat of carved wood. Tomas stood before him. Smoke rose, thick and greasy, from the low, stone-lined central hearthfire and the tallow lamps to pool at the one opening in the arched and sloping roof. Fickle light played against the empty sleeping benches that lined the walls, peopling the room with shadows.

Before this discussion, Sigtrygg's latest wife, thralls and concubines had all been dismissed, along with his numerous progeny. All but Tomas and his half-brother Olaf, Sigtrygg's oldest legitimate son and heir.

Standing beside Tomas, Olaf's heavy features were immobile; his eyes, not one whit less hostile than usual, were level and clear. None of his berserker rage, not here in his father's hall. Still, a pulse beat at the side of his throat, which was no more muscular than Sigtrygg's own. Tomas had inherited none of that breadth of chest.

Olaf said, "If Torbrand brings a complaint and starts a feud over it, our whole household could die. Down to the last child."

King Harald's law-court, where such accusations were brought, convened in a few days' time. Blood-feuds often began when the injured parties believed themselves insufficiently avenged.

"Rumor gives out that Torbrand has little evidence," said Sigtrygg coolly. "But he may well lodge a complaint. He's a prideful man, Tomas, and a hard one to cross."

Tomas nodded, and considered the facts.

Just before Torbrand's return, one of his slaves, riding a little ahead, had seen a tall blond man leave the earl's longhouse. Although nothing was found missing, the man carried something flat and angular wrapped in cloth. Despite the lateness of Torbrand's unexpected arrival, he found his young wife Sigrun, who'd unaccountably dismissed her bondmaids for the night, bridling and disheveled in a disordered chamber. Before Torbrand's thralls were silenced, these intriguing scraps of information had made the rounds of the court.

Tomas knew, additionally, that there'd been no time for Sigrun to bathe, to change the bed linens... If Torbrand had deduced the cause of his wife's disarray and beaten her, Tomas couldn't blame the unfortunate woman for whatever she might have said. Spurned or not, he felt a little sick: at least he wasn't legally bound to his accuser.

It would help his case that perhaps half the men in Vestfold were tall and blond, though few matched Tomas's height and fairness. And that cloth-wrapped object could have been many things other than the harp of a skald.

Popular sentiment could run as easily for as against him. The favored new poet at King Harald's court, Tomas had excited attention and envy before now. Others had noticed Sigrun's growing awareness of him. Some of those others, Olaf among them, had already tried and failed to attract her chilly regard.

"The sworn word of Torbrand's slave would not weigh so much as that of Tomas. He's a free man," said Olaf now, watching Tomas steadily. "Still, his word weighs less than if he'd been born free."

Sigtrygg stirred in his chair and made no reply, as Tomas met Olaf's unwavering blue-eyed stare with a grey-eyed one of his own. His long-dead mother had been a Welsh concubine, taken prisoner during one of Sigtrygg's raids in Waleis. Tomas might well have remained a thrall himself except that Sigtrygg, ambitious to number a court poet among his sons, took notice of Tomas's musical gifts, and freed him.

For which act Olaf bore him a grudge, chronic and venomous, although Olaf as the firstborn son would inherit the vast majority of Sigtrygg's estate nonetheless. Tomas would receive little if anything; too many freeborn and legitimate sons preceded him.

But at court, now, a skald could win prestige and gold, should his minstrelsy please the King. Courtiers would also pay a poet handsomely to chronicle their exploits at home and over the sea--if the poet were alive and at court.

Banishment was not at issue here. Not caught in the act, Tomas would be fined at the most. But Torbrand's sense of humiliation might prompt him to step outside the law and murder Tomas on his own. In that event, a blood-feud would follow, if Sigtrygg's household cared to preserve its honor.

With a deepening of the crow's-feet about his eyes, Sigtrygg considered his sons. "Olaf. Do you still propose to go a-viking within the week?"

Turning his gaze to his father, Olaf nodded.

"Hire Tomas to go and write of your raids. By the time you return, tempers will have cooled somewhat at court. Where Tomas should plan to recite his finest work yet," said Sigtrygg dryly.

Sail south with Olaf and his berserkers? Twinges plucked at the muscles along Tomas's spine; he'd sooner take his chances here with Torbrand. Olaf dared not lay violent hands on his own brother with so many witnesses in the crew. Still, something about that journey felt ominous indeed...

"He hasn't the stomach for it. Let him contend with his own trouble here in Vestfold, if you please, my lord," said Olaf. His tone was respectful enough, but a knot worked in his jawline.

Sigtrygg studied his heir without expression.

3

There followed a taut silence which Olaf, shifting his weight, broke at last: "Tomas must learn some restraint; he's overfond of women."

A corner of Sigtrygg's mouth twitched. "No more than you or I, Olaf. He just has more skill with them."

Olaf went rigid, then swallowed. Very slowly, he let out his breath.

"And less sense about their husbands," said Sigtrygg to Tomas, his voice now deadly soft. "Torbrand's coveted my lands since we were both your age, and he stands next to me in Harald's trust. Are you a fool, boy? If you'd create such an enemy, you'd best *find* the stomach for it." He glanced at Olaf. "Take him with you. It's as easy to disown a son as to acknowledge one."

Olaf's eyes widened. In one sudden motion, Sigtrygg rose and struck the flat of his powerful hand across his heir's face. "Get out, the pair of you, and leave Torbrand to me. Don't let me set eyes on you again until you've returned from the South." A hard stare at Tomas. "With something to sing about."

CHAPTER ONE: THE FIRST OF MAY, 871 A.D.

"Shall I take the figureheads down now?" Tomas asked Olaf.

They stood on a raised deck at the bow of the *Brilliant Dragon*, Olaf's longship, as it glided up the River Saefren that divided Waleis from Wessex. Murky water slapped the clinker-built hull, but the long wooden oars, in skilled hands, made remarkably little sound. Olaf's raiding party had just lowered the mast and lifted their iron-rimmed wooden shields from the timber rail. Axes, spears, swordhilts and the ringshirts of wealthier men gleamed in the waxing light of dawn. From a village on the Welsh side of the river, hearthfire smoke smudged a paling marsh-scented sky.

The rowers nearest Tomas tilted their heads at his question. Oddi, the navigator, looked particularly somber. "I'd have taken them down before now," he muttered. "I saw an Elf in Gotland knock holes in the hull of a ship that docked with its dragons on. And the land-spirits like it no more than the Elves do."

Ignoring Oddi, Olaf and most of his berserker guard scowled at Tomas. Both in Vestfold and on board ship, he'd chanted verses in their honor, and they bore him no personal malice. But now two or three men chewed their lips and eyed him with mindless ire as he stared back at Olaf.

In a voice that wouldn't carry to the shore, Olaf said, "I'm not taking them down. We may not be the only Norse in these waters; Ivar the Boneless sails to Dubhlinn with slaves from hereabouts. But I needn't explain the slave traffic to you."

Tomas gave a curt shake of his head.

"Closer to shore," Olaf told the oarsmen after scanning the narrowing channel. "If our dragons offend any Elves, so be it. I'm more wary of Ivar. And the Welsh are your greatest concern."

The last remark was a reference to the nerves that they both knew were splintering Tomas's midsection. Of Sigtrygg's household, Tomas had shown the least enthusiasm for weapons training, much of which Olaf gave him.

With a shrug, Tomas glanced at the crew: little enough tension there, though others besides himself made their first journey beyond the North. Almost all the men were veterans of several viking expeditions, undertaken for adventure or as likely for gain. Divided inheritance of the scant fringes of arable land that edged the fjords inspired fierce competition.

Odin might well favor their raiding party; every man aboard worshipped the Lord of Battle, though not all so fanatically as the

5

berserkers. Some of the crew invoked Odin for His other powers.

A man named Egil caught Tomas's eye. But for poverty, Egil would captain a ship of his own and could do so yet. Grinning, he jerked his chin at Olaf's massive back; the two disliked each other heartily. "Don't trouble yourself about Tomas. He turns white at hog-slaughter, but Odin grants more than one gift. The Poet-Lord's hand lies upon him," Egil said loudly.

Olaf gave no sign that he'd heard.

Egil rubbed his sun-bleached beard and said, as if the idea had just occurred to him, "Perhaps Odin gave some of His magic to Tomas. That would explain Sigrun—"

Guffaws from the crew.

Olaf rounded on them. "Enough! D'you want to be heard?"

Egil subsided, his face bland and earnest. As the longship eased closer to the bank, Tomas peered into the thick knots of trees crowding the shore, then eyed the dragon figureheads. What manner of Elf did they risk provoking in Waleis?

This foreign country, unknown people and strange lone dying god were the land, kin and deity of Tomas's mother. She had taught him to speak Welsh, and the English of the Saxon realms that bordered Waleis. When Tomas was a child, she often talked about her god from Nazareth.

"Odin hung on the World-Tree to receive knowledge of the Runes, and He survived too," Tomas would say.

She would smile. "It is not the same. But tell me a tale, for I have told you one."

Now Tomas unclenched his hands and examined them. Shaped like hers. She gave him his first harp lessons; he had her grey eyes.

The chiseled dragon-head knifed into the riverbank, and Olaf shouldered past him. "Move."

With a strip of leather, Tomas hastily tied his long hair at the nape of his neck. Hair like his father's, paler than freshly split birch wood, thick and almost straight. He caught up his shield.

Among the mossy trees and reed-choked silty underbrush, none of the Norse perceived the tall graceful figure, dressed in dark green, who had marked their passage up the Saefren. Who had tracked them, listening judiciously to their talk, and now watched them come ashore.

With Olaf and his guard leading, some thirty men disembarked, raised a shield-wall overhead and filed silently down a damp shadowy path carpeted in moss. On the wooded trail they met a short tanned boy who carried a basket and reeked of marsh salt and fish. After a panicked struggle, the youth went limp. First in Welsh, then in English,

6

he begged the strangers not to kill him. No one but Tomas understood a word.

The berserkers, some now racked with tremors from head to foot, strangled the boy. Then, as an offering to Odin, they hung the body from the nearest sturdy tree. It was the last event of that morning that Tomas would remember clearly.

Market day, it must be, or the day of a fair: the village's main square was trodden into pockmarked mud. Roaring, the Norse sprang into the small crowd. The villagers scattered, overturned stalls, dodged terrified livestock and flung barrels and benches into the path of the approaching Norse. Surprised, underarmed and demoralized, most of the Welsh fled or were gutted as the raiders advanced towards the Nazarene temple, which promised trappings of gold and silver, and perhaps refugees.

Gripped by the worst nausea of his life, his shoulders braced against a wall, Tomas stood and stared. He had grown up with stories of the rage, fearless, bloody and ecstatic, that Odin granted some of His worshippers. At the whim of the god, that violent trance possessed and deserted them, and for its sake they were at once revered, scorned and shunned.

But Tomas had never seen berserkers fully transported. He could neither lose himself in their fury nor join the rest of the crew in their cooler but efficient slaughter, all bolstered by the faith that if they died in battle, Odin would welcome them to Valholl.

Bellowing, a Norseman churned through the mud past Tomas. The man's face was livid and contorted on one side, slack on the other, and his mouth bled from gnawing his gaudily painted shield--Egil's shield. During the voyage, Egil had sometimes looked at Tomas's harp and asked questions about how it was tuned. Now his red-veined gaze speared a point directly before him. With a howl, he swung his axe at a wounded man in his path.

Tomas shut his eyes. He heard babbling, a pulpy thud and an aborted groan. Bending double, he retched into the mud. When he straightened up, having made no conscious decision, he ran towards the Saefren. He jumped over bodies, slipped on objects he didn't care to examine, dodged Norse and Welsh alike. Twice he stumbled but he kept moving. Once he heard Olaf roaring at him, calling his name.

A peculiar tingling in the air began to intrude on his attention, while at the edge of his vision, something oppressive and crackling hovered. Storm clouds? He glanced overhead.

Swirling, incandescent lines of energy seared the sky. It was a Rune: Perthro, the Web of Fate.

7

Ankle-deep in mud, Tomas halted. The air, although vibrant, was eerily still as the Fate-Rune throbbed above the trees. It was drawn with absolute, transfixing symmetry. He gaped at the long vertical slash, then at the two V-shaped lines that reached to the right from either end of the vertical: two cones, mirroring each other.

The Nornir, the three Fates, must have sketched their Rune in the sky. Was the omen meant for the village or the raiders--or for Tomas, because he was deserting? He had learned the Runes by rote, as both alphabet and oracle, so well that shock could not drive the knowledge from him. Perthro signified: "The seeker cannot comprehend the fateful flow of events, because his own lot numbers among those cast."

Never had he experienced such a vision, though skalds of Odin often did. He was abandoning a battle, but Odin's hand must lie upon him still--or the hands of the Nornir. A tremor shook him, just as the Rune blazed.

Three enormous women, grey of face and eye, their snarled ashen hair frothing down their backs, materialized in the sky next to Perthro. They stood around a tremendous loom, across which stretched heddle rods made of ash-wood spears. Arrows served as the shuttles, and the dripping crimson warp was weighted with severed heads.

Tomas bit his knuckles to stifle a moan. The Nornir wove the Fates of men and women--what if they looked down and saw him? He ached to run but he could scarcely breathe, and achieved only a painful limping gait as he peered overhead.

The Nornir--Urd, Verdandi and Skuld--walked to and fro before their loom, throwing the shuttle-arrows through the bloody sheds and beating the weft upwards. Sharper than ice-coated trees against a midwinter sky, the grisly weights were etched against the dawn. Stumbling along with his face turned towards the sky, Tomas saw the loom as distinctly as he might have seen the full Moon, with the Moon's creamy glow. But now he could focus on only one of the Nornir. Her two sisters moved in a billowy haze like fog rising above water. The one that he could still see must be Urd, she who wove the thread of that-which-has-become. Verdandi and Skuld, that-which-is-becoming and that-which-shall-become, were shrouded from his vision now.

When he reached the footpath to the river, he clutched at a willow tree for support. Urd, bending her solemn face to her work, trudged past the dangling heads. One head rotated slowly towards Tomas; its blind, swollen eyes met his. The last thread of his reason broke.

He raced down the path to the Saefren and turned north at the

8

river without slackening speed. Breathing in labored gulps of air, he ran until his chest burned, ran until his legs grew leaden, ran until smudged spots collided before his eyes.

When he came to a tributary of the Saefren that bore off to the west, he veered away from the main body of the river. His new path along the tributary's bank was narrower and more winding, forcing him to slow his pace and taking him past quieter backwaters.

By one such almost-pool there towered a vast oak tree; its branches scraped gnarled and ponderous arcs across the sky. He sprinted for the shaded clearing beneath the oak, where its leafy mass blocked the Sun. At last he collapsed in a huddle between the great tree and the Saefren. Calm brown water was the last he saw before unconsciousness took him.

Even before Tomas opened his eyes, they felt scratchy and dry. He fished a sharp toothy stone from beneath his ribs and sat up. His vision clouded, and he leaned against the hulking tree trunk. When he could see again, he glanced nervously overhead.

The Sun flared in a glazed blue sky.

Mid-afternoon, probably, on the day of the raid. He shook his head to banish the memory of the Nornir and their loom. Moving with the painstaking caution of an old man, he crept down to the water to wash.

Soon, wearing only his trousers, he perched on the riverbank. His scrubbed and drying jerkin hung from a branch of the oak. Beneath the tree lay his boots, beside his belt and short knife. He'd lost his sword, round wooden shield and leather helmet during his flight from the village.

Cool and quiet, the river bathed Tomas's feet. He stared into the mute and undemanding water, water that didn't wash away what those feet had done. They had run from their first raid.

And were there a chance to do it over, he would run again. Sigtrygg and Olaf were right: Tomas hadn't the stomach for it. Nor any shame about that. He simply was not like them.

After a while he said aloud, "Odin, Your battle-face is too fierce for me, and I fear You might take back Your other gifts. I may have no right to petition You now, but please, I cannot lose poetry."

To have music but lose words... Woe for him that Odin ruled both verse and war. Tomas waited, but the All-father made no answer.

Return to the ship was out of the question. Olaf would certainly beat a deserter and quite possibly kill him. Tomas was in Waleis to stay for a while. Warily, he glanced up and down the

9

riverbank. Any surviving villagers would cheerfully kill him as well.

But they needn't know he'd sailed here with a raiding party. He spoke Welsh like a native. Not all the Norse who traveled to Waleis came a-viking; there were plenty of merchants. Perhaps he could find passage back to the North, though not to Vestfold. In the meantime he could claim to be a trader. Better yet: a bard. His mother had taught him every song and story she knew.

But his harp was back on the ship.

Still, he could locate a large town, recite there for coins and buy a harp or a flute. Or make them, with the right wood and tools. Or a lute, a fiddle, a drum. They used other instruments here that he'd never played, but he could learn.

Consult the Runes? They hung in a small pouch at his belt, left under the oak.

No, not just yet. Not while he sat on this mossy bank, calf-deep in the soothing river. How calm it was in this sheltered spot. He could see his own reflection in the water, his tousled hair freed from its lost leather tie, his bare chest and arms.

His own reflection, and another. Someone stood on the bank not far behind him.

But he'd heard no one at all. His throat constricted as he studied the water.

His observer was slender and tall, with long hair or a veil. Probably a woman. Then the figure stirred, and Tomas saw the reflected curves of a waist and hips that could only belong to a woman.

"I mean you no harm, my lady," he said politely in Welsh and, as an afterthought, in English. "I'm going to stand up now." Moving slowly, hoping not to alarm her, Tomas pulled his feet from the water, rose and turned around.

He stared in amazement.

The woman's close-fitting silky tunic and divided skirt were a rich deep ivy green, embroidered with beryl stones. Black waves of tangled hair fell past her waist. Like ice-glazed bone, her skin was smooth and luminous, set off by the shining dark hair that formed a widow's peak on her pale forehead. Her pointed chin would easily fit the palm of Tomas's hand. High-bridged and long, her nose was perfectly straight. Beneath it, the deep coral of her mouth was lush and startling. Light moved in her heavy-lidded, enormous grey eyes. Set in a cat-like slant, they were thickly lashed in black.

No ordinary woman, this. Her eyes were too large, too tilted. All the angles and proportions of her face were slightly--yet exquisitely-- wrong. Her mouth, for instance, was wider than it should be. But it

10

looked soft, pliant...

Gazing straight into Tomas's eyes, she smiled.

He inhaled sharply. She could not possibly have intended that her smile be so enticing. Blood began pounding in his ears; his body urged him forward. Yet an even deeper instinct made him edge a few paces away. He did not think that she was human.

His mother's beliefs flooded back to him. Could it be? He'd just abandoned Odin. He dropped down to one knee and asked cautiously in Welsh, "Are you the Queen of Heaven?"

"No, Tomas." The woman's voice was warm and speculative, with an aromatic, briny resonance that made him want to hear more. "That name does not belong to me."

She wasn't Freyja, the flaxen-haired goddess of love. Odin's wife Frigg seldom left her home in the gods' realm of Asgard. "Lady Frigg?"

Tomas's visitor shook her head. Her eyes traveled over his body, lingered, returned slowly to his face.

He was breathing faster and not entirely from wariness, though that had not grown less. Perhaps the love goddess had changed Her appearance to come to mortal Midgard. "Lady Freyja?"

Triumph flashed in the woman's cobweb-colored eyes. "No, for the third time. Rise, Tomas, I pray you."

He got to his feet, then stood his ground uneasily as she approached.

Two feet away, she stopped to scrutinize him. Tomas watched her taking in his thick pale hair with its knife-cut, ragged bangs. His sparsely bearded face, widest across high cheekbones, was tanned from time at sea. The woman glanced at the faint cleft in his chin, then made a thorough study of his deep-set grey eyes. Ruddier than his hair, his heavy eyebrows almost met over his nose, which wasn't straight before Sigtrygg broke it several years ago. It was distinctly crooked now.

As the woman might have read Tomas's palm, she read the blend in his features, the Celtic strain that added a whimsical, dreamy cast to the impassive starkness of the Norse. Then she nodded slowly.

Tomas didn't object to her inspection. It allowed him to keep looking at her without appearing boorish, and not to look at her would have been more than he could do.

She was a mere hand's width shorter than he. Her age was difficult to guess. Her walk had an easy suppleness and her face seemed young, but the expression in her eyes was infinitely older. The scent of sweetbriar roses floated from her.

"How do you know my name?" he asked, hoping she'd repeat

11

it.

"I watched your ship come ashore, and what passed in the village."

Tomas winced. When the woman laid one fine-boned narrow hand on his bare arm, he almost pulled it away. But he was leery of offending this being—and once he got past his initial surprise, her touch was warm and exceedingly pleasant.

"But you wanted to take down the dragon-heads, and you did not join in the butchery—two of the reasons I have sought you out."

Then she had other reasons. Where had she been during the carnage in the town? Her sloping eyes held his; heat radiated from her pointed fingers.

Too pointed, and too long.

"Who are you?" Tomas whispered.

The speculative voice was low and mild. "I am the Queen of Elfland, which is also called Faerie."

When she started to draw languid, ascending circles on Tomas's arm, he caught his breath incredulously, but he didn't move. He didn't dare. This being was perilous in the extreme. "Alfheim?" Mortals had been lost there forever, or crumbled into dust on their return.

She shook her head. "Your Norse Elves are distant kin. My world borders theirs, and the two combined border yours. But my own realm lies closer to Waleis." A corner of her mouth turned up. "In a manner of speaking."

When her hand reached the sensitive skin of his inner elbow, her touch grew more delicate. Exquisitely delicate, and inquiring. Tomas's muscles knotted and relaxed, then knotted again, with equal measures of apprehension and desire.

It made no sense. Why would the Queen of Elfland seek out the likes of him? Retaliation for Olaf's figureheads? But she had heard Tomas asking to take them down.

Dark green silk rose and fell with her breathing, which was, surely, deeper than before? Like his own breathing, he thought despairingly. Her smile was soft with encouragement. Fighting the compulsion, unable to stop, Tomas lifted a tentative hand towards her gleaming black hair.

When the Elf twined her fingers in his, a shiver of pleasure moved through him. He took an impulsive step closer. "What is your name?"

Something ancient, solitary and alien flared in her tilted grey eyes. Abruptly, the palpable closeness flowing between her and Tomas vanished, as though a massive door had slammed shut. He flinched, but

12

she didn't release his hand. Her withdrawal lasted only seconds, but long enough to emphasize that the woman staring past and through him was not human, was not even mortal.

As though nothing had happened, she smiled again, with a new and intense tenderness that Tomas experienced physically, like water splashed across his skin. She slid her other hand from his arm to his bare shoulder. But it was her smile that gave the deeper touch, and the invitation.

He drew a shaking breath. After that mysterious contact, when the Elf reached straight into Tomas's thoughts, he found himself simply accepting it.

Had she spoken, she might have said: I know you. Your poetry; your bitter, Sighted heart; the flinty core of you, that you do not yet see. The paths that brought you here, I sense, all of your steps.

The rapport revealed Tomas to himself, as a sculptor's touch on a blind man's face can describe its features to their owner. For an astonished moment, he stood motionless, enfolded by the Elf's warm affirming presence in his mind. Then, overriding his fear, the extraordinary intimacy was both too great and not enough. Slowly and carefully, he drew her close and began to stroke her hair. It was crisp rather than soft, and all but crackled in his fingers.

Her smile was subtle, many-layered and overwhelming. "You may call me Moira," she said, caressing his face. "But that is not my name."

Tomas was past caring. "Moira," he whispered. "A beautiful name." He raised the pointed chin that fit his palm.

"It means Fate," she murmured. "It seems I am your Fate, if you will kiss me."

After a wordlessly articulate time, they made love beneath the great oak tree by the riverbank. Only much later would Tomas realize that Moira kept them as far as possible from where he had left his belt with its iron knife.

CHAPTER TWO: FEALTY

When the Moon rose, Moira laughed, ran her hands through Tomas's hair and gave it a gentle tug. "Night is falling! Will you let me be?" But she looked indulgent.

Tomas rubbed his beard over Moira's fragrant shoulder, stroked the polished softness of the skin along her spine. Sighing, he settled onto his back, content to be on a riverbank of a mild spring evening. Caught in the branches of the oak, the full Moon spilled amber light down through netted leaves, while the voice of the Saefren eddied through the hushed violet air.

Moira sat up and stretched. Moonlight blended with the Elf's hair to stipple her body with shadows. Tomas gazed at the rich sleek curves of her breasts, at the hollow where her neck met earlobe and chinline. Shutting his eyes, he tried to sort out his feelings, cautiously. How well could Moira discern his thoughts when she wasn't mysteriously present in his mind?

Physically, he was released, exhilarated--and shaken, after pleasure so intense that for some time he had lost any sensation of separateness or fear, and any memory of the events, violent or uncanny, that led him to Moira. So far beyond the realm of his experience had that communion been that he could scarcely compass it. It had changed him, he suspected, in more ways than in his sense of his own body.

With his slow return to awareness, however, he was troubled of mind. He'd been so deeply searched and perceived by the Elf that he felt--transparent, although she was tender. Although she could be profoundly tender, and generous, and he'd welcomed it. Yet by comparison, he had scarcely seen beyond Moira's surface. That he'd known it at the time, and that it had not mattered, only added to his uneasiness now.

Why had she sought him out? Her appearance followed too closely on the heels of the Nornir and their Rune. Perthro, the Web of Fate... And Tomas was in the wrong country, with precious few prospects for leaving any time soon.

Moira took his hand; he opened his eyes. She gave his palm a lingering kiss. "Are you drowsy?"

"No," he said softly. "I've never been more awake." Reaching up, he trailed his wondering fingertips over the planes and angles of her face. Not quite human. "How did you come here, Moira?" And why, most especially why. But first he wanted to know how.

She stretched out beside him again. When Tomas pulled the warm length of the Elf's body against his, she slid one arm beneath his neck, the other across his chest. "'Twould be easier to show you, than to tell," she said against his ear.

"'Show me'?" he asked, his hands full of perfumed black hair.

A soft laugh. "How I came here, witling."

"Show me, then."

She whistled. When something shuffled through the underwood towards them, Tomas let go of her and sat bolt upright.

A dapple-grey horse clopped into view, stopping several yards from the oak. The beast's saddle, fashioned of ivory or of bone, was set with shimmering green stones. Pearls gleamed from the bridle. Tied to the saddle was a roll of emerald-tinted cloth, and small silver bells hung from the braided grey mane.

The gear was too fantastic, too opulent, even for the Queen of Elfland's horse. Almost—Tomas pinned down his disquieting impression—almost farcical. And why did the animal come no closer?

Moira chose that moment to stand and stretch again from head to toe; Tomas watched appreciatively. Then she tossed him his jerkin and trousers. Surprised, he nearly failed to catch them. She slipped her ivy-colored tunic over her head and stepped into the divided skirt—a riding skirt, he now saw.

She shot him a small wicked grin. "The Elf women will welcome you as you are, Tomas, but I find the ride more comfortable in my clothes."

He shrugged into his shirt, stepped into his trousers. "The ride where, Moira?" he asked quietly.

"To Elfland."

After yanking his boots on, he stood with his arms folded. If he entered the realm of Faerie, he might never leave it alive. Or he might return to Midgard and find that everyone he knew was long since dead. But what would Moira do if he refused? He was perspiring in the temperate air.

She came to him and took his face between her frail burning palms. "We must depart this evening. The gates between the worlds yawn wide upon the first of May, but I cannot say the same for every night. Come, love; will you join my court and serve me well?"

In the moonlight, her eyes were the color of melting snow on a deep lake, tender and beckoning, edged in black.

Promises. Servitude. Time lost between the worlds.

The Elf stroked Tomas's face, smoothed his snarled hair from his temples. Her scent of crushed roses stained his own skin now; the taste of her was still in his mouth.

What better choice remains? she asked without speaking,

abruptly present in his mind again. His brother's ship was closed to him. Already exiled in a foreign land, Tomas would merely trade one alien country for another, far more hospitable.

Moira withdrew her tapered fingers from his face and took his hands. "Will you? Have I your word?" She clasped his hands together, her own hands holding them palm to palm. Tomas knew that gesture: he was swearing fealty.

To an Elf.

Her huge grey eyes took on an opaque sheen beneath the Moon. She was not mortal; she was not even human.

"What are you asking me, Moira?" Tomas whispered. His voice was hoarse.

He sensed what might have been surprise flash through her, but so quickly that he doubted the perception. Their rapport did not diminish but shifted with profound subtlety, as though some elements of that bond had been withdrawn and others added.

Holding his gaze, Moira asked, "Do you want to be with me, Tomas?" Her question was almost melancholy in its softness.

Yes: he was consumed with wanting. The hint of dejection in her voice was shattering.

Yes and no. She terrified him.

He managed to nod.

"Then swear to join my court and serve me well." She kissed him. "And come with me now."

One last spark of caution was strangling him.

That was when the faint sound of voices floated towards them from downriver. Men's voices, approaching. Tomas couldn't make out the words, but he recognized Norse gutturals, impossible to confuse with the lilt and murmur of Welsh.

"Climb!" hissed Moira, grabbing a low branch. "They might see you on the ground."

They both scrambled into the giant oak, striving to make as little noise as possible, and keeping to the side of the tree that faced away from the river. Tomas's arms and legs tingled with shock.

One branch at a time. Reach and release, no harder than rowing. A good thing he'd put his boots on. And at this time of the year, no dislodged acorns would betray him and Moira.

Shinnying up the tree above him, Moira climbed barefoot and heedless as a cat. Tomas had the impression that she could have gone faster but was matching his pace. Soon she glanced down at him. "This is a good place to stop; the leaves are thick here."

When they were settled, he remembered something. "Your

horse!"

Moira's teeth gleamed. "Never fret; they'll not see him." The Elf peered around the treetrunk towards the river. "They'll not see me either," she murmured.

The voices were closer now, almost opposite the oak. Norse voices, loud and inebriated. Tomas could isolate no words because they all spoke at once, sounding exuberant or angry. Possibly a merchanter, more likely a raiding party.

When the jabbering was almost inaudible, Moira began a brisk descent of the tree. "That was your ship, Tomas."

"Are you certain?" he asked, following slowly. Climbing down was more difficult.

"It had the same dragon-heads and the same sail. Grey, with a red B and D-Rune."

The *Brilliant Dragon*. In search of another, wealthier village on the tributary, or simply exploring—or looking for Tomas.

He jumped from the last branch to the clearing where Moira waited. The horse came crunching through the underwood, ambled up to the Elf and nudged her shoulder with his long grey muzzle. His eyes gleamed faintly red.

"We call him Aubrey," Moira told Tomas. She gave him a sober look, then took his hands, palms held together between hers.

Fealty.

Olaf wasn't far upriver.

"Very well, Moira," Tomas said quietly. "I swear to join your court and serve you well."

Their eyes met. She gave him a nod of acknowledgment, solemn and formal, with a regal quality he'd not yet seen in her. She released his hands.

Then she reached out and, very gently, spent a moment stroking his hair.

With Moira perched in front of him over Aubrey's withers, Tomas sat in the pale saddle. A wind sprang up to swirl leaves about them. Tomas shivered; it was suddenly far too cold for the season. His skin felt clammy, and the grey horse snorted and tossed his head. Soon they were in the still eye of a whirling vortex of air, the wind sobbing in the branches above them.

"Take your leave of Sun and Moon and every leaf upon this tree. While we are quit of Midgard, you shall not see them."

Tomas nodded. This deed may work me woe, he thought.

"Home, Aubrey!" cried the Elf.

17

There was a blurred, dislocated sensation. Weightlessness. Fear. Several sensations and emotions at once, with no way for Tomas to know which ones were real. Resignation. An aching tenderness. Regret. Confusing rather than painful, it was much the way he'd felt when awakened from sleepwalking as a child. Once or twice he heard distant voices but could distinguish no words.

Then Aubrey was galloping through a ruddy, phosphorescent fog. The light was different, dimmer: the full Moon had vanished. His face against Moira's crisp black hair, Tomas wrapped his arms around her so tightly that he could feel her ribs flex with her breathing.

When Aubrey began splashing through liquid, Tomas glanced down at the horse's hooves. The streaming water beneath them was a lurid madder red, shot with coppery glints like glowing blood.

Moira turned her head at Tomas's gasp and saw his sickened stare. "Yes, it is blood," she confirmed. "Running towards Faerie."

Tomas let out his breath, surprised and grateful that the air didn't reek. "Why? And whose?"

"All the blood shed in Midgard runs through the springs of my country. Your kinsmen have not been idle." Her shoulders squared. "And precisely why I cannot tell you. I don't know."

So she had limits, and had just confessed one to him. He felt honored, trusted--then terrified. What else in Faerie did Moira neither understand nor control, she who ruled there?

He could leap from the horse, into the fog and the tainted water, but where would he go?

The Elf slid Tomas's left hand inside her tunic and up to her breast, then tilted her head back to kiss his throat. Tomas stared straight ahead into the wind.

Much later, the light began to grow, steadily becoming yellow-white rather than red. Soon Aubrey stepped from the plum-colored water onto a dry thoroughfare of some packed and glittering material. A crossroads. Tomas shifted in the saddle, away from the tall motionless figure who suddenly appeared beside them. There was something strange about its head--

He was looking at a statue of a woman.

Carved of pale gleaming stone, it had three faces with differently shaped marks upon their foreheads. The figure stood in the center of the crossroads; down each path gazed one impassive set of features. Before the woman's chiseled feet lay an empty earthenware platter.

Moira swung a leg over Aubrey's crested neck and landed

noiselessly beside the horse. The Elf nodded briefly to the statue, as to an equal.

"Who is she?" Tomas asked once he'd dismounted.

Moira gave him an unfathomable look. "She represents Hecate, who rules all crossroads. This one in particular. Have you never heard of her?"

When he shook his head, the Elf sighed. "I forget your age."

Her shuttered expression and long silence gave Tomas an opportunity to walk around the statue. One face was young, a girl in the early years of beauty, with the crescent of a waxing Moon upon her stone forehead. The second image gazed at Tomas with the easy assurance of a mature and lovely woman; a full Moon glimmered on her brow. On the forehead of the third face rode a waning crescent, etched into the lined and austere features of a matriarch.

Maiden, woman, crone.

A few yards away, Aubrey stood quietly. Tomas expected to see the horse's legs soaked with blood, but they showed only traces of red. This place did not obey the logic of Midgard.

Nor had Midgard itself behaved predictably since the Nornir appeared. The very ground beneath his feet could drop away... Fighting a spasm of panic, Tomas closed his eyes: the pavement was tilting mysteriously. Moira caught his elbow as he sat down.

"Forgive me, I should long since have offered you food. My people need not eat so often as yours. I have poppyseed cakes and strawberries and wine. Will you break your fast?" Her face and voice were calm. Kneeling beside him, she kneaded the back of his neck; her fine-boned hands were incongruously powerful.

Tomas nodded and thanked her; he could not recall when he had last eaten. Moira brought a roll of green silk from the saddle. She gave Tomas a small round loaf, more bread than cake, balanced another loaf on her knee and placed a third at Hecate's feet. Burrowing in the bag, the Elf took out an ivory box of strawberries and a wineskin, which she uncorked and passed to Tomas.

In the North, wine was precious and scarce, a drink for kings and earls. The Elf's provender might carry a risk of enchantment, yet starvation seemed the greater peril. Tomas sipped cautiously; the wine was excellent. After a long appreciative pull from the flask, he gave it to Moira and was puzzled at the watchfulness in her eyes.

But the wine warmed his empty stomach, and he sighed and stretched, feeling restored. He ate a second poppyseed loaf. When Moira smiled and fed him a strawberry, he caught her hand and kissed it.

19

Releasing her hand, he saw that her appraising look had returned. He glanced aside, then back at Moira, trying to hide his uneasiness. Her huge grey eyes had narrowed.

As she studied him, her expression softened. Taking his face in her hands, she said, "Tomas, love, it is not my intention that you come to any harm."

Her voice was low and earnest. He nodded.

Appearing satisfied, she let go of him. "I would like to continue on our road--unless you are still hungry?"

"Not any more." He got up quickly, to stand scanning the featureless skies. "What time is it?"

The Elf shrugged. "There is no time at this crossroads. Not as mortals measure it."

The red liquid was gone. Tomas pointed at one of the lanes, wide and well-packed. It wound through a quiet green meadow. "Is that our road?"

She shook her head. "No. That is the way to Hell."

"The world of the dead?" he asked, stricken.

"Yes. Your people call it Niflheim."

Niflheim, where a half-decayed goddess, also named Hel, dwelt with her subjects: the dead. Those who were not in Odin's or Freyja's halls of slain warriors. The dead, and a corpse-devouring dragon.

Chilled, Tomas looked at the second track. It was choked with thorns and briars, and soon angled sharply out of sight.

"That is what this new god's worshippers call the path to righteousness," said Moira, and came to stand at Tomas's side. Her face was somber. "They are ever more numerous in Waleis and Wessex. And in Mercia, Éire and the land of the Scots. All the lands of Midgard near my own. Have they reached your country yet?"

"A few. My mother was one. She was born in Waleis."

The Elf nodded, unsurprised, and cast him an enigmatic glance. "And you?"

He rubbed his beard. There was moisture on his skin; mist was rapidly gathering in the crossroads. "I followed Odin, Who granted me the gift of verse."

Moira was giving him her full attention.

"I don't know what will befall me, now that I've fled another of His faces." A great deal has befallen me already, he thought bitterly. "Odin is capricious. The berserker trance can abandon men in battle or visit them unasked in peacetime. But I doubt it will come to me. Nor do I desire it." He stifled a shudder. "Perhaps poetry comes and goes the same way," he said, staring at the spiky hedgerow before him.

20

The Elf put two fingers under Tomas's chin and gently turned his face towards her. Her eyes were serious. "Yours has not gone." She pointed at the third trail, neither wide nor narrow, but steep; it labored up a hill that ended in a massed blue-green line of cliffs. Atop the ridge was an immense, rounded stone structure.

"That is our road," said Moira. "The road to Elfland." She mounted the grey horse.

Tomas glanced back at the statue. Thick white fog clotted the crossroads, and he couldn't tell which set of Hecate's watching features pointed towards Faerie. He took a long time climbing into the saddle.

The Queen of Elfland reined Aubrey's head towards the looming stones that waited on the hill.

CHAPTER THREE: AN ILL WIND, AND SURPRISES

As they rode, Tomas studied the faded yellow haze that stained the sky. There was neither sun nor moon. No stars, no other source of light--yet he could see. A fitful breeze began to stir, carrying the slightest trace of salt. He heard a faint roar, constant, muted, unmistakable: the sea. "Are we near water, Moira?"

"Yes. The Elvish Sea borders my country."

Tomas was framing a question about the ships of Faerie, when the wind turned icy and started to blow from directly behind them. As the gusts came with increasing force, leaves and twigs catapulted across the road, and Tomas's shirt clung to his shoulders and billowed before him. Shrieking, the wind shifted again to come from their right. A stench welled into the blade-cold air, the putrescent reek of something long dead and overlong in rotting. Tomas began to cough. What were they passing on this road? Or what, unseen, was passing them?

Aubrey snorted and danced sideways in high nervous steps. Moira shoved her frothing black hair down the back of her tunic. Her jaw was tight; her eyes narrowed, emphasizing the alien shape of her skull. She reined Aubrey to a halt, although the horse laid his ears back and made a desultory attempt to keep moving. In a language that Tomas had never heard, Moira shouted into the bellowing wind. As if in protest, the gale rose higher, then died as abruptly as it was born. The odor took longer to dissipate.

Tomas's ears rang in the silence; he flexed his chilled arms. In a moment Moira clucked to the horse, and Aubrey continued up the climbing path.

"Moira. The wind, the smell--what were they?"

Her back was rigid. "Something we should be content has departed," she said coolly.

"I am content. What was it?"

Silence. Then, "I shall tell you later. I prefer not to discuss it now."

"Why not?" It could be dangerous to push her; he felt the tension in her posture. But he understood something of Moira, and nothing of whatever caused that stench. Of the two, Moira was the known risk.

"Tomas..." She turned her head to give him a measuring glance. "Because we are in the open, and it may not have gone far. And names have power." Her voice was level. "We will speak of it again. You have my word."

Sensing that her word meant something, he said, "Very well,"

22

and began to study the circular structure of veined and weathered stone that they were approaching. It had five roughly squared doors and at least three times as many windows. Each boulder must measure twice the height of a man and wider than a hefty tree trunk. "What is that place? Do many Elves live there?"

Moira shrugged. "You see the gathering hall of my people, and the home of my household and the court. And that not at all times."

She seemed more at ease with this line of questioning, so Tomas asked, "Where else do they dwell?"

Another shrug. "Many places. Woods, fields, water, caves. And lesser halls than this. In Midgard, even. But no longer."

"Why not?"

Moira twisted around to kiss him. "Is there no end to your questions?" She was smiling. "And only for the hall. You ask me nothing of my court."

The Queen of Elfland's court... "Moira! Stop!"

Aubrey halted instantly. Moira snapped something unintelligible at the horse, drew rein and turned to look at Tomas.

He braced himself. "Is there a King in Elfland?"

"Yes," she said calmly. "He is called Rhys."

For a heartbeat, Tomas only stared at her. Sliding from Aubrey's back, he flung himself into the towering trees that lined the path. He'd known about Sigrun Bjornsdottir's husband; there, he had made a choice. Moving faster, almost running, Tomas stumbled over a root. The damp air smelled of moss.

"Tomas!"

He heard Moira churning through thick layers of leaf mold in his wake. The forest was ancient, its oaks interspersed with beech, birch and ash, vast and brooding. Beneath the girth of their branches the wood was dark and cool and at first seemed still, but soon he detected odd, quick little ripples of movement at the edge of his vision.

"I must speak with you, Tomas. Come back." There was urgency in Moira's voice. "You shouldn't trespass here!"

He slowed but didn't stop; there was a glacier in his head. He couldn't talk to her, couldn't look at her. Not now, not yet.

She was gaining on him. "Tomas!"

Something plummeted from the silent trees and landed on his back, something brown, lean and naked, and appallingly strong. Tomas caught the hands that grappled for his throat. Growling, the creature kicked at his knees, and he fell to the forest floor.

The thing was smaller than he'd thought. Tomas rolled, using all of his weight. He grabbed a bony wrist, got his knee in its chest—

23

And froze, because it set a blade of viciously whetted stone to his throat.

Its infuriated jade-green eyes had no whites at all. But the black pupils could have been human, and so could the matted black hair. Its brown arms were as long as its legs. The same sleek, chestnut-colored skin covered a pair of flexible, tendony wings, now furled, whose tips stretched above its head. Sweat trickled down between the small breasts, high and rounded, where the knife's leather sheath crossed between them. It was female.

Tomas's knee was planted in the center of her bare chest. He still gripped her other wrist.

Moving cautiously, Moira knelt down beside him and stretched out her empty hands to the wiry brown Elf, whose wings quivered. Moira said something, haltingly, as if hunting for words. Was that a note of entreaty in her voice?

Feral eyes wide with astonishment, the other Elf glanced back and forth between Moira and Tomas. Finally she leaned forward, keeping her knife against Tomas's neck, and sniffed Moira's hands thoroughly. That done, she ducked her head and muttered a few phrases. The language seemed to be the one that Moira had just spoken, but the winged being put more sibilants into it. Moira answered her slowly in the same tongue.

Looking discomfited, the creature mumbled, then gave Tomas a smoldering stare. She was still slightly out of breath.

Moira nodded. "She wants you to move your knee and let go of her arm, before she'll put the knife away. I told her that you would."

The jagged stone blade maintained the lightest of pressure on Tomas's throat, while whiteless green eyes bore into his. He released the Elf's knobbly wrist and carefully brought his arm to his side. Then he drew his bent knee back towards his chest, away from hers, and straightened his leg.

In one blurred motion, the Elf sheathed her knife and leapt to her feet. When Tomas stood up wearily, shaken and heartsick, she eyed him and said something to Moira.

Moira shook her head. The other Elf twitched her wings and spoke vehemently.

With a trace of exasperation, Moira said, "Although you were trespassing, and she did not know you were my guest, she has attacked my guest. Our laws give you the right to choose whatever punishment you wish. She in turn claims her right to request that you choose now, so she need neither suffer a long wait nor have you attack her without warning."

24

"I wouldn't attack her at all—"

"I know, Tomas. But that she would not understand. She is very old, far older than I. And quite proud, and her thoughts walk other roads than yours or mine." Moira gave him a sober look. "Tomas, I regret that this happened at all, but especially now, when I *must* speak with you. Think of something for me to tell her, so I can send her away."

Tomas studied the scowling chestnut-colored face lifted towards his. The tips of the Elf's folded wings scarcely reached his shoulder. "First, please explain that I had no intention of trespassing." He fingered his throat. "As for the rest, just ask her not to attack me again."

Moira looked judicious, then started to smile. "You chose well. That both saves her pride and protects you. And will avoid complexities..." She turned to the small Elf and delivered a short speech with several pauses.

Still gazing up at Tomas, the Elf nodded formally. She bowed to Moira, then to Tomas. He followed a sudden impulse to bow in return. The creature tilted her head, narrowed her eyes. Ceremoniously, she drew her stone knife and presented it to him, handle first.

After a second's hesitation, he took it and thanked her.

Grinning, the Elf sprang into the air. With slow, powerful beats of her leathery wings, she soared off into the trees.

Tomas sank down onto the leaf mold, where he sat cross-legged and stared at the blade in his hands.

"A mark of respect, that gift. This ends better than I dared to hope." With the air of someone forced to revise her calculations, Moira studied him. "But Tomas, some regions of Faerie would prove dangerous even for me, should I venture there with insufficient precautions. You should never move heedlessly through this realm." She seated herself in front of him, then said, "No matter how distressed you may be."

"As you wish, Moira. I wouldn't care for any more surprises," he said, keeping his voice level. When he'd tucked the stone knife into his Rune bag, he asked, "Why didn't you tell me about Rhys?"

Moira's exquisite face was unreadable. "Are you jealous, angry, or frightened?"

Tomas rubbed his jaw and the back of his neck.

"Perhaps all three?" she asked gently.

He said nothing, for the most part because she was right.

"Ask me questions."

"I just asked you why you didn't tell me about him."

Moira stared off to her left. Tomas glanced that way too but

25

saw nothing. How did Elves react when their women had lovers? He gnawed his lower lip. Perhaps Moira intended to bring him to her court, then ignore him. That stony hall could shelter many a discarded flirtation. Remembering his father's pack of sons maneuvering for position in the household, he clenched his teeth.

Images he'd been trying to avoid rose clamoring for attention. Pictures of Moira's amazingly limber body entwined with that of an as yet faceless Elf named Rhys.

"If I had told you, would you have come with me?" she asked. The question implied that there'd been a choice. Moira's face was expressionless still, and her mind was closed to him.

Tomas thought of his own half-formed plans to recite poetry in Waleis and acquire some instruments there. Plans made just before Moira found him, when his return to the North was blocked at least for the time being. And when his survival in Waleis, if more certain than an immediate return to the North, was by no means assured. But without the extraordinary intimacy with which Moira had flooded him, would Elfland have seemed his best option?

"You had a choice," she murmured just then. Tomas shot her a skeptical look; she regarded him steadily.

"I'm not sure. But I believe I would have come with you regardless," he said at last.

Moira took his left hand, traced the lines in his palm. "I wanted you to. I still do."

Back where we started, he thought. "Rhys. Is he... Tell me about him."

The ivory face grew still and inward. "We have been together long and long. Love flows between us–"

"Then why--?" Tomas interrupted furiously, dropping her hand.

He was silenced by the same alien and impenetrable energy that had flared from Moira when he'd asked for her name. The Elf's chin lifted; her pupils dilated. "Tomas. Do you know how old I am?" A simple inquiry.

Mutely, he shook his head.

"No more do I. I have lost count. Do you know when I will cease to live?" A challenge.

"You won't," he whispered.

Moira nodded, her eyes granite pits in a motionless and bitter face. "My country is much reduced from what it was. I could...change. All Elves will change, if our world shrinks as the others grow and drift away. But we neither age nor die." She crumbled a dead oak leaf into brittle flecks, the color of dried blood.

26

Tomas had so little left to lose. After a few deep breaths, he began, "I see that what you've said distresses you." When she looked at him with no trace of recognition, he clenched his fists. "But Moira, it doesn't explain why you made love to me, or why you've brought me here."

The Elf stared off into the woods again. Half a minute later, she pushed her hair back from her pale forehead, sighed, and took Tomas's face in her hands. "You will not like all that I say, but you must hear me out before we go any further."

Her expression was serious and guarded. Tomas braced himself.

"Like many Elves, both Rhys and I have taken mortal lovers." She looked directly into his eyes; her voice was low. "Rarely, in my case, Tomas. For what is scarcely a breath of time, for us." She glanced aside, then back at him. "To you it will seem much longer, when you are in our world. And longer still in yours. The two have never run apace, less so with each passing year."

A silence. Moira's palms were warm against his skin.

"While you and I are together, you and Rhys present no threat to each other. He will show nothing but graciousness to you."

Tomas said nothing.

She searched his face. "You need not dance attendance on me, nor restrict yourself in any way—apart from not venturing into some regions of Elfland unescorted."

He nodded.

"You will doubtless wish to spend much time with our musicians. And they with you."

To his surprise, he felt a faint stir of interest at that idea.

Folding her hands in her lap, Moira inquired, "Is there anything you care to ask?"

He'd always heard that Elves didn't tell direct lies--but he didn't believe her. There was so much that she hadn't said that it was difficult to know where to begin. "How often will we be--in Rhys's company?"

"Other than at a very few court functions, as much or as little as you like," said Moira, shrugging. She reached for his face again. "So long as you are with me, Tomas, there is only you. Not Rhys, and not another."

Feeling numb, he nodded a second time. When she moved to kiss him, he stopped her. "Would you hold me, Moira?" he asked quietly. "Just hold me?"

Her face went blank, then grew softer, and less remote than he

27

had yet seen it. "Of course." Her eyes looked troubled. She did not touch him again until he slipped his arms around her, and they stretched out on the thick carpet of leaves.

Without intending to, Tomas soon fell into a profound slumber, dreamless and exhausted, beneath the same tree from which the winged Elf had dropped down to attack him. Moira lay awake and held him while he slept, her black hair hopelessly tangled around them both.

CHAPTER FOUR: A CUP OF GUESTING

Apparently, Moira had not moved at all while Tomas was asleep, though his weight must have impeded the circulation in one of her arms. When he opened his eyes, her smile was spontaneous and tender. After a moment, he asked if she'd slept too. She had shaken her head, and said that Elves needed less rest than mortals did.

They continued their way in a silence for which Tomas was grateful. Moira kept a motionless, gentle hand on his knee. As Aubrey reached the level ground at the top of the path, Tomas sat tense and alert in the saddle. He made himself unclench his jaw, but there was no help for his sweating palms.

A ring of bloomless hawthorns welcomed them with grating leaves. After Moira and Tomas dismounted, the Elf removed Aubrey's saddle and bridle and set them on the lush green turf. In the middle of the hawthorns was a stone well and beyond it a clearing, where a wide grassy lane led to the immense hall. A strangely empty, silent lane, thickly lined with trees. Tomas kept scanning the length of the hedged rectangle. He felt watched.

"Aubrey, my thanks," Moira was saying.

"My honor to bear you, Lady," said a deep and throaty voice behind Tomas's back.

He spun. The dappled horse had vanished. In its place stood a very tall, utterly naked and profoundly hairy Elf, who gave Tomas a toothy grin. The Elf's bare skin was mottled with grey. Shaggy grey hair festooned with bells covered his sloping forehead and almost hid his gleaming red eyes and tufted ears. He bowed low, straightened, tossed jingling braids from his long bony face and said, "Pray believe me charmed to further my acquaintance with you, Tomas."

Moira was laughing. "You and Aubrey have already met. Aubrey is a pooka. A kind of water-Elf."

"At your service," said the pooka, beaming.

Tomas managed to thank him.

"Ordinarily, mortals are unwise to ride a pooka," Moira began. Aubrey clasped gnarled spatulate hands to his breast and cast her a look of stricken innocence. Her mouth twitching, Moira continued, "But Aubrey was kind enough to agree to serve you as he would me. And he always keeps his word."

The pooka nodded vigorously.

Tomas had heard about these creatures from his mother. A pooka appeared as a fine great horse, lured an unsuspecting mortal onto his back, then dived into the nearest river with the victim. Something

29

unspeakable happened to the mortal then. At that point in her tale, Tomas's mother usually realized that she had so far forgotten her Christian self as to talk about pagan monsters again. But her storyteller's blood allowed her to drop a few grim hints before she refused to say anything further. Tomas had a vague memory that the victim might be devoured at the bottom of the river...

The Elves grinned at his expression, and the pooka clapped him on the back. The water horse's hands were hard as horn.

"You may go, Aubrey," said Moira affectionately.

Shouldering the ornate tack he had worn, the pooka said something in a language that Tomas couldn't understand. He didn't think it was the one that the winged Elf had spoken, either. Then he caught Rhys's name in the torrent of syllables, and Moira shook her head in mock reproach. Cackling, Aubrey skipped off down the clearing.

At a loss for words, Tomas was pleased by Moira's sudden hug. Returning it, he used enough strength that she gasped a little and smiled. "Aubrey will do you no harm," she said.

Meaning someone else might?

Taking Tomas's hand, Moira led him to the well, where a rosy gold, effervescent liquid brimmed. Moira splashed her face, then sipped from her cupped hands. "Come and drink, Tomas. The water will heal you of any wounds before you enter our hall."

He hesitated. Mortals who ate or drank in Faerie fell prey to the Elves' magic and might never return to Midgard. Or find it--or themselves--forever changed. But he'd broken fast with Moira at Hecate's crossroads, so he might well be enchanted already. "I have no wounds," he said, half to himself.

Moira gave him an odd smile.

He had agreed to come to Elfland, and where else was there to go? Cupping his hands, he dipped them in the saffron liquid. It was warm; it tingled on his skin. He doused his head and neck, then drank a long draught.

In a moment, he felt as though he had awakened after a good night's sleep, to the smell of freshly baked bread and a crisp autumn morning. When he smiled at Moira, she took his hand. Arm in arm, they began strolling towards the hall.

Lights now flared from every window, shining and gem-like against the grainy porous texture of the stone. Harps, flutes, pipes and drums struck up an accompaniment to a chorus of voices as the largest double doors, carved of onyx or black jade, swung open, and a retinue of Elves filed down the grassy clearing. Their not-quite-human features, keen and mobile, marked them as natives of Faerie, although Tomas might have guessed their race from no more than the thoughtless fluidity with which they moved. They were of countless sizes and every shape, some dark like Moira, many as fair as Tomas, and of all complexions in between. Their numbers seemed to vary. Perhaps a quarter of them played instruments as they walked. Among the crowd stalked many animals both exotic and familiar.

Which one was Rhys? Tomas glanced down at Moira's fingers clasped in his.

The company halted about fifty feet away. Their expressions were polite, welcoming and deferential. But Tomas's skin crawled with a mounting sensation of being stared at, covertly and intently, by beings seen and unseen. Hearing whispers, he scanned the crowd for Elves with weapons: jealous, murderous... He saw none.

Instead, the alien, pointed faces turned towards him appeared suddenly avid and ghoulish. Another feeling shone in those watching eyes, fluttered with those long knifelike fingers. Tomas could almost smell it: the Elves were desperate, desperate with the urgency of faint but reawakened hope.

Why hope?

He took a step backward, away from the collective need and expectation. He rubbed his eyes with one hand, felt Moira squeeze the other and release it.

The strangeness passed. Tension lurking around her mouth, Moira flashed a hand signal at her subjects. "Enid, Wythe, I thank you," she said to a pair of wizened manikins who detached themselves from the crowd.

They carried a lacquered tray. A shallow bowl, hollowed from an iridescent substance glazed with swirling designs, rested on the tray beside two fragile wineglasses with curiously long and twisted stems. Mist rose from the dish, and the glasses held an amethyst-colored liquid. Nodding to Moira and Tomas, the small Elves proffered the tray. The bowl cradled two hot damp linen cloths dyed the same shade as the contents of the goblets. Moira passed Tomas one steaming towel, moistened her hands and face with the other. The Elves murmured, as if at a sign of favor from her. Perhaps Tomas should have been the one to give Moira the towel? Hastily, he swabbed his face and hands with the heated linen. It smelled of lilac. "Thank you," he said to the tray-bearers.

They measured less than four feet tall. Two seamed and puckered brown faces, rayed with lines like sun-dried leather and framed with snarled dark hair, regarded Tomas appraisingly. They had crow-black, unblinking eyes. Spiky black hairs quilled their facial skin and covered their six-fingered brown hands. Both Elves wore roughly woven breeches and tunics the color of their skin. Splayed and bare, their outsized feet ended in six prehensile-looking toes.

Hoping that he hadn't stared, Tomas returned the cloth to the bowl. The small Elves' silence made him nervous.

"Enid and Wythe are fenodyree, Tomas. The Norse call them nisse. In Wessex and Mercia, they are usually called brownies," Moira explained.

Wythe, the one with the twiggy black beard, sniffed.

"The fenodyree manage our hall. We would be in a shambles without them."

Tomas remembered the pooka's words, repeated them. "I'm charmed to make your acquaintance."

Enid giggled. Wythe's face split in a cavernous grin, revealing teeth like cracked yellow pebbles. In a deep bass voice, he said to Moira, "I'm glad it's polite, Lady," and to Tomas, "At your service, mortal."

Moira appeared relieved. "We drink a cup of guesting now."

Tomas offered her one curving glass, retained the second. It seemed the correct gesture; Enid nodded approval. Other fenodyree with similar trays circulated among the crowd.

Moira waited until all in human shape held a glass, then aimed hers, like a promise, towards the expectant Elves. "To Tomas, poet and...true friend, by nature and design. To the Fate that brought him among us," she intoned with the emphasis peculiar to ritual. "And to the deed that will mark his destiny and ours."

Her subjects cheered. Startled, Tomas looked from their intent faces to Moira. She avoided his gaze, spilled a few drops on the ground and drank the rest at one swallow. The rest of the Elves did the same. Then their glittering eyes fixed upon Tomas, and a charged silence fell.

He stared at the brimming goblet in his hand. What deed was he toasting, that would mark his destiny and theirs? The toast was probably some form of consent to that deed. How would the amethyst liquid affect him? Ominous fingers of mauve smoke pointed up at him from where Moira had spilled her few drops on the lawn.

"Tomas," said Moira, her voice pitched for his ears alone, "you must drink it, to be accorded courtesy and protection as my guest. I cannot spare you the consequences of refusing."

Consequences: a stone blade, a pooka's teeth, or something worse. Moira still had not spoken about the foul wind they'd encountered. Tomas drained the goblet. An ill-omened choice, no doubt, but probably better than the alternatives.

Turning from cool to fiery in his mouth, the liquid slipped down his throat: hot, invigorating, alive. It was not stupefying, like ale. Instead he felt transformed. Into his bloodstream flowed an alien current, rich and balmy. He sensed its tides pulling him towards the Elves, swirling him away from the faint, blind, liquid tugging of the Moon in Midgard. After an instant of nausea, of undertow, perhaps, there came a subtle shift in his center of gravity, as if countless invisible threadlike lines had unravelled all at once, unmooring him. Abruptly, and for the first time since he set foot on the greensward, Tomas heard the muffled grinding of the sea.

Blown stemware clinked in his unsteady hands as he replaced both glasses on the tray. A musky aftertaste drenched his tongue, part pepper and part tar, laced with wormwood and something like ripe persimmons.

Then the crowd parted to let a tall red-haired Elf pass. They were all bowing; it must be Rhys.

Poised and smiling, the King of Elfland came straight to Tomas.

CHAPTER FIVE: A MUSICAL INTERLUDE

Tomas's heart beat as erratically as a drunken blacksmith at a forge. His heightened senses felt each shallow breath sliding in and out of his lungs, and the parching of his mouth. Moira stepped back a pace, and the air was thick with silence.

Rhys moved with the catlike suppleness of all his kin. He and Tomas were precisely the same height. Dusky auburn hair fell past his shoulders, and his clean-shaven skin was so flawless that it might have been dusted with gold. As Moira's did, the Elf lord's age appeared to shift.

His voice was rich and calm. "Welcome," he said softly in Welsh, taking Tomas's hands and gazing into his eyes. Those of the Elf were clear yellow-gold without a hint of brown, like pale amber or the eyes of a snake, and more slanted than Moira's. All his features had a more alien shape than hers. A good deal of strong curving bone to his chin and jawline, a sharply cut and generous mouth, cheekbones and temples chiseled from a different template altogether. Moira might pass for a mortal woman among less perceptive folk, albeit an exotic woman, but Rhys was unmistakably of another caste. He released his hold and waited, his spectacular face as readable as topaz.

"I am honored to be welcomed here." Tomas silently cursed his dry throat.

"A bard is always a treasured guest. I hope that you and I will come to know each other better," said Rhys, and smiled again. Then he looked at Moira.

It was as if Tomas stood beside lightning that crackled and narrowly missed him. Grey eyes and gold widened, flashed and locked as both pointed faces shut like carved ivory fans. After a moment Tomas took a miserable step away and cast around for something to distract him from the soundless dialogue occurring at his elbow.

Aubrey waved at him so wildly from a knot of Elves that they had to dodge his flailing arms. Surprised, Tomas laughed. So did the watching court. Facing the crowd, Rhys gave Aubrey a nod and beckoned to someone near the pooka.

A mortal, a fair-skinned young woman with masses of dun-colored curly hair, came diffidently to Rhys's side. The roundness of her freckled face struck Tomas as both lush and fragile. She wore clinging, lapis-blue silk with a dull sheen, which enhanced her hazy blue eyes.

Rhys cradled the woman's hand in both of his. "Caraid, this is Tomas, newly come among us from the North. Caraid is from Dubhlinn, Tomas. She learned Norse from your people there and Welsh

34

from the traders, so you have the choice of those languages with her--unless you speak Gaelic?"

Tomas shook his head, reflecting that she might not care to talk to him at all: the Norse had taken over Dubhlinn. He and Caraid exchanged greetings in Welsh. Her voice was low and drowsy, like that of a sleepwalker. She gave Tomas a wistful smile, then cast an unexpectedly canny glance at Moira, whose expression was benign. Gazing at Tomas again, Caraid said, "You are half Welsh. You are the one who--" She stopped as Rhys gripped her elbow.

Tomas wouldn't have felt more threatened if the moon-faced Irishwoman had aimed a dagger at him. How could Caraid tell that he was half Welsh? She must know something of this deed he was to do. He started to ask what she'd intended to say, but Rhys interrupted him smoothly.

"Caraid is a Seer, Tomas. She sensed your arrival here." Another smile. "Come, let us show you the hall while the cooks and musicians prepare."

Moira took Tomas's arm. Rhys waved the four of them across an onyx doorsill into a foyer, where several silent Elves stood watching them. Guards, probably, though they carried no weapons that Tomas could see. Next Rhys opened a door to a quiet corridor. With growing anxiety despite Moira's reassuring squeezes of his arm, Tomas started down the hallway with her.

What did the Elves expect of him? When could he ask Moira, and how could he talk to Caraid? She must know; she was a Seer. Perhaps she worked like the priestesses of Freyja, soothsayers who traveled to farms and prophesied at feasts. Dressed in skins, the priestess would devour a platter of animal hearts. To the accompaniment of a ritual song, she then mounted a platform and entered trance before responding to questions and making predictions. Once, years ago, Tomas had sung the spell for such a priestess at his father's farm, but for Tomas she'd made no prophecy. Instead she had favored him with a cryptic stare, tinged at the end with what might have been sympathy or awe.

While ushered through a series of corridors, Tomas tried to catch Caraid's eye. But the Irish Seer's head drooped down; her gaze turned elsewhere. King and Queen steered the mortals unseeingly past places where the marbled floors became beaten earth, pitted with dark stained depressions, and past crumbling gaps in the enormous stones where Tomas and Caraid--had they known how and when to look--might almost have glimpsed the Sun of Midgard rising on some midsummer's day.

In the labyrinthine hallways they passed Elves who stared openly at Tomas but not at Caraid. She must be a familiar sight. Tomas longed to ask her how long she'd been here. To ask her anything, but Rhys maintained an affable flow of conversation.

Apparently trying to draw Tomas out and put him at ease, the Elf King questioned Tomas about himself at length. It was not an interrogation. Rhys's queries were courteous and perceptive, and he listened to Tomas's cautious answers with what seemed genuine interest. Subsequent questions showed that Rhys remembered every word said to him. Tomas sensed that he might have formed a strong liking for the poised Elf—under other circumstances.

They returned to the green to sit at a low table with driftwood legs and topped by a mosaic of sea-smoothed pebbles. Other Elves, including Aubrey, joined them and pressed bread and wine upon the mortals. Tomas soon despaired of all but superficial communication in that setting. Should he eat? He'd already drunk from the goblet and the well, and the scent of spiced raisins and walnuts shouted from the loaves.

The pooka declined the slice that Tomas offered him. "Not a fitting meal for me, alas. Too rich, too rare." Aubrey's eyes gleamed red.

Best not to ask what pookas ate. Tomas bit into the bread. It was moist, sweet and filling, and the wine was dry and strong. Contentment, a soothing blend of relaxation and alertness, began to soak his blood.

He became absorbed in watching the musicians. Accustomed to harps built of two verticals and one crosspiece attached to strings, with a soundbox, he studied the Elves' harps with interest. Triangular, they were carved from a single piece of wood. Several harpists played in turn, accompanying themselves or other Elves. There were Welsh songs to Moira and to Rhys, songs celebrating the Elves' history, songs whose lyrics Tomas didn't understand. Rhys absently stroked Caraid's hair as she leaned against him. At Moira's urging, Tomas drank a second glass of wine. His bemused attention floated from the music to her pointed fingertips on his thigh.

Musicians with flutes, pipes, carillons and bells joined other musicians with whistles and chimes, lutes, rattles and rasps. Still more Elves set up an astonishing assortment of drums, and all the players congregated in a loosely structured band. The drummers included a contingent of fenodyree with a bizarre collection of trenchers, spoons, clay and wooden bowls, and other items from mortal households.

Moira noticed Tomas studying the percussionists' instruments.

"Mostly stolen," she murmured, amusement in her voice.

Soon Tomas was stamping his feet with the Elves. Vibrating in the bones of his skull, the music propelled him onto the green with Moira, Rhys and Caraid. Partners lost and found one another as circles formed, dissolved and re-formed, but Tomas was never paired with the Irishwoman. Dancers and musicians kept trading places, and melodies frequently changed. Tomas played a harp for an all-too-brief time, then a flute and some pipes before the fenodyree beckoned him into their nest of drums. There he stayed until two Elf women tugged at his sleeve to plead for another dance.

Tomas followed them. They mimed steps, laughed and whirled him to other partners, stopping only long enough to offer him water from the flagons on every table. Each time he drank, he wanted to dance, resented even the interval between his first and last sips of the icy-pure liquid that soothed his heated throat. The moments blurred into sound and motion, color and rhythm. His senses sharpened; his thoughts slowed.

"I've found you, love." Moira drew him from the greensward. Usually pale, her face was suffused with delicate color from dancing, and her clothing clung to her body. She pressed against Tomas as they walked. When he felt a tremor in her hips, he caressed the side of her throat; her pulse was rapid beneath his fingertips.

She led him through a stone archway into the Elves' hall. Then there was a room, high-ceilinged and candle-lit and draped with richly patterned cloth. Before the door swung closed, he was kissing Moira feverishly, wanting it to matter, wanting affirmation, wanting something he couldn't have named. There was a bed piled with cushions. A wealth of slightly damp, crisp black hair; a fiery mouth and deftly urgent hands. A supple world of fragrant skin. More and more softness in her eyes. A low resonant voice, with a catch in it as the Elf sometimes murmured to Tomas and, much later, cried out. As did his own voice.

Music was being played well and loudly somewhere nearby. He knew that tune, but not that arrangement of it. Tomas opened his eyes.

A fabric canopy was suspended a few yards above his head, while beneath him the luxuriant bed was open to the room on all four sides. Such opulent sleeping arrangements as these were found in countries farther south than Olaf planned to sail--

No, this was Elfland. Tomas scrambled to his feet.

Moira was gone. He drew a shaky breath, remembering. Another, pleasantly visceral memory made him stretch and take some deeper breaths.

Now he recalled waking up at least once before. They'd shared a light meal at some point. Where was she? Her absence alarmed him. So did the way his head ached, faintly yet persistently. Why, when he'd accepted only two glasses of wine before drinking water instead?

The Elves might have dosed him with something, something that dulled the mind and aroused the body. Those staring desperate faces when he first arrived... What was this deed they expected, the deed of Moira's toast?

On a low table near the bed stood two goblets, a water pitcher, the heel of a poppyseed loaf, a creamy earthenware vase overflowing with scarlet roses and smoky blue forget-me-nots, half a bowl of fresh fruit, and a row of gutted candles bedaubed with rivers of hardened wax teardrops. How long had he been in this room? On the floor by the bed lay a woman's comb, carved from close-grained pale wood, and polished to the sheen and smoothness of glass. Tomas turned the comb in his hands, studied the few strands of hair caught in its tines. Black strands and blond. Yes, he'd spent a long time combing her hair. Her mouth had tasted of apricots...

Tomas washed and dressed, but ate nothing and drank only a swallow of water, wanting his mind clear when he found Moira. Or Caraid. Finding either of them meant facing Elves--facing Rhys, perhaps--and requesting a private interview.

The door was unlocked, the corridor empty. Tomas followed it till he came to an elaborately arched doorway and stepped through it onto the green. Incredibly, some of the Elves were still playing their instruments and dancing there. How long had he slept; what time was it? Time had no meaning here.

He paced along the clearing's edge, eyeing the dancers. Moira was nowhere to be seen. Near the hawthorn circle he found a small sheltered spot in the woods--close enough to a well-traveled area not to provoke attacks for trespassing, he hoped--and settled down to decide how to approach Moira with his questions.

Footsteps and conversations came and went past his hiding place. Gradually, two voices in particular threaded to Tomas's ears. Threaded and returned, until his attention fastened on them.

"The reavers felled trees needlessly this time. Not for warmth or food, merely to watch them burn," said one bitter voice.

The other sighed. "I ventured down Caerdaev way but could not pass."

"Another exorcism?" asked the first speaker, a man.

"Yes. And more of Waleis barred to us." Was that Moira's voice?

"A jealous god, the Nazarene," said the man.

"I think 'tis more his priests."

It was Moira. Tomas leaned forward.

"No, they left the dragon heads upon the ship. The captain jeered at us. I cannot reckon them for brothers, even half-blood. Yet they are."

Moira and Rhys, discussing Olaf's ship.

"Look at these hawthorns! Barren," said Rhys, frustration in his voice. "We are boxed into a shrinking realm. I've no desire to dwindle to a tale for mortal children."

"Nor I."

A pause. Tomas's back itched; he ignored it.

"You are having second thoughts," said Rhys. "Is it the risk?"

"No. Our survival merits any risk. If faith in the old truths disappears--if a single truth prevails over the many--we become nothing but myth." She sighed again. "But I would rather ask this deed of someone I disliked."

"Yet Fate sent him, and not another," Rhys observed, very gently.

"That I know. He doesn't yet, but he will." A tiny hesitation. "I must tell you... He appears to have more Sight than we first thought. And to be less easy to sway."

Rhys made a sharp, peculiar sound. "He's taken little enough food or drink."

"I noticed this before he'd taken any."

Silence. Then Rhys said pensively, "We cannot know all that Caraid saw. The more powerful the Seer, the greater the occlusion. It was not deliberate, in any event."

"Of course not." Moira's voice was soft. When she spoke again, it was in her own tongue.

Tomas stood up as silently as he could. His heart thudded in his ears, and his cramped muscles were so tense that he thought they might peel away from his bones.

So Christianity and the Norse gods, or at least Odin and his berserkers, threatened Faerie somehow and restricted its access to Midgard. As for what or whom the Elves would risk for survival, a risk that Moira found distasteful but would take nonetheless, that was only too clear. They were going to risk Tomas, by requesting some deed of him. Even if he did possess more Sight than they'd first thought--an

39

unsettling notion at every level--he still had to find Caraid and ask her what she knew.

CHAPTER SIX: THE ELVISH SEA

Keeping within the boundary of the forest, Tomas ran towards the hall. Trees leaned in close above his head, scraping their branches together like old men warming themselves over a fire. Farther back from the clearing where the woods grew dark, tangled and impenetrable, he heard chittering and glimpsed occasional pairs of eyes, mostly yellow or green, all shining damply.

He didn't stop to wonder what sort of Elves were staring at him. Color-splashed flowers, long-petaled, viney of stem, twined about trees and into his path. Lush fragrances drifted around him, turning him giddy. He held his breath and ran, stopped to gasp for air, held his breath and ran again. When he reached the section of the forest by the musicians, he stepped from the trees and looked for Caraid among the dancers.

They moved with a wild and erotic grace that gave Tomas a fierce desire to join them. At any second, the rhythm could pull him into this knot of flying limbs, or that one, perhaps... Arms stretched out to him as some of his former partners whirled past. Covering his ears with his hands, he searched for Caraid's dun-colored hair among the bobbing heads.

A yank at his sleeve: Tomas started and lowered his hands. For a disoriented instant he thought no one was there, until his gaze fell on a fenodyree. Hands on her hips, the small Elf scowled at him.

"I don't like all their music neither, but stop up my ears I would never do. A fine way to make enemies. And the worst sort, secret ones, you being friend to the Queen."

"I love the music. But I don't want to dance just now, and it pulls me," Tomas improvised, uncertain if the little Elf were the one he had met before. The fenodyree all dressed alike.

This one continued to frown, but she removed her hands from her hips. Respect flickered in her blackbird eyes. "Pull, that music does," she agreed, as if boasting of a personal achievement. "'Tis seldom that mortals fathom it. Still and all, you must be a rare one, clear-headed and apt, for the Queen to choose—" She clamped her lips together and folded her arms.

"For the Queen to what?" he asked quickly.

"Nothing!" snapped the Elf. She shifted tack. "And why don't you care to dance, young spark?"

"I'm looking for someone." With luck she would assume he meant Moira. He gave the flustered Elf a conspiratorial smile. "Is everyone dancing? Where would the others be?"

41

"Now how would I know the whereabouts of every creature in Faerie? To be sure they're not all dancing." An unexpected and unnerving cackle. "Not all of them have legs." Giving him an appraising stare, she added, "Don't fancy meeting one of those? Well, lad, you might have done already. Some of 'em change shape." She waved a hairy hand towards the side of the hall opposite the festivities. "There might be summat yonder, on the cliffs above the Sea. Or in the hall. And many in the woods." Her eyes gleamed. "Perchance you'd like to hear what kind?"

Tomas ignored the bait. "I thank you, but I'll be on my way." He started for the edifice of stone, trying not to mind the tingling at the back of his neck. The little Elf probably meant to unsettle him, to disguise her slip about Moira.

In another forty paces, Tomas rounded the great curve of the hall and stopped, transfixed at the sight of the foaming, jade-green Elvish Sea.

Veins of liquid malachite, ebb and flow of molten turquoise. Crooning, the water embraced and deserted a mutely patient shore molded from sulphur-colored, glittering sand. Moisture-laden air hung over the restless waves, while the waves pointed long curling fingers at the air, until sky and sea merged in an opal mist.

The hall crowned salt-carved grey cliffs that bathed their rocky faces in the frothing water. Drawn to the edge of the promontory, Tomas gazed with hunger at the surf. A hard wind sang in his ears and bannered his pale hair. This sea might be the heart of Faerie: evanescent, breath-taking and all but impossible to see clearly, or even to distinguish details apart from the glamour of the whole.

The ocean purred like a great cat. Like a great cat slowly stretching, lime-green water curved again and again to meet the rippled sand. Three dolphins leaped and played close to shore. Tomas felt his breathing deepen, felt tremors in his legs. To curl and sleep upon that strand, pillowed and warm...

No. He had to stop looking at the sea. With an effort that knotted the muscles in his neck, Tomas turned his head from the beckoning shoreline and sighted down the spine of the ridge towards the standing stones of the hall.

There he saw Caraid trailing with hesitant steps round the circular heft of the building, and ran to meet her.

CHAPTER SEVEN: CARAID

Caraid stopped and waited for Tomas to reach her. In the tall looming shadows of the hall above the perilous sea, he caught her hands in his. "May I speak with you privately, away from here?" He watched in desperation as her vision blurred. "Please, Caraid?"

Her blue eyes flashed glassy-clear. "Where? Make haste!"

Now Caraid and Tomas sprawled on the moss-lined bank of a shallow brook. In its water darted pearly streaks of minnows. Searching for wild green eyes and leathery wings, Tomas stared into the murky forest all around but saw nothing. He heard a faint creaking here and there, a rustling and soughing that might be merely the settling of foliage after their headlong scramble through the trees—or might be something else.

When he glanced at Caraid, she was studying him. She looked hastily away and twisted a lock of her hair about her fingers.

"Caraid?"

She turned towards him. Fright and fatigue showed in the tension around her mouth and temples, with another emotion that Tomas judged was resigned sadness. But her eyes were alert. The dreamlike lassitude so evident at their first meeting had all but left her. Still, it might be best to approach his questions slowly. "You needn't fear me," he began.

"I do not," she said with a display of spirit. "Would I have hied myself off with you if I did, when your people are staking outposts in my country?"

Tomas winced. "I hope they haven't harmed you."

"Harmed me?" Caraid's eyes slid away as if she remembered something. "No. Not myself, although—" She stopped and shook her head. "I am a Seer, and well-protected by our folk. And I could predict when your reavers would be active."

"You and Rhys," Tomas said carefully. "Did you foresee him?" He wished he'd had a more specific warning of Moira's appearance than the Fate Rune in the sky.

"Not Rhys himself. But I was aware of the Elves, and I sought to learn more. I spied upon them when I could."

"And?"

Caraid contemplated the far bank of the stream. "And one day I wandered unknowing into the realm of the Sidhe. For as you draw near them, so they draw near you." She looked meaningfully at Tomas.

"The Sidhe?"

"The people of Faerie. The Tuatha de Danaan, the Gentry."

43

Caraid laughed. "The Fair Folk. The People of Peace. They use so many names! And never the true one, for he who holds a name holds power over its owner. In Waleis they are called the Blessed of the Mothers, and the Tylwyth Teg."

Tomas nodded; he had heard the last two terms. "Where did Rhys find you?"

Caraid rubbed the bridge of her freckled nose, leaving a smudge. Her hands were grimy from her foray through the woods. "He was visiting the King of the Irish Sidhe when I was brought to that court. Rhys asked me to come with him, and I did." She studied her hands, now twisted in her lap.

Tomas nodded again, slowly. They avoided each other's eyes.

"You wish to ask me something," said Caraid. "Several things."

"First, how long have you been here?"

She chose that moment to brush drying mud from her bare feet. Surely birds were calling and Elves laughing nearby, a few moments ago? When had the woods grown so quiet? Even the voice of the water stilled; the silence settled like a shroud.

Caraid glanced up, and it was as if she had forgotten not only Tomas's question but his presence. Round gentle eyes, a darker blue than usual, met his, and she smiled. Slowly all her tension vanished, and she looked on the verge of yawning.

Her renewed vagueness didn't appear feigned. Perhaps Tomas would become as fey as Caraid, if he stayed as long in Elfland. Was the Seer always this touched, even in Dubhlinn? "How long have you been here, Caraid?" he asked again, and wiped his sweaty palms on his trousers.

Caraid's head jerked to the side and then forward, twice, a third time, before Tomas realized that the movement was deliberate. She was fighting some invisible control. Moisture beaded her upper lip; she shut her eyes and her throat contracted.

He didn't know how to help, and he hesitated to break Caraid's concentration. Her face ran with sweat, as if she expelled a poison from her body. Hands clasped behind her neck, she tucked her head and began to rock back and forth.

Distraught, Tomas gripped her upper arms, just as the Seer forced herself upright and turned a pallid face to him. He exhaled, inhaled again. He didn't let go of her.

"I have been in Faerie longer than you have, Tomas," she said in a low voice.

A shudder crept along his spine, as though a long-dead, grave-cold hand caressed him. He thought of the howes, the burial mounds of the North. Some were said to be haunted by Elves. He glanced over both shoulders.

Caraid lifted a freckled hand to his. "I am no dry-bones yet, Tomas. Nor shade, nor Elf." She squeezed his fingers. Realizing that he still held her arms, he released them. Caraid promptly took both his hands. "No more than you," she added.

"How much longer--"

"Don't ask me that again!" she cried. A brief spasm twisted her features. "I know that's not the answer you desired. But the Sight is ill-named, my friend. 'Tis like a candle flaring in a dark cave and lighting only a fraction of the blackness. It can...distort as much as it reveals. And sometimes your own arm that holds the candle blocks your view."

Tomas didn't understand. "How long we've been here shouldn't need the Sight to tell."

Her laugh held no hint of mockery, only sadness. "Tell me, then. How long have you yourself been among the Elves?"

He couldn't answer. He didn't know. Instead he asked, "What ailed you just now?"

Caraid shot him an assessing glance that softened when she met his gaze. "I cannot speak freely for long, nor fully explain why I cannot. Their food lulls us. Transforms us at least in part, though it seems to affect you less than me. Time spent here also works changes upon us, and more besides. Haven't you remarked that you feel different with a full belly than when hungry? And how we are pressed to eat?"

Tomas nodded.

"If I--strive against that transformation, against them--it is difficult for me."

"Why? Because of something you know about me?"

"No and yes. Do not speak so loudly!" Caraid started at a sharp cracking sound in the forest, but Tomas saw nothing there. Caraid's grip on his hands tightened. No wind blew, yet the nearest tree limbs shivered and stretched down towards the two of them. "Your other questions. We've no time!"

Suddenly the forest hummed with unseen life, and a newborn, squalling wind hurtled twigs and acorns at them.

"Do you know why Moira brought me here, and what deed the Elves want from me?" he asked in desperation.

Air currents shifted drunkenly as Moira materialized two feet from Tomas and the Seer. He sucked in his breath; Caraid uttered a small shriek.

Leaves snarled Moira's unbound hair. She wore dark green trousers and a belted tunic: riding clothes, old and weathered. The

45

well-worn costume seemed closer to the truth about her--to one truth, at least. Tomas rose and faced her.

Her tilting eyes were opaque and dark as slate, and she wore the expressionless alabaster look that Tomas had come to associate with self-control and the keeping of secrets. She was nerving herself for something.

"I will tell you, Tomas," she said, her voice hardly more than a whisper. "Caraid, please return to the hall with Aubrey. And fear us not, Seer; we all do as we must."

The pooka ambled up to them in horse-shape and waited. Caraid got to her feet, put her arms around Tomas's neck and hid her face on his shoulder--the shoulder farthest from Moira. Tomas was startled to feel moisture on his skin as Caraid shed a few silent tears. He patted her back as soothingly as he could.

She stood on her toes and murmured in his ear, "You will see me again, Tomas, but I don't know when." Then she climbed from a boulder onto Aubrey's bare back, and the water-horse bore her away.

CHAPTER EIGHT: THE MAGICIAN'S OATH WITH FATE

Tomas and Moira were perhaps a mile from the clearing, but from the silence there might have been no Elf within thirty leagues. Not a leaf rustled, not a mouse twitched. Had an owl, that stealthiest of winged creatures, shifted in its sleep, they could have heard the faint displacement of air fanned by its downy feathers. But no bird moved.

Moira took a small irregularly-shaped flask from her tunic pocket. She offered the bottle to Tomas; it was carved from a single quartz crystal. "To clear your head."

The liquid was icy, bone-searingly cold, when he'd expected warmth. He drank it all and gave her the empty decanter. Cold unfurled a fist in his stomach, then pierced his limbs and throat, stinging him into greater lucidity, though he'd believed himself alert before. When the glacial sensation receded, he looked warily at Moira.

She was studying the flask in her hand, but lifted her dark head to meet Tomas's gaze. Tomas had last seen her on a canopied bed in a quiet room. That asymmetrically feline face had worn a very different expression then--he pushed the thought aside.

"Sit down, please," she said tonelessly. Then, when they'd settled beside the stream: "You can accept that I am both a woman and an Elf. Most mortals prefer that something be all one way or the other."

Tomas could think of no answer. Moira gave him a small smile and glanced into the rows of trees that crowded close. When she took his hands, he decided it might be unwise to pull them away.

"Did you notice anything else not of Midgard that day, when you met me by the river?"

He nodded. The hands gripping his were warm and vital. "At the village, when my brother's men...a Rune appeared in the sky. Perthro, the Web of Fate."

"What did that signify to you?"

"'The seeker cannot comprehend the fateful flow of events, because his own lot numbers among those cast,'" said Tomas. "That is how I was taught to read Perthro. So I guessed that the Nornir were at work, even before I saw them at their loom."

Moira raised her eyebrows. "Tell me of that vision, please."

"I wish I could disbelieve it. Spears lay upon the loom, and the Nornir wove bloody threads among them." He swallowed. "The loom was weighted with severed heads."

Moira's pupils had expanded until her eyes were great pools of grey-rimmed black, pools where someone had tossed a stone to trouble the water. "You saw truly, Tomas. The loom was there, and the Rune also. And the Fates."

"You saw them too?"

"I did." When her gaze fastened on him, a mounting chill in the air woke an answering pit of cold in his belly. This was no spell from the food of Faerie, but the power of Moira herself. Except where she held his hands, frost crept across his skin. I am falling, he thought; falling, and the bones of the earth will swallow me.

"I walked in Midgard on the first of May," said Moira softly. "An inauspicious day for sailing, though some care not for omens. When I beheld your dragonship run ashore, I followed the hounds of Odin to their kill. There I saw the Nornir." She searched Tomas's face. "At times they weave an uncertain thread, and I perceived that one of those times lay upon them. Therefore I called, wondering if any mortal among those whose Fates the Nornir wove could hear me--and be loosed from the loom that day. And you came to the river, Tomas." Her voice was hushed and urgent, more alarming than if she had shouted.

"Why did you call? What difference would a mortal life make to you?" My life, Tomas almost added.

She appeared not to notice his question. "Urd, Verdandi and Skuld," she murmured. "Fate, Being and Necessity. They had spun your thread, Tomas, spun and measured it. Who can say if they would have cut it? Do you know why I might have seized that loose-held skein?"

"No, Moira," he whispered.

Her eyes were quickly extinguished flares in a remote face. "My reasons--on that day--were that you paid Odin homage as lord of poetry and magic. But had discovered you could not follow Him as lord of war and the dead."

Tomas's expression must have changed, for Moira added quickly, "Nor do the Elves honor those two aspects of Him. His berserkers encroach upon lands in Midgard too near our own. They fell and burn our trees." Her chin lifted. "Celts and Saxons cleave to a new god and limit our movements in Midgard with their rites and one-sided creeds. All this your Norse gods know, the Aesir and the Vanir both. Yet they do naught to prevent the constraint of my people, who were once... We would learn why this is so."

Guarded and restive, she glanced into the trees again. For a long moment she said nothing and seemed to weigh some decision. "You followed Odin, whom you well know does not allow mortals to pick and choose among His guises. Had you died fleeing that raid, your lot would have fallen to Hel in Niflheim, not to Odin's hall of warrior-dead. But you did not die, Tomas. You came to the river, and I brought you here with me." She paused. "Do you recall the wind and the smell that pursued us?"

Tomas nodded. He stared numbly down at his hands, still holding hers.

"As we passed through the gates between the worlds, Hel wanted to claim you."

"Why didn't She?" asked Tomas after a short silence. Not that it mattered now.

"For one thing, that particular crossroads is free to all travelers. She had no power there, and we both knew it."

Not I, he thought. I knew nothing.

"She comes here next."

He shot to his feet. "Here!"

Moira stood and gripped his arm. "You should return to Midgard immediately. Hel does not lightly venture there. She seldom leaves Niflheim at all, but I'd wager She would like to find you."

"Why?" The goddess Hel, Queen of the dead. She must want to bear him across the icy river Gjoll into the misty freezing darkness of Niflheim, Her underworld realm. There She would hurl him onto Nastrond, the strand of corpses, among the mouldering dead. If Tomas were still alive, how would the newly rotting bodies and the ancient, dry and animated bones react to his arrival? None of it would happen with merciful speed, for Hel and Her subjects moved slowly, slowly, in that crushing murky cold.

Moira was saying something. "For many reasons. She is an ill loser, the daughter of Loki, when She loses at all. She hungered to lay claim to one who might have been Odin's, and to gloat. But She was cheated of you at the loom. You eluded both Odin's grasp and Hers, and became still more a prize."

"So Odin knows that I left—"

"Who can say what One-eye knows?" Moira released Tomas's arm. "You have precious little time for questions."

"Then we go to Midgard now," he said cautiously.

The Elf's face was the color of sun-bleached bone. Leaf-studded black hair coiled like snakes around her head. Arms folded, she said, "Perhaps."

It was here at last, the thing that Tomas had dreaded: Moira's motive for bringing him to Faerie. No doubt the only reason she had touched him—he could not think about that yet. The deed she would require of him. "You wish me to agree to something. Before you'll take me back," he said dully, then looked her full in the face.

He thought she might have turned a shade more pale. After a moment she nodded. "You would be removed from Hel's proximity a second time. And I will give you a gift or two, to help you do as I request...if you will swear by the Magician's oath with Fate to perform a certain task." She spoke the last phrase with the same ritual formality she'd shown when mentioning the task before the assembled Elves.

Acutely aware of the overhanging trees, the stooping vines, Tomas said, "I'm not a Magician."

One corner of Moira's mouth moved, but her voice was gentle. "No? Perhaps not yet. Perhaps then you are a Fool."

She must intend the word in the sense of jester or mummer. Fool to the Elf Queen. He said with acrimony, "That is the truth, by all the gods. What is your task?"

"Go to Asgard by way of the temple at Uppsala, in the realm of the Svea people. Steal Odin's ravens, Thought and Memory. Bring the birds to me."

Tomas stared, until the air between him and Moira swarmed with unspoken words. Finally he shook his head and laughed in despair. She might as well have asked for the Moon. Mad, she was, and he was already a dead man. "Why?"

Moira gave him a chilly look, unwavering and eminently sane. He would have preferred bluster and rambling. She said: "If we can rob Odin, for even a short time, of the birds who fly through Midgard each day and tell Him what they see, His berserkers' raids might be hampered. And the Elves would hold His ravens with which to bargain. To learn why the Norse come to our borders, they who do not fear the sea, the woods, the dark—and who no longer worship us. And why the Christians move against us with their one-pointed choking faith. The ravens themselves may know these things." She touched Tomas's shoulder. "What I ask is most difficult and perilous, but lies within the realm of possibility. Each night the ravens fly back to their cage to sleep, for what lives, and especially what thinks and remembers, must sleep and dream." Her face was frozen. "Take the ravens in that cage and bring them to me."

"What's to protect me from Hel, once you have what you want?"

"Why, then She can be deflected from you once and for all, while you are living," Moira said quietly. "Accept this task, and I will return you to Midgard, where I will give you counsel and the gifts I promised." She gave him an enigmatic look. "Refuse, and Hel will find you here. I pray you, Tomas, do not feign acceptance now and balk in Midgard." A pause. "If you do, your Fate will move to claim you there, and I doubt that I could find the Nornir weaving in just that way again. You must work quickly, too, while your link to us is fresh."

It was impossible. The god of magic, whom Tomas had deserted, would discover him; the god of the dead would kill him. Terror mingled with a growing urge to strike Moira. "Why didn't you tell me in Waleis?" he blurted. Knotting his fists, he tried to slow his shallow breathing. "Did it occur to you that I might have preferred Hel then and there to being lured here and forced to this? Or didn't it matter to you?" Lunacy, to say those things to the Queen of Elfland, but he barely managed to choke back more dangerous words.

Moira neither moved nor gestured, but there was a sudden tightness in her face. A different expression welled into her eyes, a look so incalculably old and stark that he retreated a pace. "It is a matter of my survival. And were you not whom you are, Tomas, you would regret those questions," she said formally. "What do you prefer now?"

In a trice the atmosphere had turned moist and heavy, and the trees appeared to bristle with alarm. Glancing over Moira's shoulder, Tomas was appalled to see countless leaves curl and shrivel, and branches huddle against the trunks. With a great crashing, Aubrey snaked out of a thicket to Moira's left. Neck extended, ears flat, the water-horse scudded up to them. White ringed his red-sparked, rolling eyes.

At first his arrival deafened Tomas to the sounds that echoed through the cringing trees. Then he heard footsteps, ponderous, creeping. Immense weight shook the ground at irregular intervals, arrhythmic not from the entity's gait, but as if the feet dragging themselves along were of unequal size and indeterminate solidity. Into Tomas's face plummeted a vicious wind like an evil scavenging bird. With it came a carrion stench that he recognized from his journey to Faerie.

Knowing whose footsteps lurched closer, Tomas made his choice before Hel could stagger into view. Before Hel's putrescent legs and hips heaved Her troll-green upper body to where Moira stood and stared bleakly at Tomas, he shouted, "I swear by the Magician's oath with Fate that I will take Thought and Memory from Asgard and bring them to you. The curse of all the gods be on your soul!"

Howls began to mingle with the reeking wind as Tomas and Moira vaulted onto Aubrey's clammy back.

"Elves have no souls," Moira told Tomas in a flinty voice. "You'd best hold onto me; this will be a worse ride."

Shuddering, he clasped her waist. Just before Aubrey leaped into swirling nothingness, the Elf Queen smiled grimly. Tomas's last coherent thought was that he had never noticed how sharp and white and numerous were Moira's teeth.

51

CHAPTER NINE: THE FIRST OF MAY, 878 A.D.

A different smell: pungent, dank and earthy, faintly redolent of reeds and salt. Tomas opened his eyes. He was sprawled on his back on soggy ground. Four mud-caked hooves stepped closer, and the pooka rubbed his shaggy grey head against Tomas's jerkin.

"We're both pleased you have awakened," said Moira, and smoothed a lock of hair from his eyes. Only then did Tomas realize that his head was in her lap. He sat up and got dizzily to his feet.

Moira went to perch cross-legged on a flat hulking rock, on which lay a large satchel of finely tanned, sturdy leather. Tomas eyed it suspiciously. They'd left Faerie with nothing but the clothes upon their backs.

They were in Midgard now, he judged, because the Sun had reappeared. From low in the east, it stretched elongated sallow fingers over level scrubby terrain that edged into marshy fens. Vine-choked clumps of trees and brushy hillocks sprouted from mud flats, and puddles of brackish water dotted the landscape.

"Where are we?" asked Tomas.

Moira lifted one shoulder and let it drop. "Wessex." She twined her arms around her knees. With a quantity of leaves still riddling her black hair, she looked waifish in her riding costume, like a girl masquerading as an Elf.

"Not where you found me before," he said.

"No, that was Waleis. We have come east of there."

"Why?"

She exchanged glances with Aubrey, who had assumed two-legged shape and joined her on the rock. Aubrey was dressed like Moira now, but Tomas found himself staring at the pooka's ears, too long and oddly shaped to be human. In a futile attempt to hide their tufted tips, he had fluffed and snarled his coarse grey hair.

Moira said, "This site is the one most likely to serve our various ends. To drive Odin's followers from these isles. To suppress the exorcisms that restrict our movements here. And to begin your journey to Uppsala."

"You chose this particular spot?"

"Not I. Caraid named us this region of Wessex long before you set foot in Faerie." Moira patted the boulder where she sat. "I merely followed the path where the most forces converged."

Her attitude was patient, egalitarian and informative, and Tomas mistrusted it. He glanced at Aubrey, but the pooka's gleaming eyes and faintly twitching ears revealed only wary interest and amusement.

"Caraid counseled you to bring me here," Tomas muttered. Perhaps he should give no credence to anything Caraid had said; she might have been coerced to mislead him. He felt a pang of sympathy. Perhaps, on the other hand, Moira was lying. Elves were reputed not to lie--and not to tell the complete truth, either. "So you consult mortal Seers?" he asked.

Another shrug. "In conjunction with our own, mind you. But power is power, wherever it may manifest."

Tomas took a deep breath. "Why send me to fetch the ravens? Why not an Elf?"

The pooka whistled, a high-pitched whinnying sound that had not died away before he looked aghast. Moira glared at him; her eyes flashed redder than his. Aubrey quickly composed his face.

"Why you?" Moira repeated as if nothing had happened. "Many reasons. Your reaction to the violent trance that Odin sends. You are half Norse and might pass unremarked through Asgard, and a bard travels with ease among mortals." She gave Tomas an appraising glance. "And your Welsh blood is attuned to us. The affinity would be clear from no more than your music, but that blood flows surpassing strong in you. Or you would not have responded when the Nornir's thread worked loose, and I called." She looked away. "Nor would you have been able to perceive me and accompany me to Elfland."

Tomas studied her: the sloping eyes; the warm and bloodless skin; the improbably long and tapered hands. "And I'm mortal, and vulnerable to you," he said, keeping his voice level.

Moira blinked. "That also, in some ways. Some of those vulnerabilities I share."

He cast an involuntary glance at the pooka. Aubrey hunched forward in a close-ranged scrutiny of the rock where he and Moira sat. From his bird's-nest hair the tips of his ears protruded, flattened and immobile.

A sigh from Moira brought Tomas's attention back to her. Her face had grown utterly still, and the frozen dislocated focus of her eyes disturbed him. "We must speak of the temple in Uppsala now," she said. "When you arrive, do not linger on the howes, the burial mounds. Pay homage at the altars. Then await a night at the dark of the Moon to approach the tree by the great Well." She paused. "You are not looking at me, Tomas."

Reluctantly he met her eyes. They were glassy and shallow.

"Stand alone and unobserved between the tree and the Well. Plunge your hands into the water for three breaths' time. Then raise

53

your arms, palms outward, to make the Runic passes I will teach you."
She glanced down at her own hands clenched in her lap. "They are not
to be drawn in another's presence or elsewhere than between the tree
and the Well. Do not fail to hold your hands beneath the water before
you begin."

Tomas nodded; the words of any language had deserted him.

A moisture-laden wind blew, soft and dream-like. Sliding from
the boulder, Moira beckoned Tomas to a level stretch of sand. Among
the murmuring reeds the Elf found a sharp twisted stick, then turned to
Tomas, who shrank back a pace. Moira had fixed him with the pebble-
grey staring eyes of a crone, wounded and imperious, horribly at odds
with her flawless face.

"Form the Runes precisely as I do, in the same sequence. Attend
me well." Moira scratched a mark into the gritty sand. She asked
Tomas to trace the design after her, then close his eyes and trace it
again.

Many such lines he learned, distinct and unmistakable, while
in his sweaty grip the stick grew hot and dry as grains of sand crumbled
away from it. He recognized only a few Runes, drew far more that he
didn't know, although their shapes and meanings seemed familiar.
Sensing the staggering antiquity of this latter group of symbols, he felt
little surprise when they shifted and glimmered like insects on the pale
rushy ground. Afterwards he could recall the primitive scrawls, the
living ones, only as part of the complex and fibrous pattern that he and
Moira carved into the earth.

The Sun had wheeled to the top of the sky before Moira
conceded that Tomas would not forget the passes. After examining the
heat-shrivelled branch, she gave him an approving glance. "Well done
and with much power, to scorch the stick. When your hands have
shaped these lines, a bridge to Asgard will be visible. Cross it.

"You will enter near Valholl, Odin's hall of warrior dead. Feign
that you are of that caste. The slain are too drunk on battle to know
differently. As for the gods, Thor is unlikely to be troublesome; he has
more strength than wit. But Freyr..."

She made a decision. "The Harvest Lord spends much time
with the Norse Elves. And some with ours, in former days." Plunging
a hand into her tangled hair, she retrieved a small perfumed flower.
"Should Freyr recognize whence you have come, give Him this apple
blossom. Say it is from me."

Tomas stowed the flower in his jerkin. Little use to bolt and
run, when Moira--or Hel--could track him down in any of the worlds.

Moira asked Aubrey an abrupt question in their own language.

54

The pooka shook his head and lifted his bony hands in an ascending arc. With a quirk of her mouth, Moira said to Tomas: "Loki misses little that happens in the nine worlds, in Asgard most of all. Should the Father of Lies approach you, take heed: he is a trickster, inclined towards chaos, not order. Reveal your errand to him only if you must; he may or may not assist you. Yet I doubt he would betray you. For Loki's Fate is to help topple the Norse gods, the Aesir and the Vanir both, and he might regard an encounter with you as a step along that path."

Moira fished among her garments, took Tomas's hand and pressed into it a sprig of faded green leaves clustered with white berries. "This is mistletoe. If Loki presses you, give it to him. Remind him it is sacred to us, to the old beliefs." She paused, then added, "And to the ancient rituals." Her eyes dark and narrow, she waited until Tomas stowed the mistletoe in his shirt. "Inform Loki that this plant the Norse gods may overlook only to their peril—and that a day may come when he deems this knowledge useful.

"Still, none of the gods may even take notice of you. Wait for evening when the ravens fly in. After Odin converses with them, He will fetch an iron key from the world axle-tree. You call it Yggdrasil, though it has other names. The key unlocks the room with the ravens' cage. Follow Odin; He will secure them there and replace the key."

Moira drew closer to Tomas. "While Odin attends His warriors' feasting, steal the key. Discard it as soon as you take the cage. Then carry the ravens to the bridge and reverse the sequence of the passes. Will you remember?"

Tomas nodded, hypnotized, adrift in a haze of grey. Moira's eyes were immense silvery lights, as warm and promising as when he first had seen them. Frightening, how much he ached to hold her. He could have, easily; she stood a mere foot away. He didn't move.

"You will return to Uppsala, within the temple itself," she murmured. "Should priests or priestesses see you, do not speak. Let them assume they were granted a vision. Leave the temple and the sacred grove. At the largest oak due south of the grove, call my name three times."

Tomas wet his lips. "But Moira is not your name."

"It is not." The Elf Queen smiled a feral smile, wide and swift and tantalizing. "But it will do." She glanced up at the quilted clouds and the westering Sun. "I spoke of gifts, Tomas, and their time has come."

The enormous leather pouch sailed through the air into Moira's outstretched hands, narrowly missing Tomas's head. When he looked at Aubrey, still sitting on the boulder, the pooka appeared to have thrown nothing. From the satchel Moira pulled a bundle of clothing and tossed it to Tomas. "Put them on, please."

He unfolded a dark green tunic and trousers much like the ones Moira wore, then a cape-like garment in the same color. They were wrapped around a pair of well-oiled leather shoes and a belt. All too aware of Moira's gaze, Tomas turned away to peel off his old clothes. He tucked the apple blossom, the mistletoe and the winged Elf's knife into the new jerkin. Then he tied the soft leather belt at his waist and stepped into the shoes. Finding no brooch to pin the cape at his shoulder, he fumbled with unfamiliar bone and leather fasteners.

When Tomas finished dressing, the Elf lifted two identical harps from the bag, each carved from a single block of dark wood. These she set on the flat-topped rock. A case for both instruments followed, and a flute fashioned from the same gleaming wood. "For you, love," she said, elaborately casual, then chuckled at Tomas's expression.

"Moira..." He ran a reverent, greedy hand over all three instruments. Gods, he had missed his own harp and flute, left on Olaf's ship. "This is almost too great a boon. How can I take them all to Uppsala?"

"One harp only will you carry down the entirety of that road, for quite soon you shall offer the second one to a man who aids you. Keep the flute, and the harp that you now touch."

It flared hot, singeing him, and he jerked his hand away. Examining the instrument, he found imprints from two of his fingers, like grainy oval eyes burnt into the wood. But his skin bore no scar at all.

"You have my deepest thanks for this, Moira," he said quietly.

"Have I indeed?" Moira contemplated him with the abstracted air of someone musing at the edge of a cliff. "A bard partakes of mysteries, but to win his bread, this mongrel age of yours requires diversion from him. Yet in times not long past and in lands not far away, bards had no enemies, and their persons were sacred." Flicking sand from her sleeve, she muttered, "Rather like priests."

The pooka slid from the boulder, trudged up beside her and glanced at the empty sack.

"The hour grows late. A third and final gift," said Moira, who suddenly wore a self-contained smile, a mask that Tomas could not read. "And you shall choose. Which will it be, poet? Harp or carp?"

With something like affection in her eyes, she laughed as Tomas drew his brows together in confusion. No words came to him, no thoughts at all.

"That is to say, Tomas: more minstrelsy? Or, to truly speak

and prophesy?"

He shut his eyes to think. She must mean to grant him either musical or poetic skills. Which did she expect, and which did he prefer? His fingertips still tingled where they'd touched the harp. At last he said, "Might I choose to truly speak and prophesy? I have more need for that than for minstrelsy now, thanks to these instruments." Opening his eyes, he caught the end of a flash of motion.

Moira swayed like an ice-laden sapling, her face ghostly and rigid. Fingers fanned so wide that her frail extended palms were nearly convex, she had just finished sketching a Rune between herself and Tomas. He could not tell how he knew it was a Rune. The air glowed faintly silver and he wrinkled his nose at a peculiar smell, resinous and scorched, but with no trace of the carrion reek that signaled Hel's proximity.

What Rune had Moira drawn? A spasm of mild nausea gripped him, followed by a curious sensation of weightlessness. He reached for a nearby branch, but his shaking hand refused to move quickly and seemed instead to float up of its own accord.

When the giddiness passed, Tomas pulled himself onto a large crumbling rock whose fissures were padded with moss. Something around him had changed, or perhaps the change lay in himself. Yes, that was it: the mutation had occurred within him. He could tell by the bitter, oily flavor that coated his mouth and furred his tongue, a taste like the sodden green scent of the marshes, tainted with salt and mud. He twitched his clammy shoulders.

Aubrey rested two tentative fingers on Moira's arm; she gently brushed his hand aside. Perspiration beaded her face, while from Aubrey came a whiff of a distinctly horsey odor. Yet the air felt more cool than warm. Propelled by the restless breeze, a thin drifting cloud had cloaked the Sun.

Folding the satchel in his gangling arms, the pooka sat down on the sand. Moira joined Tomas on his boulder, facing him. He studied her, with restraint at first and then more closely, noting her colorless skin and the smudges, faint as bruised petals, beneath her eyes and at her temples. Her cheekbones jutted skull-like above hollows. Look for haunted look she gave him, and her eyes gleamed almost black.

"You are weary," said Tomas, startled by this undeniable new perception. "Years weary. And dispirited--" He stopped, more in response to the warning expression on Moira's face than because of her uplifted hand.

"That will suffice, Tomas. Temper your true speech and prophecy with courtesy, and with the wit to know when to say nothing.

I am an Elf who warns you, and you'll find that mortals love truth less than we."

Deciphering her words, he flinched. "'True speech,' then, signifies—"

"That your tongue will never lie," Moira finished for him. "And that you will discern truths. Therefrom you have also a gift of prophecy, that sees where in Midgard the lines of truth might run."

Her voice, reasonable and measured, twined round and away from two words. Tomas repeated them: "'In Midgard.'"

Surprise, then respect, shaded the Elf Queen's eyes. Tomas had the impression that she had taken and lost a calculated risk. "Time does not flow in ordered lines in Faerie. There, one event does not dog the heels of another quite as happens here."

"I cannot lie," he muttered, questioning it.

"You cannot knowingly utter a falsehood. Cannot bear false witness. Not in words." Moira shook her head. "'Twould please a follower of the Nazarene, but you are not one of them." She shot a level glance at the pooka, who appeared to be stifling a grin. To Tomas she said, "I have not left you entirely without resources. Your gift applies to words only—deeds are another matter. And nothing compels you to relate a truth completely, when a partial truth is not in itself a lie." A speculative pause. "You may appreciate what unfolds in your poetry and music. They are a truth of sorts."

Tomas stared, then flung himself off the boulder. She was in earnest. "Gods, Moira, I've no mind to belabor points with you! Don't you know that the Danes are enemies to the Saxons here? One look at me and the Saxons will think I'm a Dane! And you'd have me find the coast and cross the sea to Uppsala without a ship, without a horse, with not so much as a piece of silver.

"Though I'm grateful for the fine harps and the flute," he added and stopped, confused. He *was* grateful, but he hadn't meant to say so just then. "If I reach Uppsala alive, how do I know those Runic passes won't do more than conjure a bridge?"

Again, he'd said more than he intended. More, even, than he was aware of thinking before he began to speak. Moira and Aubrey surveyed him without comment, but Tomas saw an infinitesimal change in their eyes. Then he understood that they recognized his consternation at his newly heightened awareness, and that they had expected such reactions on his part.

From the Elves' stillness and from the way they held themselves isolated from each other and from him, he also saw that neither Elf had anticipated experiencing this degree of pity for him, an emotion they were trying to conceal, yet it emanated from them like a scent. Pity beat in the soft pulse at the hollow of Moira's throat; pity hovered in the muscles that suppressed the twitches of the pooka's ears. Tomas detected other feelings too, darker and more turbulent. That how much he could already sense surprised and disturbed the Elves, that it was more than they had bargained for, and sooner come. And that, knowing Tomas guessed the cause of their uneasiness, they felt exposed.

Good, he thought bitterly. So do I. "Supposing I even reach their cage, how will the ravens react? What is this 'Magician's oath' with the Fate that you deflected from me? And is Hel still searching for me? *You* needn't worry; Elves have no souls."

The errand was impossible, even before Moira robbed him of his ability to lie. A curse, that gift, that last one.

"Either I save your world from fading, or my Fate finds me and Hel takes my soul--and I cannot lie, not even to protect myself." Tomas slammed a fist against the trunk of an alder tree. "But the worst of it is the truths I can see, and that you--"

Moira's face, resolute and brittle beneath her moon-pale skin, silenced him. Her frozen grey eyes did not meet his. Moving with exaggerated care, he went to her and took hold of her shoulders.

When she looked at him, her face cool and white, he asked, "You knew it would come to this, that day by the river. Didn't you?"

She glanced at Aubrey, who was levering himself to his feet. The pooka strolled off towards the nearest clump of trees.

Returning her gaze to Tomas, Moira nodded. "You presume on our relation," she said softly. Her expression was taut. "Do not presume too far."

Tomas suppressed a tremor in his hands as he grasped her shoulders. Between himself and Moira the air grew charged, and prickly where it touched his skin. In Elfland he'd believed he had very little left to lose, but now... He could just as easily die now as at any point along this road she'd set him. More easily, perhaps. He lowered his voice to match hers. "Does that relation matter? You also knew I thought you cared."

Meeting his eyes, the Elf said stonily, "I do care." Then she twisted out of Tomas's grip and turned her face away.

"Not in any way I understand. And it doesn't stop you from fettering me with a deed that I can sense you think is futile." Damn her. Flexing his hands, Tomas stared at her rigid profile. "*Why*, Moira?" Under his ribs, a landslide of fiery stones began to fall.

Knots worked in her jaw and temples. "I have told you.

59

Survival. I had no more choice than you."

"How much choice was that?" he demanded. Let her kill him. "Couldn't you have simply requested that I perform your task or simply compelled me, one or the other? Why make love to me too? To get me to Elfland or to addle my wits like the food? They were addled already, or I might've drowned myself in the Saefren!"

Moira leapt from the rock and shook him, so violently that he lost his balance and staggered. He didn't fall, but only because she pulled him to his feet. He'd no idea she was so strong.

There was a knife-edge in her face. "Tomas, my country is at stake. With the last loophole of our Fate and whatever twist of mine or yours, you came to the river when we made a summoning in our need." Her voice was hoarse. "I *had* to know more of why your Fate sent you, and gather in your thread to run together with our own."

"If a troll had come to the river, would you have bedded him?" Tomas flared.

The Elf's eyes turned molten red. Her fist swung back, with all her weight coiled behind it. The motion was faster than Tomas would have believed, too fast for him to duck. Almost too fast for him to see.

As Moira's arm began its descent, Aubrey grabbed her wrist. She spun to face the pooka, who flung himself to his knees and bowed his head. He was still gripping her arm. Moira stared at the nape of the pooka's neck; her free hand clenched convulsively. She closed her eyes.

They'd catch Tomas if he ran, not that he could. His legs were made of melting ice.

Aubrey said something cautious and deferential in low-pitched Elvish. Moira, eyes and fists closed, stood like a stone carving.

The damp air smelled of salt, and a feeble breeze sighed through the nearby woods. Webbed feet folded against its mud-spattered belly, a marsh duck winged overhead. A procession of ants began winding its laborious way past Tomas's feet.

His stomach cramped with hunger. The Elves' food could no longer impair his wits, not since they'd granted him the discernment of truths. But were he starving, he'd have none of that fare now.

Truly speak and prophesy. In the name of all the gods, why did Moira give him such a gift?

At last she murmured something in her own language. Aubrey released her wrist but remained kneeling until she rested a hand on his craggy head and spoke to him again. Then she came to stand in front of Tomas. Her face was white and drained, and the gaze she bent on him was remote.

"I'm sorry, Moira," he whispered.

60

Her eyes widened a trifle. "So am I, for many things." Her voice was lifeless and formal. "The least of which is that I forgot myself just now."

Behind her, Aubrey laid his ears back and gave Tomas a smoldering look. "You're not alive because we need you, though we do," the pooka told him.

"Aubrey," Moira said without inflection.

"You're alive because I swore to serve you as I would her." The pooka turned on his heel and stalked away.

Tomas swallowed, remembering Aubrey's bony hands and huge protruding teeth. "Moira," he began, and had a sudden notion to try to read her name, her true one, in her eyes.

Elusive and palpable as cold-running water, she dodged his attempt, but her voice echoed in his mind: *My name isn't easy to learn. I am older than you, Tomas, and more artful--yet I believe your courage is greater than mine.* Aloud, she said wearily, "Ask me what you will. But be swift about it."

"Why did you give me that last gift?"

"Ahh." Her expulsion of breath was almost a hiss. "There is no simple answer. Because Truth, Thought and Memory are--intertwined. Because danger and perplexity may follow you to Uppsala and beyond." Aubrey trotted up to them in horse-shape as Moira gestured rapidly with both hands. Before she finished, the sky was seared with light, and a series of booms split the blinding air.

When Tomas could see again, Moira sat bareback on the pooka. "And because," she said, "you may have need of that last gift. Do not tarry; delay is perilous."

Aubrey plunged into a stand of gnarled drooping trees. Tomas shouted and ran after them but the Elves disappeared, mottled grey horse and green-clad rider blurring like wet glaze into the stunted woods.

CHAPTER TEN: A CONVERSATION IN ELFLAND

Moira rode up the hill to find Rhys waiting for her among the withering hawthorns. He was as silent as the trees. When she half-fell from Aubrey's back, Rhys caught her. Bounding away in great skittish leaps, as if the greensward were thick with snakes, the pooka left without a word.

His arm around Moira's drooping shoulders, Rhys coaxed her towards the well. Leaning against its stones, she raised her cupped hands to her mouth and sipped, then took a second draught and a third. She splashed her face, thrust her arms in the well up to her elbows, and finally laughed when Rhys slowly poured a cupful of warm sparkling water down the back of her neck.

Later they lay on the wind-carved sand and gazed at the Elvish Sea. They were half-dreaming, the endlessly veiled musing of immortals who have all of Time and nothing by which to measure it, no Sun or Moon, no signs or seasons. Long-submerged memories, a kaleidoscope of images and emotions whirling around no constant center, floated to the surface and passed others that, in turn, were slowly sinking.

After one such long suspended space, Rhys said softly, "I sent Caraid back to Dubhlinn."

Moira glanced at him; this was an area where they did not trespass in each other's thoughts.

"At her request," he added.

"Then you did right." Moira tossed a rounded pebble into the ocean, watched it arc and hit with a foaming splash. "Though we shall miss her. There are few Seers with such gifts now."

Rhys evaluated the slant of Moira's left eyebrow, lifted higher than the right, the tension in her forehead, and the angle at which she held her chin propped on one fist. Before her, the sand was laced with fleeting spiky patterns, drawn with her fingernail and blotted with her palm.

As the elder of the two, it fell to him to make the suggestion. He said delicately, "If you feel there is need, we could seek out those who live apart..."

"I find no need to disturb them. We know enough." Moira rolled onto her back and threw an arm across her face. "We know what Caraid foresaw: that the Nornir's hands might falter and someone could be summoned to us, and where he should re-enter Midgard. Now the burden rests with Tomas, and I wish to see no more. We'll learn what becomes of Elfland soon enough."

She turned over again and settled on her stomach next to Rhys, with her side touching his. Holding hands, as if they both needed an anchor, they stared out to sea.

"He took it very ill," said Moira flatly.

"Did you expect he would take it otherwise?"

"No."

"Then what troubles you, Moira?"

She did not answer right away. "How much truth Tomas could perceive, and with what speed. That will grow, and quickly, and I ask myself how he will respond."

"We cannot know," said Rhys. He caught her chin and turned it gently towards him. "You fear that Tomas will fail, and Elfland will be lost?"

Moira's shoulders moved in a tiny shrug; her eyes were wide and grey and brimming with fatigue.

"All that could come to pass," Rhys said. "And would be just as likely to come to pass, had you not spent time with him and granted him those gifts. Do not reproach yourself! On the paths that Tomas follows, we need as strong a link to him as possible, and he needs to discern truths."

"But with discernment comes true speech. They can't be separated."

He nodded patiently; they both knew the gifts were linked. Moira went on, speech tumbling from her as if she feared that silence now might still these particular words forever. "Tomas is mortal; how will he bear so many truths so fast? Too much of Elf nature can accompany our gifts. He may go mad."

"So will we all," said Rhys, folding himself into a cross-legged position. She would continue to gnaw at herself like an animal in a trap--which in a way she was, as were they all--until she recognized that they'd had no better choice.

He felt quite dispassionate himself, and briefly wondered when he had ceased to agonize over their Fate. His own emotions came and went in long slow cycles rather like the tides, but not nearly so predictable and with wildly varying intensity. Just now he was numb, and had been for some time. The numbness would pass, and so would the volatility that he knew would take its place. But for now he felt virtually nothing.

Moira was watching him, digesting his last remark. Rhys scooped up two palmfuls of sand and let glittering saffron rain cascade from his pointed fingers. Holding Moira's gaze, he said: "So will we all, my heart, if our boundaries keep shrinking. Did you mark how the hawthorns wilt, and how exhausted you and Aubrey were on your return? Was it not harder to find your way with fewer landmarks and dwindling paths? The Norse lose respect for us, if not belief, and the Nazarenes bind us on all sides. I will not live forever trapped, not even in Faerie. Nor do I wish to go mad and join those who live apart. I will not cling to consciousness as wood or stone or water for eternity."

He did not say, "or as sand," but they each cast a brief uneasy glance at the shimmering minaret that now lay between them.

"How much longer do we have, before blood stains the well and fouls the Sea? Look how she froths, who was so clear and still." Rhys waved a hand towards the churning water. As if in answer, a dolphin leaped. The surf calmed slightly but soon resumed spitting out long green tongues of translucent spray. Rhys ran his fingers through his auburn hair and wiped the mist from his forehead. "Should Tomas's gifts render him more like ourselves, why, then he has all the more reason to help protect Faerie."

"I know that. But does Tomas? He is loosed from the Nornir's loom--and I can see nothing further of his Fate."

This was news. His brow furrowed, his amber eyes half-closed, Rhys grew very still. At last he said quietly, "You and Caraid and I all saw some distance down Tomas's road before he came to you. Before we even knew his name."

Moving with difficulty, as if from weariness or pain, Moira climbed to her feet. When Rhys rose and offered her his arm, she leaned against him. His golden face impassive, he held Moira and stared over her shoulder out to sea. "Tell me," he murmured into her hair. He had to bend his head to catch her words.

"No sooner had I given Tomas true speech and prophecy than I could not see his road. It did not vanish, nor did my link to him. But his road went black, Rhys, and full of shadows. Shadows where I could but dimly sense twists and turns that were not there before." A caught breath, almost a sob. "What have I done?"

CHAPTER ELEVEN: ALFRED, KING OF THE WEST SAXONS

When Moira and Aubrey faded from sight, an invisible crackling barrier closed behind them. Cold air hissed past Tomas's ears as the surrounding reeds shivered down to their sodden roots, then all was still. He stared despairingly into the alder trees. However thin were the borders between Midgard and Faerie in this and every other marsh, the door was barred now.

Keeping his face to the afternoon Sun, for a while Tomas meandered in the direction of the coastline where there would be ships, and towns where he could sing to earn the fare to Uppland. The boggy terrain was treacherously slow going, just when he ached to dull his grief with a hard steady run. Little by little, fatigue dragged at his steps, and he began to stumble with increasing frequency.

Soon there was no help for it: he could go no farther without rest. He found a relatively dry and sheltered nook by a fallen trunk in what woods there were, now predominantly alder trees. Burrowing into a pale gold carpet of dead leaves, he pulled his new green cape over his head and sank into the dreamless sleep of exhaustion.

He awakened to rough hands seizing him. He tried to strike them away, to get to his feet, all the while knowing he was sadly outnumbered. There was a confusing glimpse of grim dirty faces and boiled leather caps, just before something solid struck his head. Pain blossomed; blackness followed.

"Heart of Christ, he might wake up after all," said a grudging voice in broad thick English.

"Then count yourself lucky, Edgar. We bade you tap him gently, but that blow could have felled an ox." The second man spoke English too, his accent more refined than the first, his tone softer and far colder. Edgar did not reply.

A third voice, mild and low, said thoughtfully, "Can we be certain he's a Dane?"

The others shifted their weight. At least two more people, their footsteps muffled and uneven as if picking their way across soft ground, joined the little knot of Saxons discussing Tomas.

He didn't want to betray the fact that he was conscious. He lay on his back--they had taken his satchel, then. The top of his head throbbed like another small separate heartbeat. No doubt he had a lump there. It would probably pain him more when he sat up, if the Saxons let him. Around his wrists they had knotted what felt like a cord of rough hemp, and tied a similar rope to one ankle. His muscles wanted to twitch; his chest was tight, and he was cold.

The mild voice spoke again. "Danes are darker-complected than this man, as a rule. I never yet met a Danish scout with only two harps, a flute and a stone knife for arms, nor one dressed in clean new clothes. No helmet, not even a hat, and the fashion of the cape is odd."

Someone gave Tomas's shoulder a hard shake. A dozen suns exploded behind his closed eyes; he could not suppress a moan and a start, and the rope tugged at his ankle.

No use dissembling now. Opening his eyes, he blinked warily up at the Saxons.

A circle of bearded faces stared down at him, half a dozen men in belted tunics and tight trousers, their calves and ankles wrapped in strips of cloth or leather. All of them were armed with sheathed knives of varying lengths. Some carried swords as well, long ominous swords whose scabbards dangled from belts or from chest straps. All had helmets, mostly of leather although two were of iron. Those two men wore mail shirts.

Where were their shields, and their axes and spears? This must be the Saxons' camp, since they had put aside weapons and armor not carried on their persons.

One of them—Edgar, by his voice—said in rudimentary Norse, "You! Might you speak a Christian language?"

"I do; my mother was Welsh," Tomas answered in English, eyeing the swelling neck, formidable shoulders and sunburnt arms of the man who had hit him. Under medium height, Edgar more than compensated with breadth. He had thick, greasy brown hair, sullen brown eyes and enormous hands. He gaped down at Tomas, while the others frowned and exchanged glances.

An older, rangy man with colorless hair and eyes and a thin, peaked face took a step forward and surveyed Tomas coldly. He sensed that this man was the second speaker, and the one who had just shaken him. The Saxon's dry sallow skin looked as if it might tear away from its underlying flesh. He said tightly, "Excellent; that will save time. Tell the King who you are and what you were doing in the marshes."

Without thinking, Tomas glanced at the one man who had not scowled, the owner of the mild voice, the mail-shirted, clear-eyed man who stood quietly listening. Looking straight at the Saxon monarch, Tomas said, "My name is Tomas, my lord, and I am not a Dane. My father Sigtrygg lives in Vestfold, up the North way, and my mother was from Waleis. I am a skald—a bard, in your tongue. I'm traveling through your country on my way to Uppland." Best not to mention

Uppsala itself; they might have heard of the Norse gods' temple there, and they were probably all Christians.

There was a quickly stilled murmur of consternation—and some furtive gestures to ward off witchcraft. Shaking his head at two men who made as if to restrain the prisoner, the King came and knelt down beside Tomas. "Sit up, if you can."

When the world stopped tilting and spinning, Tomas took a quick survey of his surroundings. He was in a damp, stumpy clearing in an alder forest. Trussed game dangled from the trees, and pots hung from wires stretched over crumbling piles of ashes. Not all of the tents appeared makeshift: the Saxons must have been in the wild for some time.

"You know who I am," the King said calmly. Perhaps thirty years old, he had maple-brown hair streaked lighter by the Sun. He still knelt near Tomas; their eyes were at the same level. Those of the Saxon were a dark intense blue, blue as the glass bottles from the country near the Rhine. Around his neck, a heavy cross hung on a golden chain, but he wore no royal insignia at all.

Tomas nodded. Detecting no enmity in the Saxon monarch, he breathed a little easier. He'd spent enough time at Harald of Vestfold's court to know how to handle himself. But he was wary of the other men, who were full of qualms because he had divined their King's identity. Curse these gifts of truth and prophecy. He *must* remember to speak with caution, despite his pounding skull.

"What else do you know about me?" asked the King.

What news had Olaf's crew received of Wessex during their journey? At every stop on the route through the south-lying isles, they had heard talk, and listened well to all they heard, for Danes warring elsewhere would offer little trouble to a raiding party.

"Your name is Alfred," said Tomas slowly.

"That it is."

"And your brother—" Tomas drew his brows together, ignoring the pain in his head. "Aethelred. Your brother, the late King Aethelred, just died of wounds taken while fighting the Danes led by..." He hunted for the names; he almost had them. "Bagsecg and Halfdan," he finished triumphantly. "At a place called Meretun. And so the crown has passed to you. A fresh Danish army came to join their camp at Reading, and you have been sore beset by them."

Alfred's healthy color had drained from his face, now pinched about the nostrils. His eyes dark and wide, he stared at Tomas. The King did not see him, but something else, some ancient wound.

Two or three Saxons crossed themselves. What had Tomas

67

said?

Alfred let out his breath and glanced aside. The pain left his eyes, yet shock remained, and an emotion midway between awe and fear. After studying Tomas's expression, he seemed relieved yet deeply mystified. "Tomas of Vestfold, Tomas the Poet, all you have said is true. Now tell me, what year is this?"

"In the Christian reckoning?"

Alfred's face relaxed, but only a fraction. "Aye, in the Christian reckoning."

"Eight hundred seventy-one, my lord." Suddenly Tomas knew what was wrong, and his stomach knotted. Why had he not realized before? Alfred should have been younger.

The Saxons were murmuring. Wonder and compassion mingled with alarm in the King's eyes, but he said levelly, "No, Tomas the Rhymer. It is now the year of our Lord eight hundred seventy-eight."

No reply had seemed possible when Tomas heard the date, so he'd merely nodded. From behind the King someone said wildly, "It be one of the Fair Folk and an ill omen."

Alfred frowned. Another man muttered, "Didn't I say bad luck would follow if we camped near the marshes? Now the Fair Folk will want one of our men--"

"Nonsense!" snapped the Saxon who had shaken Tomas.

"Enough talk for now," said the King. His voice was courteous, but an immediate and respectful silence descended. "This man has suffered a blow to the head; I want it tended before we speak further. Edgar, escort Tomas to my tent. William, have Simon sent for. And Linley; he'll know how to care for these instruments."

Edgar hauled Tomas to his feet. Once he was standing, his head hurt less than he'd feared. Alfred's thoughts appeared to have turned elsewhere; he had nodded at Tomas in an abstracted way and waved him and Edgar across the clearing.

Now Tomas sat in Alfred's tent like an honored guest. But why? Perhaps because guards stood outside, who would stop him should he try to leave. Alfred might wish to interview Tomas in private, or to prevent others from questioning him first. To protect him?

At that idea, a chill eased down Tomas's spine and lifted the hair on his arms. So that was it. To protect Tomas from the Saxons who thought he was a Dane, or the ones who believed him an Elf? But if they feared the Elves, would they try to hurt one? There should have been time to ask Moira these things. She should have told him.

The tent flap lifted. Two men, both short, slight and dark for Saxons, with smooth round faces and watchful eyes, ducked through the opening and introduced themselves to Tomas.

Simon was the one in priest's garb. The other, called Linley, was carrying Tomas's pack as if mindful of the harps and flute inside. With what could only be a musician's reverence, he set the satchel down in a corner.

"I possess some skill in healing," Simon said diffidently, his hands folded in his coarse brown robe, "and the King has requested me to examine your bruises, if you permit."

Tomas liked these two at once, liked their slow smiles and careful eyes, and said he would be grateful. Stretched out on a pile of furs, he let Simon probe his scalp with gentle fingers.

Even without his gift of discernment, Tomas would have guessed that Simon and Linley were brothers. Besides their coloring, they had the same small, neat, clever hands. They both spoke little and quietly. But they listened to the words of others the way that a parched field drinks water, their faces growing more secretive all the while.

Tomas sensed one difference, however, where a shadow fell between the two and made them as unlike as salt and bread. Simon, the priest, was afraid, and the bard Linley was not. The priest feared that which his eyes could perceive, and the wisdom in his hands, and the words that drifted to him on the wind. But the bard ached to see further into the heavy air of Midgard, and wondered at the magic in his fingers, and often walked bare-headed and listening in the rain.

Now, watching Simon's ministrations, Linley said, "You look well enough to me. A wonder after Edgar's handiwork! But bards have impossibly thick skulls, so Simon tells me."

"Thick skulls that keep the music in," murmured Simon.

Tomas surprised himself by laughing. He couldn't remember the last time he had laughed. From Linley's smile and fleeting glance at Simon, the brothers had shared an old familiar joke with Tomas.

"Those are fine instruments you have. Might we hear you play?" Linley asked, hope in his face.

"Whenever you wish," Tomas said promptly.

Linley looked pleased. Simon informed Tomas that the abrasion was superficial, but the swelling would remain a while. The priest inquired about pain; Tomas said it was decreasing. After scrutinizing Tomas's pupils and observing him walk around the tent, Simon shrugged, said he would prepare an unguent for the scalp, and pronounced Tomas fit, with a caution to report any dizziness or sudden pain.

"Good," said Alfred, pushing through the tent flap. "I am content to hear it is no worse than that." The King motioned them to sit, then joined them on the reed-strewn floor.

"What do you suppose has happened in Wessex these past seven years, Tomas?" Alfred asked with no preamble. He sat quite straight, gracefully, as though the posture were second nature to him. His hands lay relaxed upon his knees, and his glance at Tomas was amiable and curious, but Tomas knew that the King was following Simon's examination with one of his own.

"I don't know all that's come to pass, my lord. But I would guess that your army camps here in hiding from the Danes, and that you raid them from this base, while the neighboring farm folk aid you as they can."

Alfred blinked. Simon and Linley both sat quietly, but Tomas felt the concentrated force of their attention. "You are correct. And how can you tell these things?"

Judging from the clarity in Alfred's eyes, he had no thoughts of magic and few of spying. He was trying to determine if Edgar had damaged Tomas's wits, and if he were quite sane.

He could provide an answer to Alfred's first concern, at least, thought Tomas wryly. "Edgar and I passed an old man carrying a chicken and some freshly churned butter. Your men go too heavily armed for a mere hunting expedition, yet I see game hanging from the trees. And men who divert themselves for a short time at the hunt have little need for a priest."

Simon nodded. Tomas went on, "And you've been away long enough to look--" Reddening, he stopped and searched for an elliptical phrase, but Alfred, unoffended, was grinning.

"Scurfy?" the King suggested. "A villainous, nasty lot we all look, and you Norse are particular about your persons. Be easy, you said nothing amiss. Never hesitate to speak the truth to me."

Tomas swallowed and said nothing.

"Who leads the Danish host invading Wessex?" asked Alfred, abruptly sober.

"Bagsecg and Halfdan, my lord."

Alfred's face went blank, and the brothers exchanged glances. A wrong answer. Tomas's heart gave a painful thud.

"Do you know the location of our camp?"

"Only that it's in Wessex." He remembered the alder trees. "On higher ground in the marshes, from the lay of the land."

"Can you tell me how we came to be here?"

Tomas had no idea.

"Or when we arrived?"

"No, my lord. I would estimate that you have been in the field...more than a month and less than six."

Alfred tilted his head to one side. "Almost four. What month is this?"

Tomas shrugged politely and said, "Late spring? Early summer? Our months in the North are different from yours."

In the dim light of the tent, the King's eyes shone lapis blue. He twisted a heavy ornate ring on his right index finger. Simon and Linley, dark and sleek as a pair of seals, sat listening. The skin around Simon's eyes and mouth tightened; he furrowed his brow and looked from Alfred to Tomas and back. Linley leaned forward, his face intent, his breathing quick and shallow.

"It is the first of May," said Alfred.

Moira had said it was the first of May when Tomas came to the river. He failed to control his expression, and the King asked quickly, "That surprises you?"

"No more than the year," Tomas stammered. Linley opened his mouth, hesitated, and closed it again. When Alfred glanced at him, he shook his head.

"The first of May," continued Alfred, "and Guthrum leads the Danes who occupy Wessex. They drove me from my manor at Chippenham last Epiphanytide." He folded his arms and looked at Tomas. "Your story puzzles me. But you reason well, your wound does not appear serious, and you seem quite sane in most regards. You speak English as an educated poet might, and carry a bard's instruments, quite good ones, Linley says. Your coloring and build are Norse, yet I could see some Welsh blood around your eyes and nose. But your people spend more time in Éire than in Wessex, and no love is lost between them and the Danes just now."

His face grave, Alfred waited. When Tomas was silent, the King went on, "Norse raiders sometimes strike our coast, and your merchants trade there and in Waleis. But I cannot fathom what might bring you alone and virtually weaponless, Tomas, all the way to the heart of the Somerset marshes. This camp is not easy to find."

How much Tomas could safely reveal? Alfred was a Christian, as was Simon; they might well dread or deny the Elves and all connected with Faerie. While Linley--Tomas glanced at Linley's expectant face, and guessed that the Saxon bard would not respond with disbelief or abhorrence.

But Linley did not command these men. Studying Tomas, Alfred said, "You wished to travel to Uppland, yet you had no notion

71

where you were."

Tomas shook his head.

"Uppland lies well to the east of your home, and its merchants and pirates seldom come here. I'm told that they press east and south, from the port of Birka across the Varangian Sea. Do you still want to go to Uppland?"

"I do indeed."

"You realize that you are well inland here, and that to reach the coast you must cross territory, on foot and unarmed, where skirmishes are likely between my people and the Danes? And that you must find passage on a ship and sail for many days?"

"Yes, my lord."

"Why endure all that to go to Uppland?"

Tomas took a deep breath. The close, dim light of the tent shimmered as if with heat, but no one besides himself appeared to notice. Blue and transparent, the air trembled around the four men in Alfred's quarters. A streaky line of energy wavered through the haze. Pointing everywhere and nowhere, the line left patterns in its wake. Just as Tomas understood that he perceived a crossroads of the possible futures of four people, suspended like a roadmap on his next words, the wildly complex geometry of choices vanished.

Perhaps fifteen seconds had passed. He rubbed his eyes. The other three watched him, Alfred patiently, Simon frowning, and Linley with the frozen, wary attitude of a cat who hears a sound that it can't identify, and waits to hear again.

All of Tomas's carefully prepared half-truths had fled with the vision, and he blurted the first words that came to him. "Begging your indulgence, my lord, I would rather not say why. I doubt you would believe me. And while it is not precisely a confidence, much of it is personal."

For a long moment, Alfred stared. Then he threw his hands in the air, laughed and got to his feet. After rummaging in a small chest, he took out a wineflask and four crude wooden cups. "I can recognize a stubborn man, which you are, Tomas. And I have learned to spot a Danish scout, which you are not, as God is my witness. I believe you pose no threat to me and mine, so I'll not pry into your affairs. Simon, may the patient drink some wine?"

A sullen, peculiar expression on his face, the priest was studying the trampled osiers on the floor. Some conflict seemed to grip him, as if he were hungry and seasick at the same time. "Wine should do him no harm, my lord," he said shortly.

Linley scrambled up to help serve. Wine sloshed over the brim

72

of the mug he handed Tomas with a smile and a slight nod, his eyes tinged with what might have been awe.

They toasted one another's health, then the King asked, "Will you share our evening meal and give us a story or a song, Tomas, before you go on to the coast? Linley would be glad of reinforcements to keep us entertained."

Tomas said he could do no less after such gracious treatment. The mention of food--or the good potent wine--made him light-headed with hunger.

Alfred was still speaking. "Someone may find his ale a trifle strong and forget you are not a Dane. A stone blade presents little deterrent, so perhaps we should loan you a scramasax." From a chest in the corner, he fetched a leather scabbard and unsheathed a short iron knife, whose blade had one sharp edge and one dull. Balancing the scramasax lengthwise on both palms, Alfred presented it to Tomas, dull edge towards him.

Surprised and touched at this sign of trust, murmuring his thanks, Tomas accepted the knife. Its flat chilly weight lay heavily on his open hands. Then he winced, nearly dropping the weapon, and stared down at it in astonishment.

It had grown colder, had turned icy-hot, so that he thought his naked skin must have adhered to the blade. To his disbelief, his hands were unmarked. But vicious cold gnawed its way through the bones of his fingers and bit into his knuckles. His knees felt spongy. As Tomas stood and gingerly held the pointed scramasax between the curled tips of his thumbs and forefingers, the ravenous deadly cold began to swallow his wrists.

Then Linley grabbed the knife and sheathed it. Tomas had not noticed him taking the scabbard from Alfred. "The iron-sick," muttered Linley.

A damp pallor crept across the faces of King and priest alike. Simon gripped Tomas's arms and gently pushed him down to sit on the pile of skins. "It could well be only the blow to his head, my lord." The priest's strained whisper was loud in the silent tent. "Tricksy they are, and sometimes you cannot tell until much later." He clamped sweaty fingers on Tomas's wrist. "Trouble with balance, confusion: it all could come and go." But the priest's gaze went straight to the scramasax in its scabbard, lying on the earthen floor by the chest where Linley set it.

Alfred had not moved since Tomas took the weapon. Also staring at the knife, the King held himself straight and tense as a spear. Linley sat down beside Tomas and looked from Alfred to Simon and back.

73

"His heart is fine." Simon released Tomas's wrist. "Perhaps a rest before supper. And some food now, come to think of it. We don't know when he last ate."

Tomas started to agree that he was hungry, but Alfred came and stood before him. In the Saxon King's gaze, Tomas read fatigue and pity, mingled with apprehension and a certain refusal, a firm establishment of boundaries. Yet he also saw wonder, and a flicker of hope that made the depths of Alfred's eyes flash indigo and jet.

"Rest then, and welcome," Alfred said at last. "Accept the scramasax or not, as you please." Beckoning to Simon, Alfred turned to go. "God be with you," he said to Tomas.

Simon followed the King from the tent. They left Tomas and Linley sitting bathed in the filtered light and shadows within.

CHAPTER TWELVE: ELF-COUNSEL

When Tomas said nothing, consternation crept into Linley's face. His head tilted, he glanced from the sheathed knife to Tomas's satchel and finally down at his hands, turning them over to inspect their calloused fingers. Then he sighed, rubbed his chin and gave Tomas a preoccupied scowl.

Linley picked up the scramasax in its scabbard. Gesturing with it, he said, "First, if you must carry iron, keep it cased in leather or wear gloves. Do not handle it unprotected. Did they teach you nothing, then?"

How much had Linley guessed? Tomas tried to use his gift of discernment, as he had when attempting to learn Moira's name.

Nothing happened: no shimmering, no faint crackling of otherworldliness. The air remained dim, close and unremarkable. Tomas saw only Linley's dark brown eyes on either side of the scramasax, which he held before his round and earnest face. The sheathed knife blocked Tomas's view of Linley's nose, and the sight might have been comical but for the Saxon's increasingly concerned expression.

It was past time for Tomas to reply. "I was trained in the use of weapons," he began.

"You know perfectly well what I mean. You've been with the People of Peace these past seven years," said Linley, exasperated. "If you don't care to speak of it, very well, but for pity's sake let me instruct you more than they seem to have done."

Tomas pulled his knees to his chest and wrapped his arms around his shins, then realized he'd taken one of Moira's characteristic poses when she was tense. The back of his head throbbed. Assuming what he hoped was a friendly, non-committal demeanor, he told Linley, "I am grateful for your good will. Instruct me, you say?"

An unexpectedly wry smile. "Your pardon, if I was overbearing. You could likely teach me more than I can offer you." After setting down the scramasax, Linley crossed to the corner of the tent and poured two mugs of water, his motions slow and deliberate.

When he came back, his tone was crisp; he might have been reporting for duty with Alfred. "Do not lay hands on iron without protection. I wish I could say how ill it will make you, or how that may change with time. But I don't know." An intent look at Tomas. "So have a care, though I doubt that Alfred and Simon will expose you to iron any more than is needful."

"Do they know—"

75

Linley grinned, sloshed his mug in the direction of the camp, then drew an oversized cross in the air. "Faithful Christians both. They don't want to know. Want to hear nary a word about where you've been and what you did there. Of course they know, Tomas, but they won't admit it, and you'd best not remind them overmuch. Ah, the sight of their faces when you touched that knife!" Chuckling, Linley shook his head. "But let us remember your head injury, my lad! That's why you lost seven mortal years of your life and turn faint sometimes for no reason. Humor them, and abide by that explanation." Linley's tone was light but his eyes were grave, and he waited until Tomas nodded.

"But I thought... Linley, I don't understand. Elves seldom receive the offerings they once did, but most of us in the North still honor them." The Saxon looked interested, so Tomas went on, "Every year, for instance, when my father's household moved to its summer steading, we'd walk the whole farm with a torch to let the land-Elves know we'd come. The Elves are a race apart, powerful and immortal. Not gods, precisely, but not of Midgard either."

Linley was nodding.

Tomas said, "But there's little room in the minds of many Christians for any power but their one God. They seem to name all else "devil," and fence themselves in with words. If Simon and Alfred know, why didn't Simon propose an exorcism? Why has Alfred been so kind?"

Linley rested an elbow on one knee and put his chin in his hand. "I have only partial answers, and one can always misunderstand." For almost a minute, he studied the earthen floor before gazing at Tomas again. "My brother and I have a bit of the Sight. Not much, mind you. And I would that it were more, but Simon wishes it were less. It frightens him. I might be frightened too, if my portion of the Sight were his. He could be a healer, Tomas, such as this day and age have rarely seen."

Remembering Simon's gentle fingers on his scalp and the easing of his pain beneath them, Tomas understood. He also remembered how Simon often hid his hands in his robe as if ashamed of them, and the ambivalence in his voice when he spoke of his skill.

Linley fidgeted with his empty mug. "When people started coming to Simon with their hurts, asking him to heal their livestock and their children, and begging him to mend—" He plunked the cup down, and with its uneven base began to gouge a hole in the dirt where he sat. "It was after a battle with the Danes. Simon had loved Aegytha since they were children. He'd never told her; he told no one except me. And Aegytha was blind to it. But had she known, she would have had

76

none of Simon, for she was betrothed to a great hulking thane named Godfric. Half an idiot, but a face like a whole choir of angels.

"Godfric was mortally wounded by a Dane who left the deed for loss of blood to finish. Which it would have done in private on the battlefield, but for Aegytha. She had Godfric found and brought to Simon." The rawness of Linley's glance made Tomas bite his lip. "Can you guess what happened next?"

"Godfric died, through no fault of Simon's. But Simon blamed himself," said Tomas.

"Aye. Godfric died. I saw him, and I tell you as I told Simon that all the gods in all the worlds could not have preserved the life in that flayed body. But Simon was not sure. Simon feared that he could perhaps have done something, and had failed to do it out of jealousy. Aegytha was sunk in grief and made him no reproach, but fear and guilt consumed him. He lay awake and could not eat, until soon he would have no traffic with me or any other, save the priests."

Linley pushed his mug aside. "A month later he entered holy orders. He does not speak of that time; there's much he no longer speaks of at all. But I believe he was persuaded that he'd abused a God-given gift and must be cleansed of his sin. And the price seems to be that Simon feels obliged to reject everything else, Tomas, all that the Sight revealed to him of any world save this. Now he mistrusts the knowledge that has graced his hands since birth, because he thinks he chose to fail where none could have succeeded."

Tomas rose, took both cups and refilled them. He wasn't thirsty. But water was something he could offer Linley, although it couldn't erase the bitterness in Linley's eyes or ease Simon's self-imposed constraints.

Linley seemed to understand the gesture. With a half-smile, he accepted the mug and drank the water almost at one swallow. "But Simon remembers, and he cannot dismiss the Sight by denying it. He remains a healer, and he knows you are not evil. He'll perform no exorcism and will aid you all he can."

"I'll endeavor to give him as little reason as I may to regret it."

Linley nodded, then looked down at the rush-strewn floor. "Alfred, now," he said, "Alfred is another matter. A Christian all his life. Made a pilgrimage to see the Pope in Rome. Hears Mass every day or almost, even now. And he's a good man, Tomas, and a wise one, and I'd follow wherever he led. So would every man here."

"I understood that," said Tomas, "as soon as I heard his voice."

"He's taken to you, too. And he sees further into the heart than most." Another quick smile. "Even if you'd come errand-riding from the King of Elfland himself, Alfred wouldn't harm you, for at least two reasons."

Tomas winced. Linley gave him a curious glance but continued, "Alfred strives to leave judgment to his God. He says we cannot hope to comprehend the whole of God's creation. Besides, there's his name."

"His name?"

"Alfred. Alf-rede. Elf-counsel." Linley was serious. Leaning forward, he said, "Alfred has great respect for mysteries. In some ways, he's more a pagan than he ever would admit. And you suddenly turn up near camp, fresh from seven years in Elfland, though you'd never hear Alfred say that aloud. You look Norse when we're at war with the Danes, and that bodes ill for you. But Alfred, being fair-minded, doesn't assume you're a Dane and doubtless saves you from his men thereby." He stopped, his face expectant.

"I don't understand," said Tomas, though he could see that Linley followed some line of logic of his own.

"Tomas, I've no knowledge of how your Elves behave in the North. But in Wessex, we hear countless stories of Elves who appear in a suspicious guise to mortals in difficult circumstances. And when a kind-hearted person helps the Elf regardless, the Elf aids the mortal in turn. Gives him advice or a gift or performs some service for him."

Tomas considered. "I am not an Elf," he said cautiously.

Disappointment flickered in Linley's eyes. He seemed to conduct a brief silent argument with himself, and then shrugged. "But Alfred doesn't know that. And you've come from Elfland or someplace like it--" He stood, lifted the tent flap to cast a glance around outside, and returned to sit across from Tomas again. "And the Danes have rendered us fugitives, and Alfred wants his country back." He lowered his voice. "We are not desperate, but we crave any aid that may appear. Alfred prays daily; I think he importunes Heaven for a miracle. Enough of the old faith lives in him that he won't be overly choosy where his miracle comes from. Do you see, Tomas? He won't hurt you." He paused. "What disturbs you?"

"If Alfred asks-- But from what you say he wouldn't ask, because that would be admitting... Linley, I may not be able to give him whatever he expects from me."

"Ah," said Linley, studying Tomas. Hands steepled, index fingers resting on his lower lip, the Saxon's eyes gleamed with speculation. He resembled nothing so much as a young otter contemplating a foamy splash into black river water. "Well. We shall see. Perhaps something will come to you. You know more of the Danes in general than we've learnt about this lot of Guthrum's, I'll warrant."

Besides Alfred's expectations, another concern gnawed at Tomas. He said, "Linley, I'm grateful for all you've told me, and you've eased my mind over some matters. But why--"

"Why am I helping you?

Tomas nodded.

"Because neither Alfred nor Simon can, at least not past a certain point. And I believe you may be able to help us." Linley glanced at Alfred's scramasax. "And because your response to that knife puzzles me." He waited, but Tomas said nothing. "Iron pains you as if you were an Elf. Yet you looked surprised, while an Elf would have expected it and hidden his reaction. Unless he were pretending to be mortal. But you just said that you aren't an Elf, and Elves don't lie--"

Linley ducked as Tomas, cursing Moira in Norse, hurled his cup across the tent. Not at Linley, but the Saxon had quick reflexes. He straightened up when the mug rebounded on the packed earth and trundled to a halt in front of Tomas.

"I beg your pardon," muttered Tomas, feeling foolish. Elves don't lie. How many other little bequests, such as the iron-sickness, would he discover had come with Moira's gifts? "I beg your pardon," he repeated.

"Granted," said Linley, blinking at the cup. A guard stepped inside the tent and gave Linley an inquiring stare. "At ease, John. I'm learning a Norse drinking song." John rolled his eyes and withdrew without a word.

Linley grinned. Tomas felt his embarrassed flush receding, and managed a smile in return.

"You're not an Elf, then," said Linley cheerfully. "But I never yet heard of a mortal who took the iron-sick home from Faerie, and that makes me curious. Another reason to help you." He pointed at the large leather satchel. "And three more: your harps and your flute. I want to hear you play, Tomas the Rhymer."

"Gladly. All the drinking songs you want, and more besides." They both laughed. Reaching for his satchel, Tomas was gratified to see the blaze of pleasure in Linley's expression.

And so he was completely unprepared when Linley touched his sleeve and said, his tone more dignified than the naked pleading in his face, "Would you speak to me of Elfland? All my life I have dreamed of it but had nothing but glimpses now and again, till I am almost sick with longing. If I have been a friend to you, could you take me there?" The Saxon's eyes burned until they shone like melting copper.

Tomas swallowed, twice, feeling the sweat break out on his

forehead. "Linley," he said, and his voice rasped in the silence that hovered between them. "Linley," he said again, "because you have been a friend to me, that is the last place in all the worlds where I would ever take you."

CHAPTER THIRTEEN: HARP AND CARP

Tomas would always remember telling a skald's tale of the Norse gods at this Saxon camp in the thick black hours of the night, while low-burning fires transformed men's faces into the starkly shadowed profiles of half-carved icons. The same ruddy light lapped at the trunks of the alder trees that seemed to creep closer to listen.

His story was not the evening's first entertainment. After a meal of roast meat, boiled cabbage, thick crusty bread and dried fruit, the Saxons began peering expectantly towards where Linley sat with Simon and Tomas. Before long, Linley ducked into the trees and came back tenderly carrying a lute.

Its wood gleamed in the firelight, so that at first Tomas assumed the instrument had been freshly sanded and polished. When Linley passed him, headed for a huge flat stump in the center of camp, Tomas saw that the lute was old, skillfully made, and burnished only by the oils left by the oft-repeated touch of Linley's hands.

The Saxon bard had been taciturn during the meal. After one or two tries at conversation, Simon gave his brother a sharp glance but refrained from comment. Tomas was equally silent.

After Tomas's response to Linley's request for an escort to Elfland, Linley had stared at him for perhaps six heartbeats. Then he whispered, "So this is to be the way of it. I had suspected as much: that I shall continue to thirst, perhaps my life long. And for poisoned water, you who have tasted it tell me. I cannot say if I would trade Fates with you or not."

Few words had passed between them since, not from any sense of strain, but because, on that subject at least, nothing remained to be said.

Upon the lute Linley's hands spoke now. He leaned over the instrument, dark straight hair falling into his eyes, and his fingers travelled the frets in trailing sequences of notes. Swaying gently, his round secretive face tilted to one side, Linley played as if abstracted and alone.

Tomas heard one theme after another dropped, altered and evaded, only to be taken up again and relentlessly repeated. The music was Linley's dialogue with himself, the latest episode in an ongoing attempt to reason with desire. He bent so far forward that he appeared to be trying to kiss the strings, and his hands slid up and down the neck of the lute in an audible, articulate caress.

At Tomas's right, Simon pushed his trencher of food away and rested his chin in one hand, his eyes intent upon Linley. In the priest's face, Tomas saw something that might have been respect, melancholy or recognition. Simon did not return Tomas's glance. He watched no one but Linley, as if he and his brother were the only men present. As Simon stared, the bruised twilight swiftly curdled into night.

His touch as gentle and deliberate as if he laid his fingers on a woman's lips, Linley rested his hands upon the strings to still them. For half a moment the Saxons were silent. Then a few of them cheered, while others applauded and called out praise.

A somewhat inebriated voice near Tomas said, loudly enough to carry over the noise, "'Twas fine, lad, but sad enough to make a corpse weep. Play something more lively, now!"

"I will," Linley promised, smiling. "And I'd welcome a flutist to play it with me." His head turned in Tomas's direction, and Tomas went to fetch his flute from Alfred's tent. Bringing the harps as well, he joined Linley on the stump.

Linley shot him a grin and leaned into the frets, fingers flying. Tomas's flute came in on the next phrase, as smoothly as if they'd rehearsed for years. It was as easy as playing music with the neighboring farm's cowherd, Gunnar, whom Tomas had known all his life. The Saxons were whistling and stamping their feet. Without warning, a short, chicken-necked man with a scraggly ginger beard hurried to the foot of the stump. Exchanging nods with Linley, he produced a small mallet and began beating a wide, shallow wooden drum.

After Linley began a few pieces and the drummer one or two of his own, they glanced expectantly at Tomas: it was his turn. Catching Linley's eye, he sailed off into some tunes heard in Elfland. The lutenist followed him readily. On the ground below them, the drummer's hand was a loose-wristed blur.

Tomas lost himself contentedly in the music. Sometimes Linley sang alone, and sometimes the scrawny little man sang with him. Several times Tomas recognized an air he had learned from his mother, and the other two musicians appeared pleasantly surprised when he joined in. Once he looked up and glimpsed Alfred nearby, and Simon with him.

Almost an hour passed at that furious pace, before Linley stopped at last and wiped his forehead on his sleeve. Someone brought the three players a round of ale. Studying the flute Moira gave him, Tomas realized that he'd played as rarely before, with fiery, effortless grace--and with foreign material and musicians. He turned the instrument wonderingly in his hands.

The drummer bounded onto the stump and gave Tomas a

vigorous handshake. "Bones of God, you can play. Even music you don't have in the North! You'll be well-guested at Alan the Cobbler's hearth whenever you care to visit. And your name might be?"

"Tomas. And thank you!"

"Tomas the Rhymer," added Linley.

Alan narrowed his eyes. They were dark and shrewd and, in the uneven glow from the fires, reminded Tomas of the fenodyree. "Rhymer, eh? Give us a poem, then."

"Please!" said Linley, thrusting a harp into Tomas's hands. His fingertips fit into the two burns on its otherwise sleek wood. "Give us a poem or a tale, won't you? And accompany yourself on the harp? Or I could play the other one, if you permit."

Tomas recognized the hunger in Linley's face. "Would you join me?" he asked.

Linley gave a small shout and reached for the second harp. As Alan hopped down from the stump, Linley was already making an introduction. "Tomas the Rhymer, a bard from the North, and our guest here this night."

Scattered murmurs, rustling sounds; then silence fell. Tomas spotted Alfred, who nodded at him encouragingly. Most of the men had sat down after Linley's announcement. Bearded faces under boiled leather caps stared up at Tomas. Some of the Saxons appeared reserved and others hostile, but they all looked curious or expectant, peering from Tomas to Linley and back again.

Alfred kept good order here. There were surprisingly few drunken men, at least not belligerent or obvious ones. Tomas saw no women at all in the crowd, though there'd been several about the camp during the day.

They were mostly farmers and earls, these men--thanes, Linley called them--whose country had been overrun by invaders, whose King's rulership was usurped. Tomas knew, with no conscious decision, which story he would tell the Saxons to while away one late evening of their exile.

He began strumming his harp, and for a moment closed his eyes in delight at the pure, strong notes that rang beneath his fingers. Like a waterfall, or the voice of an Elf. Clearer than hers, though.

Best not to pursue that thought. Tomas looked at Linley, whose harp echoed his. Amazement suffused Linley's face, rendering him young and wistful over the music that floated from his hands. The harp opened Linley, in contrast to the lute that had sealed him into communion with himself alone. When he threw Tomas a giddy incredulous glance and the slightest of nods, Tomas knew that he might play as he wished: Linley would follow.

Tomas settled into quiet, rhythmic patterns that would blend with the rise and fall of his trained voice. He'd never recounted this myth while speaking English, but some aspects of storytelling transcended language, he hoped.

"I will tell you a tale of the Norse gods, an ancient tale, well-loved by my people. A legend, as true and as false as legends are, about the theft of power, and the wit and courage that reclaimed it."

He glanced at the Saxons, at Alfred with Simon beside him, but their faces were bemused with listening. No one appeared to object to the mention of Norse gods. Tomas began:

"Once upon a time Thor, the powerful god of thunder, who by virtue of His hammer Mjollnir protects free men in Midgard and the gods in Asgard both, awakened to find Mjollnir vanished.

"Thor confessed as much to clever Loki the Trickster, and how Thor feared that with Mjollnir gone, the Jotun-kind, the frost giants, would overrun Asgard. Now Loki was himself the son of giants, but also Odin Allfather's foster-brother, so Asgard was his home. And if Loki was not always well-disposed towards the gods, neither was he always an unfriend to them.

"So from the goddess of love, Freyja, Loki borrowed a falcon-skin. Wearing Her feathery cape, he flew far into the west, so far that he came to Jotunheim, the land of the giants. Where he saw Thrym, their king, fashioning leashes for his hounds.

"'Greetings, Loki Sky-traveler,' said Thrym. 'How fare the gods? How fare the Elves? And why have you come to visit me?"

"'Elves and gods alike fare ill these days,' Loki replied. "'Tell me, have you stolen Mjollnir?'

"'I have indeed. Nor will I return it until Freyja lies in my bed."

"This word Loki carried back to Thor, and the two of them to Freyja in Sessrumnir, Her hall. And the goddess refused. At the force of Her rage, Her golden necklace Brisingamen flew apart, and its pieces clattered throughout the hall.

"To determine how else Mjollnir might be restored, all the gods and goddesses held a council. Even Heimdall the Watchman left His post near Bifrost, the rainbow bridge to Asgard. He it was who proposed that Thor should go to Jotunheim in Freyja's stead.

"Over shouts of laughter from the other gods, and Thor's protests that they would mock Him, Heimdall said, 'Adorn the Thunder Lord like every other bride, with homestead keys at the waist of His gown. And don't forget the veil!'

"This they did, and Loki offered to go dressed as my lady's maid. So it seemed that the goddess and Her servant drove to Jotunheim. Where Thrym, beside himself with glee at winning such a bride, escorted the two damsels to his feasting hall.

"Thor in His hunger devoured almost two oxen and half a dozen salmon, washed down with a barrel of mead.

"'Never have I seen such an appetite!' said the giant, amazed.

"'My lady Freyja is so thrilled about Her wedding that She was unable to eat these nine days past,' the bridesmaid whispered helpfully to the groom.

"Liking this response, Thrym sought to steal a kiss, but flinched away from what he saw beneath the bridal veil. 'Her eyes! Like raging fires!'

"'Why, for Her passion the lady Freyja has not slept in several nights. Did you not see Her burning glance of love?' explained the bridesmaid.

"Indeed Thrym had. 'Let us now consecrate the bride,' he ordered. 'Bring me the hammer to place between Her knees while we plight our troth.' For such is the custom in the North. Thrym himself laid Mjollnir in Thor's lap. Thor seized His hammer, tore off the veil and slew every giant at that feast.

"Thus Thor regained His hammer. When Odin Allfather next gazed toward Jotunheim, He saw that Thor had claimed Thrym's lands, and on them sprouted tender green shoots that promised to bear fruit."

Tomas stilled his hands, curious about how the Saxons would receive a tale that was probably new to most of them. He'd done his best to act out the various parts while he spoke. From smiles and approving rumbles, the Saxons quickly progressed to loud stomping cheers. Tomas was obliged to tell two more stories before they let him and Linley down from the stump.

CHAPTER FOURTEEN: ANOTHER ERRAND

At Alfred's invitation, Tomas sat with Simon and Linley in the King's tent late that night. With them was a fifth man, William, several years older than Alfred. Lean and brown and quiet, William rarely met anyone's eyes, but listened with intense concentration to everything said in his presence. An advisor to Alfred, and a trusted one, Tomas judged. William had given Tomas a brief scrutiny, neither warm nor hostile, when they met, but Tomas would have wagered a hefty sum that his features were graven in William's memory by that one glance.

"Have you ever met Guthrum?" Alfred asked Tomas now. "Do any acquaintances of yours number among his men?"

"No, my lord, to both questions. Danes sometimes visited the court in Vestfold, but none of them were Guthrum's men."

"How seem these Danish raids to you?"

Images edged in red came to Tomas: the destruction Olaf had wreaked on a Welsh village. With memories of a vibrant glowing Rune and three grey-haired figures who weaved at a bloody loom. Fidgeting in the stuffiness of the tent, Tomas glanced longingly through the open flap, where he could see stars speared by the alder trees. He'd not had a second alone to think since the Saxons found him.

He pushed an untouched mug of ale aside. "They seem an unjustified slaughter, coupled with the theft of your country," he said, and heard the tension in his voice.

The others looked at him, concurrence in the grim set of their features. Tomas began to sense a separate attitude behind each gaze, four reactions as distinct as voices, as recognizable as faces. With this heightened awareness came an odd, almost painful itching, as if invisible fingers were stretching his skin away from the underlying muscles. He glanced at his hands and forearms; their color was normal. The peculiar sensation must be subjective, an accompaniment to his still-increasing powers of discernment. A sudden fancy struck him that Elf fingers were peeling shreds of his skin away, to replace it with strips of their own flesh.

He shook his head to dismiss that idea, then relaxed and let the impressions from the Saxons flood his mind. It was like lifting the lid from a cauldron to better appreciate the savor of a stew.

Resolution and a trace of sadness from Alfred. Physical, visceral empathy for the pain of the land and its people from Simon. Linley's awareness that Tomas's last statement stemmed from more than his reaction to the Danish raids on Wessex, and a courteous reluctance to probe further into Tomas's past. And from William: single-minded

86

loyalty to Alfred and a persistent, throbbing anger, a fury bargained with daily, sometimes hourly--but harnessed and set to work. After one shattering picture of mutilated bodies hanging in a row, Tomas wrenched his mind away from William's.

The Danes had murdered William's family.

Tomas suppressed a wretched urge to rush out into the silent, undemanding alder trees and breathe deeply of the anonymous night air. There seemed no way to tell when he was about to discern one truth too many. Perhaps no one had noticed his malaise. Quiet filled the tent, wedding each man to his thoughts.

A few moments later, Alfred came to sit directly in front of Tomas. In the lamplight, the King's eyes shone murky blue, and the lines around his mouth appeared more deeply etched. "Tomas the Rhymer, I would ask a favor from you. Nay, a gift--" He cleared his throat. "You are Norse but not a Dane. Not much nearer kin to them than to us, I suppose, since your mother was Welsh. Still, should you refuse what I ask on the grounds of blood in common with the Danes, I would not take it amiss, and hope that neither would you hold my request against me."

With no idea what Alfred would propose, Tomas waited.

"God be praised, we defeated them in Devon not long ago, and they lost many men," Alfred continued. "I must learn how it is with them since. Their numbers, their spirits, and the mind of Guthrum concerning us, now that it is doubtful he'll attack us here, after his losses." The King leaned forward. "However, my scouts can tell me little, while near Chippenham the countryfolk are wary of the Danes, and close-mouthed. I cannot fault them much for that. To gain information, I proposed to enter Chippenham fort myself, disguised as a tinker or a bard, but that plan met with nothing but opposition from my ealdormen."

Across the tent, William nodded, scowling.

Alfred said, "When I heard your tales tonight, I said to myself, 'Now, here is one who would require no disguise to go to Chippenham, and could understand the Danes' every word while he played his harp for them.' Would you consent to go, and bring back those words to me?" The King studied Tomas's face. "This quarrel is none of yours, and what I ask has dangers. I will reward you as best I can now, and better in the time to come." He paused. "What are your thoughts?"

They were of Moira, and the deed she had forced upon him. How would he have responded if the Queen of Elfland had treated him with Alfred's openness and courtesy, had begged a boon, had left Tomas any kind of choice? A stone's weight lay upon his heart.

87

At last he said, "If it pleases you, my lord, speak further of your proposal. I find I cannot decide upon the instant."

"Very well," said Alfred promptly. "Someone will guide you to Chippenham--"

"I will, your Highness," said Linley, in the voice of one who states an obvious and irrefutable law of nature.

Simon shifted where he sat. William frowned. Linley gave his brother a dark level stare and an infinitesimal nod; Simon lifted one shoulder half an inch, let it fall and looked away.

Alfred ignored these reactions, though the flickering of his eyes showed that he had noticed them. "Thank you," he told the Saxon bard. "Linley will guide you to Chippenham, Tomas, but will enter neither the town nor the fort."

Like a marionnette whose strings have just been severed, Simon sagged with relief. Linley's face grew still.

The King said, "He will wait hidden outside the town. How you choose to enter it, to present yourself at the fort, to comport yourself while there, and to leave and find Linley, I trust to your discretion. Once you tell Linley what you have learned, you may return here. Or you may take the horse and the seal of safe conduct I will give you--Linley will hold and hide it while you visit the fort--and go wherever you like."

"When would we leave?" asked Tomas.

"Tomorrow morning--this morning by now--after hearing Simon say the Mass with us, if you would."

A seal of safe conduct and a horse. Tomas hadn't seen many horses in camp. "You could spare me a mount, my lord?"

"I could do no less. A horse, the seal, and what silver can be set aside from feeding my men. With greater reward and a hearty welcome if you return to Wessex, which you may do whenever you wish. The safe conduct holds for your lifetime or mine." Alfred's earnest expression bespoke his sincerity, even without the current of good will that flowed from him.

Tomas said, "Your generosity humbles me. I will perform this errand for you."

Nodding slowly, Alfred searched Tomas's face. "Then I am in your debt. You are quite certain? The Danes are not your countrymen, but..."

"I find I have less and less in common with those, even my countrymen, who raid these islands," said Tomas, very low. "I accept your task, my lord."

Alfred's eyes kindled; he clasped Tomas's shoulders. "Accept also my gratitude. I am well-served! There is room for you at my court, and lands could be given you in Wessex, if such is your desire. I would be honored to number you among those under my protection. Would you swear fealty to me?"

Into Tomas's mind sprang a memory, swift and certain as a lynx and, as lynxes do, this memory had claws. A great oak tree by the river Saefren under filtered moonlight. A tall, pale Elf Queen who held Tomas's hands between her narrow burning palms, whose grey eyes pulled him to her like an undertow.

"I cannot." His voice was a lacerated whisper. "I am pleased to perform your errand, my lord, but I cannot swear loyalty to you or any man."

Alfred removed his hands from Tomas's shoulders and sat back, his face full of concern. He started to speak, stopped, then said gently, "I regret that. But my offer stands. You have a place at my court and lands in my realm, whenever you wish."

Stunned, Tomas thanked him.

"I request your Highness's permission to question Tomas the Rhymer," William said formally. His voice was harsh and grating. The others turned to look at him.

"Granted," said Alfred, his tone neutral. He stood up and moved aside.

William crossed the tent, crouched on his heels a yard from Tomas and stared him full in the face. The Saxon's expression was unreadable, but Tomas sensed the deliberation behind it.

"Have you broken another such oath?" asked William.

Tomas met the cold brown eyes. "No. I have not."

William considered. "Have you sworn loyalty to someone else?"

Alarm began a slow ascent of Tomas's spine. "Yes." So much depended on the wording of the next query! Fool: he should have forestalled it with a more elaborate answer than the monosyllable he'd just uttered.

Mistrust radiated from William like midsummer heat from granite. The man's emotions were all the deadlier for their impersonality. "To what lord?"

Trying to prevent his relief from showing, Tomas said, "To no lord. To a lady." The title was less human than the word "woman," and less specific than "queen." None of the Northern countries was ruled by a Queen when Tomas left Vestfold; he took a chance that such was still the case.

It apparently was. William's features went blank and still, like a knife-blade dulled by frost. Then his eyes widened with comprehension. A corner of his mouth drew down; he glanced aside and tugged at an earlobe. Tomas thought he recognized an older man's slightly nostalgic empathy with a younger one. At the last he felt William's amusement, directed only at William himself. Suddenly Tomas understood why this silent, rage-driven man stood so high in Alfred's trust.

William said to Tomas, his tone still formal but warmer, "I beg your pardon if my questions seemed presumptuous or offensive, and offer my gratitude for your service to us."

"Granted and accepted," said Tomas, smiling.

William nodded unceremoniously and returned to his former place, standing by the wall near the doorflap.

"Sleep, all of you," said Alfred. "I am well content with this night's work, but the Mass will come early after it."

Linley said nothing on the short walk back to his tent, where he and Tomas slept. But Tomas knew, from the single commiserating glance that Linley cast him from parched and dreaming eyes, that Linley guessed to what lady Tomas had sworn fealty.

CHAPTER FIFTEEN: A MASS CELEBRATED AT DAYBREAK

Mass was said beneath an ill-thatched square roof that rested on tree trunks and crooked pillars of stumps. The Saxons had filled in one wall with turfed and wattled posts and stone. On that wall hung a crucifix, and before it stood an altar, a tall, narrow wooden table draped with a linen cloth. The altar was flooded with the delicate climbing light that immediately follows dawn.

Tomas, who had never attended a Mass before, was trying not to stare. On the altar were arranged something that resembled a brass lantern, a shallow brass bowl of water beside a neatly folded towel, an oblong brass platter of bread, and a carved and chased silver goblet of what must be wine.

He shifted from foot to foot. With him waited Alfred, William and Linley. Tomas could not account for his wariness, nor why the mute trappings on the altar seemed to warn him.

Gazing around the open pavilion, his voice so soft that the others leaned closer to hear, Alfred said, "One day I will build a church upon this site. A church whose nave is a square such as this, but at the center of four aisles that reach from the nave like the arms of a cross."

"A new design, my lord. I like it well," said William thoughtfully.

Without a word or a glance, his profile tense and brooding, Simon appeared and trudged straight to the altar. He had changed his robe and draped a long embroidered strip of fine-textured cloth around his neck. He stopped with his back turned to the others. Alfred, Linley and William bowed their heads. Taking his cue from the Saxons, so did Tomas.

Simon dipped his hands in the bowl of water and dried them painstakingly with the towel. In a language Tomas did not know, whose vowels and consonants alternated in flowing patterns innocent of dipthong or guttural, Simon intoned a series of phrases. Some of these the Saxons answered, in no order that Tomas could detect. But the priest spoke without expression, and the others responded as if by rote. Not until they all chanted together, their words overlapping and muddling rather than harmonizing, did Tomas's perceptions start to change.

First he heard the drone of other voices rising and falling, men and women who lamented in a tongue different from the one the Saxons used for their responses. With the extra voices came a trilling and piping of flutes. Tomas aimed a surreptitious glance around the pillars that supported the thatched awning but saw no one else near. From their somber faces and pensive eyes, he guessed that the Saxons heard nothing but themselves, although the singing and the flutes wailed with increasing volume to his ears.

Simon was burning something in the lantern-like object, swinging it to and fro in a cramped arc. Dusky perforated smoke swirled from the filigreed metal, and Tomas caught the mingled scents of myrrh, roses and other perfumed oils. What did the others smell? Suddenly Simon's robes turned a billowing crimson, ruddy as anemones and pomegranates. Red as damp clay and trampled grapes. Red as blood.

Like a high wind, power welled into the air, reverberated from the chunky wooden posts and seethed beneath the tattered roof. Knocked off balance, Tomas just managed to keep his footing.

Could this be the early stages of a gale? But the Saxons stood immovable as mountains, their clothing limp against their bodies and their hair unruffled on their bowed heads. So the atmospheric tremors marked a turbulence that was tangible to Tomas alone.

But what was happening, and why? Clenching his hands, Tomas stood very still at Linley's side and tried not to draw attention to himself, sure that what he sensed would be reflected in his face. Linley, intent on the various gestures that Simon was making by the altar, seemed to notice nothing amiss.

Then the altar blurred, dissolved and re-materialized. Ripe fruit and cakes and flowering plants now layered it, most of them unfamiliar, their colors lurid in the fragrant dissipating smoke. With a slow, awkward reverence, his mouth drawn tight as if with pain, Simon took the platter of bread into his hands. The Saxons pounded their chests with stiff, ritual blows of their closed fists.

A procession of women, bare-breasted ghosts, filed between the Saxons and the priest. Fighting the panic that was rising in his throat, Tomas began to shiver uncontrollably. He could see through the sobbing apparitions, who beat their breasts in rhythm with the Saxons. The women carried what seemed to be a shrouded corpse.

They passed through the trailing edge of Simon's red-stained robes, melted unharmed into the hilts of the Saxons' swords and marched straight through their grimy leather boots. Tomas's ears rang with the women's cries and with the roaring of an unglimpsed sea where, he sensed, the phantom assembly would hurl the body that they bore aloft.

As the last woman stepped beyond the pillars, the procession faded from Tomas's sight. Shaking, his fists squeezing empty air, Tomas opened his mouth, but no sound came from his dry throat. Turning his

92

head as little as possible, Linley was giving Tomas a puzzled sidelong look, but didn't stir.

The wattle-and-daub wall evaporated from behind the altar, denuded now of fruit and greenery, holding bread and wine again, bowl and towel and censer.

I am exhausted, Tomas thought. Never have I been so drained; I've scarcely strength to breathe. What did I see? If I stand here and rest, perhaps the wall that should be in front of Simon will reappear.

But whatever Tomas's vision was, it had not ended. Beyond Simon's unhurried movements, fields of barley, wheat and corn now appeared, and throngs of small dark men and women, all pleading and lamenting. Then stakes, whittled into wicked points, and scythes with long curving handles rose and fell, and fell again. There was a single, pulpy scream, quickly aborted. Gods above, the huddled crowd was hacking at a human body.

Limbs were torn apart, scattered and buried, staining the field with clotted red. Tomas's own heart thumped painfully in his unmarked chest and he breathed in shallow gasps, but in every other way he was immobilized. Even his eyes refused to close. None of the Saxons showed the slightest awareness of the grisly scene, although Linley was still casting the subtlest of worried glances at Tomas.

As Simon bit into the wine-soaked bread, the harvest scene vanished and a great tree sprang up to tower above the altar. Hulking transparent branches filled the sky; sunlight trickled down through roughened cylinders of bark. From the shimmering trunk and limbs hung an immaterial figure, thorn-scratched and bleeding: a man; a god; a sacrifice.

The suspended image shifted, transmogrified into a series of faces, each set of features superimposed upon another, until the thorns twisting about the forehead gradually stretched and swelled into long spreading antlers. And as the figure changed, the tree alternated with other backgrounds: woods and temples, fields and caves. When the being raised his rippling head and stared, Tomas could not endure that gaze.

As if breaking free from a thin confining layer of ice, his body jerked and shuddered. With a convulsive groan, he whirled and fled from the Mass.

CHAPTER SIXTEEN: A SEAL OF SAFE CONDUCT AND A HORSE

Linley found Tomas huddled in the clump of alder trees where they'd stowed their packs just before the service. The Norseman was breathing hard and fast, almost panting, his arms locked around his knees. Beneath his mariner's tan, his face was waxy and painfully taut about the mouth and nose.

Great dark pupils encircled by a narrow ring of grey peered up at Linley, who was relieved to find recognition in their depths. Whatever Tomas had seen at the Mass had not broken his mind. Still, it might be wise not to ask too many questions, especially at first.

Linley said hello and gave the him a tentative smile. Tomas nodded back. He expelled air from his lungs in a whistling sigh, and his respiration began to slow and deepen. Deciding to let Tomas speak first, Linley sat down and started arranging pebbles and twigs in aimless patterns on the damp ground. Not yet warmed by the young morning Sun, the air was moist and smelled of marsh salt.

Soon Tomas unfolded his long body and stretched out on his back, one arm cradling his pale shaggy head, the other flung across his closed eyes. Linley moved to a spot where he could see Tomas's face, and waited.

"Where are Alfred and Simon?" Tomas's voice, still quiet and well-modulated, was huskier than usual. For the first time, Linley detected a trace of Norse accent.

"Just outside camp, with our horses. The ostler is checking their gear."

Tomas sat bolt upright and frowned. "I'm still to go through with this?"

Linley thought of several replies and two questions, but discarded them all and merely nodded. When Tomas's face remained incredulous, Linley asked, trying to sound neutral, "Have you had a change of heart, then?"

Tomas's eyelids quivered, and he gave a short muffled gasp. Slumping onto his back again, he said, "No and yes." A brief silence, during which he stared bleakly overhead. "But not about Chippenham. I'll go there gladly, if you and Alfred are still agreed."

Linley nodded a second time and gazed quizzically at Tomas. A strand of snarled blond hair played about his face in the light breeze. When a thrush called nearby, both men turned towards the sound.

"Why did Alfred not change his mind?" asked Tomas after a moment. His color was better and his shoulders less rigid.

"Truly, I could not say." Tomas was giving him an odd look

but said nothing, so Linley continued: "Alfred doesn't shift course with every wind that blows. We need whatever tidings you might bring, and he's inclined to trust you. In part out of liking, and also for the reasons I gave you yesterday."

"After what just happened?"

"Aye. You're a Norseman. This was your first Mass?" At Tomas's silent nod, Linley shrugged and said, "We supposed as much. So he and Simon can tell each other that you found it new and strange. Or misinterpreted the talk of sacrifice, perhaps, and felt endangered--"

"Sacrifice!" Heaving himself to a sitting position, arms wrapped around his knees, Tomas stared at Linley. His eyes were as unfocused as they had been during the Mass.

Linley chewed his lower lip. Now that he thought of it, Tomas probably hadn't understood a word of the service, since it was doubtful that he spoke any Latin. "Pay no mind, Tomas. It's over now. I wish that Alfred hadn't asked you to attend."

"Why not?"

Tomas's face was strained and nervous, but free of guile. He truly did not know. And therefore was probably not an Elf, concluded Linley for perhaps the tenth time in an ongoing private debate.

Then why was Tomas so fey? What manner of Elf had spirited this man away for seven years to return him here transformed in so many ominous, telltale respects, of which Tomas himself had apparently been left unwarned?

Dark and incomprehensible are the inhabitants of Faerie, thought Linley, marvelous though they are, and their ways are not the ways of men and women.

Choosing his words with care, he said, "The Fair Folk cannot bear the touch of the consecrated Host or wine. Or holy water, or any relics. Nor a crucifix, some claim. Though I have never heard it said, it might also be difficult for--one closely associated with Faerie to hear a Mass, or even to be near those objects."

Tomas looked away. His throat moved as he swallowed, and his head sank into his hands.

A sudden worry struck Linley. Scrambling to sit in front of Tomas, he said, "You must believe me when I say we did not know the Mass would pain you. We are all aggrieved for your sake."

The grey eyes that met Linley's were no longer remote. The Saxon saw wistfulness there, and a temporary lowering of defenses. But most of all he saw fatigue, a deep, chilling weariness that welled up from far beneath the surface, as if Linley gazed into the cold clear water of a lake.

"I believe you," Tomas said quietly. "And I never thought otherwise." A small lopsided smile appeared and disappeared beneath his crooked nose.

A silence fell and lengthened. It might have been an awkward silence, but it wasn't. Still, from the height of the Sun, they should leave for Chippenham soon. Linley gathered up his pack and got to his feet. But first there was something he wanted to say.

"Tomas," he began, studying the sky. "I do not know what befell you in Elf--these past seven years. But I perceive they were not easy. I don't know what you saw at the Mass and I don't want to know, unless you care to tell me. I can only guess when some act or word of ours might trouble you, and I'm loathe to question you too closely. But if I can aid you or avoid causing you hurt in any way, tell me what it might be." He glanced cautiously at Tomas.

After a moment, Tomas nodded. Very straight and still he sat, hands folded in his lap as if he considered something in the distance that Linley could not see. "Thank you," he said, his voice low and clear. "You have given me a gift, perhaps the one I most needed just now. This I ask of you: when we join Alfred and Simon, would you help me turn the talk from the Mass, if need be?"

Fascinated by the new-minted glitter in Tomas's eyes and the vibrancy in his tone, Linley agreed without hesitation.

Tomas thanked him again, then turned and reached for his pack. As he did, his demeanor returned to what it ordinarily was, and Linley saw only a disheveled, gangling young Norseman rummaging through an oversized leather satchel. Tomas pulled out one of his harps, wrapped in its case, and offered it to Linley.

"We've no time to play now," said Linley, taken aback.

Tomas was smiling. "I know. You gave me a gift, and now I give you one. Take the harp, please. It's yours. I suspect it always was."

It was one of the two finest harps that Linley had ever seen. To have played it last night was something he expected to remember fondly for the rest of his days. Now this astonishing man wanted to make him a present of the instrument, was waving it under Linley's nose, laughing, and urging him to keep it.

At last Linley extended two reverent hands. Tomas the Rhymer promptly put the harp into Linley's arms and closed his fingers on its leather case.

As Linley held the instrument, a current of excitement and delight seemed to run from his hands up to his heart, the same exuberance and buoyancy the harp had given him the evening before.

96

When he thanked Tomas, Linley couldn't keep a slight quaver from his voice, but he didn't care.

Giddy over his new harp, Linley forgot about Tomas's horse until they'd almost reached the clearing where Alfred waited. "John is loathe to surrender you the grey you'll be riding," said Linley, pelting down the path beside Tomas.

"I'm not taking his mount, I hope?"

"No, nor anyone's. Anyone here, I mean. We've not many horses, as you know. But this one wandered up to where ours were tethered last night, and that old horse-nurse John contrived to catch him," Linley explained. "Meek as milk, John says, till you're in the saddle. Then he struts like a charger. Someone's prize stallion must have strayed; I expect they were sick to lose him."

Linley glanced curiously at Tomas. Intent on the slightly uneven ground, he ran in practiced reaching strides, and showed not the faintest interest in the fine animal he was to borrow. Not a horseman, then. Something occurred to Linley. "Ah--you can ride, can't you?"

Tomas nodded without enthusiasm. They vaulted a fallen log, Tomas in one sailing bound, and Linley in a huffing scramble that was calculated to protect his harp at all costs.

Anyone who could move like that should be able to manage a horse. "Good," Linley panted. "Even if he's a handful, it's pure luck we've a mount to spare at all, let alone one that can carry someone your height."

They sprinted the final yards to the clearing, where Simon and Alfred stood talking quietly. The King did not refer to the hour and aimed no tell-tale squint at the Sun. With an alert, assessing expression, he merely looked from Tomas to Linley and back.

Tomas met Alfred's eyes. The King smiled, but not before Linley had glimpsed the concern beneath Alfred's warmth and detected the minute, awed hesitation preceding his smile: an acknowledgment of the size and nature of the gulf that separated Alfred of Wessex from Tomas the Rhymer.

As if the Saxon bard were the doorway between the skald and the King, Alfred turned to Linley and pressed a small disk of carved metal into his hands. It was the seal of safe conduct. "Bury this outside the range of their scouts--and mark where you hide it. I will not lose either of you, God willing."

To Tomas he said, "My thanks again. You are my welcome guest, whenever you choose to return. I must leave you now; John is bringing the horses." A slight pause. "God be with you." Another

97

smile, and Alfred swiftly walked away, shoulders squared and braced. While the King spoke, Simon had maintained a courteous distance. Now he gave Linley a quick, rough hug that did not quite conceal the shifting of his eyes towards Tomas. Linley thumped his brother on the back and released him with a small significant nod.

"Go with my blessing," said Simon. Dark smudges blotted the skin beneath his eyes, and his speech came with more difficulty than usual, as if each word were a living thing escaping his lips. He and Tomas gazed at each other until something invisible passed between them.

His face suddenly wistful, Simon looked down at his clasped fingers—and made a careful, measured gesture that Linley had not seen in years, not since Simon's ordination. He reached up to lay his left palm on Tomas's forehead and his right hand on Tomas's heart.

The skald's eyes widened, but he stood quite still beneath Simon's hands. After holding the pose for perhaps five seconds, Simon whispered, "Go in peace," then turned and left without another word.

On his way he passed John the Ostler, a seamed and chunky little man, bull-shouldered and cheerful, with a lame right leg. John led the saddled and bridled horses into the clearing, lecturing the recently acquired dapple-grey. "And mind where you set your great ugly feet."

The grey and a shaggy little roan mare clomped to a halt and stood with their eyes on Linley and their ears cocked towards the sound of the ostler's voice. John fastened the packs to the saddles. Reluctantly, Linley handed the ostler his new harp to entrust to Simon's care. In the middle of John's admonitions, Linley glanced at Tomas. He was eyeing the tall grey horse.

Noticing Tomas's scrutiny, the ostler beamed. "Aye, he's a rare one. Look at the size of him, and the chest! Big as a bear's, his heart must be, and legs straight as treetrunks. And not a scratch nor a tare on all that pretty hide." John gave the horse a sociable whack on the rump, then chuckled at the fleeting alarm on Tomas's face. "Don't take on; he'd not kick in a thousand years. Sweeter than a lass in love, till you get on his back," said the ostler, grinning. "And then full of tricks. Likes company, he does, so tether him near you where he won't miss anything."

John's weathered face sobered. "His mouth is perfect, so it would be a kindness and a courtesy to pretend the reins are cobwebs," he said to Tomas, who nodded. "Finest animal I've seen in twenty years, and I'd a mind to train him proper for the King's use. But I reckon this amounts to the same thing. Luck to you both." He yanked his leather cap down over his thinning hair and walked off with Linley's harp.

Linley took a moment to admire the grey's short back, springy pasterns and powerful hocks. Truly, a magnificent beast, though just now he looked bored enough to fall asleep where he stood, blinking into strong sunlight that reflected from his luminous black eyes in reddish glints.

Tomas was staring at the dappled animal with the mesmerized attitude of someone who has narrowly missed treading on a sleeping snake.

"A lot of horse, eh? We'll go gently at first, so you two can get acquainted," Linley offered somewhat enviously, and swung onto the roan mare's padded back. Like sitting on a haystack. She flicked an ear back towards Linley and snorted. But he could trust John to cinch her saddle tightly, against her bad habit of inflating her belly as soon as she felt the strap.

Finally Tomas turned his head and looked at Linley. His face was blank, his features immobile.

"We should be starting," said Linley, hoping fervently that Tomas was more cautious and green around horses in general than frightened of this one in particular. What could make his mount more approachable? "Shall we give your friend there a name?"

The question seemed to work; Tomas chuckled. Nervous laughter, perhaps, but genuine. He shook his head, gathered up the grey's reins and hoisted himself into the saddle. "Let's call him Aubrey."

CHAPTER SEVENTEEN: THE BOGGY ROAD TO CHIPPENHAM

At first, half-expecting that the pooka would retaliate for Tomas's parting scene with Moira, Tomas was relieved when Aubrey neither kicked nor threw him. The pooka behaved much like any spirited horse. Then it became clear that he was clowning.

He whipped smartly left or right at the slightest pressure on the reins, and bounded forward the instant that Tomas's heel grazed his side. When Aubrey jumped, he sailed majestically across fence or stream with ostentatious inches to spare. From time to time he crested his neck, danced sideways and produced a series of theatrical, deep-chested snorts. The stout mare responded to this equine burlesque with long soulful looks, whose effect was rather spoiled when she stuck out her neck and scuttled to keep up with the highstepping pooka.

"Sorry, Linley," Tomas called over his shoulder. He tried to rein Aubrey in--gently, to give the pooka as little excuse as possible to rear or to sashay sideways into the mare's earnestly approaching nose. "I don't mean to leave you behind, but he's hard to hold."

"I can see that." Linley was grinning. "When we reach the road, give him his head for a while, to fatigue him. Perfect mouth or not, he needs a bit with more muscle. I'll tell John."

His hands full, Tomas grunted. Plague take the pooka; had he returned to enforce Moira's requests or to bring a message from her? Would Moira reappear too? The muscles along Tomas's breastbone knotted painfully. "Which way when we come to the road?" he asked Linley, as the pooka flattened his ears and did another pirouette.

"To the left."

Yes, he would let Aubrey run. And he would by the gods try to talk with him as they galloped out of earshot. Tomas had never heard Aubrey speak while the pooka was in horse-shape, yet felt sure that he understood every word said in his presence.

But Linley was signaling them to stop. "Look," he said, pointing. "The wetlands shift quickly, Tomas; that boggy strip wasn't there a year ago. We must cross it to reach the road. It's that or double back into country held by the Danes."

Glumly, Linley surveyed the sodden turf that was dotted with hillocks of quavering grass. From small pools of brackish water, there jutted rotting tree stumps and tangled knots of reeds whose heads drooped on scrawny necks. Sniffing the air, Tomas caught the sulphurous reek of marsh gas.

They had ridden the better part of the day. In the west, a ruddy Sun trailed down the sky towards glowing cloudbanks.

100

"I like this not one whit," muttered Linley. "I intended to cross the road, make camp and bury the seal, then send you to Chippenham on foot this evening. But look at the will-o-the-wisps in the bog." Tomas spied a flickering yellow gleam in the gathering mist, and another, and a third. As he tried to trace one saffron flare through the marsh, it lengthened and stretched itself into a wavering shape. He saw a mournful face, its features blurred by long dripping hair. The figure stood with one wasted hand cupped around a weak sickly light that poured through its fingers. With its other hand, it beckoned to Linley. When it vanished with a hushed tremulous wail, others appeared to take its place.

Linley was watching Tomas. "What do you see?" asked the Saxon. Wanting confirmation rather than reassurance, his eyes were round and dark against the growing twilight--the eyes of someone who prefers not to endure his visions all alone.

"Lights. Forms that come and go. One of them cried out."

"I heard a duck calling. And I can see only lights, but so many of them, and all so bright." A fine layer of perspiration glazed Linley's forehead. "I could never understand why men followed will-o-the-wisps down to die in the mud...but I keep thinking those lights point the way to dry land and a cottage." He stared into the syrupy glittering mist that swirled above the marsh. "If I could see the forms as you can, Tomas, I might not feel so drawn."

Absently, Linley gathered up his reins. Of his own accord, Aubrey stepped between the roan mare and the bog. A crowd of figures stood and beckoned now from mere yards away, their pale arms swathed in torn linen and plastered with mud and marsh grass. Every drowned face was turned towards Linley, as if Tomas were not there at all. But their cold eyes narrowed and glinted as Aubrey shouldered his way in front of the mare, and the foremost wraith retreated three measured paces.

Jostled, the roan horse stepped backward and snorted. Linley lifted one hand to shade his eyes from the phantom lights. "I cannot tell where the solid ground lies, and where the treacherous. Can you see a clear path? I won't take the horses into a bog while my vision is clouded."

The will-o-the-wisps had drawn into massed ranks. Their faces tight and avid, they now stared at Tomas as well. Thin light haloed their heads, while every cadaverous hand cupped a matching phosphorescent flare.

One stood in front, slightly apart from the others. It said in a voice like drifting leaves, "Suffer them to come to us, pooka. We are your brethren. It ill beseems you to dance attendance on mortals and mongrel creatures."

Wheeling to face the speaker, Aubrey bared his teeth and hissed: "You know whom I serve. These men are under her protection and his. It is you who will suffer them to pass unharmed."

The pretense was over now. How would Linley react to the pooka's voice? Tomas looked despairingly at the Saxon.

But Linley merely said, "Aye, Tomas. We'll follow you and Aubrey." He urged his mare towards the pooka's hindquarters.

Relieved, Tomas loosened his hold on the reins. The pooka's doing, no doubt: Linley must have heard something different.

The wraith who had spoken was scowling. "We have always had sovereignty here," it said with an attempt at dignity.

Aubrey snorted. "Since you were exiled. Do the chained rule the free? Begone!" He lowered his head and plunged into the marsh.

Tomas clung to the pooka's back, gripping fistfuls of coarse grey mane. The mare stayed at Aubrey's heels. Among the hummocks of marsh grass the pooka traveled a circuitous route, and his hooves made wet sucking sounds as the blackened mud reluctantly released them for each step. The will-o-the-wisps shrank away on either side. One or two called out, "Traitor!" and something that sounded like "Mongrel!"

"Traitor" was probably Aubrey. A pooka was a water-Elf, and Moira had said that mortals were generally unwise to ride one. Aubrey himself had said that Tomas was alive only because the pooka had sworn to serve Tomas as he would Moira. But what was "mongrel"?

When at last they clambered onto the higher ground of the far bank, directly before them lay the road to Chippenham. It was hardly more than an uneven cow path, muddy in places and choked with weeds, but blessedly solid.

They made camp a few miles down the road. After burying the seal of safe conduct near a grove of holly trees, Tomas and Linley sprawled, exhausted, before the low-burning, lapis-centered yellow embers of a small fire.

"I believe you saved my life today," said Linley. It was the first time either of them had spoken since they reached the road. "I could never have found the path alone."

"It was Aubrey," said Tomas quietly, feeling the damp right down to his bones. His muscles were already cramped and sore. "He picked his own trail through the bog."

The next morning dawned crisp and clear, with a quickly evaporating chill in the sun-washed blue air. Not without misgivings, Tomas shouldered his pack and set off on foot down the muddy track towards Chippenham fort. He left Linley alone with the roan mare and the pooka.

CHAPTER EIGHTEEN: A RESIDENT OF CHIPPENHAM

At twilight of the day after Tomas left for the fort, Linley slept in the deepening lavender shade of a thicket. Aubrey and the mare dozed a few yards away.

The drowsy pooka was dimly aware of the amorous boasting of frogs and crickets, the softly hooted challenge of an owl and the snapping fangs of a disappointed fox who had missed her kill. Their voices mingled with the soughing of the breeze in the hollies, a hedgehog's deliberate waddling gait—and the faintest of snores from the half-Sighted mortal, an accompaniment to such dreams as mortals have.

Once one of them had told Aubrey of his dreams... Blowing air from his delicate nostrils, the pooka shifted his weight from one hind leg to the other, tempted both to pursue that newly emerged memory and to wander elsewhere down the inviting paths of his own slumber.

That was when a remarkably solid kick, given the size of its source, landed just below Aubrey's kneecap, and a brownie's dry waspish voice said loudly, "Hsst! Don't make a sound!"

Aubrey glared down at the excited Elf, the tip of whose red knitted cap didn't even reach the pooka's shoulder. A long unraveling tassel bobbed as the brownie hopped from side to side. He wore one ancient, cracked leather boot which, from the weathered appearance of his other foot, he didn't need.

The pooka's shin smarted. "And what might you want? You make enough racket for seven brownies, leaping about like that."

Scowling, the little Elf planted himself in front of Aubrey, waved a hairy simian hand at the still-snoring Linley and demanded, "Are you with that?"

"What do you think?"

The brownie looked meaningfully at Aubrey's halter, then down the length of the rope that ran from it and tethered the pooka to a tree near the Saxon.

"Very well, I am. For the moment," said Aubrey, exasperated. "Come to the point, brownie!"

"Can it understand us?"

"Not very well. He's only half-Sighted and he's sleeping. And I am losing patience," Aubrey said sweetly, and displayed his teeth.

The brownie took two dignified steps backward. "I reside in Chippenham fort," it said in a self-important tone. "So naturally I remained there to mind things when the Saxons left and the Danes arrived. Someone had to."

Aubrey nodded. A household Elf, then, fond of a particular

steading rather than a person. What could have induced the brownie to leave the fort? Curiosity began to temper Aubrey's irritation.

"And it were well that someone stayed, I tell you, Pooka. Cleaner about their persons they are than the Saxons, but the Danes build their fires and gut their deer smack in the middle of the great hall. And I flummox 'em as I can, hide their gear and spoil their food, but do you think a drop of porridge has passed my lips since Alfred's cooks departed?" The brownie shook his head so hard that the tassel of his cap almost wrapped around Aubrey's knees. "What do the Norse feed their own nisse, I ask you? Little wonder they leave their freezing land up yonder. And with it a pack of nisse turned spiteful, I warrant, and helping the mortals with naught. Well, these Danes took a prisoner--"

"What?" Aubrey felt his ears go flat, and the slight stinging of his eyes that meant they had flared red.

"They took a prisoner, I said, though he was one of them, or nearly. A bard from Vestfold he said he was, up the North way. At first they had him tell stories and sing yestereve, while they feasted. But soon there was muttering that 'twas men from Vestfold who murdered some Danes of their number, so why should they let this bard go free? Then some offered to kill him, while others gainsaid that but wanted to force him to fight the Saxons with them. It grew from a blather into a brawl, that Guthrum himself stopped by taking the bard prisoner. On the morrow they decide what to do with him."

Wheezing from the long speech with no pause for air, the brownie squinted over his shoulder at Linley, who hadn't stirred. Aubrey studied the brownie's huffing little face. How much did he know, and would he help? Brownies were an anarchical lot, quirkish and xenophobic, especially when attached to a site and not to a person. Lord Rhys and Lady Moira's authority, the threat to their territory and indeed to all of far-flung Faerie, might well mean nothing to this self-absorbed, house-proud creature.

Yet unlike the rebellious lunatics imprisoned in that bog, the brownie wasn't incorrigibly malevolent, nor was he confined to Chippenham. Still, something odd was going on...

The brownie had begun to squirm beneath Aubrey's gaze, but did his best to fix the pooka with a defiant stare. Suddenly Aubrey realized what was bothering him. Out of mischief he made his voice as grave and helpful as he could, and asked the question that he guessed the other had hoped to avoid. "Brownie, why have you come to me with this mortal's quandary?"

"Because," said the brownie, more loudly than before. Grunting in his sleep, Linley curled himself into a cat-like ball. With a guilty

105

glance at the Saxon, the brownie continued, "Because when he came into my hall, he stank of pooka."

It was not the answer that Aubrey expected, and for an instant he saw a tiny wicked gleam in the brownie's eyes.

Ah, this one possessed some subtlety. The pooka grinned, happily anticipating a quality of verbal by-play he had thought to leave behind in Elfland for a while. Mortals, even Tomas, were so utterly transparent. "And because?" Aubrey prompted.

"Because I sensed the hand of the Lady Moira upon him."

Aubrey nodded. Excellent. "What did you think then?"

"I? What would you have me think?" A twitch of the bony shoulders. "The ways of the Queen and any Fool of hers are none of mine to judge." Then a perplexed look crept into his eyes. "This one seems more ignorant than most."

The pooka nodded a second time, and waited.

"But from the first he could see me, and watched me as he sang. While the Danes jabbered, he would glance at me where I sat by the door, as if he wanted to speak. So I thought, whatever pooka this bard has been Fool enough to ride, perchance Herself means to send me a message by him. Maybe he could tell me when the Danes might cease to kennel in my hall. For Fools know many things, even when they know not all they know."

Squinting at his unshod foot, the brownie wriggled his bare toes. "Finally some men made ready to sleep, him among them. So I sidled closer, and he caught my eye and contrived a pretext to move away from the man who was conversing with him." The brownie thrust out his lower lip. "That selfsame man, Knut, is the only half-Sighted one in all that pack of Danes. A great slyboots who uses his Sight to pry and bedevil his fellows. Perhaps Knut sensed there was more to the bard than met the eye. But I forgot all that in my hurry—and trod on a live coal, which broke my attention to my spell of concealment. Knut caught a glimpse of my burnt foot and grabbed for it."

He scowled at Aubrey as if daring him to laugh. Aubrey gazed earnestly back, until the brownie heaved a disgusted sigh and went on: "The bard saw it all, lunged at Knut and knocked him aside. In the end all he got was my boot, and upon that I cast an unglamour to make it seem naught but a dry brown leaf. He threw it in the fire."

"Ah," said the pooka. They both considered the brownie's naked foot and its coarse black hair. Almost captured by mortals. The brownie curled up all six toes and shuddered fastidiously.

"Knut started the muttering against the bard then and claimed he was attacked. He wouldn't admit a live coal needed quenching. Of course they neither one would say what else they'd seen."

Aubrey allowed himself the pleasure of prodding. "But why have–"

"I'm getting to it!" snapped the brownie. Linley murmured something in his sleep, and Aubrey cast a mild concerned glance at the Saxon. Red crept into the brownie's bark-colored cheeks. "The Danes confined the bard for the night. And I went to see him." Clamping his mouth shut, the brownie dug his toes into the earth.

He looked like a dwarf apple tree, topped with one huge ripe glowing fruit. The court would relish that description when Aubrey returned. "And?"

"And I told him that because he'd prevented my capture, I was in his debt and that I, Brownie of Chippenham, owed him one service with good cheer," said the brownie with a steaming glare. "While privately I gave thanks he'd not done more and bound me longer to his will." Drawing himself up to his full height, the little Elf puffed out his chest in indignation. "And then he laughed!"

"Laughed?"

"Aye! Folded double, holding his belly as if it pained him. Laughed silently and long."

"Meseems 'twas not at you, Brownie," suggested Aubrey. The other Elf nodded and coughed, and they both chose to look elsewhere for moment.

"I could not grant his first request, to release him from an iron cell that locks with an iron key," said the brownie in a small voice. He shot Aubrey a quizzical glance. "I believe he's in some discomfort there, and knows not why."

Aubrey decided to say nothing.

"But I could follow my nose to you, Pooka, to tell you what had befallen him and to beg your aid."

"Well," said Aubrey, sighing. "Well, well. When this one awakens, I suppose I must commence a rescue." He frowned in Linley's direction. The Saxon had rolled onto his back and flung an arm across his dreaming face. "Were a harp and a flute in the cell with him?"

"Yes. He plays them well." A grudging concession.

"He does indeed. Now I must question you about the fort and the Danes, as part of your service with good cheer. Agreed? But first, Brownie, why have you never called our bard by his name?"

Bristling eyebrows drew together, then shot upwards. "Because he would not give me his name."

The Fool grew wiser, at least in part. Aubrey shook his head at the thought, and began to consider what he should ask the brownie.

107

CHAPTER NINETEEN: A CONFERENCE BY THE ELVISH SEA

Before Aubrey left to confer with the Lord and Lady about his plans, he assigned the brownie to watch Linley and keep him sleeping with whispered illusions, if necessary. "Should all else fail, I give you leave to smite him on the head," he told the little Elf.

Anxious to return to Chippenham, disgruntled about being embroiled in the affairs of long-avoided Elves more powerful than himself, and peevish at having to play nursemaid for a mortal to whom he was not indebted, the brownie brightened at the prospect.

"But don't hurt him!" Aubrey said, suspicious of the anticipatory glee that lit the crinkled face.

"Aye, aye. 'Smite him, Brownie. But nay! Gently, I say.' If I'm to detain him here, your worship, I might have to do more than kiss his hand." Taking sudden aim, the brownie spat a long stream of greenish-yellow liquid from a wad of leaves he was chewing.

The pooka dodged just in time. "Do no more than you must. Agreed?" His eyes flaring a dark and turbulent red, Aubrey stared until the brownie nodded reluctantly.

That done, the pooka traveled to Rhys and Moira's court, taking what could be called the shorter road, the route through mortal Time instead of Space. He waited until the Earth spun into the proper angle to the Sun, waited until the Sun's light slanted just so across the purblind contracted face of Midgard, waited until the Moon looked the other way and all the planets inhaled together. And then Aubrey leaped into the void that mortals cannot see, because they live it, just as mortals cannot see the air they breathe.

Holding his own breath, the pooka skimmed through the measured wastes of Time, bounded by the great slow heartbeat of each star, until at last he landed in Faerie. Where Time is not, nor Sun, nor Moon.

Round hooves dug four great gouts in the amber-colored shoreline of the Elvish Sea. Through the salty air, sand spurted, frosting Aubrey's hide, Moira's streaming dark hair and Rhys's amber skin.

Maintaining the embrace in which Aubrey found them, standing with their arms wound about each other, Rhys and Moira regarded the pooka without surprise. But Aubrey thought that Moira's tilted grey eyes shifted a little, as though she scanned the beach behind him.

Calmly, Rhys said, "You would not arrive thus without great need. What brings you here?"

Aubrey explained how he learned what had befallen Tomas, and how he proposed to free the mortal from the cell at Chippenham. After the pooka assumed two-legged shape, all three Elves sat down upon the sparkling beach.

"Risky, to use Faerie as a route through that section of Midgard," said Rhys, shaking his head. "Or through any section. There are more blockades each time we pass."

Aubrey looked at Moira, who was drawing maps in the sand and watching the lines as they shifted. "I believe it is feasible," she said, not meeting Aubrey's eyes. "There have been no exorcisms at Chippenham fort itself."

"There may be one after they leave," Rhys told her. She gave him a quick smile, then furrowed her brow. "In that event, what of the brownie?"

"A priest would most likely mention shape-shifters and demons," said Rhys. "I doubt that would disturb the brownie. He's dwelt there many of their years, and his roots drink from that soil."

Clearing his throat, Aubrey said, "Begging your pardon, your Majesties. But you misremember that these are Danes, who number few or no Christians among them. Perhaps we would be propitiated as before, after the rescue. But not expelled."

The other two Elves exchanged glances. "You are right, and our minds are wandering," muttered Rhys. "Are you certain that you wish to chance that road?"

"With what lies in the balance, it seems I must." To Moira, Aubrey said, "The gifts you gave him grow apace, my lady."

Moira gave him one swift bleak look but said nothing.

Rhys got to his feet and stood gazing at the foamy sea. "Much lies in the balance," he said, his voice weighted with a fatigue that didn't mark his features. "More labyrinthine Truths work here than I can understand. But I sense that as the other worlds surrender to the rule of Time, Faerie swings free of it." He turned to face the pooka. "We've become the shrinking hub round which the others turn. The more that they fence themselves in with an unyielding mortar of only one belief, or two, the more I perceive that we are shut in."

Sighing, Moira asked Aubrey, "What of the half-Sighted mortal?"

The pooka shrugged. Rhys and Moira looked at one another, and continued looking. Just as Aubrey began weighing the merits of a solitary stroll down the beach, Rhys said, "Go then, and attempt what you propose. We in turn will keep the paths as open as we may." His golden face softened as he added, "You have our blessing, for wherever

109

it may still take you."

Bowing, Aubrey said, "M'lord, m'lady. Wherever indeed!"

And back he went the longer way for this half of the voyage, through elfin Space and not through mortal Time. Panting, he danced an entirely different and fatiguing dance, until he found himself again in Midgard.

Beside the sulking brownie Aubrey emerged, not a yard from the spot where he had disappeared, near the grove of holly trees and the thicket where the Saxon slumbered on.

At the brownie's impatient expression, Aubrey stifled a grin, knowing he would be accused of dawdling shamefully and a-purpose. But if Linley had been awake, he would no doubt have sworn that the interval between Aubrey's departure and return had taken only a moment of Time and perhaps a foot of Space.

CHAPTER TWENTY: LINLEY'S VISITOR

The brownie liked Aubrey's plan still less than had Moira and Rhys. "Are you daft, Pooka? The mortal will run away! Think of something else, for pity's sake."

"Would you be delivered of your debt or not?"

"I've no debt to this one here." The little Elf eyed Linley with disdain.

"Weren't you charged to seek my aid?"

Muttering, the brownie squatted down by Aubrey, who sat in his two-legged Elf shape beside Linley. "I never knew one to sleep so much. Perchance it's ill," the brownie said hopefully.

"He's not ill. He's had but little sleep these past few nights and much to distress him. Sighted and half-Sighted mortals have more need of sleep, for they have more dreams."

With a grunt, the brownie began nibbling its ragged fingernails.

"You'll hold his ankles fast if I make you a sign? And stay invisible?" Aubrey asked one last time.

"Aye."

The pooka stretched one pointed grey hand towards Linley's arm, then pulled back with a sigh. How to seem less threatening? He'd conjured up some clothes and shoved a hat over his tufted ears. Sitting would mask his height, at least till he had to stand. But the mortal would probably be frightened regardless.

Within as short a time as possible, Aubrey must accomplish two things: invoke Linley's fascination with Faerie, and reassure him. If the Elves had to restrain the Saxon, Aubrey's scheme would prove far more difficult.

At the pooka's prolonged hesitation, the brownie puckered his face and snorted cynically.

Aubrey laid his fingertips on Linley's shoulders. "Linley," he whispered. "Singer, lutenist, half-Sighted one. Brother to Simon, follower of Alfred. And friend to Tomas the Rhymer."

On the last words, Linley opened his eyes. They were fogged with sleep, and he blinked at Aubrey with the unquestioning acceptance of a child awakened from a nap. Then his eyes narrowed in alarm, his dark brows drew together and his mouth clamped shut. Beneath Aubrey's hands, the mortal's stringy muscles began to bunch and slide. Shifting his grip, the pooka allowed Linley to sit up but didn't release him.

"Please listen to me," Aubrey urged. He added just enough strength to his hold to make it difficult for Linley to pull away, and put

111

as much gentleness as he could muster into his raspy voice. "I too am a friend to Tomas, a friend from another country. I bring you tidings of him and beseech your aid. I will swear upon anything you like not to harm you, Linley, but I pray you to hear me out."

Beneath his tawny complexion, the mortal had turned the shade of dirty parchment. He stopped struggling. Sitting straight and to all appearances relaxed, although Aubrey knew better, Linley looked the pooka up and down, then cautiously met his eyes. Those of the Saxon showed a great deal of white around the irises. "Who are you? You're not a Dane."

Ignoring the brownie's wicked chuckle, too low-pitched for mortal ears, Aubrey said, "No, indeed. I am friend to Tomas the Rhymer, and friend therefore to you. So fear me not."

Linley's gaze flickered down to his upper arms, where the pooka's hard knotted fingers clutched him, and back to Aubrey's face.

"Ah," said Aubrey. "Then why do I restrain you? It displeases me that I must show you this unkindness. But without it you might depart in haste, before you heard my news from one end to the other. And Tomas has need of you." He glared at the brownie who was still hovering around Linley's ankles, until the smaller Elf flounced off to perch on a fallen log a few yards away.

"Has Tomas sent you, then? How can I know you come from him?" asked Linley.

"I come from Elfland," Aubrey told him slowly, trying to sound reassuring. He smiled.

Perhaps that was imprudent, for Linley's eyes flared wide. With a twinge of guilt, Aubrey realized that his yellowed teeth would seem ominously large and protruding to the mortal. Behind Linley's back, dead leaves churned into the air as the brownie gleefully drummed his heels.

"I believe you," said Linley. He mustered a weak smile in return. "But how can I know that you mean Tomas well?"

Aubrey found himself admiring the Saxon's nerve. "You cannot know. So you must trust me. If I release you now, will you stay and listen?"

Before the mortal finished nodding, Aubrey let go of him. Linley flexed his arms but otherwise sat still, his head tilted and his wary brown eyes on the pooka.

"Tomas was taken prisoner by the Danes at Chippenham," said Aubrey. "Not for reasons that concern your King."

"Why, then?"

The pooka shrugged. "Do men require reasons? Merely

112

because Tomas is not one of them, perhaps. Maybe one of the Danes senses something strange about him. Or because they drink and quarrel and grow restive."

"Can you free him?"

"Not without your aid, Linley."

"What would you have me do?"

Aubrey considered. The Saxon leaned forward, impatient, and his face had almost lost its earlier pallor. "First, you must swear to do precisely as I say. No matter if you think it foolish. Have I your word?"

Linley gave his word.

"Excellent," said the pooka briskly. "In a moment I will leave you. Hide your pack, kick ashes over your fire and tether your mare deeper in the woods. Carry neither sword nor knife; you will not need them. A horse that you may recognize will approach you. Get on his back and give him his head. He will bear you to Chippenham by a route that will be foreign to you. Do not dismount. You might be terrified, or overcome with wonder or with joy. But you must not dismount." He stopped to assess Linley's reaction.

The mortal's round secretive face was a mask of concentration. "I won't," he promised.

"Good. You see, Linley, I must trust you, too." Aubrey took a moment to review the brownie's information. "The horse will arrive at Chippenham before dawn, in the courtyard by the stables. Some stalls have been converted into cells. At the left end of the double row of stalls, keys hang on hooks upon the wall. Take the rusted iron key that hangs alone. The stall just opposite is Tomas's cell. Unlock it and drop the key into the straw. It must not remain upon your person!" He paused until the Saxon nodded. "Tomas will grab his satchel and get on the horse with you. You'll be returned to this campsite by that same foreign route." Something occurred to Aubrey. "Discourage Tomas from dismounting, should he try. Although I doubt he will. Are you agreed? Will you remember?"

"Yes. But if I have no weapon, and the Danes--"

"Give the horse his head. And hold fast, to keep your seat," said the pooka grimly. He caught the sullen eye of the listening brownie. "I've reason to believe the Danes are unlikely to disturb you. They will have drunk much oddly potent ale and fallen onto pallets of unusual softness. And in other ways their slumber will have been encouraged."

The brownie looked dubious, then nodded.

Somewhat to Aubrey's surprise, Linley grinned and said, "I think I understand." He stood and began raking ashes over the remains of the small campfire.

The pooka had dreaded this moment, but there was no escaping it. Slowly and awkwardly, he clambered to his feet. When Linley glanced up at him, the mortal's face tightened, but he didn't seem unduly alarmed.

Relieved, Aubrey said, "I thank you, Master Linley." Bowing low, he backed away from the mortal and into the thickest part of the forest. The brownie had already bounded off towards Chippenham to inform Tomas they would soon arrive.

Even though the strange mottle-skinned Elf had warned Linley that he might recognize the horse, Linley was startled when Tomas's mount, Aubrey, emerged from the underbrush. Had Tomas ridden an Elf horse all along? Linley remembered the way that Tomas had stood stone-still at his first sight of the beast, and how he'd ascribed their successful journey through the bog to Aubrey. But how had the horse escaped his tether, and where were his saddle and bridle?

Aubrey rested his warm grey chin on Linley's shoulder and sighed. "And hello to you, too," said Linley, absurdly pleased at the display of friendliness. Elf horse or not, this was a splendid animal. Linley stroked the curving neck. "How am I to get on your back, my lad? You're no pony, and there's naught for me to hold onto but that fine thick mane."

The horse tossed his head, clumped over to a large boulder and kneeled down on his two forelegs.

"As you wish," muttered Linley after what seemed like a long time. "I gave my word. And may I not have taken leave of my senses." He thought of Tomas; he thought of Alfred. Squaring his shoulders, Linley marched over to the rock where the dappled horse waited. Gingerly, he settled onto Aubrey's muscular back.

The horse got up from his kneeling position and stood still while Linley fidgeted. He was used to riding bareback, on ploughhorses and ponies and his own little mare, but not on such a great highstrung animal as this. Finally he decided he had his weight distributed as best he could, but he didn't care to touch his heels to those glossy sides. Feeling both ridiculous and uneasy, Linley took two handfuls of Aubrey's mane and said, "I'm ready."

Then he forgot his scruples and clung to the mottled grey barrel with both legs. With Linley leaning low over his neck, Aubrey shot away through the woods--and into a shifting netherworld the likes of which Linley had never thought to see.

CHAPTER TWENTY-ONE: ANOTHER ROAD TO ELFLAND

For the mortal it would be a bewildering journey, and most disorienting. But it would be almost impossible for Linley to ride unmolested through mortal Space into Chippenham fort, and Aubrey needed a roundabout road, partly through Elfland and partly through Midgard, to reach the row of keys on the stable wall.

So many things for the pooka to hold in mind. Jostle Linley as little as he could. Detour through elfin Space often enough so that when they emerged at the fort, sufficient mortal Time would have elapsed to bring them there before dawn. In that hushed hour when sleep enfolds men and women most tightly in its heavy arms, the Danes were least likely to stir.

Aubrey must risk several blind leaps into Midgard, not only to prevent himself and Linley from arriving too late in mortal Time, but also to guide their route through mortal Space lest they appear, in that still and magic hour, somewhere other than by the stables. In the main square of Chippenham town by the watering trough, the pooka could set all the dogs to barking. He should also avoid the great hall, where he might awaken Guthrum and his men. If Aubrey miscalculated badly enough to arrive in Tomas's cell itself, he would keep Tomas unwilling company behind bars of unyielding iron, that harshest of metals, too searingly cold and madly self-absorbed, its particles whirling in their insular clannishness, to be tolerated by the ambivalent Elves with their complexity of vision.

Yet the pooka's navigational sorties into Midgard, indispensable though they were, held perils. For he could not predict exactly where they might materialize, be it town, field or churchyard, nor who might see them there. Nor could he discern in advance if the entry sites he chose were barred by exorcism.

Once his hooves touched the soil of Midgard, however, he would know immediately if that rite had been performed nearby. In such places, ghosts of chanting voices echoed in his ears, and the scene invariably looked icy-grey and wintry, slashed with thick black lines where human hands had drawn the fear-laden, deadening symbols of certainty and exclusion. All the mortals' emotions, all their thoughts, had lingered at such places, trapped and swollen by the half-truths of the ritual, until the charge in the atmosphere became a wall, oscillating and palpable, like a current of lightning encircling the spot. Where rigid belief, fed by anxiety and guilt and empowered by ritual, filled and closed the air, anyone with the intricate, sensitive awareness of the Elves could not pass without great pain.

Therefore, each time that Aubrey trespassed into Midgard, he must move tentatively, ready to retreat at the first hint of what Linley would call danger, or at the first sensation of that other and more deadly contamination. Neither could the pooka be careless of where he entered Elfland. In Faerie lay many a remote and savage region where mortals were unwelcome, where the inhabitants chose to dwell apart even from other Elves, and where the Lord and Lady's sovereignty was questioned as much as accepted. Even among the natives and the places that Aubrey loved best were many that he'd wager Linley wouldn't care to see.

Now Aubrey raced along a well-trodden path just outside the perimeter of Faerie, near the marshes, where he knew that the mortal could perceive no more than curdled mist. He flicked an ear back towards Linley. A far better horseman than Tomas, his weight perfectly balanced, Linley rode as if trying to dissolve into the pooka's back. He sat lightly, moved with rather than against Aubrey and kept his hands and feet quiet.

Excellent. He could probably handle fancier footwork than the pooka had first supposed. Aubrey gathered himself for a not-quite-sideways leap from the trail and into Faerie.

At first Linley was queasy. The big grey horse ran smoothly, effortlessly, with a clean springing stride that delighted the Saxon, accustomed as he was to choppier-gaited animals. After a time he found that his pleasure in the horse's motion distracted him enough to settle his stomach. But his nerves remained on edge, because their road would probably take them through Elfland.

Elfland! Where he'd always longed to travel, where Tomas the Rhymer had assured him he should never set foot, and where he still desired to go. They weren't there yet, because the topography of Faerie must consist of more than this strange doughy fog that surrounded them at the moment.

He would see marvels there. Maybe he would have further speech with that towering polite Elf with the big teeth and gleaming red eyes. Or meet other Elves, musicians, with any luck. That explained Tomas's uncommon skill: time with the musicians of Faerie.

As for their women... Tomas might have sworn fealty to an Elf woman and suffered grief thereby. A tiny chill raised the hair on Linley's arms. But he would remain upon this horse and so was unlikely to enter into such entanglements. To behold the women of Elfland, however, that at least he might do.

And the men also. Elf warriors, riding into Chippenham...

Linley shook his head and laughed aloud at his own foolishness. That was when Aubrey's muscles knotted and flexed, and by long habit Linley bent low over the dark coarse mane so as not to hinder the horse's leap to Otherwhere.

The terrain near that particular border path had become unexpectedly treacherous, as had its population. Something was amiss. The watchful stillness in the murky air, the lingering sour odors of hostility and of immeasurable age, gave Aubrey a growing certainty that he'd set off a vast and complex system of alarms not quite perceptible to him. When a viciously barbed arrow streaked past his nose to bury its resin-dipped head and two inches of shaft in an alder tree, he knew that he'd stumbled into one of the malign, crazed and isolated sections of Faerie.

Hisses and jeers echoed around him, directed partly at the mortal and the pooka, and partly at the archer who'd just bungled a clear shot. Aubrey yelled an apology for trespassing, then mumbled a half-forgotten spell of protection, one that he could trust little if at all in these particular woods. Summoning all his strength, he propelled himself into a long-reaching bound back to Midgard.

He alighted on roughly plowed earth. The impact made him stagger a few paces, and Linley shifted but kept his seat.

By some kind whim of the Fates, Aubrey stood in an empty field at the foot of a low hill, under a black star-strewn sky illuminated by a half Moon. To his relief he heard no dogs, no human voices. When Linley patted the pooka's shoulder, Aubrey sensed that the action was more for the mortal's reassurance than for his.

Not that he wouldn't welcome some reassurance of his own. He edged across uneven ground, away from the hill, guessing that a farmhouse might lie on the other side. The damp silty scent of his intended trail filled his nostrils. Soon he came to a sodden cowpath, where he stopped and tossed his head to communicate his intention to re-enter Elfland. Seeming to understand, Linley grasped the pooka's mane.

This time Aubrey selected a destination in Faerie that he knew quite well. His choice might be unpopular with the Elves, perhaps, but not dangerous—at least not in the same way. Leaping off the muddy cowpath, the pooka twisted in mid-spring and headed for the circular hall of stone that overlooked the Elvish Sea. But he didn't take the road he'd followed with Tomas and Moira. That way required too many years of mortal Time and might work too many transformations upon Linley.

Instead, Aubrey picked a route often traveled by water-Elves in whatever shape they wore, horse or human or some other creature. For the sole reason that Linley accompanied him, the mortal would find the trail passable as well. Aubrey wished he had some way of reassuring the Saxon as they dived into the narrow murmuring river that bordered the farmer's land.

At first there was a prolonged moment of nothingness. Then the horse was running among immense trees of astonishing girth, galloping full out through crumbling masses of leaves. Linley had barely time to sense that something was irrevocably wrong with this place, to feel a twisted, hovering rage in the giant trunks that erupted from the shrouded earth, when a long pointed stick flew whistling past Aubrey's nose. All the nearby tree limbs, like so many fists, began to shake at once.

There came the infuriated screeching of owls, and for a terrified instant Linley heard garbled words interspersed with the shrill raucous hoots. And his own name, too; wasn't that his name?

Then Aubrey neighed, and Linley felt the big animal collect himself for another jump. He hung on tightly and, despite his horseman's better judgment, closed his eyes. He re-opened them as soon as he felt Aubrey land.

To Linley's delight, they had escaped from the horrible forest and were in a ploughed field at the foot of a hill. A familiar hill. Why, it was the Wickes' farm; he knew it well. But how they'd arrived here in so short a time he didn't care to ponder. The farm lay a good two hours' ride east of the campsite they'd left at twilight.

Past midnight it was now, from the look of the sky, but they'd spent only minutes in that uncanny wood. Was all of Faerie like that? Linley shuddered and gave Aubrey a few pats on the shoulder.

The horse began to cross the field towards the Wickes' cowpath and the river beyond. Linley squinted up at the half Moon. Yesterday it had been close to that size, so he doubted they were traveling very far through Time. Besides, what good would it do to arrive at Chippenham years after Tomas's imprisonment? Still, one could never predict the behavior of the Elves with complete certainty.

Then he screamed aloud as Aubrey dived without warning into the river.

A weak swimmer, Linley knew he'd tire quickly in cold water, and he clutched at Aubrey's mane. The horse sank beneath the surface of the river just as Linley inhaled to scream again. He got a lungful of water as he tried to kick free of the horse. And then he stopped, astonished, and rearranged himself on the animal's back.

He could breathe! The water hadn't choked him, seemed neither foreign nor threatening to his lungs and moreover was not cold. It didn't even feel wet. It felt like air, and he could see in it. He exhaled, inhaled again, with no difficulty at all.

Beneath him Aubrey swam in great powerful strokes. His ribcage expanded and contracted with less effort than when he ran upon dry land. Aubrey could breathe this water too, then. They both could.

Stay on the horse's back regardless of what may happen, the tall polite Elf had said. Linley grinned: he certainly wasn't going to dismount now. Marveling, he glanced around beneath the surface of the water.

Linley couldn't see with absolute clarity, more as if peering through a wafer-thin, rippling veil of amber that trembled with his breathing--but well enough to count the scattered stones half embedded in the river bottom and the dark twisted chunks of decaying wood. He recognized the unnatural man-made angles and curves of long-lost tools, the occasional flash and wink of metal, and sometimes the mute jutting white of bones.

Neck craned with curiosity, a turtle paddled towards Linley and the horse, its shell gleaming ochre and yellow before it veered away in alarm. The slower-witted fish heeded them less, gliding around them as if they were driftwood or the hull of a boat. A frog fled at their approach; Linley recognized it only by the narrowing diamond shape of its rear legs as it kicked. Aubrey was not the least graceful creature in this flowing yellowed waterscape, merely the largest. The horse swam as elegantly and thoughtlessly as any fish, his mane streaming back toward the Saxon's torso.

Linley's heart kept racing and slowing down again, as his unbelieving body resisted a recurring urge to panic and struggle up towards the surface. An occasional fine tremor shook him. He experimented with deepening his breathing. In and out of his lungs the river water slid, silent and imperceptible as air, except for the extra wavering of the liquid curtain that surrounded him.

How strange, how unnerving--and, ultimately, how intoxicating. Pale light glinting down through the water. Moist sheen on the warm skin of his arms, their fine layer of dark hair floating free. Each small sound the water carried to his cushioned ears was oddly stretched and slowed, sometimes clear and sometimes distorted, like voices heard upon the threshold of sleep.

The first of the water-Elves didn't bother Linley at all. He hardly noticed it: a larger, darker and more rounded shape than the derelict wood along the riverbed. But this form had smoother surfaces than wood, had muscles and tendons and sleek black hide, and eyes that were red and shining. The other water-horse allowed Aubrey to swim by, then came abreast to pace him for a few strokes. Turning its head, it stared at Aubrey, then back at Linley, finally leaving when Aubrey gave it a gentle shove with his nose.

So there were other such creatures in the river. Linley wasn't sure how much time had elapsed before he saw the second one. He might not have spotted her if he hadn't happened to glance up at the surface, wondering why what illumination there was had suddenly grown less. And perhaps she would not have noticed Linley, had he not lifted his head and caught her eye.

A dead body, he thought, horrified. A woman's corpse floating face-down in the river. Entangled with water lilies, her long red hair fanned out around her. Strong legs and arms and much of her curving hips were revealed by a torn grey gown. When the half-curled fingers of one of her hands flexed ever so slightly, Linley stammered something and pointed.

Her eyes flew open. She pushed ruddy trailing hair from her face and peered down at Linley, meeting his terrified gaze. Laughing, she lowered her head and trunk into the water, raised her long-muscled legs and arrowed down to hover beside Aubrey. Shrinking away from her, Linley clutched the horse's mane. Aubrey glanced back at the red-headed woman and swam faster.

The woman seemed to want a better look at Linley, and without visible effort she accompanied them, swimming on her side with lazy scissor-kicks. She breathed water as easily as Aubrey did. All the fear Linley had felt when the horse first dived into the river returned four-fold, almost paralyzing him. Not wanting to see this woman, still he could not turn his head away.

Her complexion was so pale as to be almost green. Perhaps the eerie tint was an effect of the water flowing all around them, but Linley didn't think so. The woman was smiling; her teeth looked like yellowed ivory next to that fish-white skin. A long blade of marsh grass was trapped between her upper left canine and the molar behind it. Her brown eyes were huge, tilted, rather bulging and quite bloodshot, glittering with intelligence. But her features were dainty and appealing, and her tattered clothing clung to the curves at the small of her back.

"Hello," she said softly to Linley. "And what might your name be?"

Some instinct told him not to answer. Laying his ears back, Aubrey increased his pace, but so did the woman.

"Who are you? What brings you here?" As she reached a hand towards Linley's shoulder, her gown fell open. Her breasts were full and rounded, their nipples surprisingly small. He caught his breath.

Then four bony fingers clamped upon on his arm. She shoved her face up beside his.

Aubrey's head snaked back in an appallingly supple motion, and his teeth closed on the woman's wrist. The water blossomed red. With a shriek, the woman released Linley. Tearing her arm from Aubrey's second strike, she heaved herself up and backwards, away from them, and left a trail of beaded crimson drops behind her.

121

The horse let her go, to streak downstream in the direction they had been traveling. Linley slumped against Aubrey's neck. Would this journey ever end?

As Aubrey waded out of the water, Linley lifted his head and looked around. The river had narrowed to a brook. Aubrey clambered onto its shallow bank, crashed through some underbrush and emerged in a long grassy clearing.

It was utterly deserted. Linley frowned at the sight of a ring of huge standing stones. Grey and weathered horizontal slabs crowned vertical ones, like the stones he'd heard tales of in Wiltshire. On Salisbury Plain, they were. Had Aubrey brought him to Wiltshire?

Then a tall, dark-haired, graceful woman stepped from behind one of the stone pillars and walked lightly towards them, and Linley knew they were not on Salisbury Plain.

Dark green silk she wore, the color and sheen of holly leaves, and she was barefoot. Aubrey moved forward at a leisurely pace, neck arched and ears pricked. Abruptly, Linley was conscious that he was soaked to the skin, his clothes plastered to his body, his hair lank against his neck. He and the horse were both daubed with mud from head to toe.

Linley shifted his cramped muscles, longing to dismount and stretch. But he stayed on Aubrey's back, remembering the uncanny fierce woods and the water-Elf who'd just attacked him. With apprehension, he eyed the elegant figure strolling closer. Was she hostile too?

At Aubrey's shoulder, she stopped and said something to the horse, who lowered his head as she patted his neck. Linley didn't know the language, didn't even recognize it, and that made him more uneasy. Then the woman looked up at him, and he forgot his fear.

He could not even have imagined such a woman. Her long black hair gleamed like a sheet of liquid onyx. Huge slanted eyes, the shade of polished pewter, dominated a delicate, wistful face with a pointed chin. Her features were asymmetrical in some shifting way that Linley couldn't pinpoint or define, but the effect was mesmerizing. A porcelain face, he thought, with all its color poured into a lush coral mouth. As she gazed up at him with a faint welcoming smile, it suddenly came to him that she was the saddest woman he had ever seen.

He heard himself say, "What troubles you, my lady? Might I be of service to you?"

The grey eyes narrowed, became watchful and guarded, just

before all emotion left her face.

Linley felt a shocked loss of balance, as if he had unexpectedly fallen into a ravine. He didn't know whether to hope she would accept his impulsive offer. Had he offended her somehow? Dread crept over him: whatever this being might need was far removed from the likes of him.

The woman laid a warm long-fingered hand on Linley's knee. "Yes, you might," she murmured, eyeing him, her face gone paler still. "You already have. So yours is a proposal that I think I should best refuse. In all particulars but one."

Her voice was low, steady and hauntingly rich. Linley dared not answer.

"When you see Tomas the Rhymer, please tell him that I wish him well. And that is all," she said, glancing over her shoulder. Linley stared in alarm: a handsome auburn-haired man was hurrying towards them across the empty stretch of lawn.

"Now go," the woman told Linley, and gave the horse a tap on the shoulder.

Aubrey seemed to leap straight up into the air, then thundered across the clearing and into the woods. Dizzy, Linley clung to the horse's neck and shut his eyes.

He didn't open them until much later, when Aubrey at last came to a halt. To Linley's relief, the horse stood in the familiar courtyard of Chippenham fort. To the east, the sky held the barest promise of illumination, of purple upon smoke, or perhaps Linley only imagined it. He blinked at the row of keys, shining faintly beneath the Moon, that hung on the stable wall in front of Aubrey's nose.

CHAPTER TWENTY-THREE: IN CHIPPENHAM FORT

The Danes kept a reasonably well-maintained stable at Chippenham, though Tomas wondered if the credit went to the few miserable Saxons pressed into service here. There were only a few rats, and the hay smelled more fresh than musty. From the stall where he was imprisoned, he could see part of the courtyard and a watering trough. In this particular stall, some carpenter had done a workmanlike job of constructing the sturdy wooden feed bin, its weathered corners gnawed by rodents or restless horses. A smith or another carpenter had recently completed a crude but quite adequate job of walling off the stall with iron bars, converting it to a cell. Tomas gazed at the oversized lock and shook his head.

Midnight, perhaps. He sat cross-legged in scratchy straw beside his satchel. Cast by burning rags atop wooden staffs thrust into the ground outside, shadows and torchlight flickered on the stable walls, which appeared alternately to lean in on him and then recede. From the nearby hall resounded shouts, laughter and thickened Norse voices singing out of unison and out of key. A sharp gamey odor of roast venison, the Danes' evening meat, lingered in the humid air. An untouched trencher of the same broiled flesh lay a yard from Tomas's left knee.

He reached for the earthenware jug, swallowed a long cool draught of water and felt his stomach knot again. No, he could not eat; the nausea that had descended on him as soon as he was locked in this cell showed no signs of abating.

The queasiness must have to do with being enclosed by iron. The Danes had shoved him, and he'd fallen hard against the bars and felt a singeing cold, as if his skin adhered to the metal that it grazed. After a time the numbness faded, became a tingling ache and slowly disappeared, but left Tomas nauseated. How could he accomplish Moira's task, how could he even pass through Midgard unimpaired, if he were saddled with an increasing sensitivity to iron?

There was one swift, easy way to determine if he had the iron-sick. Get up, walk three paces to those bars and lay his naked palms against them.

His stomach heaved, and his hands twitched with anticipated pain. Folding them in his lap, he continued staring glumly at the lock.

That touchy little brownie had flatly refused to fetch the key and release him, which made him all the more certain that his discomfort came from iron. Somehow the sight of the brownie in the hall among Guthrum's apparently oblivious men hadn't startled Tomas, nor had the Elf's visit to his cell to thank him for his intervention with the Dane and to offer help.

The unsettling surprises were that lone Dane's odd half-awareness of the brownie, and the Dane's sudden unmistakable sighting of the Elf when he burned his foot. Why was the brownie invisible to everyone else before then, and what had changed so fast? Some ill-perceived taint of otherworldliness about Tomas might have aroused the Dane's suspicions, even before he saw the little Elf. For the man had haunted Tomas's footsteps, eyeing him strangely and asking many abrupt, double-edged questions.

He sighed, propped himself on his elbows and stretched his legs out before him in the straw. Try as he might to occupy himself with thoughts of iron and Elves, his mind circled back to two questions. What would Guthrum do to him on the morrow? And what would Aubrey do when the brownie found him?

Deep in conversation, Guthrum had at first ignored the scuffling around Tomas, finally shouted for it to stop, then demanded to know who had started it and why. His mouth a thin hard line, Guthrum stared wordlessly at Knut, the Dane who'd seen the brownie's foot and instigated the muttering about Tomas. Knut stood respectfully enough as he explained, but thrust out his jaw and stared back. A troublemaker.

Reading their faces, Tomas decided that Guthrum probably wouldn't go so far as to kill the prisoner, because that would create too much justification for Knut's actions. But what would Guthrum do instead?

Sworn to serve Tomas as he would Moira, Aubrey would most definitely do something, but the gods alone knew what. Not for the first time, Tomas wondered how Linley would react when the preternaturally strong pooka broke his heavy tether as if it were the thinnest twine and bolted off into the underbrush. Was Linley worrying at Tomas's long absence, or fearing he'd defected to the Danes?

Nothing to do save wait and count his flea bites. Or... Eyeing his satchel, Tomas tilted his head to gauge the scraps of song floating in from the courtyard. He didn't care to attract attention, taunts or thieves. The voices outside were still energetic, but fewer and slower, so he decided to risk taking out his flute.

Lost in rich woody trills, tapping his foot, Tomas didn't notice the brownie until the Elf heaved a double handful of grain through the bars.

"You've come back," said Tomas softly, and gave the flute a shake to clear it of any stray kernels.

125

"Aye," said the brownie, exasperated. "I'd come back three measures ago, too. And you'd do well to quit tootling now; your great stinking friend of a pooka is on his way to collect you. Wait and watch, and stay awake. They'll be here sometime before the Sun."

"'They'?" asked Tomas, stowing his flute in the satchel.

"The pooka and the other mortal. The Saxon."

Staring, Tomas started to ask how that had come about, but the brownie interrupted him. "I have discharged my debt to you now. I shall see that you're safely off with your pooka, but I doubt we'll meet again. Farewell!" With a faintly sarcastic flourish, he bowed low and bounded away.

Tomas jumped to his feet and peered through the bars, but the courtyard was empty and palely lit beneath the stars. Did the watering trough quiver under the spring of vanishing feet? There was no way to be sure, and nothing to do but compose himself and wait for Linley and the pooka.

CHAPTER TWENTY-FOUR: ESCAPE

Brown eyes rounder than ever, Linley clutched Aubrey's mane with white-knuckled fingers as the pooka walked noiselessly to the barred door of Tomas's cell. Partially dried mud smeared the Saxon's face, while from his damp clothing and matted hair rose a faint brackish odor. One sleeve of his tunic was in shreds.

Grabbing his satchel, Tomas leapt to his feet. "The key—"

"Shh! I've got it." Linley's voice was a hoarse whisper. When the pooka sidled up beside the heavy lock, Tomas saw that the Saxon gripped a large rusted key in his fist. Leaning sideways, he fumbled with the lock until the weighted door, half iron and half wood, swung in its frame and bumped against his leg.

Linley tossed the key into the stall. Moving as fast as he could, Tomas scrambled onto the water-horse's back behind Linley.

It was almost not fast enough. With a thud, the key hit the stall's wooden slats. Low-pitched growls and barks promptly broke the silence of approaching dawn. A yell rang out, followed by other voices thick with interrupted sleep. Laying his ears back, Aubrey charged into the muddy courtyard and knocked a helmeted figure aside. The Dane fell to the ground; his ax described a harmless arc through the air. A spear whistled past Aubrey's head. There was more shouting and the sound of running feet, but the pooka had already hurtled himself into a spiraling twist in mid-air.

Much of the voyage blurred in Tomas's mind, both then and later. He cried out when Aubrey's hooves struck solid ground after that initial leap, for they landed in a dim ominous place with still more bars. Not of iron this time, these bars seemed wrought from coruscating bitter-orange light, pouring and swirling in self-contained, vaguely cylindrical shapes, like dust motes in the rays of a bloody sun. Then he heard echoing words that he couldn't understand, although the voices' fright, determination and refusal were plain.

Directly before him, two intersecting lines glowed in the murky air. The sight stung his eyes, and he blinked. The symbol looked like a Rune—the Christians' cross-Rune. But why would he see it between the worlds, on a pathway such as the one he'd traveled with Moira?

Or was it? Linley didn't appear to see what Tomas did; the Saxon peered in all directions through the gloom with no sign of focusing on anything. He was trembling slightly.

Aubrey stood motionless, staring at the dull coppery lines of force in front of him. At last the pooka snorted and flung himself back and to the left.

Through a formless white world the water-horse galloped, with no ground beneath his feet and no sky above his head, only an unending stretch of stark flat emptiness. After a while Tomas shut his eyes; he kept inventing hideous figures in the gloom. He didn't look again till Aubrey halted.

They were at Hecate's crossroads where Tomas had stopped with Moira. The place was clabbered with fog and chillier than before. Wanting a good view of the statue, Tomas started to slide down from Aubrey's back.

Linley grabbed his elbow. "Don't! Mustn't dismount, no matter what. Please, he said so." His grip was strong, though his arm was shaking.

"Who said so?"

"A tall grey Elf. Said Aubrey would take me to Chippenham to fetch you. Please, he said not to dismount."

"All right," said Tomas gently. He had a suspicion whom that tall grey Elf might be, but apparently Linley didn't. His shoulders slumping, the Saxon relaxed his hold.

Aubrey began to move again. As if sensing Tomas's wish to study the figure of Hecate, the pooka passed directly in front of it. Tomas shifted to one side and peered at the statue through the mist.

Before Aubrey bounded a third time into some nameless corridor between the worlds, Tomas realized that he couldn't focus on the maiden's face among the three. Yet whether the fog blurred his vision, or the stony features themselves were blurred, he could not tell.

Back in the enveloping blankness, Tomas glanced down and saw blood streaming beneath Aubrey's hooves. He covered his face with one hand.

"Tomas, true Tomas. Tomas the Rhymer--" The voice was faint but insistent, calling till he opened his eyes.

Who had spoken? Linley sat and stared blankly ahead; the pooka's gait was swift and efficient. Around them swirled a sulphurous haze, unaccountably translucent. Then, with a sickening start, Tomas saw Moira.

She stood on an enormous jagged rock that seemed to rear its granite surface out of nowhere and float unanchored in the air. Ivy-green silk billowing around her in the wind, she stretched her hands out towards him. Black hair whipped and tumbled across her bloodless face.

"Make haste!" she cried, and another phrase that might perhaps have started, "I regret—"

But Tomas couldn't hear the rest. Twisted around on Aubrey's back, he stared until he could see Moira no longer. Then he turned his head away and closed his eyes again.

CHAPTER TWENTY-FIVE: WHERE IN MIDGARD THE LINES OF TRUTH MIGHT RUN

After digging up the seal of safe conduct, Tomas and Linley rode a serpentine route through the woods and halted close to Alfred's camp in the marsh country. Over a small fire, Tomas told Linley everything he'd learned about the condition of the Danish troops and their intended movements—no small amount of information, since at first the Danes had spoken freely in his presence.

Clear and remote, the summer stars shone overhead as Tomas and Linley rushed through that necessary portion of their remaining business together. Now that it was finished, everything else that had happened since Tomas set off to Chippenham lay between them undiscussed.

From the economy of Linley's movements, he was even more tired than Tomas. "I'd like a wash before I get within hailing distance of Simon," he said at last, trying to comb his dank hair with grimy fingers. Flakes of dried mud sifted down onto his knees.

"Did Aubrey throw you into a bog?"

"A river. And he didn't throw me."

Linley was watching sticks and branches shrivel in the flames. Radiant heat, welcome on this chilly evening in late spring, warmed Tomas's face and hands. Idle breaths of wind stirred the leaves against the hovering night. A few yards beyond the fire, Aubrey dozed beside the roan mare. Since they'd made camp, Linley had avoided Aubrey and offered him no horseman's admiring glance or pat. But neither had Linley behaved as if the pooka understood their conversation.

Tomas was tired of wondering how much Linley guessed. "What happened after I left you? How did you come to the fort?"

A brooding look from Linley. "Don't you know?"

Tomas wanted to say no, but the denial was not strictly true. He would attempt the lie regardless and see what happened. His lips parted; his tongue moved into position against the ridge of gum behind his upper front teeth. He felt an abrupt, physical reaction, like a vicious hand clamped on his mouth and nose, suffocating him.

Startled, he reflexively gulped for air. As soon as his vocal cords abandoned the effort to say no, he could breathe again. "Some, I know," he said, measuring the words, and was relieved when the choking sensation didn't reappear. "But I should like to hear your part of the tale."

"Very well." Linley poked the fire with a long crooked stick. He did not look at Tomas. "A tall grey-skinned Elf woke me. He said that you were taken prisoner at Chippenham, and that a horse I might recognize would come to take me there. I was to unlock your cell and drop the key. And not dismount, no matter what I saw on the journey."

"What did you see?"

"Aubrey, first; he was the horse. We ran through some mist and entered an evil wood that moaned and threw branches. Next we were in a farmer's field I know. Then we dived into the river that borders the field, and swam beneath the water." Linley shook his head in wonder. "I could breathe it, Tomas. I could breathe the water. Did you know that?"

"No," said Tomas in a low voice, unsurprised. The pooka was a water-Elf, after all. "But I counsel you not to attempt it alone."

"Small chance of that." Linley shivered. "A red-haired woman tried to unhorse me in the river. Or a fiend, in the likeness of a woman." He took a swallow from his leather flask of water and wiped his mouth on the back of his hand. "Then we came to a great ring of standing stones in an empty clearing." He hesitated. "I saw a woman with dark hair. She bade me give you a message."

Wrapping his arms around his knees, shivering in his turn now, Tomas stared at Linley. At first the Saxon wouldn't meet his eyes, but at last he turned his head. In the firelight it was hard to read Linley's gaze, but Tomas saw mingled awe and pity there--and, perhaps, an unwilling trace of envy.

Frowning into the airy darkness all around, he kept his voice dispassionate and asked, "The woman who called after us on our way back? She is imposing; I doubt you would mistake her."

Linley gave him a puzzled stare. "She was lovely. Long hair black as heartbreak, and haunted grey eyes. But I met her on the way to Chippenham, Tomas. No one called after us on the way back, and I saw nothing but fog."

"No cross-shaped Rune?" Tomas asked, though he'd suspected it was invisible to Linley.

The Saxon spread his hands apart and shrugged.

"No statue with three faces? And the dark-haired woman standing on a rock?"

Eyes big and solemn, Linley shook his head and drew closer to the fire.

"Gods!" muttered Tomas. He slumped onto his back to scowl at the night sky caught in the treetops. The ground was damp; he didn't care. She might reappear. He might never see her again. And Linley had spoken with her. "What word did she send me?"

"She said, 'Tell Tomas the Rhymer that I wish him well.'"

"That was the whole of it?"

Linley nodded. "And I saw someone else, an auburn-haired man."

Rhys, probably. Sparks scattered from a collapsing log. Grateful for an excuse to hide his face, Tomas got up to collect more wood and set it on the flames. It was difficult to find something dry enough to burn.

When he rejoined Linley, the Saxon asked, "Where does your road lead now? To the coast, for passage to Uppland?"

"Yes." Tomas's voice sounded curt in his own ears. Haltingly he added, "Linley, I've no words to thank you and your companions for all your aid."

The Saxon smiled and shook his head. "Yours was the greater service, as Alfred will be the first to say when I report. Now we can take the battle to the Danes and be done with hiding in the marshes."

"I hope so," said Tomas, his thoughts turning to the route to the coast and the long ocean voyage ahead. Then in the half-light of their campfire, he felt rather than saw Linley growing tense beside him.

"Tomas. Can you tell me somewhat of Alfred's Fate?" The Saxon's face was tight with concern.

Moira's words came back to Tomas: "Therefrom you have also a gift of prophecy, that sees where in Midgard the lines of truth might run." He could probably discern something of Alfred's Fate. But how much, and how reliably? In his vision of the delicate web of energy that connected the men in the Saxon King's tent, Tomas had sensed how easily that fragile living balance could be disturbed and re-aligned. Where lines of truth ran today, they might not run upon the morrow.

"A small portion of it, yes," he said slowly, wondering how to explain. What had Caraid said about the Sight? None of her words came back to him; he would have to use his own. "I can tell you something of what Alfred's Fate may be now, at this moment, as we sit together, you and I. But when you go to his camp and I to the coast, for the morrow I cannot say if that Fate will still hold true. Your return may alter it, or my departure, or a thousand other things that are not given me to see." He had a sharp frisson of certainty.

Around them the trees stood tall and still, with stars peering down through the branches. A spark or two floated from the fire, fanned by the light breeze. When the roan mare whickered plaintively at nothing, Linley glanced over his shoulder, then back at Tomas. "I think I understand." The Saxon's eyes were pensive.

"Do you still wish me to speak?"

"For Alfred's sake, I do. If you would be so kind."

"It may be no kindness."

Linley nodded. "Yet what I hear I might be able to avert."

"Very well. I'll try." Fixedly, Tomas stared into the fire, envisioning Alfred of Wessex hidden in the Somerset wetlands. Breathing deeply and evenly despite his apprehension, he waited for the lines of possible truths to appear in whatever form they chose to take.

At first it was difficult to focus on one image among the multitude that shimmered in the flames. Tomas saw not merely lines this time but tiny pictures, carved of fire-blue and molten yellow. They twined together and danced apart, sometimes holding motionless for a few clear glowing seconds, only to waver and change shape again. He found that he must concentrate on Alfred alone and not allow himself to be distracted by the figures of people he recognized: Simon, Linley or Guthrum--or himself.

But I won't be there, he thought, after the initial shock of identifying his own face at the periphery of the crowding images. I will have gone to Uppsala, he insisted silently, and squinted into the leaping tongues of fire until he located the figure of Alfred once again.

Now the motion slowed and the pictures seemed both sharper and more distant, as if he watched them from afar but with falcon-keen vision. Outlines grew more distinct, colors more vivid, lurid enough almost to hurt his eyes. Flames bracketed the images, yet something was missing; something was different...

It was his hearing. He could no longer hear the fire's steady crackling, nor the occasional sputtering hiss of immolated wood. For an endless moment he heard nothing whatever, his ears so thoroughly insulated that they didn't even ring. Slowly, as the deafness passed, he began to detect the sounds that accompanied the visions.

With solid shield-walls, Alfred's forces fought the Danes upon a hill, routed them and pursued them to Chippenham. The clash of iron mingled with shouts and groans; the fort was besieged, and Guthrum offered hostages. Next Guthrum stood meekly in a church with Alfred at his side. Chants rose in the smoky air, while on the Dane's forehead a priest traced the cross-Rune with oiled fingers.

That sight was obscured by falling leaves and snowflakes in thick wadded clumps, until Guthrum and the Danes rode out of Wessex on a carpet of white that gleamed beneath the newly risen Sun. Through a rapid succession of images, Alfred's face flickered and changed, growing older and more care-worn, studying plans for streets, ships and churches, or conferring with advisors. He fought again, battling the Norse at sea and on land. When a large town burned, glimpses of Guthrum's enraged face came and went behind the conflagration.

Then Tomas saw a map of what he guessed was Waleis, Wessex, Mercia and the country to the north. On a rough diagonal from north-west to south-east, a great line slashed across the map. By the time he understood that the Danes took what lay east of the line and Alfred what lay west, the images started to fade. Soon he saw only the small campfire and heard nothing but the sizzling thud of a fallen log, and a stamp and a sigh from the horses.

After a stretch to ease his cramped muscles and a long pull from the water flask, he looked at Linley. His expression wary, the Saxon was watching him.

"You're back," said Linley softly, and Tomas nodded. There was relieved anticipation in Linley's smile. So his wariness was for whatever Tomas had divined, not for Tomas himself.

Parched, he drank again. To sleep... Not yet, not until he explained what he'd seen. Or tried to explain. Even if the visions hadn't left him stupefied in both body and mind, it would have been difficult to interpret the story in the flames.

Best to start now, before his fatigue grew worse. "Alfred will fight the Danes. On nearby terrain, I believe, because they retreat to Chippenham. He besieges them there until they surrender and hear some sort of Mass with him. One winter morning they leave Wessex. Riding east, facing the sunrise."

A triumphant exclamation from Linley. Suppressing a yawn, Tomas went on, "Alfred designs villages and buildings, and works with many counselors. They looked like they were at a Thing."

"A what?"

"A Thing, such as we have in the North. Where the King and his earls—his thanes and advisors meet, and declare laws."

"Oh. What an odd name for it. But Tomas, these are good tidings!"

"You've not heard them all. More fighting with the Danes; I don't know when, but Alfred looks older. An important town burns, a big one." Tomas hesitated. "He and the Danes divide this island, and they rule the eastern part."

"Mercia?" Linley was frowning.

"I think so. And farther north. I don't know the island, so it was hard to tell."

"But Alfred keeps Wessex? To the west and south, between Mercia and Waleis?"

"Yes. Of that much I'm certain."

"When?"

"I cannot say, Linley. I've no idea."

Silence. Chin propped in his hand, Linley scowled into the forest. Gratefully, Tomas stretched out on his back, folded his arms behind his head and considered the stars. He was almost asleep when Linley asked, "And you saw all of that?"

"I saw images that moved, then I heard sounds. They came fast, and I had no sense of when these things would happen. Some may already have, for all I know."

"I think not. But where did you perceive them, Tomas? Where were these images? Not in your mind; your eyes were open, and you were gazing at the fire."

"I saw them in the flames."

Linley raked his hands through his hair. "I wish I had your gifts. However you came by them."

"You say that, after your passage through Faerie?" Tomas sat up for a better look at the Saxon.

Firelight played across Linley's round subtle face. Biting his lip, he said softly, "Yes." There was hunger in the monosyllable.

"I would not wish my gifts on you," Tomas told him.

Neither man had spoken for some time. Tomas sprawled on his back again, half-dozing, while Linley sat with his chin in his hands. Twice they heard an owl. The wind had all but died; the air smelled of night and spring, and possibly some rain upon the morrow.

"Don't go to Uppland. Come back with me. Alfred has need of you," said Linley in a sudden rush of words.

But Tomas had sworn to complete the task laid upon him. Sworn by the Magician's oath with Fate, not fully understanding that phrase either then or now. He remembered the Nornir at their loom, and Perthro, the Web of Fate.

And Hel. Moira said she had called him from his death that day, and so from Hel. Was Hel searching Midgard for him; was that why Moira had urged him to make haste? He was snared in another kind of web, his thread entangled with those of the Elves.

"What do you say?" asked Linley.

Gods, he wanted to say yes, to forget the very existence of Faerie. What would happen if he did? "Your Fate will move to claim you there, and I doubt if I could find the Nornir weaving in just that way again," Moira had told him. But what exactly did that mean?

Linley watched him, waiting. Perhaps Tomas could delay a

while and spend some time at Alfred's camp. He might at least ride back with Linley before going on to the coast.

Hesitantly, Tomas began, "I would like to come with you--" Then he clapped a hand to his mouth and nose. The stench!

The fresh night air had fled, and it was as if he lay within a howe packed with corpses a week dead. Choking, he sat up and groped for the water bottle. The smell coated his nostrils, filled his lungs, crept into his hair and clothes. He shuddered as he drank.

When he lowered the flask, Rhys stood across the fire from him. The Elf King's eyes were narrowed in a bitter golden face. "Would you be foresworn, Tomas?" he whispered in a voice that echoed the hiss of the flames. "Would you indeed?" Rhys moved one coiled pace closer. Like a second fire about his head, his auburn hair looked molten in the wavering light, and his pointed hands were twitching.

Tomas grabbed for Linley's scramasax. Shouldering the Saxon aside, he caught one glimpse of Linley's bewildered face as the smaller man fell beyond the illuminated circle cast by the blaze. Tomas drew the blade, to hurl it if he had time--or to use at close quarters if he must.

But before he could balance the knife for a throw, he groaned and dropped it from his nerveless fingers. He'd forgotten that the scramasax was made of iron.

Laughing, the Elf turned on his heel and faded from sight before his pivot was half-done.

Gathered in a defensive stance, Linley edged into the firelight. In his right hand he held a good-sized rock. "What happened?" he asked, so cautiously that he sounded almost formal.

Tomas sank to his knees and clutched his deadened sword-arm. "What did you see?"

"You choked, and drank some water and glared at something across the fire. I couldn't see it, but I felt a presence." Linley paused, concentrating. "I think it wanted to frighten you. Then you grabbed my knife and dropped it, and the presence left."

"No more than that? No stench?"

"No." Linley picked up his scramasax, wiped it clean of dirt, sheathed it and sat down.

"One day, I would like to return to Wessex," said Tomas when the numbness left his arm. "But I can't go back to camp with you. I leave for the coast at dawn."

"I gathered that."

A prolonged silence.

"I knocked you down. I'm sorry."

Linley twitched his shoulders. "No harm done." His voice was mild, but he shot Tomas an odd look. "I don't suppose you'd care to talk about it."

"No."

"All right," said Linley, gazing thoughtfully up at the stars. "Might there be some way I could help?"

"I wish by all the gods there were."

Linley looked at him for a long time, then at the ground, then back at Tomas. The Saxon's face was troubled. Finally he muttered, "Well, I've seen her."

"What?"

"Nothing. Pay me no mind." Another silence. "Pay you! Save me, I'd nearly forgotten. And how would you barter for passage to Uppland with no silver?" He scrabbled in his pack.

Too dispirited to ask questions, Tomas watched him but kept seeing Rhys's eyes instead, and the Elf lord's twitching hands.

With a triumphant flourish, Linley produced a tightly knotted, bulging leather pouch and tossed it to Tomas. "Here you are." It hit his palm with the metallic thump of coins. "From Alfred. I meant to give it to you when we dug up the seal, but it slipped my mind. That should get you to Uppland and back twice over."

"Please convey my gratitude to Alfred. This is unlooked-for generosity," said Tomas quietly. "As is your friendship." They each studied the fire.

More thanks were spoken on both sides before they slept, so none were needed at dawn, when they embraced without a word and rode their separate ways.

CHAPTER TWENTY-SIX: LINLEY'S DREAM

The night before he and Tomas the Rhymer parted ways, Linley dreamed.

In that dream midsummer was in full flower, and he dawdled beside a well-loved pond where he used to play as a child. In later years, he enjoyed walking there in the company of women.

He and Simon had swum and fished and idled in that pond, drifting on their backs to gaze up at the brilliant puffy clouds that floated in the watching sky. In winter they ventured across the ice on crudely whittled wooden skates, laughing and slipping, taking turns with neighbor children when they could be spared from farmwork or, as more often was the case, when they could steal away. All the youngsters counted it well worth the subsequent beatings.

By that pond, in a treasured, highly secret game, he and Simon had often pretended to be Elves.

Now Linley dreamed that he cradled his lute and gazed at the tranquil water, quite alone. Beneath the glossy surface of the pond, a fat carp lazed past with sluggish flicks of its fins. A lark called; another answered, and a soft breeze came to finger Linley's hair. Then a small turtle slid hurriedly into the water, and Linley realized that someone stood near him on the bank.

Turning, he recognized the graceful, dark-haired woman he had met on the way to Chippenham. He set his lute down carefully, then rose to greet her.

"Good day, my lady." He felt awkward and tentative.

"I came to thank you for your aid to Tomas, and to present you with a choice of gifts." Her voice, low and resonant, carried an undertone of something that Linley couldn't quite identify, though it was familiar. Bemused, he stood and gazed at her. She was just as lovely as before. And just as sad, despite her smile.

At last she asked indulgently, "Shall I describe them to you?"

Describe what? With a twinge of anticipation, Linley remembered: gifts.

Gifts from the Fair Folk.

The woman watched him, her smile deepening. He could not remember precisely why such presents were said to be hazardous. "You needn't give me anything, my lady," he began.

She lifted an all but translucent palm to silence him. "Perhaps not. But I will offer, nonetheless."

They scrutinized one another as Linley's hands slowly grew cold.

"Consider these your choices," she said. "Should you wish to enter Elfland, you may do so now and again at our discretion. If it pleases you to remember your recent visit, then you will. But you might prefer to forget you ever passed that way, and never to return."

Her expression was patient. When Linley said nothing, she went on: "The possibilities are fourfold. To cross our borders with no memory of your first experience there. To cross and to remember. To recall but not return. Or to forget, and never travel there again." She gave him an expectant, curious glance. "Tell me, which is your desire?"

While she spoke, Linley understood each alternative, but now his head swam with the echoes of that smoky voice. He had to look away from her melancholy grey eyes before he could think.

To enter Faerie with no recollection of its dangers seemed foolhardy and senseless. But a sojourn there marred by dread of vicious wood and water Elves would be terrifying.

Yet never to return, and always wonder what he might have seen that was high and magical... Did he truly want to erase his memories of traveling in Faerie--and of this woman's perilous fragility?

"I do not know," he whispered, unaware he had spoken aloud, until the Elf's fine black eyebrows drew together.

She made a short staccato sound that might have been a laugh. "As you wish," she told him, and turned to go.

"Wait, please, my lady," said Linley hastily, and was astounded when she stopped and faced him. "What have I chosen?"

"You have yet to choose."

"But what will I remember? And what if I try to go to Elfland?"

"You will remember that which any mortal might. I do not know what governs the retention or the fading of mortal recollections." She showed her teeth; it was not quite a smile. "Nor of my own. And should you attempt to enter Faerie; well, do you not think that constitutes a decision?"

He had to clear his throat. "If I don't try, will I remember being given a choice?"

"Ah," she said softly. "Now that, at least in part, I can answer, Linley. You will believe you had a dream."

She whirled and was gone, leaving him shaken, and wondering how she knew his name. Suddenly he realized that her voice reminded him of the deep hypnotic murmur of the Sea.

139

CHAPTER TWENTY-SEVEN: AUBREY'S FAREWELL

No sooner had Tomas ridden out of Linley's sight than the pooka snorted, laid back his ears and abandoned the potholed trail. Ignoring Tomas's attempts to guide him, Aubrey set off in a distance-eating gallop across the countryside. He veered farther west than Linley's suggested route, calmly leaping thickets and brooks and an occasional moss-covered stone wall. A startled flock of starlings whirred chittering overhead, carpeting the pale sky with churning black wings.

Tomas heard the deep baying of a far-off hound. Whose land were they crossing, and how would the owners react to trespassers? To judge from his steady rhythmic gait, Aubrey was pacing himself for a long run.

When the pooka thundered through a stream instead of jumping it, Tomas shouted in exasperation: he was wet to the knees and precariously overbalanced. They were traveling north-west now, from the angle of the Sun. At least the Saefren lay in that direction. "Why are you headed upriver?" demanded Tomas. "Norse traders would be farther south along the channel!"

The water-horse did not alter his course, did not so much as flick his ears. Tomas could swing one leg up and over the pooka's neck, slide off and take his chances on a tumbling roll across the ground. Not so marshy as before, the terrain was overgrown with briars and thick scrubby underbrush, and liberally studded with rocks.

Too easy to break a limb, damage the harp, snap the flute in two. It would delay his arrival at the coast. Besides, nothing would prevent Aubrey from coming back for him. He thought of the pooka's towering human shape and Linley's underwater journey. Twitching his shoulders to redistribute the satchel's weight, Tomas settled in for the ride wherever they were going.

They reached level country, its blackened soil rich with silt. A salt-laden river-smell permeated the air. Tomas spotted gulls winging overhead; he'd been watching for them. He was still farther upriver than he cared to be.

Perhaps traders sailed this far up the channel and north-east along the Saefren. Traders with relatively established routes might even make regular stops here, once they were familiar to a populace who realized it had little to fear from merchants.

Would the natives assume Tomas was a merchant or a raider? His only weapon was a stone knife, but a hostile and wary farmer might take a foreigner by surprise without waiting to find out how he was armed. And Tomas would have to ask people when and where Norse traders came to the river. Merchanter ships were built enough like the long flat-bottomed warships to run right up on the strand. They could come ashore virtually anywhere, and Tomas remembered seeing no port this far inland marked on Alfred's maps. Plague take the pooka for not heading farther south along the channel.

Just then Aubrey ground to a shuddering halt, as if he'd collided with an invisible wall. Lowering his head, the pooka began to buck in deliberate leapfrogging jumps.

Swearing, Tomas tried to wrap his legs around the water-horse's barrel. Long as his legs were, however, they couldn't have reached if Aubrey had been standing still--and the pooka's barrel was never where Tomas expected it to be. Too late, he made a grab for the coarse grey mane.

He missed. He saw a dappled neck and shoulder, plunging fetlocks and hooves--

Cushioning his head, Tomas twisted to try to land on his side rather than on the satchel. He barely succeeded. The ground was soft, thanks to the gods.

Lunatic pooka-cackling faded rapidly into the distance.

CHAPTER TWENTY-EIGHT: THE *PRIDE OF SKIRINGSSAL*

Seething, Tomas got up and dusted himself off. Nothing was broken, but he would have bruises a-plenty. When he opened his pack, he was relieved that the harp and flute were unharmed in their oiled leather cases, and that he'd lost neither Alfred's seal of safe conduct nor his coins.

After a whiff of the brine in the air and a glance at the slant of the Sun, Tomas continued due west. Should he carry the seal openly, so the populace might be less alarmed by a tall and grimy young Norseman prowling about? No, there could be Danes this far upriver. Perhaps word had spread of a mysterious escape from Chippenham fort.

He'd neither wanted nor expected Aubrey to sail to Uppland with him. Why had the water-horse tossed him unceremoniously onto a dune and run away? Damn the pooka. Moon-mad and wood-wild, like all of the Elves. Crackbrained and shatterpated. Bereft of all reason.

So absorbed was Tomas in variations on that satisfying theme that he'd stomped up a sandhill and almost started down it before noticing that he'd reached the river. He scrambled back to the other side of the dune, where he flung himself onto his belly and peered cautiously at the men and the boat pulled up on the strand.

No one looked in his direction; the gritty sand must have muffled his footsteps. The ship was a knorr, a Norse merchanter. Perhaps fifty feet long, she was broader than a warship and rigged with a taller mast. More sail power meant fewer oars and fewer men than a warship's crew. He counted a dozen sailors.

Gods above, they spoke with Vestfold accents, not a Danish voice among them. He took back some of the names he'd called Aubrey.

Tomas eyed the men's soft-skinned boots, coated with a dark sheen of grease for protection from the ocean damp. An occasional jewel winked from a sword hilt, and embroidery brightened hems and sleeves. Successful traders, these.

His own cape, jerkin and trousers were travel-stained an even darker green and freshly smeared with clinging sand. His hair and beard needed trimming. And gods, he wanted a wash.

The merchanter's crew appeared to be breaking last night's camp, loading skin kitbags and cooking gear on board. They were talking and laughing: a good sign. And they were nearly done; the incoming tide was beginning to lap against the hull.

He'd better approach them now. His mouth went drier than dead leaves.

Fool, he chided himself: these are your countrymen. You've

no time to waste worrying. Just go speak to them before they get underway.

Standing, he gave his clothes a hasty brush that only succeeded in grinding the sand deeper into the fabric, then walked towards the man who'd been giving orders. Both weaponless hands visible, Tomas called, "By your leave, captain; may I make a proposal that could profit us both?"

"Be quick about it," the captain began, turning to see who had spoken. Sandy-haired and heavy-set, he had a map of smile lines that creased a sunburnt face. His exuberant beard was combed into a braid. Ruddy hair escaped from the neck of his tunic and grew thickly down his gold-banded arms.

His shrewd blue eyes were wide and startled. "Who are you? Thought you were one of us, I did. You hail from Vestfold, by your voice." He looked Tomas up and down. "Where'd you come by the clothes? Been bedding down in the sand?"

Which question should he answer first? Over the captain's shoulder, Tomas could see that the crew had already finished loading. A few rummaged in sea-chests placed by the oarports on the raised decks, fore and aft, that flanked an open cargo hold amidships. To the sides of the hold, men were fastening skins to be stretched over the cargo in rough waters or rolled up and tied for easy access in fair weather. A couple of the crew were removing the woolen sail cover, and some lingered on shore near the captain. All of them were listening to his conversation with the stranger, and most of them watched.

"I'm called the Rhymer," said Tomas, prompted by some obscure instinct to conceal his first name. He indicated his satchel. "I'm a skald; I've a harp and a flute here. And you have keen ears; my people live in Vestfold." Perhaps these merchants did too, but he recognized no one, which was probably just as well.

The captain was nodding, taking Tomas's measure. "My name's Hrolf. I can generally place a man by his speech. Useful, in trade." He waited.

"My clothes I got in Wessex, where I've been traveling. They look like this because my horse just threw me onto a sandhill."

"Catch him?" The captain squinted up and down the strand.

"No, he bolted before I could even stand up. I only acquired him recently, and I guess he didn't take to me enough to want to stay."

"They can be ornery," Hrolf said politely, though from his expression he didn't rate Tomas as much of a horseman.

"Where are you bound, Master Hrolf? I'm going to the temple at Uppsala. Might I buy passage for part of the journey?" He noted the subtle change in the captain's face at the mention of Uppsala, and the quick assessing glance at Tomas's pack. He could almost hear what Hrolf was thinking: some witless skald tired of this backwater. Worships Odin and fancies a pilgrimage—but has he got any money?

"Plain Hrolf will do, thank you. We're off to Ljodhus in the Sudreyjar, then all the way to Birka and back home to Skiringssal. Can you pay? In coin, Rhymer, though we'd be glad of your songs."

A stroke of good fortune: the major trading port of Birka lay on an island in Lake Malar, not far south of Uppsala on the mainland. "I've Saxon silver," Tomas offered. "Shall we weigh out a mark?"

"Twelve aurar," Hrolf said promptly, raising his eyebrows.

One mark weighed eight aurar. "Ten," said Tomas.

The captain grinned and said, "Done! Passage to Birka, ten aurar. And with it you've bought some advice. Don't go telling strangers you carry so much silver! What was to keep us from robbing you, I ask?"

Having sensed Hrolf's intrinsic friendliness, the possibility had never occurred to Tomas. He blurted his thought: "I just knew you wouldn't."

Howls from the crew. Hrolf was slapping his thigh. "I like you, Rhymer," he said, sputtering with laughter. "Never yet met a skald who was right in the head. Do us all good, you will. Welcome aboard the *Pride of Skiringssal*."

Tomas joined the mariners who were pushing the ship down the strand, aided by the rising tide. The tallest man among them, he waded in up to his hips, welcoming the cool water that drenched his filthy clothes. He was last of the launching party to climb aboard.

When his feet touched the planking, he staggered for an instant and gripped the rail, to stand frozen and stare down at the deck. Then someone handed him his pack and asked him a question. He moved, answered, concealed his reaction to the wavering images he'd just seen.

As soon as his feet had made contact with the deck, the clinker-built hull appeared to crack and split apart, leaving a yawning black hole through which poured an angry sea.

The next day they cleared the channel and bore north, up the throat of the Irish Sea towards the islands called the Sudreyjar. "A small sea, though rough betimes," said Hrolf. "With a fair wind, we should make Ljodhus in about three days."

Hrolf shared all the watches, though he owned the major interest in the ship. He and Tomas were finishing their stint at baling-watch, a two-man operation. Hrolf stood below in the baling-well, a cleared space between the planks laid down in the hold to support the cargo and keep it out of harm's way. He filled a wooden bilge-bucket with water and passed it to Tomas up on deck, who carried the bucket to the rail and emptied it over the side. From long practice, both men reflexively adjusted their balance to the ship's motion as they handled each heavy pail.

"Tar and caulk, and caulk and tar. But there's no end to baling," Hrolf said cheerfully. "Cloth rots, wheat and honey spoil, and silver tarnishes in the wet."

The next baling team came, two men named Svein and Thorkel. "And boots crack," said Svein, grimacing as he leaped down to take Hrolf's place in the hold.

"Have yourself another pair made on Ljodhus," Thorkel suggested, as if weary of the topic. He gave Hrolf a long-suffering look.

Grinning, Hrolf climbed up on deck beside Tomas, who stood eyeing the skins fastened over the cargo. "What else are you carrying?" Tomas asked on impulse.

The other men exchanged pleased glances. "We're having a right good run. And a long one," Hrolf said. Thorkel nodded, and Svein heaved a contented sigh.

"Amber from Truso," Hrolf went on. "Frisian cloth and Rhenish glass. We traded Telemark whetstones for jet from Eoforwic. From Waleis and Wessex we have wheat, honey, wool and tin. Here, I'll show you."

Untying some knots, Hrolf drew back a fold of tanned hide to expose a section of the cargo. He raised the lid of a sturdy wooden sea-chest stuffed with straw. "Go through it all if you like, Rhymer, and tell us what you think," he said with pride. "Tell all of Uppsala, and steer some custom our way."

Curious, Tomas reached into the straw and carefully pulled out the first item he touched. It was a large wide-mouthed jug, painted in surprisingly brilliant colors. Turning the vase in his hands, he tried to guess its material. It wasn't the familiar soapstone of most Norse cookware but something coarser, with a different surface to take such pigment.

Hrolf was chuckling at the expression on Tomas's face. The baling slowed as Svein and Thorkel craned their necks to watch.

"Beautiful. Where'd you come by it? What is it made of?"

"Baked and painted clay, from the Rhineland," Hrolf said. "I've half a mind to keep it for my daughter. Now look inside it."

When Tomas cautiously upended the vase, a small, cloth-wrapped parcel landed in his palm. He stowed the jug back in the straw before examining the rich maroon fabric.

It was silk, about the right amount for a woman's headscarf. Very smooth it was, and fine-woven. Its knotted corners formed a pouch that concealed something knobbly, flexible and nearly oval, open at the narrow end.

"A neck-ring," he said, and looked a question. Hrolf nodded, so Tomas undid the cloth and held up a beaded silver necklace that glittered in the Sun.

From the largest central bead, the others ran in a graduated series of smaller pairs, down to the ones that flanked the opening. He'd seldom seen such fine craftsmanship. Each bead was deeply and intricately carved, and many were ornamented with minute granules of silver. The filigreed effect was airy and delicate, though the neck-ring hung heavily from his fingers.

"Smithied by a master--" he began. Then without warning, impressions came thick and fast. He had no chance to blink them away, to make himself concentrate on the salt air and the wide pale sky and Hrolf's expectant face. An immaterial curtain shimmered before Tomas's eyes, wiping away the skin-covered hold, the open sea-chest, Hrolf and his men, in a dizzying meld of color and form.

When the curtain lifted, Tomas perceived another scene entirely. He saw Hrolf bartering with an amber carver, and somehow knew this was a recent event in Truso.

The carver was a fair-skinned man with high cheekbones in an otherwise flat face. His hair was thick, brown and almost straight, and he spoke excellent Norse. After weighing Hrolf's silver, the artisan unlocked a small iron cask to make change. In the coffer lay the necklace, and Hrolf praised it.

"Ah," said the carver, his green eyes turning cold. "It's not come to me honestly. Some berserkers paid in silver last year. Threw me a bag, and I didn't ask them to stay while I weighed it. It hefted right, and I deemed it worth a few coins to get that lot out of my shop. The neck-ring was in the bag." The artisan frowned. "My brother's a silversmith, up the coast towards Grobin. It's his work. Made for his wife, but berserkers killed his and mine both, these five years past. He and I were off hunting when it happened."

Hrolf shook his head in sympathy.

"Later I'm paid with that neck-ring. If I'd opened the bag while they were here...." The amber carver stared at his scales.

"It might not have been the same men," Hrolf observed.

The other gave a brief nod, then knuckled his chin when Hrolf politely offered to buy the piece. "My brother doesn't know I have it,

146

nor anyone in Truso. But I took care that every berserker who came here should see it. None reacted. Not that they would. And not many come in." A brief silence. "It's yours. I'll be glad to get it off my hands."

The curtain re-descended. When it rose again, the images were much hazier, flickering by faster than before, and Tomas heard nothing at all. But he saw raiders burning a house on what he sensed was the Varangian coast, after they raped and killed two women.

Sharp and clear and all too familiar through the hallucinatory flames, one of the assailant's faces came into focus. The necklace grew cold in Tomas's fingers. The berserker was his half-brother Olaf.

Rather than fading, the vision stopped all at once. Still light-headed, fighting a touch of nausea, Tomas lifted his gaze from the neck-ring and met Hrolf's narrowed blue eyes.

The merchanter captain was sitting back on his heels, his hands resting on his knees. He appeared intrigued and a bit wary, but not surprised. Open-mouthed, Svein stared, ignoring his soaked boots. Two men who were off-watch hovered on deck near the hold; Tomas felt their puzzled glances.

Water sloshed: Thorkel remembered to empty the bilge-bucket. When it struck the side, everyone jumped.

"Lose that bucket and spend your off-watch time making another one," said Hrolf, his tone abstracted. He seemed not to hear Thorkel's "Aye," as the baling resumed.

Tomas knotted the maroon headscarf around the necklace, slipped it back into the vase and closed the sea-chest. As soon as he moved, the queasiness vanished and he felt more alert, but he knew better than to leave the hold. Hrolf was going to ask questions, and they had avid listeners. Seated across from the captain, Tomas waited, trying to keep his face open and calm. The sight of Olaf had left him a trifle shaken, even though the events occurred five years ago.

"Touched by Odin Witchlord, are you, Rhymer? Well now, what can you tell us about that neck-ring?" The captain looked neither hostile nor frightened, just highly interested.

Tomas took a relieved breath: Hrolf had produced his own explanation for Tomas's rigid posture. How long had he sat there distracted, clutching the neck-ring? He would have to recount part of what he'd sensed. But how much would satisfy his audience, and how much make them leery of his presence on board?

The Irish Sea slapped the *Pride of Skiringssal*'s hull as she pitched and rolled. Cold and deep, the water was, and land a long distance away.

"You got it in Truso," Tomas said carefully.

"That I did. You needed to ask where the vase was from, but not the neck-ring. Why is it different?" Hrolf's voice was pleasant; still, he wanted to know. The listeners nodded, absorbed.

It might be best to stay within the rough outlines of the story. "It was taken by violence from the woman for whom it was made." Noticing a frown or two, he added, "Not taken by your hand, nor that of anyone on board."

"Right you are," said Hrolf. "And?"

"I sense amber and silver around it, and the grief of two men." He assumed a serious expression and folded his arms, to imply that was all he had to say.

Hrolf, already deep into a somewhat exaggerated narration of the amber carver's tale, asked no more questions. But the awed faces of the silent men told Tomas that more would come of the matter.

He finished a watch standing look-out. Some flute practice now, or a nap in his borrowed bed-roll? The crew slept as their watches permitted, in whatever spot on the fore or aft decks where their cramped presence was least likely to impede the sail-handlers.

Tomas had just picked up his flute when Svein approached him with a diffident question. "Could you read the Runes for me, Rhymer? I'd gladly pay."

Tomas's hand crept to his belt, where he carried the Runes he had brought to Elfland. The small drawstring bag was still there, although the leather beneath his fingers was a shade rougher from the ocean damp.

Suddenly he felt chilled; the abrasive tang of salt water sluiced down his throat and was gone. He did not want to draw the Runes. "I'd save my coins if I were you. I've not read for anyone but myself before," he began cautiously, aware that Svein had seen the Rune bag.

"But you could?"

"Aye." The word escaped almost of its own volition, and Tomas stifled a grimace. Truly speak and prophesy. He could find no plausible excuse to refuse and had no time to fabricate one now, not with Svein's solemn expectant face, younger and darker than most of the crew, waiting there before him. If he'd anticipated this request--but he hadn't. Sighing inwardly, he gestured for Svein to sit down, then unwound just enough of the skin bedroll to serve as a backdrop for the Rune stones.

"I would learn something of this voyage's outcome for me," Svein told Tomas without being asked.

Salt rose in Tomas's mouth a second time. "I'll draw three Runes," he said, concentrating on the texture of cracked leather in his hands and willing any visions to stay away. Groping in the bag, he chose the first three stones that seemed to tingle and pulse against his skin.

Svein saw Fehu, the Rune of Nourishment; Kenaz, the Rune of Ingenuity; and Laguz, the Rune of Release. These Runes appeared to strike him as promising, and he studied them with pleased anticipation.

But Tomas saw Fehu, the Rune of Possessions; Kenaz, the Rune of Opening or of Fire; and Laguz, the Rune of the Sea.

Moistening his lips, he cleared his throat to banish the parching savor of brine. Fehu meant movable possessions, as opposed to land... He resisted the temptation to look at the cargo hold. From the way the Runes before him gleamed as if dripping wet, he sensed that if he glanced that way, he would see frigid water pouring in through a ghostly hole in the planking.

"Well now, Svein," he said, "it would seem that you've gained some wealth by the use of your wits, and that further journeying lies ahead before you're rid of what you've acquired. Did you plan to sell nothing until you reach Skiringssal?"

"Huh." Svein peered at the Runes. "No, I was going to trade at Birka. But I could hold off till Skiringssal." He rumpled up his brown hair. "What I should sell, and when?"

Laguz: Rune of Release, Rune of the Sea. "It doesn't appear as though you'll keep anything."

Svein grinned, revealing stained and broken teeth. "Sell it all at a profit, eh? I just might. I would if I could. The Rune of Ingenuity... I've been hankering to buy my own ship, or at least most of one, like Hrolf here. Thank you, Rhymer." Clapping Tomas on the back, Svein stood and made his way aft, a slight swagger in his walk.

An easy escape. Amazing how folk heard only what they cared to hear. Tomas picked up the three Runes to return them to the bag. He half-expected them to be wet, but when he turned them over in his hands, the stones were flinty and dry.

Then a substantial shadow fell across his lap and blotted out the Sun. Thorkel squatted down beside Tomas and politely asked for a reading. Gods, he hated to risk another one, but again he had no good excuse to refuse. "One more, friend Thorkel! And then I must sleep."

Isa, the Ice-Rune, Rune of Waiting.

Ansuz, Rune of Oracles or Messages. Tomas kept his face still. Ansuz was Loki's Rune, and Tomas didn't care to see any hint of the Trickster's hand at work.

149

Hagalaz, the Hail-Rune, Rune of Irresistible Forces. It implied sudden, unexpected and usually irreversible changes.

Abruptly, Tomas saw the *Pride of Skiringssal* becalmed in fog so thick that her crew could not find the horizon, so thick that even the transparent sunstone Hrolf held up against a leaden sky gave no hint of their location. They floated lost and as if suspended in a shroudlike mist. Isa, Rune of Waiting.

Tomas lifted his hand to his eyes but could not dismiss the images, nor the grinding headache that descended on him. He saw someone--Thorkel, Tomas realized with a kind of numbed irony--grab him, Tomas, and demand that the Witchlord's servant tell them where the open sea lay beyond the shoals. Ansuz, Rune of Oracles.

The image of Tomas babbled, that of Thorkel shouted and others shouted with him. Finally Hrolf at the steerboard bore hard in the direction of Tomas's shaking hand. There was a loud sickening crack, and black water lashed across the heeling deck. Hagalaz.

"What ails you, Rhymer? Are you seasick?"

Tomas shrugged and said nothing. The vision had mercifully stopped, and he looked straight into Thorkel's bearded, sunburnt face. The merchanter's expression was a mixture of sympathy and amusement. "Best not to sleep, then. Watch the horizon; that helps seasickness pass." Thorkel put the stones back in the bag. "I'm not surprised to see those Runes; no, indeed," he said, standing up. "Isa and Ansuz. I expect that midwinter will bring me word of my father's death. And Hagalaz--only the gods know what will come of his land with eight quarreling sons, and my uncle a greedy man and a violent one. Mind you keep those eyes open, Rhymer, and look out to sea."

Staring after Thorkel's departing back, Tomas dreaded reading the Runes a third time, but could no more have stopped himself than he could have stopped breathing. This time was for himself.

Good: everyone else was either on watch or asleep. He pulled three Runes, gave them a hasty squint and returned them to the bag. Then he lay down and shut his eyes, heedless of Thorkel's misguided advice.

Ehwaz the Horse-Rune, Rune of Movement. And cooperation.

Raido, Rune of Journeys.

Berkana, the Birch Goddess. Rune of Growth, Rune of the Mother. It might also mean Birka; the port was located on Birch Island.

But how could Tomas travel there by horse, when he felt sure that the pooka had stayed behind?

Small comfort that this last reading did not look disastrous. How would Tomas escape the Fate that evidently awaited the others?

Perhaps the Runes showed only probable events that could be avoided, if he were wise enough to find a way. He should stay awake to consider the possibilities.

Sleep took him quickly instead.

CHAPTER TWENTY-NINE: THE DRAUG

Night, grey and heavy, enveloped the crew, pressing moistly against their eyelids. After a freakishly violent day-long storm, during which they lowered the sail and let the sonorous wind drive them where it would, fog thick as stale curds rolled in before they could take a reckoning. Now the wind had failed; the sail was reefed, and they drifted in a high-running sea.

Overhead near the stars of Odin's Wain, no Lode Star burned to guide their way. No stars shone at all. Blown off course, adrift and directionless, the ship lay wrapped in a blanket of fog so dense that from where Tomas stood amidships, he could focus on neither stem nor stern.

They were lost. Hafvilla, Norsemen called this state.

"There you are, Rhymer," said Bjarni, making his way towards Tomas. Bjarni's soft boots made no sound on the deck. He was to have shared steering watch with Tomas. A seasoned trader about Hrolf's age, Bjarni's hair had already turned completely grey.

He cut off Tomas's question. "No, no point in the watch; the fog's like sheared wool. Hoped it'd blow over, but instead it's got thicker, and we've wholly lost our reckoning."

"Does the sounding-lead--"

"It's not much help. We're running it down every quarter-hour; depths vary in these waters. Can't use the sunstone till dawn. With luck the fog will break up enough to see the horizon by then."

"Birds," said Tomas without thinking, his mind still slowed from his long sleep.

Bjarni chuckled. "Do they fly in the fog? All the birds in Galloway could circle fifty feet off the bow, and we'd not see them for the murk. But if you spot one, sing out. I'm off to find Hrolf." He made his way towards the stern, where Hrolf had just finished the last steering watch.

After strapping his satchel on--and telling himself firmly that was more to prevent anyone from stepping on it, than that he expected they'd sink--Tomas peered over the rail into the fog. Had someone ventured out in the ship's boat they towed astern, to look at the color and run of the sea? But these men weren't novice sailors. They would have decided not to bother with the ship's boat yet, since they could better judge such things once the fog lifted.

He squinted through the leaden haze towards the bow, where he heard a hushed conversation. Should he join it, or the group with Hrolf at the stern? Where was Thorkel? Perhaps Tomas could avoid

Thorkel's Rune-predicted request to point out a safe passage. Maybe that image was a probable event rather than an irrevocably Fated one. If only there were some way to tell the difference!

Water gurgled over the side as someone wearily emptied the bilge bucket. Sooner or later, Tomas should approach Hrolf and volunteer for baling. That watch went on regardless of hafvilla.

Except for the ship's gentle rolling, they were motionless now. Over the deck and around the mast floated shrouds of mist like tattered ghosts of the lowered sail. For a moment, the *Pride of Skiringssal* seemed to be a clumsy wingless beetle slowly foundering in a turgid sea of dark honey. Tomas shivered, although the air was more damp than cold. His skin was slick with clinging moisture, and he tasted salt on his lips.

And in his throat. If they sank... He tugged his satchel straps tighter, then went aft to find Hrolf.

With the ship's captain were Svein, Bjarni, Thorkel and two other men. Hrolf gave Tomas a nod and went on debating their position with Bjarni. Svein was hauling up the line from which hung the sounding-lead. Every face looked pale and tight and clammy, and Hrolf's beard curled furiously in the sodden air.

"If we could just get a good look at the water," said the captain. "Curse the fog! Even if we had our reckoning, we might be drifting into a tide rip that could run us onto a shoal. And we'd break up fast. There's a high sea still running after that storm."

Bjarni, staring over the rail, gripped Hrolf's elbow with one hand and pointed with the other. "Is that a light?" he asked. He sounded as if his throat were full of hot pebbles.

The other men all turned to look. A greenish-yellow glow welled through the mist, growing rapidly brighter as something neared them. The dwindling fog itself seemed to part in two and flow away from the source of the sickly illumination.

"It's not torches on headlands," Hrolf muttered, seizing the steerboard and bearing to port, out of the path of the oncoming light. The gesture was useless, made from sheer habit and nerves. It was flat calm and they were making no headway, so the ship could not be maneuvered.

The fog was evaporating. By then Tomas had already glimpsed the apparition and its fragmentary craft, but it was Svein who saw it next, and Svein who screamed: "A draug!"

Another man cried, "Odin Draug-lord, have pity on us!"

But the draug, that evil spirit whose appearance spelled disaster at sea, steered its scrap of boat directly and impossibly towards them, trailing phosphorescent foam in its wake. The same glimmering sulphurous light hovered around its pallid corpse's face.

A draug, and not an Elf. Some whispered tales hinted that a draug was a drowned man's ghost. Tomas stared at the seaweed that festooned the draug's flapping oilskins. More seaweed hung in rank dripping lengths from shards of the half-boat's rotten planking. The craft flew no sail from its shattered mast, yet it ran with bare poles over the Irish Sea until it pulled up alongside them, so close that it could have rammed their clinker-built hull.

Hrolf's hand fell bonelessly from the tiller. Bjarni sank to his knees, one hand clutching his chest. With a wild moan, Svein covered his face, but Thorkel stood like one turned to ice. Louder than the wails of the men on the foredeck, Tomas could hear his own heartbeat booming in his ears like surf on a gravelly shore. Clenching the rail, he waited.

From out of nowhere a hard wind began to blow, driving them towards the apparition across a now choppier sea. The remainder of the fog rapidly dissipated. In the air floated draug-laughter: breathless, high and thin. Two pale lights flickered in hollow eye sockets beneath the phantom's oilskin hood.

Tomas flinched as something sang through the air past his head: a short knife, hurled at the draug. The weapon passed through the half-boat's deck without a sound. Its head snaking around at an impossible angle, the draug bent its smoldering gaze on Thorkel.

The trader gave it an answering glare. Thorkel's hands twitched convulsively at his sides; spittle ran from his mouth. Recognizing the beginnings of a berserker-like rage, the other men edged a step or two aside. All but Svein, who stood swaying with his face still hidden in his hands.

"Draug!" croaked Thorkel. "It's said that sometimes you help sailors and take a soul in payment. Is that true?"

A thready gurgling chuckle emerged from the shadowy depths of the oiled hood. "Not for you. You're all lost this night--save one, whom I perceive is beyond my reach. His time has not yet come." To Tomas's lasting horror, the draug waved a shriveled, flipper-like hand in his direction. He shrank away from the stares of the crew.

He was grabbed and violently shaken. "It's lying!" Thorkel screamed, a pulse jumping at the side of his throat. "You both serve Odin, damn you! Which way to open water?"

"Don't ask me!" Tomas gasped, bracing himself as best he could. Thorkel was almost Tomas's height, and much heavier.

"But you know! Tell me or lose your arm!" roared Thorkel.

With Hrolf yelling at them to stop, Tomas pointed hastily down at the deck, and groaned as his right arm was doubled behind him.

Draug-laughter echoed around them, but Tomas felt a soft cold whisper brush the inside of his skull. "As well to tell him, Mortal, and spare your arm. They're all mine regardless."

With his free hand, Tomas pointed over the rail. Hrolf at the steerboard bore hard in the direction of Tomas's shaking arm.

There was a horrid, grinding, splintery sound.

The ship had hit the reef that lay between it and the open sea. Black water lashed across the heeling deck, soaking the crew. Tomas ducked Thorkel's punch, which was already deflected by the trader's loss of balance as waves lifted the vessel and drove it back down with punishing force. Shouts, and a howl from amidships: a man or men overboard.

Again, and a third time, they crashed onto the reef, heeling more and more steeply. Wood crunched and tore. They weren't clearing the reef; the ship was breaking up.

Hagalaz, thought Tomas incoherently as he pitched into an angry sea. Thorkel shrieked as he tumbled onto the half-boat with the draug. Just before something struck Tomas's shoulder and he sank beneath the waves, he saw the draug open its oilskin-covered arms and enfold Thorkel in a crushing grip.

155

CHAPTER THIRTY: LANDFALL

Tomas resurfaced. Spat out briny water. Kicked off his boots. The Irish Sea was cold enough to weaken a man before long.

What was happening to the ship? The waves' troughs blinded him with sea water; he could be dashed onto the reef. Had the ship's boat or some part of the hull floated clear?

The *Pride of Skiringssal* was torn open just aft of the cargo hold, and the sea tossed with boxes and coffers and barrels rendered deadly by the waves. Only two other heads bobbed in the swells. When Tomas shouted, no replies came over the clamoring waves. The crests towered taller as the wind picked up, driving the ship away from him. There was no sign of the draug.

"Hrolf! Bjarni!" Tomas shouted again. Gods, he was cold.

The only answer was the huge racketing voice of the sea. With the ponderous boom of a slowed thunderclap, the mast cracked--and toppled towards him. He swam desperately beyond the arc of its fall.

The great pole slapped into the water. Was there a faint human cry? When the next crest bore him up, he saw no one. Most of the ship had sunk beneath the Irish Sea, and the rest was following after.

Shivering, Tomas tread water in a sea of breaking waves. The ocean chill bit deeply, stiffening his limbs, tiring him. His teeth chattered.

It was only drowning, drowning in cold water. No ravens, no spirits, no goddesses--not yet. Better this way than being dragged alive to Niflheim. Would Moira find someone else to fetch the ravens? Moira...

But he wasn't dead yet. Snagging the largest piece of barrel he could find, Tomas let it support part of his weight. He looped one end of his belt to the barrel staves; it took several attempts.

He was shuddering violently, the first sign of succumbing to the cold. Next would come feeling drowsy. He'd remain awake as long as he could, and go where the ocean bore him.

The entire world was dark flowing water and rolling swells, and always had been. Waves, lapping at the night sky as if thirsty for the bright pale moon overhead, rocked Tomas and murmured in his ears. He was more tired than ever in his life before. Salt no longer stung his eyes and his swollen lips, and the cold had agreeably disappeared. There was no sensation in his limbs at all.

Close his eyes, rest for a moment, and he might feel stronger. Sleep: he wanted to sleep. But sleep was perilous. Why?

There was an obstruction in the neighborhood of his knees. At least now he knew where his legs were.

Directly below him in the water, something was moving.

Gods, not a shark! He sucked in a terrified breath. A shark hit on the snout might retreat until it smelled blood, or until Tomas grew too weak to strike. He reached for the barrel staves with some hazy notion of swinging them as a club.

From the end of his arm, a piece of deadened meat--his hand-- hung and groped with agonizing slowness for the wood.

Something was surfacing between his knees. A sleek wet body, smelling of fish and glistening in the moonlight, came up supporting Tomas's belly and chest.

Sprawled on a long curving back, he stared at a blowhole, a snubbed and beaky nose, and the glint of small dark eyes. Between mingled fear and amazement, he slid off, and lost the pieces of barrel from the awkward knot in his belt. The big dolphin promptly ducked, and rose again with Tomas slumped in front of its dorsal fin. This time he stayed on and patted its sides in a daze.

The dolphin's skin was extraordinarily soft, and once or twice quivered under Tomas's touch, like the muzzle of a mettlesome horse. But most of all the dolphin was warm, with a radiant, blessed, contagious heat, and the open air into which it lifted Tomas was warmer than the sea.

It seemed disrespectful to keep stroking the living creature beneath him. To keep his balance, he rested his hands lightly on the dolphin's back. "Thank you," he said fervently, his frozen mouth barely able to form the words. He had no doubt the animal was taking him to land, but no idea where. It didn't matter.

The draug had spoken truth: Tomas would not die by drowning this night. Remembering Hrolf and the others, he shook his head.

But sorrow and shock could not lessen his wonder, for he rode a dolphin.

Pale glowing streaks appeared low in the sky behind them, increasing in number and intensity until they sent long ripples of peridot-green light over the waves. The big dolphin made for a dark uneven smudge on the horizon directly ahead. They were headed west, most likely for the eastern shore of Éire.

Tomas frowned, wincing as his cracked lips split further. Now that he wasn't quite so cold, he could try to think. Various port towns were held by the Norse, but their relations with the Irish princes were uneasy at best. With luck, the dolphin would approach a Norse-ruled region.

Why was the beast rescuing him? He felt sure that he would recognize Aubrey in any form the pooka took, and equally sure that the dolphin wasn't Aubrey. Could it be another sort of Elf sent by Moira? There was no way to tell yet. No way, perhaps, to tell at all.

Staying awake was the crucial thing just now. Tomas settled himself on the dolphin's supple back as best he could, and waited.

The Sun burned well above a light-raddled sea when at last they entered a harbor. As soon as Tomas's feet grazed the ocean floor, the dolphin began a slow careful duck from underneath him. Nauseated and swaying, he managed to stand clear in hip-high water and watched the dolphin swim to a deeper section of the harbor. After rearing out of the waves as if to stand on its tail, and chittering loudly and at length in Tomas's direction, the dolphin started circling the mouth of the bay.

Tomas blinked; his eyelids were salt-creased and puffy. Beyond the wooden docks, lush green turf thickly studded with rocks rose gently from the waterline and up into the low hills. Ah, good: some of the buildings were Norse longhouses, narrow rectangles of wood with curving roofs. Smoke seeped from window slits high on the walls, and carved animal heads grinned in ferocious blankness from corner staves.

Smaller dwellings, built of wattle and daub and turf, huddled together like so many sheep among the great horned cattle of the longhouses. Up on the slope, now, that was probably a Nazarene temple displaying the cross-Rune.

At the edge of the shoreline towered a twelve-foot stone pillar. A wide brown river emptied into the bay, and the docks were lined with ships: slender Norse dragon-craft, beamy merchanters, and small round flattened leather boats that looked like upturned shields bobbing in the mud-colored water. Tomas smelled silt, bread and fish, some rotting nearby and some freshly cooked. His empty stomach knotted and churned.

With varying degrees of alacrity, sailors and dockhands loaded and unloaded cargo. Men and women chattered, argued, cleaned fish, hawked their wares and tracked mud over the rough planking laid down on the bare sandy earth. On the portion of the docks directly opposite Tomas, people were beginning to cluster. They pointed at him and jabbered.

Sick and dizzy, his eyelids nearly swollen shut, he cast a wistful glance behind him at the dolphin who cruised in lazy zigzags around the harbor's mouth. But his finned friend came no closer.

158

Wade towards the docks. One foot, the other foot, the first foot again.

He aimed for a break in the expanse of weathered wood, where the water spat seaweed and refuse onto the strand. The interested crowd, which now included a few beggars, several children and some wildly frisking dogs, headed for the same spot. A lean cat streaked past in pursuit of half a dozen seagulls who flapped, shrieking with belligerence, into the tepid blue sky. Some of the sailors stopped passing crates to each other, wiped their hands on their trousers, and sauntered down to the gap in the planking to join the men and women gawking at Tomas.

Many of them wore Norse clothing, the women in sleeveless dresses pinned at the shoulders with a pair of heavy brooches, the men in breeches and shirts and tunics. A few fair-skinned Norsemen wore billowing trousers like those of the small dark hook-nosed men in turbans who prowled through the crowd. This harbor catered to far travelers. The sturdy round-faced folk with freckles and curly hair must be the native Irish, along with the creamily pale, black-haired men and women who were dressed in cape-like garments belted over shifts and trousers.

Wading closer, Tomas attempted a smile, hoping to establish his harmlessness before he collapsed at the edge of the scummy water. When it lapped around his ankles, he stopped and spread his hands wide to show they were empty of weapons.

The crowd fell almost completely silent. Elbowing one another, they gaped at him. One or two backed away. A few made the White-Christ's sign and several others a far older gesture.

Not good. Not good, when they were so noisy before. At least no one had drawn a weapon, although a couple of men laid their hands on their belts. Tomas tried to say something in Norse, but his throat produced only a squawk.

A grubby little boy in a torn shift broke away from the throng and dashed down to meet him, babbling with excitement and pointing towards the harbor's mouth. Grabbing Tomas's hand, he tugged violently and motioned for Tomas to wade back out with him. Unprepared for the sudden yank, Tomas lost his tenuous balance and sat down hard in silty mud and five inches of water.

Looking aghast, then concerned, the boy started to giggle.

The crowd chuckled, its tension apparently forgotten. Soon the only people not convulsed with laughter were Tomas and a plump woman with a wild mane of frizzy brown hair. She stormed into the water, seized the child and showered Tomas with a torrent of red-faced invective, not a word of which he understood.

Still sprawled in the mud, he looked up into her furious blue eyes—not very far to look; she was quite short—and croaked an apology in Norse.

That stemmed the tide, though her eyes still snapped, and her every freckle stood out like an apple seed. She muttered something and gave the little boy a shake. He stopped dancing in her grip and began to sniffle. Tomas expected a final simmering glance thrown his way, but the woman set her chin, lowered her gaze and marched off to the docks with the protesting child firmly in tow.

Tomas stood up. It seemed to take an uncommonly long time, and he would much rather have gone to sleep right there in the mud. To no one in particular, he said, "I come in peace—" Then he stopped and stared at the three men walking towards him.

One was perhaps forty, of medium height and build, and dressed in long robes. His eyes were brown and quiet and deeply lined, and his lips twitched with suppressed laughter. The crown of his head was shaved bare, the rest of his graying black hair pulled back in a long plait, and he carried what must be a skin of fresh water or of wine. Tomas's mouth felt drier than ever, and his knees wanted to sag. Reaching him before the others, the tonsured man took Tomas's elbow and pressed the precious skin into his hand. "Drink," he said in accented Norse.

It was water. Tomas drank it all.

The other two men joined them. One was a few years older than Tomas, round-faced and muscular, with blue eyes, brown curls streaked red-blond by the Sun, and a scar on his chin. He gave Tomas a blanket and a smile. Tomas thanked him in Norse, but didn't realize that he was shaking until the curly-haired man gave him a judicious look, took the blanket gently out of his hands and settled it around his shoulders.

The third man was about Tomas's age, nearly his height, and dressed like a courtier in a fine linen shirt under a lightweight tunic with an elaborate silver pin. Gold bands cuffed his arms, and the hilt of his sword was inlaid with beaten gold. He had a well-kempt head of fine blond hair, pale expressionless eyes like polished chips of aquamarine, and an elegantly trimmed beard. "Welcome to Dubhlinn. Shall we all get back on dry land?" he asked in cultivated Norse.

Steered onto the docks, Tomas took a final awed glance at the sparkling water beyond the harbor's mouth, but the dolphin was gone.

CHAPTER THIRTY-ONE: KING IVAR OF DUBHLINN

Even if Harald, the well-dressed man among the three who waded out to meet Tomas, hadn't regaled King Ivar's court with the story of the young Norse skald who'd entered Dubhlinn harbor on a dolphin's back, the tale still would have reached the King's ears. The town buzzed with it, Norse and Irish alike, and the monastery where Tomas was recovering received more visitors than it had in some time. Brother Daren, the man in long robes who had offered Tomas water, was heard to give innocent-sounding thanks for the sudden popularity of the monastery's cheese and produce.

Brother Daren introduced himself to Tomas when he struggled awake from a day-long sleep to find the monk sitting calmly by his pallet. After inquiring how Tomas felt, Brother Daren said that King Ivar of Dubhlinn himself had conceived such a fervent desire to meet this dolphin-rider that Ivar had sent his courtier, Harald Thorfinnson, to fetch Tomas to court as soon as he might go.

Still sorting through hazy recollections of being helped to a Nazarene temple and stumbling into bed after a light meal, a bath and some unguent for his face, Tomas blinked stupidly at the monk and asked, "Now?"

Brother Daren laughed and said in his sing-song Norse, "No, my friend, you don't appear ready yet to me, and the abbot is of the same mind."

Soon Tomas found himself eating a more substantial meal and talking about the shipwreck and the dolphin, although the monk hadn't asked about anything beyond Tomas's health. He named himself Rhymer and refrained from mentioning the draug.

When he finished, Brother Daren said, "I have heard of such with dolphins. Truly, they are wondrous creatures."

Tomas nodded. After a moment's silence, he blurted, "Why was I brought here?"

The monk looked sober; he steepled his fingertips and spoke slowly. "Because you needed care. And while Brendan O'Quinlan and the abbot both offered, there are more of us with the skill to tend you here at the monastery."

"Brendan O'Quinlan?"

"The man who gave you a blanket in the harbor. He has a scar on his chin."

Tomas remembered. He also noticed that Brother Daren didn't say that Harald Thorfinnson had offered any help, on his own behalf or

161

on that of King Ivar.

The large hall was dim and smoky, aired by slitted windows at
ceiling height and carved wooden doors propped open. Tomas stared
moodily at the low flames on the portion of the long central hearth
directly before him. He awaited an audience with Ivar, the Norse King
of Dubhlinn.

Not with Ivar the Boneless, that fabled Viking who, the
Dubhlinn-men had given Tomas to understand, had been killed four or
five years ago, while Tomas was in Elfland.

He had slept another deep and lengthy sleep in the White-
Christ's temple under the auspices of Brother Daren. Now the monk sat
next to Tomas on the smoke-blackened wooden bench, his back straight
and his hands folded. Since entering the hall he had said very little.
Tomas wasn't sure why Brother Daren was there. When Harald had
arrived to escort Tomas to King Ivar's court, the monk had simply
appeared and fallen into step with them.

On Tomas's other side lounged Harald. Resplendent in a new
gold-stitched tunic, with freshly washed, braided and be-ribboned hair,
he appeared to be enjoying the curious murmurs that drifted their way.

Tomas suppressed a sigh. He would probably have been
obliged to come here and give an accounting of himself in any case. The
wait and the smoke, the drone of voices and the flicker of the hearthfire
could have lulled him to sleep again, but for the unforgiving wood of
Ivar's benches. Tomas shifted to ease the bite of the hard planking into
his thighs and backside, thinner now than they had ever been. He'd
occupied this seat for well over an hour.

Stifling what would have been a cavernous yawn, he shook
himself awake and looked about for something to distract him. A
surprising number of people, Norse, Irish and foreigners, awaited the
King's notice. By the look of them, they were mostly nobles, soldiers or
merchants. Slaves tended the fire. Occasionally more slaves walked
past with platters of food and jugs of water or wine. The hall had at
least one other wing at right angles to this one, but smoke prevented a
good view. Voices floated towards Tomas from farther up the hall, and
people hurried by him towards the voices. Ivar must hold court there,
beyond the great hearth.

Tomas glanced down at the clothes that Moira had given him.
Freshly washed and mended now, thanks to the monks, they were much
worn from time in the water. Brendan had brought a pair of soft leather
boots to the temple--the monastery--where he and Tomas exchanged
smiles and a few friendly words. Brendan's quizzical blue eyes asked

far more questions than he did, although he spoke adequate Norse.

Brother Daren had given Tomas his satchel, saying only that the monks had cleaned and oiled both instruments and replaced the harpstrings. Tomas had not yet brought himself to see how badly the sea had warped the harp and the flute. They might never sound the same. He heaved a sigh, partly for their ruination and partly because the thought made him miss Linley, not for the first time.

"Patience," said Harald, responding to Tomas's sigh. The gentle remonstrance of the courtier's tone clashed with the hard stare in his flat pale eyes. Ignoring him, Tomas squinted up at the oily smoke that pooled near the curved ceiling. Let it appear to anyone watching from a distance that Harald had silenced him, but show no diffidence to Harald in person. The race of courtiers Tomas understood; he'd had dealings enough with them in Vestfold.

But of this King Ivar he knew very little, though the fame of Dubhlinn itself had spread to all of the North and beyond. Ivar was lord of a Norse-founded harbor town, hub of the Viking piracy lanes and a major port of legitimate trade routes. Goods from the far-flung corners of the known world found their way to Dubhlinn. Silk, silver and spices procured in Itil and Bulgar, brought there from as far off as the trade roads in the uttermost East. More silver from Sun-scorched Moorish lands, south of the Franks with their wine and salt. Falcons, furs and walrus ivory from the Lapps and Finns of the frigid stretches near the White Sea. Trade in slaves and other merchandise from these and less remote places was brisk, with much trafficking in items such as the cargo that sank with Hrolf's ship. Hired mercenaries wintered in Dubhlinn; men loafing between Viking raids made the town their headquarters, and merchants of all stripes scrambled to establish a foothold there.

Over this lucrative and restless outpost ruled the King of Dubhlinn, Norse for the moment, sometimes collaborating with the Irish chieftains and sometimes at odds with them. The political climate changed so often that even if Tomas had lost far less than seven years in Faerie, he would have had no idea how the balance of power now lay.

In Faerie. How much time had elapsed there since he left, and was Hel looking for him? Could Rhys appear on this island, on another visit to the King of the Irish Sidhe, perhaps, as when they had taken Caraid?

Drawing another scowl from Harald, Tomas shifted on the bench and peered through the murky air at the assortment of people. How long would it take to learn the intricacies of this court? Perhaps he could profit from his notoriety about the dolphin, and earn enough gold arm-rings with his poetry to buy passage on a ship bound for Uppland. There would be vessels bound for Uppland, beyond a doubt. From Dubhlinn ships sailed in all directions.

A tow-headed boy approached Harald and said something in Gaelic, his tone low. A slave, probably; he maintained an edgy distance from the courtier. Harald stood and motioned Tomas to follow. Along the glowing strip of stone-lined hearth they made their way, and people pressed back to let them pass. Brother Daren trailed mute and uninvited in their wake, until they stood before the looming carved pillars of Ivar's high seat. The fire blazed brightest there.

As Harald made the introductions, Tomas studied the square watchful countenance of the lord of Dubhlinn. The King was in his early middle years, tall and powerfully built. Hooded blue eyes considered Tomas calmly. Ivar's brows were thick flaxen tufts, the only softness in a remote, stark face. His protruding cheekbones were as sharp as the great ivory tusks supporting his chair, and reptilian shrewdness lay in the gaze that he bent on the newcomer.

An icy man, thought Tomas, and a deep-minded one. He waited. The court was absolutely silent.

At last Ivar said softly, "Where did this dolphin find you, Rhymer?"

"I could not rightly say, my lord. In the Irish Sea, near where the ship broke up."

"What ship was that? Was she yours?"

"The *Pride of Skiringssal*, my lord. No, she was captained by Hrolf Sorenson, a merchant from Vestfold."

Ivar did not take his eyes off Tomas and gave no signal that he could see. A pale sweating man, with an oddly fat face for his slight frame, stepped to the King's side and muttered something in his ear. Ivar nodded and sat back in his chair. Some of the intensity left his face, and for an instant a touch of amusement softened the lines of his mouth. "That one has been known to stop here before, and to complain of my harbor taxes. Although he paid them."

The court laughed; Ivar did not. Nor did Tomas, though he thought it behooved him to smile. A knot tightened in his chest, and his mouth was growing parched. But all he could do was wait for these questions he must answer and over whose course he had no control--and little opportunity to steer the conversation away from channels rendered treacherous by his inability to lie.

"You are not a merchant, are you, Rhymer?"

"No, my lord. A skald."

"Why were you on board?"

"For passage to Birka, on my way to Uppsala."

Ivar nodded, his eyes moving from Tomas's face to his hands, from his frayed green clothing to the leather satchel slung over his shoulder. "You carry your instruments in that bag?"

"Such as they are." Moving slowly, Tomas took the harp and the flute from the case and held them up to show the King.

He almost dropped them. Still smooth and glossy, the wood showed neither swelling nor cracks. It merely looked older and more weathered. Hours in the sea had changed it only as might years of playing.

Ivar reached curiously for the harp. He turned it over in his huge calloused hands, the hands of a warrior still, not those of a man who spent every day warming himself before the fire in his hall. "Oddly made," he said. "I do not recall having seen the like, and a river of goods flows through Dubhlinn. Well, the world holds many things that I have never seen."

He returned the harp to Tomas, who put it away and ventured to ask if the King played.

"I? No. But I listen. I listen well." Ivar was silent a moment, his eyes boring into Tomas. "Your harp is well-preserved, and the sea is cruel to wood. You must have soaked the case in the fat of an entire herd of sheep. How long were you in the water?"

Tomas swallowed. "I don't know. Only minutes before the dolphin came, I think, and longer afterwards."

"The dolphin. Such a creature has not aided you before?"

"No, my lord. Only this once."

"And the remainder of the crew?"

"All lost, I fear."

The King transferred his stare to the flames, and his face grew mask-like in its stillness. No one moved or spoke, no courtier, law-speaker, petitioner or slave, no member of the royal household. A vast feline elemental being, the fire hissed and spat and stretched itself within its trough of stone. Blotted shadows leaped against watchful faces, and a high hammering beat of apprehension began to pound in Tomas's skull. The atmosphere was too close, too still, too full of wariness. Was the wariness all his?

No. It had a heaviness, a weighted center that tugged at him like quicksand. The tugging emanated from somewhere in the hall, somewhere quite close. He looked at Ivar.

Around the monarch the air seemed to thicken and become almost opaque. Then it was diluted by an oily grey so dark it was

165

nearly black, and by an angry clay-red shot with bilious yellow. The colors radiated from Ivar's head and shoulders like a halo, as if he exuded the billowing stain from his pores.

These were the sooty hues of a morbid, gnawing anxiety, not a constant terror, but one that periodically arose and engulfed a personality otherwise forceful and self-contained. The other faces in the hall, not cognizant of the erratic attacks of Ivar's particular demon, shone puzzled and greasy in the flickering light.

In a burst of unwelcome insight, sluicing over him like a bucketful of tainted water, Tomas grasped the source of the King's dread.

Ivar was haunted by the fear of drowning.

With that perception, the uncanny tinctures in the air around the King's head began to ebb away, until nothing filled the hall but the smoke that had always been there. Tomas closed his eyes with relief but immediately opened them again.

"The favor of Odin must lie upon you, Rhymer, to have escaped the grasp of the waves. The sea-gods give no quarter. It was not they who sent the dolphin." Ivar fixed Tomas with a measuring stare and added, "Is there something you wish to say?"

"No, my lord." He did not care for any mention of Odin, nor of his own brush with death. For all he knew, Hel might be drawn closer by such talk. The Elves might also seek to learn his whereabouts, to hold him to his task. An image of the jade-green Elvish Sea rose in his mind, and he repressed a shudder.

The expression crossing Ivar's face was that of a man who tastes an exotic new dish and finds it not quite to his liking. "I would hear more of this dolphin, how it came to rescue you, and what was in your thoughts. All that you remember." He glanced over Tomas's shoulder. "But I must tend to other matters now. Harald Thorfinnson will escort you to my table tonight."

"Your invitation is an honor, my lord." The appropriate response was not, strictly speaking, a lie--though Tomas knew of no table in Dubhlinn where he would less care to dine.

In a speculative tone, the King added, "I'll presume to advise you on your calling, Rhymer. That dolphin is the stuff of a fine poem. But we will speak more of this at our evening meal."

Harald and Tomas bowed, then turned to go, with Brother Daren following. Ivar's attention was already on the next man who sought an audience, and who had just stepped out of the shadows to stand before the King's high seat.

As Tomas passed the new petitioner, the man's head swiveled

towards him. There was a truncated gasp. Then a hard hand shot out, seized Tomas's arm and spun him around.

He found himself staring into the furious face and twitching eyes of his half-brother Olaf.

CHAPTER THIRTY-TWO: MANSLAYING

With one hand on Tomas's elbow to hold him braced at arm's length, Olaf's other hand swung back. His short cloak parted at the shoulder. Corded muscles bunched; an axe glittered in the wavering light.

Into the air welled the sour taint of iron, flowing stain-like from the blade--but Tomas sensed no iron below the axe's head. A wooden handle, then. He had a chance, one narrow chance.

Just as the weapon began to descend, Olaf's face, which had gone still as bone, twitched once, and his slitted eyes flicked down at Tomas's knees.

So. Olaf considered a crippling blow to the legs, a surer stroke than to the neck, less likely to go wild.

With a sly wisdom of the body, a visceral perception of his opponent's intentions, and a wild viperish agility, Tomas moved. But he neither fought his brother's braced arm nor stepped in close to make the stroke too dangerous to complete. Centering his weight, he leaped backwards, with a fierce yank along the line formed by Olaf's extended arm and gripping hand. At the same time, Tomas thrust his caught elbow against his brother's thumb joint and towards the midline of his own still-balanced body.

The vicious pull when Olaf must have expected a push, and the heft of his axe abruptly deflected from its trajectory, combined to trip him. He stumbled forward. As his weight ground his thumb backwards, he let go of Tomas's arm.

Tomas grabbed for the axe with one hand, made a fist of the other and clouted the nape of Olaf's descending neck, adding to the force of his fall. A jump to clear Olaf's torso; a twist in mid-air. With a back-handed motion, Tomas wrested the axe from his brother and swung it around through the arc of his own twisting leap. He landed facing Olaf, the wooden axe-shaft clenched in both hands.

His knife already drawn, the berserker scrambled to his feet. Blood from his scraped forehead streamed into his eyes. Aiming high, he feinted at Tomas. When Olaf changed tack and plunged in, stabbing low, the sharp whetted edge of his own Rune-carved axe-blade caught him square in the heart.

The same thick pulpy sound, grating against resistance, that used to drive Tomas from the farm at slaughtertime and earn him Olaf's scorn, awakened him from his ritual dance of defense. Staggering, he almost fell with Olaf, but recovered his balance to stand gripping the wooden handle of the axe that still connected him to his brother. When he finally released the weapon, it was wet, and the whites of Olaf's staring eyes were as flat and opaque as those of raw fish.

At that precise moment, a cloudy form began to trail from Olaf's mouth. The dingy grey, shredded substance appeared moist and dull, with no firelight reflected therein. Roiling and swirling in upon itself, the column of fog loomed taller and denser by the second. From it wafted a faint sour odor of brine and rotten grapes, and something that Tomas couldn't identify. The apparition shivered and rippled, as slushy water will when struck by a tossed stone. When the entity coalesced, it took a human shape, its edges blurred in the smoky air.

Pallid and distorted, its texture that of bleached and watery clay, Olaf's face peered blindly out into the hall. Rage stamped each sodden feature, and a colorless liquid trickled down the porous forehead and welled from the gashed chest.

With infinite slowness, Tomas turned his strangely heavy head to the left, to the right and back again. His neck stiffened and cracked like splintered kindling, and his legs were numb. Was it possible that no one else in Ivar's longhouse saw the ghost? No one pointed; no one shrieked and wailed, although many had cried out during the fight.

Instead they all stared at Tomas, their faces appalled, incredulous or frightened, but the match of his particular brand of terror he saw nowhere. Voices rose and fell, and rose again. Moving with exaggerated calm, a few massive, well-armed men began to make their way towards him.

He looked back at Olaf's ghost, the outlines of which had started to run and the features to dissolve. Like a creature made of melting ice, it stared with furious empty eyes. A violent shudder took it from head to toe, leaving only an attenuated wisp of vapor. Tomas could not tell if the apparition vanished or receded into the corpse's open mouth. Parts of it seemed to do both, until nothing remained in the air but the hearthfire's oily smoke.

Tomas was swaying on his feet but had not taken a step, nor uttered a word, nor let himself collapse when Ivar's guards reached him.

Slumped on a thin pallet of straw in his room at the monastery, Tomas stared out the window. Lavender cloud banks riddled with light filled the rocky square of sky. The setting Sun glanced across a sill of crumbling stone, turning it to cold grey velvet, and illuminating the dust motes that floated in the air along with the resinous scent of peat.

Halfdan, one of Olaf's men acting as plaintiff in the absence of relatives other than Tomas, would come to the monastery in the morning, formally accuse Tomas of manslaying and summon him to appear at Ivar's law court that same day. Ivar's arbitrators would certainly consider Tomas's claim of self-defense--witnesses abounded. But they would also weigh the fact that Olaf's men accused Tomas not only of manslaying, but also of deserting Olaf's raiding party in Waleis seven years ago. And the fact that Tomas had no silver to pay the price of a free man's life, since Alfred's coins had gone down with Hrolf's ship.

Sighing, Tomas reviewed the possibilities again. If the council accepted his self-defense plea, they would declare Olaf's attack "unholy," and his men could legally claim no recompense and no right to blood-feud--though such rulings presented little deterrent to the practice of that popular Norse custom. Should the arbitrators declare for Halfdan, however, even if Tomas could produce the requisite pieces of silver, he might be sentenced to banishment or full outlawry.

Banishment would grant him time to arrange his departure unmolested by Olaf's men, and thereby aim to prevent a vicious and costly blood-feud that could target all the relatives of those involved. A sentence of outlawry, left to the plaintiff to carry out, would forfeit Tomas's property to Halfdan. Such as it was. Tomas glanced at his salt-ravaged satchel and almost smiled.

If he didn't flee Dubhlinn, outlawry would make him fair game, free of judicial reprisals for anyone who slew him. He gave a tiny shrug. What would happen on the morrow would happen.

Olaf.

Lying naked on the straw, Tomas shivered in the chilly air. From crude wooden pegs near the window, his damp green garments hung drying in the feeble breeze. No stains remained on the clothing. He had taken great pains in laundering it; the skin of his fingers was still puckered from long immersion in the washtub. Of all wounds, those to the chest produced the most blood. He had known that.

Olaf would have killed him.

Where would Tomas be now, in that event? And where was Olaf? He might already have arrived at Hel's strand of corpses. He would stalk furiously among them, would strike aside the groping fingers of the dead who hungered to touch the barely rotting flesh of the new arrival. Olaf with Hel, both of them cursing Tomas for his absence.

Ivar's retainers had removed the corpse from the King's longhouse through a hole they knocked in the wall, so that Olaf's violent ghost couldn't find his way back through the door to haunt them. Tomas got up to light a wick stuck in a bowl of congealed tallow, and twilight crept reluctantly from the room.

Once he was back within the monastery walls, released to the custody of Brother Daren, the monk had said, "You acted to preserve your life." Tomas nodded. When Brother Daren asked, his voice gentle, if Tomas might wish to talk about it, he shook his head. At his request they gave him lumpy soap and a washtub. At the monk's order, they had brought Tomas some food and left him alone.

He went to the window to feel of his clothes: damp only in spots now. Leaning against the sill of grainy stone, he stared at the sky until the last streaks of light died away. Then he returned to his pallet and sat hugging his knees.

What had happened to Olaf's ghost, if ghost it were? What else could it have been? The apparition had seemed unaware of its surroundings and incapable of thought: rage incarnate, frozen in time. A demon, a soul, or a vision culled from guilt?

Dearth of answers. Mystery. The worst truth that Tomas had yet perceived.

He'd slaughtered his own brother, granted in self-defense, but slaughtered him, with a cool intuitive skill he'd not possessed before his journey to Faerie. With something like a berserker's Odin-inspired rage, but colder--far colder--he'd performed the very act that had sent him running from berserkers and entwined his Fate with that of the Elves.

The violent favor of his deserted god hadn't fallen upon him. No, that deadly calculating grace must come from the same Elfin transformation that made him see spirits, shun contact with iron, perceive ever more complex truths--and would not let him give voice to a lie.

Closing his eyes, Tomas thought: I have become, at least in part, that which I fled. Where else will these gifts lead me? Likely to Asgard, if I live, but where else within myself?

He did not sleep that night.

CHAPTER THIRTY-THREE: IVAR'S LAW-COURT

Walking from the monastery to the walled section of Dubhlinn, Tomas and Brother Daren trudged along a cow-track thick with mud and potholes, and flies that rose with the heat of the morning. Tomas's head ached. He didn't speak; neither did his companion.

At the beginning of the cursory wood-planked roadway that led into the town and Ivar's hall, a man in Irish dress ran towards them. His gait was steady and he didn't glance about to find his way. A Dubhlinner. Probably.

Scowling, Tomas hurried the monk forward a few paces, into an open area where two narrow streets crossed. A hen startled at their appearance. She squawked and half-flew a few yards away as Brendan sprinted past her, dodged a rotten plank and stopped beside Tomas.

"Have no fear," said the Irishman, panting. "Who did you think I was?"

"I'd no idea. You could have been one of Halfdan's men."

Brother Daren, who had shown no surprise at Brendan's arrival, furrowed his brow and then nodded. "They might try to keep you from the law-court. Who fails to appear, loses."

Continuing towards Ivar's hall, they passed men wheeling strapped and covered cart-baskets up from the waterfront, and women carrying buckets of milk and baskets piled with wet clothing. A lone pig scudded squealing down one street, and ragtag chickens scratched around doorways.

Everyone who crossed Tomas's path eyed him, more openly than surreptitiously. Conversations dwindled at his approach and resumed behind his back. If the Dubhlinners spoke Norse, he caught the same words time and again. Dolphin-rider. Skald. No, berserker. Manslaying. Self-defense. Ivar's law-court.

Still, no one blocked their way. Why was Brendan there? He'd also been in Ivar's hall during the fight on the previous day. The Irishman's manner was friendly, but he didn't explain his presence and after his initial question said nothing more. He seemed to ignore the scraps of Gaelic heard in passing, yet more than once Tomas caught Brendan studying him quizzically.

Brother Daren, gazing blandly at the turfed or staved roofs of Duhblinn, at the merchants' stalls and the wandering livestock and the tinkers, clasped his hands and strolled along as if alone.

Ivar's hall was full to overflowing. The law-court's arbitrators

172

and courtiers. Halfdan's men--a score, perhaps--stood apart in a taciturn little knot. Numerous other folk sought audience on different matters, and a throng of onlookers were in attendance.

On this morning, warmer than the previous day, the fire burned just as high. Despite the oil-lamps sputtering on iron poles thrust into the floor, the hearthfire was needed to see as well as to cook. Tomas could scarcely breathe for the smell of scorching wood and unwashed flesh. Odd, when such an atmosphere had seldom bothered him in Vestfold. Perhaps it had something to do with the amount of iron in Ivar's hall.

A summons: "The skald Tomas Sigtryggson, who is also called the Rhymer."

His real name: Olaf's crew must have given it to them. Standing before the King's chair, Tomas studied Halfdan, lean, tense and balding, who grimly ignored him and stared straight ahead. They both swore to abide by the arbitrators' decision.

"This man," said Halfdan in his role as plaintiff, "murdered his half-brother Olaf Sigtryggson yesterday, and deserted Olaf's raiding party seven years ago. That desertion looms all the larger because Tomas Sigtryggson possesses unusual skill with arms. Anyone who saw the murder will agree."

There were nods; most of the people in the hall had watched Olaf die.

"Indeed," Halfdan continued, leveling his close-set dark eyes at Tomas for the first time, "he acted as might one of Odin's chosen, not in the slaying of his half-brother and comrade-in-arms, but in how that deed was done. We question whether he possessed such skill these seven years past. Odin who gives poetry might grant another of his gifts."

When Olaf had first learned to cast spears with both arms at once, he paraded the feat relentlessly before his younger brothers. Tomas, who had seen perhaps ten winters, could already recite long lays from memory. Yet what did that matter? He could jump higher than any of his brothers to evade a blow to the legs, but just one of Olaf's spears dragged Tomas's arm earthward with such weight that he could cast it scarcely a dozen yards.

Someone cleared his throat. They were waiting for Tomas to speak.

"I acted in self-defense," he said. No more words emerged.

Ivar shifted in his carved seat and gripped its bony arms of walrus-ivory. The monarch's look said plainly: Is that all? And what of the other charge? Explain yourself.

Why did Ivar want Tomas exonerated? The dolphin, most likely. The King must be eager to take that postponed evening meal with Tomas, and to ask why he'd not drowned in the Irish Sea.

Terms from other cases, heard in other law-courts, came back to him. Provocation. Compensation for deaths and injuries. Relative worth of each party involved.

Ivar's stare intensified. Tomas had to speak the truth, or some partial truths.

"I did not provoke Olaf Sigtryggson yesterday," he said slowly. Seven years ago, perhaps, but not yesterday. "I was unarmed. He gave me no warning; he merely attacked, breaking the peace of King Ivar's court." When he stopped to cough, no one spoke. "I left Olaf seven years ago. He had not seen me since, and the...spaciousness and warmth of this hall demand a fire that renders clear sight difficult at times." Now he sounded like Caraid. "And what if Olaf had mistaken me for another?"

Murder and desertion he had now addressed. Dissimulation? "I was not a berserker. Nor am I one now." Careful, careful. "How I came to defend myself as I did, I cannot understand." Cannot comprehend the Elves' transformations, nor how they work in me.

Folding his arms, Tomas waited.

Witnesses verified the statements, then established Olaf's legitimacy and position as oldest son and heir of a Vestfold earl and that Tomas, the child of a slave, was not himself a thrall only because his father had freed him. Further testimony noted that Sigtrygg hadn't legally adopted Tomas, which would have increased his inheritance and decreased that of the legitimate sons. Rank of the two brothers: unequal.

The arbitrators conferred, sent one of their number for a hasty word with Ivar, and conferred again. Once or twice Tomas wiped his forehead with the back of his hand; he felt Halfdan's gaze on him and heard muttering from the crew. He did not look their way and stared at the fire instead, aware of Brendan and Brother Daren standing silently a little to the right.

When the deliberation ended, the expectant crowd grew still.

"Tomas Sigtryggson," intoned the arbitrators' spokesman, "is guilty of manslaying, but in self-defense and with ample provocation."

Black stares from Halfdan's men.

"However," the arbitrator went on, "there remains the price of a hundred and twenty aurar in silver for the life of a free man. In this case, one hundred and seventy-five for an oldest son and legitimate heir."

174

Everyone looked at Tomas. "I have no silver at all," he said quietly.

"Would the plaintiff accept the skald's possessions instead?"

Halfdan refused with a mute shake of his head. His jaw was set, and his gaze hadn't wavered from Tomas.

"Given these circumstances," the spokesman said smoothly, "King Ivar of Dubhlinn will pay the aforementioned price. And deduct it from Tomas Sigtryggson's fee for a previously commissioned poem, to be completed within the week."

Shocked silence at what must be the high price of that poem: Ivar had a reputation for tight-fistedness. Then murmuring rose from all sides.

"Those present have sworn to abide by the arbitrators' decision," the spokesman said in a voice pitched to carry well. The mutters subsided.

As for the other charge, what had passed seven years ago in Waleis occurred beyond the confines of the royal law-court of Dubhlinn who, none of the principals being King Ivar's subjects, declined to rule thereon. The law-speaker pointedly reminded his listeners that no further legal action would occur, since Tomas had received no sentence of banishment or outlawry.

Ivar's bursar paid Halfdan the fine. Case closed.

A few hours before dawn the following morning, Halfdan's men attacked the monastery.

Tomas opened his eyes to the sound of voices shouting in Gaelic. Flames stained the sky beyond his window a lurid greyish-yellow. He heard running feet and more shouts in Gaelic--and in Norse. Halfdan's men.

Fully awake, Tomas scrambled off the pallet and into his clothes. Brother Daren, carrying a wide bowl of burning tallow, burst into the room. The uneven light threw the bony planes of his face into prominence, and his brown eyes glittered in their shadowed eye sockets.

"We had anticipated as much," he said, his tone surprisingly calm. He thrust Tomas's satchel into his arms. "Follow me. Can you see?"

Tomas said that he could. The monk held the bowl aloft, and they hurried across the stone threshold and down a cool dark corridor. Keys clanked at Brother Daren's belt. A left turn and another, then a right. A robed figure ran past them, carrying a tallow lamp and a squarish container draped with cloth.

Three more turns and a door. They rushed down a flight of

175

stairs, at the foot of which Brother Daren gasped and stopped short to avoid colliding with two other monks. One clutched a few cloth-covered plates and the second some decanters of liquid. With some hurried Gaelic words thrown over their shoulders, both pairs of men kept moving in opposite directions.

A large, well-swept, high-ceilinged chamber lined with barrels. Another corridor. Then a room with whitewashed walls and the rich smell of milk: a dairy.

Brother Daren lifted the heavy wooden beam that barred one of its doors, and gently pushed Tomas outside. "Peace be with you, Tomas the Rhymer." The door swung shut; the bolt fell.

Sod beneath his feet. Above his head, stars. And flames, farther down a grassy slope. They came from the main entrance, and not merely from torches.

Within the encircling stone arms of the monastery wall, a man stood waiting some ten yards away.

"Hello, Brendan," Tomas said quietly.

"You've the eyes of a lynx, to see in this murk. Hurry!"

They scaled the rough moss-covered wall and hung by their hands from its grassy top for an instant before leaping down to the opposite side.

"Put these on. Pull the hood over your face and keep your pack hidden. If we meet anyone, say nothing at all. I'll speak for us both."

Struggling into one of the voluminous woolen capes that the Irish favored, Tomas followed Brendan down the hill. Behind them the flames appeared less. By the gate Tomas saw a crowd of men in both Norse and Irish dress. "What will happen at the monastery?" he asked.

Brendan looked too but kept walking. "Hardly anything, since they won't find you there. Ivar will fine them for any damage they've done." He chuckled. "Brother Daren might offer a tour to show them you've gone. Now that I'd like to see."

They trudged through a series of fields, slowed by thick springy grass, clumps of manure and scattered boulders. Tomas made out the huddled forms of drowsing cattle and other livestock. A curious young goat followed them for a few yards and then bounded away, head held high.

"Why are you helping me, Brendan?"

"Cannot speak of that here."

"Where are we going?"

"Not much farther. Shh!"

They jumped a rambling stone wall by a cluster of buildings, some wattle-and-daub and some stone, with turfed or thatched roofs.

Brendan started down a muddy footpath between two houses.

Tomas shook his head and followed. No questions, no answers; at least not yet. Still, he was alive.

The Irishman led him to a round squat stone dwelling with a flourishing garden and a haphazardly thatched roof. Brendan pushed through the garden gate, opened a door without knocking and waved Tomas inside the house.

He ducked through the low doorway ahead of Brendan, to stop by a briskly burning hearth-fire and let his eyes adjust to the change in the light. The house smelled of apples, fresh bread, stewed cabbages and onions.

It also smelled of iron, acrid and penetrating.

"Welcome, Tomas," said a soft voice to his left. A woman's voice, one he recognized. Somehow not surprised, he turned and smiled down at Caraid as she took his cape.

CHAPTER THIRTY-FOUR: A THING ENTIRELY APART

Inordinately pleased to see Caraid again, Tomas was startled when she put her hands on his shoulders and gave him a tentative kiss. He welcomed the caress but refrained from returning it. Such a gesture seemed an inconsequential thing among the Elves, but he was unfamiliar with Irish customs, and the Seer might be married to Brendan. From the way he'd come in without knocking, he knew Caraid well.

"Brendan is my brother," said the Seer, with a trace of a smile. She offered them towels, soap and a basin of water. "You'll both want a wash, I expect. Then we'll dine,"

Brendan was already scrubbing his face and hands. Tomas did likewise, while casting what he hoped were covert glances at Caraid.

Paler than she'd been in Elfland, her expression was warm but her blue eyes were somber, and shadows lurked beneath them. She seemed relatively calm in that her speech and movements were unhurried, but fatigue could produce the same results. Tomas sensed an underlying alertness in the Seer: not anxiety, but a fine-edged awareness of her surroundings. He caught a few looks coming his way as well.

And Brendan was her brother. They had the same face, round as the Moon, the same fresh glowing skin and dun-colored hair. But Caraid's glance was still bemused if no longer vague, her walk trailing and her voice soft, while Brendan's gait and gestures were quick and decided, like his speech, and his eyes were never dreamy.

How old had he been when she was taken to Elfland? He was a few years older than Caraid now. When had she returned from Faerie? Was Rhys nearby—or Moira?

"Are you hungry, Tomas?" Caraid asked. "I was certain you'd both be famished."

"I am," Tomas told her.

Brendan grinned at him. "So am I. I'd no wish to befuddle you out there, but there's no telling who might have been listening. We're closer to the harbor here than you might think. I took you across the common fields on our way, and that got you turned round, I expect."

Sitting at a low table, they tore hunks of bread from a brown-crusted loaf. A substantial meal and a costly one: there were thick slices of salted beef marbled with fat. They drank cold water in mugs whose outside surfaces were beaded with condensation. For nearly half an hour no one spoke. Then Caraid looked up and asked, "Ale?"

"You are a treasure," said Brendan, one hand on his heart, and Tomas nodded.

With their tankards, they settled down on piles of sheepskin and cowhide near the fire and rested in meditative silence for a while.

"You must have many questions, Tomas," Caraid began. She sat cross-legged on the bed of skins between him and Brendan, who lay back with his arms crossed behind his head. Caraid was close enough to Tomas that her abundant hair, floating loose about her shoulders, brushed his arm.

He gazed at the curving stone walls coated with some kind of whitewash. From them and from the wooden beams hung pots, ladles, kitchen knives, garden tools and what must be Brendan's weapons, along with strings of garlic, onions and herbs. Tomas smelled ale and the remnants of supper, musty straw overhead in the thatch, tanned leather and an intriguing whiff of lavender from Caraid's hair. Piercing through all the scents, the rusty tang of iron stung his nostrils.

Tomas glanced down at Brendan sprawled beside his sister. His eyes were closed.

Caraid said, "You may speak freely. I've told Brendan that I was in Faerie and you also, with Moira and Rhys. And what happened there. What they required of you."

Squinting up at Tomas, Brendan said, "I've never seen nor spoken with the Gentry; I've not a particle of the Sight. But I know Caraid does. And yourself." He yawned, sat up to drink some ale, then stretched out and closed his eyes again.

Not a particle of the Sight. Tomas stared at him enviously. Sighing, he rubbed the bridge of his itching nose. "What did they require of you?" he asked Caraid, not looking at her.

"What do you mean?"

"Moira said that you advised her where in Wessex to bring me." He had not said her name for some time, not even to Linley.

Caraid rested a hand on Tomas's arm; he turned towards her. Her brows were drawn together with concern. "Yes, I did."

"What else did you tell her?" The question sounded rougher than he intended. He cast a swift glance past Caraid to her brother, but Brendan didn't move.

"Ah," said Caraid, comprehension in her eyes. "You would know my part in this deed they assigned you." She thought for a moment. "They called upon me as a Seer. Called greatly, for all that my gift knows fewer bounds when I am in Faerie. They sought to learn when and where the Fates might next weave awry, and a mortal's thread could work free."

"And you knew that? Where my brother's ship would come ashore, and on what day?"

"I did not." Weariness showed in the set of her mouth. "Nothing so precise. There are far more times and places where the Fates might weave awry than I would have guessed before that Seeing." Her voice sank to a whisper. "I had to name them all."

Tomas gripped her shoulders, pulling her around to face him. "Did you name the man whom Moira could call?"

Brendan sat up, his expression darkening, but Caraid looked at him and shook her head. "Do you think I could see whose thread might drift loose from the Fates?" she asked Tomas. "Do you think They Themselves see that?"

"I can answer in riddles now too, Caraid. Moira gave me gifts of my own." Her eyes betrayed no comprehension. Tomas felt his jaw tightening. "Don't take me for a fool. I don't believe you can lie any more than I can. Did you name me to Moira, yes or no?"

"No! I named no one!" White to the lips, Caraid stared at Tomas. Brendan glanced back and forth between them, shrugged, then got up and went to the table.

Tomas's hands fell to his sides. She spoke truth; the air rang with it. "I beg your pardon, Caraid. After all the kindness you and Brendan have shown me, I'm behaving like an ingrate."

"She warned me you might not be right in the head for some time," Brendan said helpfully, returning with three brimming tankards.

Caraid scowled at him, then turned a distraught face to Tomas. "You needn't apologize. But what do you mean, you don't believe that I can lie any more than you can? What gifts did Moira give you?"

As succinctly as possible, Tomas described them.

Brendan said, "Jesus, Mary and Joseph. I'd not be right in the head myself."

"Little wonder you thought I twisted my words to mislead you. 'Truly speak and prophesy'..." muttered Caraid after her first shocked silence.

"Is that not the Sight?" asked Tomas. She hadn't known what had befallen him, but she might understand it better than he did.

"Prophecy, yes; although the Sight has other aspects. Many others. But not true speech. That's a thing entirely apart."

"And you don't possess it."

"I do not. But Tomas, you must believe I speak the truth when I say I did not name you to Moira."

"I believe you," he said softly.

She gave him a tenuous smile. "I told them where a thread might work loose from the loom. And the most auspicious part of Midgard for the journey to Uppsala to begin. Was I not right?"

180

Tomas glanced at his satchel and thought of Linley. "I don't know how to answer. I made a friend. And met the King of Wessex, and earned his good will and the price of the voyage. My friend got his wish to see Elfland, but his peace of mind may have-- And the ship sank. There was a draug."

Caraid and Brendan stared at him, their eyes round and dark in the firelight. He decided not to tell them how the draug had spoken with him and the traders. Then his gaze fell on his hands; he shoved them under the hem of his shirt. "And I killed my half-brother."

Brendan looked relieved at the mention of something he could understand. "Trouble yourself no more about that. I saw it all. He would have killed you."

"Brendan told me how a dolphin brought a Norse skald into the harbor, and I knew it was you," Caraid said after a moment.

Remembering something, Tomas turned curiously towards her. "Did you guess I would be here now, Caraid? In Elfland you said you would see me again."

"When, I did not know. Where..." Caraid's face appeared to have more color, though he couldn't be certain for the dim light. She wouldn't meet his eyes. "I knew you would come to Dubhlinn."

A mystery. He decided not to probe, not yet. Instead he asked, "Do you know why Moira didn't take me straight to Uppsala?"

Caraid flashed him a startled glance. "Because of the Norse Elves, I suppose."

"I don't understand."

"The Elves have factions, Tomas."

"Like Irish chieftains," Brendan put in, settling back on the hides and closing his eyes again. He sounded resigned.

Caraid grinned. "Well said. I don't understand it all myself, but Moira would have to cross the Norse Elves' territory to bring you to Uppsala. The power of all the Elves is waning, as that of Odin and the Christ increases. Yet I'd wager that the fortunes of the Norse Elves are more tied to Asgard than are those of the Celtic Elves."

"So if I were taken through Norse Alfheim, they might warn Odin?"

"Perhaps." Caraid made a helpless gesture. "But I do not claim to comprehend the Elves, Tomas. That's more than mortal minds can do."

Tomas made a sound halfway between a laugh and a sigh, and put his face in his hands. When he lifted his head, Caraid was studying him, but she quickly averted her gaze.

Since his explanation of Moira's gifts, he'd sensed a certain ambiguity in Caraid's attitude, neither the easy courtesy one accords an equal, nor the deference granted a superior. She treated him as if he were--what had she called "true speech"?

A thing entirely apart.

No, not that. He was not that. She could not think him that, when she was the one person who could understand, even better than Linley, what had happened to Tomas.

But just then the delicate tissue lining his nostrils gave a painful twinge of protest at the iron-taint in the air. And Caraid said carefully, not looking at him, "You yourself could perhaps comprehend the Elves better than I, at this pass."

All his muscles went rigid, but his bones felt made of porridge. Wrapping his arms about his knees, Tomas stared into the hearthfire. From the corner of his eye he saw Caraid's glance at her brother.

With a remark about Kate lying awake, Brendan got up to take his leave of them, and waved away Tomas's thanks for his help. Caraid gave her brother a prolonged hug as the two of them stood in the doorway. After a brief low-voiced conversation in Gaelic, Brendan stepped out into the night and shut the door behind him.

CHAPTER THIRTY-FIVE: QUESTIONS AND ANSWERS

Caraid bolted the door. "Kate is Brendan's wife," she told Tomas when she settled beside him again.

Her sleeve touched his. Through the drift of her long hair and the fabric of their clothing, he felt the warmth of her arm. The firelight deepened her patient blue eyes almost to lilac. She gave him a faint smile and looked away, lips parted, her earlier tension gone. The pressure of her arm increased, slightly yet unmistakably.

Moira's ivory face rose in his mind, with another image: Rhys's elegant, narrow hands entwined in Caraid's mass of springy hair.

"Did Moira's gifts change me into an Elf? Is that what you meant?" Tomas asked in Welsh, and his voice sounded flat in his ears. They had been speaking Norse before Brendan left, but Caraid's Welsh was better than her Norse.

A long pause. Her face withdrew a little. "Why do you think they may have changed you?" she asked, also in Welsh.

He sighed. Always, she went round in circles. "I cannot touch my bare skin to iron without pain now, for one. And Elves have true speech--not that they don't lie in other ways. As we've both had occasion to learn."

Caraid said nothing and did not move her arm away from his.

"I don't know how Sighted I was, before she found me." He didn't care to say Moira's name aloud just then. "But now I can see Elves and spirits. Sometimes I sense the thoughts or feelings of the folk near me."

The Seer glanced at him and almost spoke, but Tomas went on, needing to talk, the words tumbling out. "Sometimes I touch an object and feel its past, Caraid, or even see it. I've had visions of possible futures. And different layers of truth."

He'd not realized that before, but as he said it, he knew it was so. Of course it was; he had true speech. Using the arm that didn't touch Caraid, he pushed another log onto the fire. "Layers and visions and everything besides are growing more complex. And happening more often, and I have less control of them."

"How do you know you have less control?"

Tomas considered. "I suppose I don't know, at that. I've not really tried to master it."

The Seer was nodding. "In that, I can offer you some instruction."

"I'd be grateful for it."

"But I cannot promise you that you can learn."

He closed his eyes in exasperation. Caraid shifted position; her shin touched his through his trousers. Something about the contact felt different. Opening his eyes, Tomas saw that she'd hiked her skirt up to her knees, and her warm bare calf lay against his leg. Hers was firm, rounded and covered with tiny freckles. His breath caught in his throat.

"I'll learn," he said after a moment. "I must. Do you think I was turned into an Elf?"

Measuring her words, Caraid said, "The gifts have transformed your Sight. But I do not believe she could alter your essence, and you are mortal."

At last a straight answer. Did he agree? "But she altered my Fate," he pointed out. "And the gods themselves are subject to Fate. Even Odin."

"Did she alter it? Might your thread not have worked free regardless?"

Mulling that over, Tomas shook his head. "I don't understand the difference between Fate and essence."

For an instant Caraid stared at him. "Who does? Not the Fair Folk, not the gods, and not the Fates themselves."

Shrugging, he glanced away, down at his legs. Their legs; her calf still rested on his shin. He looked at the fire instead. "Very well," he said. "But why the gifts? Why the Sight and the iron-sick?"

And the way Olaf had died.

"The dolphin--" began Tomas, stopping at the memory of the draug's thin lunatic cackling.

Caraid rubbed her temples and slumped a little. The pressure of her arm on his increased. "As regards true speech and prophecy and the iron-sick, Tomas, I don't know. The Elves do nothing without a reason. Many reasons, but their reasons are not ours. They have eternity to spin out their motives and feel their way, all the twists and turns." She bit her lip, and Tomas feared she would begin rocking back and forth as she had in Faerie, but she merely sighed. "Now that I have met Rhys and--experienced something of the Elves... Mortals simply cannot know them, ever, for we do not live at the same--we are too different in almost every way. I do not believe, now, that I would care to be immortal."

For a time Caraid was silent, her face pensive, staring at the fire. Then she said, "Moira might have believed your errand would be sped by her gifts and by the waxing of your Sight, or even by the iron-sick. But I couldn't say how or why." She gave Tomas a searching look. When he met her eyes, she asked gently, "Your brother's death is what most disturbs you just now. Is it not?"

He nodded tightly.

"Brendan told me about it. He is right, Tomas: Olaf would have killed you." Her eyes were sober and compassionate, and not repelled.

Tomas drew a breath. "You heard how he died, then."

"Yes," she said, with no alteration of her expression.

"Caraid—" He swallowed and glanced aside. The need to talk about it was so great. "Before I went to Elfland, I'd killed a calf once. I was forced to, when I'd seen about eleven winters. Then I got beaten for disappearing at slaughtertime, until I was too big to hit." He studied his hands; he'd never discussed that with anyone. "When Olaf raided that village seven years ago, I deserted. Once my stomach quit heaving."

The Seer waited.

"How did I turn into someone who could murder a berserker with his own axe? Without even thinking; my body seemed to move by itself. It felt different. It still does. I've no wish to kill again, but I'm sure that I could."

He had said it, which was relief of a kind. But how would Caraid react?

Her face showed no revulsion. "I'm sure you could as well. As sure as I am that you've no wish to. Tomas, here again your gifts have changed, or your skills, if you prefer. But not your nature."

Hoping she was right, he nodded.

Caraid said slowly, "As a race, Elves are generally stronger and more agile than mortals. Their physical consciousness is different." She glanced aside. "So are their senses. Think of the iron-sick."

"Do you mean it might have come with some other physical changes?"

It was Caraid's turn to nod.

"And increased Sight, and true speech and prophecy," Tomas muttered. "Gods." And what else?

"As for the dolphin, perhaps they sent him and perhaps not," said Caraid. "Did you notice the dolphins in the Elvish Sea?"

"Yes. But they've aided sailors in Midgard before."

The Seer looked thoughtful. "Among our Irish horses, some are pookas, and few mortals can tell the difference."

"Pookas!" said Tomas. "The dolphin wasn't Aubrey, if that's what you mean." He told Caraid how the pooka had trailed him to the Saxons' camp and brought Linley to Chippenham. Listening, the Seer began to giggle, until Tomas found himself laughing too.

"That does me good," she said. "What a plague Aubrey can be!"

185

She leaned comfortably against Tomas's shoulder.

As he closed his eyes, his inner Sight opened of its own volition. First he caught a glimpse of his brother's gleaming axe-blade as it fell, and the draug's tattered half-boat skimming across a dark and angry sea. He saw himself in the prison stall at Chippenham, and watched the forest floor of Elfland shudder at Hel's approach.

Somehow he blocked the sight of Moira. Like the woman whose head now rested on his shoulder, he was mortal, and still alive-- though transformed and compelled.

Was Caraid also transformed and compelled? So much remained to ask. When Tomas opened his eyes, Caraid's face, round and lush, was tilted confidingly towards his. "Did Rhys give you gifts?" he inquired after a moment, fearing that the question might distress her.

"Nary a one," she said calmly. "Unless you count returning me to Dubhlinn."

"And have you changed since you were in Faerie?"

She sighed. "Of course. What mortal would not change? My Sight has deepened in many ways, some that I understand, others that puzzle me, and some I expect I have yet to discover."

"Their food. Are you still--"

"Bewildered? No. No more than you." Her voice grew softer. "Nor prevented from speaking with you as I wish, Tomas. All that passed once I departed."

"When did you leave?"

A tiny laugh. "After you did. 'When' means nothing there."

"Would you have warned me if we'd had more time to talk?"

Caraid's eyes darkened. "Yes. Though I doubt it would have done any good."

"Then why warn me?"

"We are both mortals who..." From the curtain of dun-colored hair that draped her shoulders, she took a long curling lock and began to twist it with one hand. "Once you were in Elfland, I saw us--" Her mouth looked full and soft in the firelight, and Tomas thought he saw her lower lip tremble for an instant. "No one warned me," she said at last, very low.

"'About?'" he prompted, putting both arms around her. He'd intended to wait a while before doing that, had intended to wait as long as he could.

She stopped tugging at her hair. "About the Sidhe compelling my Sight while I was there. About the time lost from this world." She gazed fixedly before her. "Or about Rhys."

That, Tomas understood. But he said only, "You must have lost more time than my seven years."

"Eleven." Caraid's voice was harsh and level. "Brendan was still a boy when I was taken. I scarcely recognized him when I came back. But he knew me; I hadn't changed at all." She smiled, but her eyes looked pained. "Kate didn't know me from before. We had the devil's own time convincing her I was really Brendan's mad sister. The famous disappearing Seer, back from wherever I'd been spirited off to by the Gentry."

A long silence. Caraid's lavender scent almost banished the stink of iron in the room. Tomas rested his face against her fragrant hair; it was heavy and warm and rather coarse. When a few moments had passed, she trailed an exceedingly gentle hand from his throat down to his breastbone where his jerkin lay open.

One more question. "You just said, 'Once you were in Elfland, I saw us--' Was 'us' you and I, Caraid?"

She gave him an almost imperceptible nod. Her thumb began a tentative stroking motion of the bare skin of his chest.

Two more questions, then. "What did you see?" Lifting her chin with one hand, he kissed her lightly on the mouth.

"This." Her expression serious, she looked him straight in the eye. "We were here, under this roof." She touched her fingers to Tomas's lips and said hesitantly, "You were making love to me."

After a startled second, Tomas drew her onto his lap. He cradled her delicate face in his hands for a series of prolonged and unhurried kisses, which gradually built in intensity as her mouth opened under his. Before very long she reached beneath his shirt; her small, slightly calloused palms caressed the length of his spine.

Easing Caraid's shift from her freckled shoulders, Tomas kissed them, and the hollows at her collarbone, and her throat. Her eyes closed, Caraid tilted her head back as his mouth moved slowly down to her breasts. At a taken breath that sounded like a sob, he stopped, concerned, but she gently pulled him back onto the pile of skins.

This time, Tomas could not banish from his inner Sight one fleeting image of Moira's porcelain face, grey eyes wide and dark and glittering with self-containment.

CHAPTER THIRTY-SIX: SOME INSTRUCTION

The deep burring rumble of bees floated to Tomas's ears. A weight lay half on his stomach and half on his chest. A light weight, soft for the most part, with a few nubbly spots and an occasional pinprick.

Bees... He remembered a garden outside a round house of stone. Had there been a hive? Did Caraid keep bees? Caraid. Tomas started awake.

Two half-closed, pale green eyes, black pupils slitted in the morning light that spilled through the open door, regarded him contentedly from inches away. Tomas blinked at the black cat that purred on his torso, then lifted his hand and scratched the little animal behind the ears. The left one was crumpled, folded forward. The cat kneaded Tomas's bare skin with its front paws, claws sheathed, and purred more loudly.

"What's your name, friend?" he asked, almost expecting it to answer. Raising himself on one elbow without dislodging the cat, he looked around. He was alone. A sheepskin half-covered him; a tangled, dark green knot of clothing lay nearby. Caraid had placed the remnants of last night's bread, a pitcher and a mug by his left shoulder. At the sight his parched mouth felt drier than ever.

Settling the drowsy cat beside him with an apologetic pat, Tomas sat up, drank some cold water and munched the bread. It had kept surprisingly well. Feeling that his every act wedged him more deeply into the life of this house, he found a basin, used the rest of the pitcher's contents to wash, and hurried into his clothes. Then he sat at the low table and propped his chin in his hands. The wood was comfortingly solid against his elbows.

Caraid must be in the garden. Tomas studied the utensils hanging from the rafters and the walls. Despite the fresh air from the open door, the tang of iron was stronger than it was last night. His nose stung. The twinges would probably lessen if he went outside. But that meant greeting Caraid, embracing her, coming back indoors...

She was far more kind than he'd imagined or felt he deserved, infinitely responsive--and vulnerable to an aching degree. Not just in contrast with Moira's profound reserve, Caraid's innate vulnerability was compounded, Tomas sensed, by her recent encounter with Rhys. And she knew that Tomas couldn't stay. They both knew.

Damn the Elves.

He should leave, now, while he still could. Go down to the harbor, down to the ships, and barter for passage to Uppland.

Barter with what? He owned the clothes on his back, a harp, a flute and their cases, a satchel, a stone knife, and one seal of safe conduct from the King of Wessex, whose disputed realm lay beyond the Irish Sea.

But King Ivar of Dubhlinn had commissioned a poem from Tomas, to be completed within the week. He would write and recite it, collect his fee and buy passage to Uppland.

In the meantime, he would listen to Caraid's instructions and hope they would help him better tolerate the augmentation of his Sight. And trust that Halfdan's men would be brought to account for their attempt on the monastery and cause no further trouble. And try to leave Dubhlinn without--

Caraid came in, her arms overflowing with flowers and cuttings from her garden, and glanced around the cool dim house with its walls of pallid stone. In her eyes, he detected a trace of disappointment that she tried to conceal when she saw him at the table. Evidently she wished that he had followed her outside.

He should have; he could have given her that. Tomas got up quickly and went to her. Without a word, Caraid tossed the greenery aside and kissed him. His resolve fled at the touch, but his misgivings remained. Her mouth had a faint dry undertaste of despair.

Holding the Seer, Tomas murmured her name, smoothed her hair. He would try to leave Dubhlinn without hurting Caraid any more than was inevitable.

She spoke words she might have better left unsaid; Tomas feared she would regret them. Unable to make an answer that would not wound her, he made none--not in words.

"Decocted elder blossoms are a tonic for the skin," Caraid said, arranging herbs and flowers in little heaps upon the table. She slapped the plants down on each pile with rather more force than was necessary. She didn't look at him.

Tomas sorted cuttings and kept up a gentle stream of questions, any question that came to mind.

"To be sure, they think I'm the local witch," she told him. "The village wise woman. The whole town comes here for unguents and potions. And begs me to tell fortunes, not that they listen when I say I can't with any certainty. Careful, those are stinging nettles. Slice off the tips."

Tomas shook his head at the knife she offered him; the iron set his teeth on edge. He found a sharp wooden cleaver instead. Caraid looked at the knife, slowly turned it over in her hands, then carried it outside.

She came back with a fresh armload of plants. "Chamomile, for infusions against stomach ills. Sage, to bathe sore muscles and ease breathing," she explained, when Tomas fingered a couple of stalks and raised his eyebrows. They worked in silence for several minutes.

"And I'm called on to remove curses, and reason with ghosts and boggarts if the priests have failed. Or if a priest won't do to begin with," said Caraid, returning to an earlier topic. From a tin coffer near the door, she fetched several squares of coarse-grained cloth and some twine. She indicated to Tomas which plants to set on the cloth, and which to gather and knot at the stalks for hanging in bundles to dry. "Now that rumor has it that I've been off with the Fair Folk, I'll no doubt be consulted on more matters touching them."

He glanced up; her expression was composed. It seemed as good an opening as any. "I'll consult you too, since you offered me instruction," he said lightly.

After a minute she said, "First, mind where you speak of them. It's believed that conversations in the open may be carried to their ears by the winds. Or by spirits, the air Elementals."

"Is that true?" Tomas asked.

Caraid jerked her shoulders. Her mouth was set. "I don't know. Indoor speech could reach their ears as well. It all depends on who's listening."

"Then they might hear us now?"

"It's not impossible." The Seer turned her face away. "She doubtless bends her thoughts upon you now and again, and we cannot tell how far they reach. But there's no spying house-Elf here; we both would see it."

Tomas had been eyeing the open door, ready to suggest that they sit in the garden. He decided not to propose it just yet.

"Your friend Linley warned you about iron," Caraid went on. Last night Tomas had told her about Linley. Told her, with immense relief at her unflagging comprehension, virtually everything that had happened between when Caraid last saw Tomas in Elfland and his arrival here with Brendan.

"You would learn to control the Sight..." Frowning, Caraid studied the table, still littered with scraps of green. A fresh, succulent, faintly medicinal smell permeated the house. Tomas helped her tie the last of the bundles to a wooden beam. She swept the floor with nervous efficient swipes of a broom whose bristles Tomas recognized; they had just hung some of the fresh plant to dry.

Noticing his glances from the broom to the rafters, Caraid smiled for the first time in hours. She wiped the table and motioned him to sit. "Well." Her tone was brisk. "Spells there are to call forth the Sight. You've no wish for those, I believe."

He shook his head, grimacing.

"Some do," she said dryly. "Both wish and need. But yours is rather to restrict it. You cannot banish the Sight once and for all, nor dismiss it at will," she added, anticipating his next question.

"Can I learn not to be so overwhelmed by it that I lose awareness of this world?"

Caraid's face softened with empathy. "Sometimes. But not always, I fear."

He had suspected as much; still, disappointment settled in his stomach like a hunk of gritty bread. The iron-stink in the air seemed stronger. "Even sometimes would be a help," he said at last.

She tilted her head. "What I do--and I don't know if it will prove useful for you--well, one sense can impair another. When I want to enfeeble my Sight, I give my body other messages. To distract it."

When Tomas said nothing, she rumpled her hair. "I might weed the garden, or just go out to take the air." She looked around the room as if for inspiration. "Or prick myself just the slightest bit with a knife--oh. You shouldn't."

"It might distract me, at that," he said quietly. "This is helpful, Caraid. What else would you suggest?"

"Sometimes it helps not to resist the Sight." One corner of her mouth jerked. "To embrace the vision can help it leave you more quickly. Or when you sense the presence of a creature, ask what it wants, rather than ignore it."

Had Caraid asked what Rhys wanted? If Tomas had asked Moira, and insisted on answers--either on the riverbank or in Elfland-- would it have made any difference? "That I can do," he said. "And have done. I'd rather hear more about resisting."

The cat, who was dozing under the table, chose that moment to leap into Caraid's lap and nudge her hand. Smiling, she stroked his glossy black fur. The cat lifted his chin, half-closed his eyes and started purring.

"Then try anything to help anchor you in the here and now. I can always pet Finian here. Concentrate on what those around you are doing; resolve to see and hear only what they see and hear." The cat butted her hand again, until she transferred the caress to his head and behind his ears. "Unless those around you are cats. They may see more than we do. Yesterday before you and Brendan arrived, Finian acted the

191

way he does when the Moon is full. He yowled until I let him out, then lurked in the tree by the gate all evening. I couldn't coax him in till this morning. Perhaps he knew you were on your way here."

Tomas reached out a hand to stroke Finian too. At the extra attention the cat rolled onto his back, hooked one paw over his nose and favored Tomas and Caraid with a blissful green-eyed stare. A pigeon-like trill crept into his purr. "Would he know if any Elves were going to appear?" Tomas asked.

"I believe not. I think he can tell when something important's afoot, but I'm not sure he knows what it is. Nor can he explain it to me." Then Caraid's eyes widened, and her pupils dilated to an unnatural size. "Why? Do you sense any coming?"

"No, Caraid," said Tomas gently, touching her hair. "I was just asking."

There was a delicate pause. Caraid stopped petting Finian and grew very still, staring steadily before her. The cat mewed once, then made a dignified passage into Tomas's lap and began taking an elaborate bath, bracing himself with a paw against Tomas's stomach. He loosened Finian's claws. The cat shifted position, overbalanced and slid from Tomas's knees onto the floor.

He and Caraid laughed; the cat flattened his ears and stalked off into the garden. Tomas picked up his satchel, brushed Caraid's hair with his lips, and followed Finian.

An hour before sunset, his flute cradled in his lap, Tomas sat cross-legged on a stone bench by the garden gate. He had just finished polishing his song for Ivar and was lazily enjoying the fresh air.

A filthy barefooted boy about nine years old drove a dozen still more filthy cows along the path towards Tomas, using a long crooked stick to hit stragglers on their swollen udders. Carrying two mugs, Caraid emerged from the house. She gave one to Tomas and seated herself next to him. He sipped; it was water. He thanked her and drank half of it.

"You seem more at ease outside," she observed.

"Fewer tools," he said elliptically, just as the cowherd passed them. Staring curiously at Tomas, the boy exchanged greetings with Caraid.

Tomas and the Seer lapsed into a companionable silence. The air turned crisp, tinted indigo and mauve. Shadows lengthened until a chill crept across the stone beneath them. Settled at their feet with his small black paws neatly folded, Finian eyed the birds that flew calling overhead. Tomas stowed his flute away against the damp.

"You and I, Tomas," Caraid began, "have lived through similar events. We are both Sighted, and share a knowledge..." She scuffed at the grass with the toe of one shoe.

Tomas waited, but she seemed to have finished. After a while he nodded. It was probably best to let it go at that. He put an arm around her.

"You wish to ask me something," she said a bit later.

It was almost dark now; he couldn't see her expression clearly. "Can you tell me how my errand will end?" he asked carefully.

"No," she said, shaking her head. "Before today I tried, and again all afternoon. I cannot see the end."

"Could you see anything?"

"From Dubhlinn harbor, you will sail for Uppland," Caraid interrupted in a brittle voice. "And dock at a place called Birka." There was an inquiring lift of her chin.

"Birka is a major port, on an island in Lake Malar," he said. "Uppsala's on the mainland just to the north."

"I know where it is. You will go from Birka to Uppsala. To the temple grounds." She shuddered. "The sacred grove, the trees... It turns black then, Tomas. I cannot see beyond the grove."

"Could that mean--"

"I don't know what it means!" she cried.

"All right," he said quietly, holding her. "All right."

They both knew he had to leave, and why. Tomas made a resolute attempt to talk about it, and about Caraid's desire for him to stay--and his own desire. But she declined to discuss it. Not in words.

CHAPTER THIRTY-SEVEN: THE FAHEYS' BIT OF WOOD

The following morning, Brendan arrived early to guide Tomas to Ivar's court. Caraid and Tomas, half-dressed and yawning, had not yet broken their fast. The Seer gave her brother a sleepy hug and, still tugging at her shift, trailed outside with a bucket. She left Tomas in a state of elaborate calm. How would Brendan react?

Seating himself opposite Tomas at the low table, Brendan put down the flour-dusted round of bread he had brought. "I believe she'd do well to take up with a Norseman. Life in Dubhlinn is easier for your kind these days," he said gravely. He tore the loaf into thirds. "You've spent time with the Gentry, so you'd not heed any blather about witchcraft and such. Nor let it get out of hand. The way you handled yourself the other day..." He gave Tomas an approving look. "She'd be far safer. And you're in Ivar's favor as well." His tone was cordial. "Might you be planning to stay?"

"I can't." Tomas's voice was very low. He met Brendan's gaze squarely and added, "I wish that I could."

Disappointment clouded the Irishman's frank blue eyes. "Ah, well," he said. "If you can't, you can't, and you'd have your reasons." He chewed and swallowed a bite of bread. "Thinking of coming back, were you?"

"That would please me, Brendan. But I don't know yet whether I can."

Brendan gestured vaguely towards the door. "Does she know?"

Know what? That Tomas couldn't remain, that he had no idea if he'd return, that he would like to? He said merely, "Yes."

Seeming satisfied with that reply, Brendan nodded once, then turned his attention to breakfast. Tomas had no appetite. But when Caraid appeared with a bucketful of fresh milk, he accepted a mug and a small portion of bread.

Caraid walked Brendan and Tomas to the gate, where she hugged them both. For a moment her head lay on Tomas's shoulder; she gave him a fleeting kiss. She said nothing. Neither did Tomas. Her eyes were wide, not quite focused and refused to meet his, but not, he suspected, because of her Sight.

A steady rain had fallen the previous night. On their way to the Norse part of town, Brendan and Tomas crossed fields whose grass shone sleek and dark with moisture. Every low stone wall seemed on the verge of crumbling into streaky powder from the damp. For the most part they walked in silence, though now and again Brendan whistled to himself, always the same air. Once he grabbed Tomas's arm and said, "Not through there. A bull stands in that pasture."

Finally Brendan halted at the tree-lined edge of a field. "It's shorter if we pass through the Faheys' bit of wood here." The faintest of frowns creased his forehead, and he shifted from foot to foot.

"I've no objection," said Tomas, raising his eyebrows.

With a resolute air, Brendan stepped between the towering trees, and Tomas followed. The forest was dark, still and rather cool, smelling fresh and mossy after the rain. The trees were old and boasted considerable girth. Overhead, their branches intertwined stout arms and twiggy fingers, and no footprints disturbed the leaf mold that carpeted the underwood. Not a path in common use, then. Why not, when it was so pleasant in this moist green world? Stretching some knots from his arms and shoulders, Tomas drew deep breaths of ferny air into his lungs.

Soon they descended a gentle stony slope and came to a noisy rill of water, where Brendan stopped short. A slender yellow-haired man sat cross-legged on the opposite bank, watching them.

Or watching Tomas. To Brendan he paid no attention at all, although at the sight of the stranger, Brendan had removed his cap and backed away a few paces. He muttered something unintelligible and threw Tomas a look full of alarm.

The fair-haired man's eyes were slanted, green, and half-closed with concentration. His face was long and pale; he wore clothing of dark, finely-woven cloth, and the graceful hands that rested in his lap bore six fingers each. An Elf, beyond a doubt.

He beckoned to Tomas. "Come, cross the stream and converse with me a while. Your companion will wait." His voice held no trace of warmth, but it was pleasant and clear, and very soft.

Brendan was already edging several yards back down the path they'd just walked. Feeling cautious rather than frightened, Tomas remembered what had almost befallen Linley in the river. "Move away from the water before I cross," he suggested courteously.

The Elf blinked at him, then laughed, tipping his head back until golden hair spilled past his shoulders. "Ah, no," he said. "I am not one of *those*, young man, though I am of the Sidhe." His teeth gleamed. "But I shall do as you request." He stood; he was taller than Tomas would have guessed. With a deep bow whose politeness bordered on mockery, he retreated two or three yards from the bank.

Tomas jumped the rill and, his breath coming faster, approached the Elf. While not so big as Aubrey, he was still freakishly tall, and Tomas was obliged to look up to meet the haughty green eyes. "What do you want?" he asked warily.

"I?" The Elf's gaze slid aside and then back to Tomas, reminding him with piercing suddenness of Moira. "Innumerable things. Few that you are like to give me, I fear. Yet I have something for you."

"And what might that be?" asked Tomas, mimicking the other's tone.

"Why, merely two small tokens that you let fall into the Sea. And a message, or a warning, if you will. My kindred across the water bid you hurry, Fool." He disappeared without fanfare; he simply was no longer there. Where the Elf had stood, the leaf mold bore no impression. But where his feet had been lay a faded sprig of mistletoe and an apple blossom, crumpled but still almost fresh. Tomas stared at the plants for a long time.

He had just finished tucking them into his satchel when Brendan, ashen and sweating, came up to him. "You always hear tell that the Gentry frequent this stretch of Faheys' wood," Brendan said in an awed voice.

"You might have said so before," Tomas observed mildly. It hardly mattered now.

Brendan goggled at him. "Why, I thought you knew. And Himself there seemed to know you. The first one I ever saw, and the last, I hope." He stopped; color flooded his face. "But yóu, are you all right?"

Tomas said he believed so, and they continued on their way to Ivar's court.

CHAPTER THIRTY-EIGHT: A SONG FOR KING IVAR OF DUBHLINN

Ivar could not receive Tomas before dusk. At the close of a day spent rambling through Dubhlinn with Brendan, Tomas was hungry. They'd strolled through alleys and visited tanners, goldsmiths, a shipwright and an alehouse or two. Brendan went by himself to a smithy. At a comb-maker's shop, Tomas lingered over amber-work nearly the shade of Caraid's hair, but decided that the contrasting color of jet suited her better.

"If you're minded to buy it, go ahead," Brendan said patiently.

"I've no coins till tonight," Tomas reminded him. He put down the black comb he'd been holding, which was finely carved with a leafy design.

"Then I'll buy it. You can pay me this evening."

Thanking Brendan, Tomas had stowed the comb in his shirt. It was almost dark by then, and they made their way to court.

The King of Dubhlinn dined that night upon a leg of roast mutton, boiled leeks and close-grained wheaten bread. The plates were hammered brass and smoothest soapstone. They sipped wine from cups of fragile Rhenish glass tinted a rich blue, and the board was spread with a boldly colored cloth. Servants hovered just out of earshot, keeping an anticipatory watch upon the diners' needs.

The opulence didn't awe Tomas, who was accustomed to a similar court. Still, seated on a carved wooden bench opposite Ivar, he wished silently for different clothes: perhaps a gold-embroidered tunic of pale linen such as the ones that Ivar's courtiers favored, and new boots of supple leather. His own dark green garments, although relatively clean, were roughened and stained from the sea.

He ate and drank sparingly and in silence. Ivar, after a formal greeting and an inquiry about Tomas's health, spoke very little until the meal was done. Then, over a bowl of nuts, apples and cranberries, the King remarked, "Halfdan paid a fine over the fracas in the monastery and made sail for Vestfold."

"I am content to hear it."

"But not so content as you will be to make sail yourself."

Tomas looked up quickly. Ivar wasn't smiling, but his eyes were less remote than was their wont. "Yes, my lord." How best to restate this? "I must thank you again for your assumption of my own fine."

"I wished to have further speech with you and to hear you sing," said Ivar calmly.

197

And that was the whole of it: Ivar made no reference to Olaf at all.

The King signalled his retainers; a young woman hurried over to pour from a flask, then hastily retreated. "Before you recite, I would pose a few more questions about this dolphin."

Tomas bade him ask whatever he wished, though they both knew that Ivar would do so regardless. The King drank deeply of the wine. From the country of the Franks, it was rich and dry. His hooded eyes held a brooding look, as one immured in his own thoughts, and he toyed with a heavy ring upon his finger.

"Did you do aught to call the dolphin to you?" His voice was mild, a trifle careless, as though the answer mattered little to him.

Tomas suspected otherwise. "No, my lord."

"Nothing whatever?"

"Nothing at all."

Silence. Tomas drained his glass, then shook his head and smiled at the silent woman who offered him more wine.

"Leave the flask on the table," murmured Ivar. He asked Tomas, "Know you any reason why the dolphin might have approached you alone among your shipmates?"

None he knew for certain. Perhaps because the Elves had wrought changes in him. For all he could tell, Moira herself might have dispatched the beast across the Irish Sea. "I must reflect on that," he said. "I think that I alone was still alive when the dolphin came."

Cold blue eyes bore into his. "You are quite certain?"

"I believe I was the last man afloat by the wreckage. I'd drifted and not seen anyone for some time, my lord."

"Yet sailors seldom see one solitary dolphin."

"True. I cannot remember having encountered one by itself before."

Ivar considered him. "If ill fortune were to send you another shipwreck, do you think that a dolphin might appear a second time?"

Tomas shook his head as politely as he could. "I do not know."

"Nor do I. Yet I would wager that such a beast is more like to assist you than another," said Ivar, watching Tomas's expression. "And I believe you would agree, for all your careful speech." He smiled grimly. "Ah, that found a mark."

Tomas's face and neck burned; he said nothing.

Sipping wine, Ivar regarded him. "You are young yet, Rhymer," he said. "If you would be advised by me, learn to school your features as well as you do your words." He leaned forward and asked, "Do you know why a dolphin would come first to you?"

"No," said Tomas, clipping the word. He didn't know; he only guessed.

"Could you explain how one might be summoned to me?" Ivar's voice was very low, his eyes intent.

"I regret that I cannot, my lord." Tomas met the austere gaze and held it. A servant, approaching to replenish the bowl with cranberries, stopped a few yards away.

But Ivar settled back in his chair and beckoned the man closer. "Very well," he said to Tomas. "Declaim your piece; I am listening."

After the first few measures from Tomas's harp, Ivar closed his eyes and rested his head against the tall scrolled back of his wooden chair. The bitter lines around his mouth softened a trifle, and he didn't stir again until the music was over.

Tomas sang:

> I took passage on the *Pride of Skiringssal.*
> Ship lay a-lading on the sandy shore:
> Amber, wheat and honey for her cargo,
> Near Uppsala, the town she's making for.
>
> Hoist the sail; the south wind is a-rising.
> Blow us home, nine days passage time.
> The captain spoke and he took my coins of silver:
> Poet, praise our fjords with a rhyme.
>
> As my name is the Rhymer, I make you a vow:
> I had no desire to see Dubhlinn town.
>
> Moira, why did you curse me with this vision?
> I see the truth and the Fate of every man.
> No gentle lies to ease me in my burden;
> There were hard truths off the coast of Ireland.
>
> I look in the eyes of the crew and their captain.
> I hear the sound of the keel as it cracks.
> The cruel shoals of the Irish Sea are boiling.
> Twelve men drowned and me on a dolphin's back.
>
> As my name is the Rhymer, I make you a vow:
> I had no desire to see Dubhlinn town.
>
> Washed to the shore like the body of a bloated fish,

I was found by a boy and a monk on the kelpie strand.
Carried to the court of the King of the port of Dubhlinn,
'Mid the silver and the gold and the glories of Ireland.

Hidden in the court of the King of the port of Dubhlinn,
My brother Olaf, to kill me he has vowed.
He swings his axe, but the Faerie strength is in me.
I killed my brother in the port of Dubhlinn town.

As my name is the Rhymer, I make you a vow:
I had no desire to see Dubhlinn town.

As Tomas sang, the faces of Hrolf and his crew came to his mind's eye and drifted away, while the fog that had overtaken the ship seemed to curdle the air of Ivar's hall. Blinking, Tomas shook his pale hair from his eyes and tried to attend only to his harp. He neither missed a note nor banished what appeared to be his own private mist. Did Ivar and the servants notice it? Their expressions bemused, they listened calmly.

Remembering Caraid's advice, Tomas set one heel atop the toes of his other foot and pressed down hard, in the hope that the discomfort would clear his vision. He didn't care to see the draug a second time.

The room cleared, but as Tomas recounted the shipwreck, he heard the crack of outraged wood and the roar of sluicing water. Faces floated in the air before him. Hands, closing on nothing, scrabbled and missed their hold.

When he ground his heel into his toes, the faces vanished. He no longer thought of the verses, but words flowed from him nonetheless. Had he written them, those words? Not all of them were familiar.

His audience looked half-asleep and dreaming, Ivar motionless in his chair, the servants standing hipshot several yards away. Did they see anything uncanny? Stretching his awareness towards theirs, Tomas willed himself to share their perceptions.

With a start, he abruptly saw himself as he must appear to them: a blond and haggard young man in weathered clothes of dark green, who played a glossy harp. Although his face was thinner, it seemed no older than he remembered, and his sun-warmed skin was as unlined as before. But the look in his grey eyes, now: that had aged. Beyond a harper's concentration, his expression was removed, inward and stark. Some quality in his face had worn away, revealing a tangible sense of loss.

Yet what, precisely, had eroded? And what had come to

replace it: harsher than detachment and more raw; self-contained but fragile, volatile, still changing...

No. He wished to see nothing further. Wrenching his awareness from that of Ivar's retainers, Tomas slowly reeled his mind back towards his body.

It was as if his thoughts were weighted and swam through something more viscous than water. It was far more difficult than sending his perceptions outside himself had been, and surprisingly draining. But at last his calloused fingers felt the supple tension of the harpstrings. The hard edge of the bench dug into his thighs; his heel pressed into his toes. His stomach gave a half-hearted churn, and he felt chilled.

He was singing about the dolphin now. Good. That meant he was past any word of the draug. To his relief the hall remained solid, and he saw only the faces of those present at the start of the meal. Relaxing, Tomas turned his attention to the music. The song took him through the meeting with Brendan and the monk, then to Ivar's court and the encounter with Olaf.

Wait. What was this mention of "Faerie strength"? Tomas had written no such words in Caraid's garden. And gods above, now he remembered an earlier verse, something about seeing truths, and Fate, and a dearth of gentle lies. What had he done?

Words and music trailed away into silence. He glanced around the quiet, nearly empty hall and across the table at Ivar, whose eyes remained closed. The servants, goggling at Tomas, gradually rearranged their expressions to convey soberness and rectitude.

With his palms, Tomas stilled the harpstrings. Would these revelations continue to happen; could he induce them, stop them, control them? With a cold little knot of fear and awe taking root in the pit of his belly, he bowed his head and waited.

But Ivar found the song much to his liking, or so he said.

After opening his eyes and directing towards Tomas a look of wary appraisal, the King observed, "There is much in the world and on the seas that we do not comprehend. So. I am well entertained and you, Rhymer, are well paid."

A scrawny dark-haired man leaped to Ivar's side and presented him with a knobbly purse. Ivar gave it to Tomas; it was heavy. "Look within," said the King.

Tomas took a perfunctory glance at the silver coins and began his thanks.

"Enough," Ivar said coldly. "Three ships sail for Birka at dawn;

you will doubtless find one to your liking. Should you have more to tell me of the ways of dolphins, send me word. If ever you return to Dubhlinn, I would prefer that news of your arrival be brought to me promptly." His level blue gaze flickered. "Do you understand?"

Tomas understood quite well. The King of Dubhlinn was leery of sorcerers, though he judged it wise to pay them well and to treat them with respect. Ivar had decided that he, Tomas, was a sorcerer.

And why not reach that decision? He was a skald journeying to the temple at Uppsala—and skalds served Odin, lord of poetry and magic, of war and of the dead. Tomas had not only escaped death with the mysterious aid of a dolphin, he'd disarmed and slain a crack berserker before Ivar's eyes. And lastly, Tomas's song hinted at considerably more arcane knowledge than he'd professed in the immediately preceding conversation.

But the King was far from challenging him on that account. Tomas read the wariness in Ivar's mind: he suspected the sorcerer of toying with him.

Bowing low, he said he would make sail at dawn.

Moira, Rhys and Aubrey were at the center of the hawthorn circle. Massed round the Elves, the trees leaned and swayed in the tarnished air, and their shedding twigs and branches grated together like the thin dry scraping of insects' wings. No lights shone from the stone hall. On the shrinking greensward beyond the hawthorns, knots of subdued Elves stood, sat or wandered aimlessly. Now and again, pipers played a few measures of some all-but-forgotten air, letting the final notes echo into silence.

Stretched out on her back upon the withering grass, one white hand flung across her closed eyes, Moira stirred and sighed.

"Ah," said Rhys, relaxing his grip on her other hand. Aubrey stopped pacing and came to hunker down beside them. The shape he wore was neither horse nor human, and one no mortal would have recognized. Rhys and Moira, her eyes now blinking open, scarcely noticed it.

Moira shook her head at Rhys's offer of assistance. Propped on her elbows, she levered herself to a sitting position as, beyond the ring, a piper resumed playing.

"Far traveler," Rhys said gently to Moira.

"As is he." She shook her dark hair loose about her shoulders. "Finvara met him in the wood, and returned what he'd let fall into the Sea."

Rhys nodded, unsurprised. "Fortuitous, the dolphin," he said somewhat later.

"Indeed it was," the pooka agreed, leaning forward, his eyes gleaming red. "But mark you how the draug revealed to Tomas that he would survive. How came it by such knowledge? I would that we ourselves had known."

"Aubrey," said Rhys, raising an eyebrow, "a draug is an ocean-spirit, who in its malignity can divine much of which we Elves remain ignorant. And such divine in ways we cannot hope to match."

The pooka snorted, not impolitely. Rhys smiled at that, an ever-widening smile of comprehension—for the most part--until the pooka lowered his eyes and looked away. "Perhaps it told the dolphin," Aubrey muttered, shifting back to his own Elf-shape.

Rhys laughed, and Moira said, "The People of the Sea follow no instructions from the draug-kind, or any kind save their own. We were fortunate, was all."

The piper stopped a second time. From the nearby trees there came an intermittent rain of dropping leaves, each detaching from its twig with a soft desiccated tearing sound, to ride the air currents earthward in a spiral.

Watching the scraps of yellowing green float down to die, Moira said, "Finvara bade him make haste."

Watching Moira, Rhys asked, "Does he comprehend the reasons?"

"Some. Not all, and not entirely."

"Hel's pursuit?"

"Mm," said Moira, gazing through spiny hawthorn limbs at the starless sky. The grey of her eyes reflected the grey overhead. Rhys and Aubrey looked up as well.

No stars, and neither sun nor moon. Elfland hung motionless beneath a cinder-colored, slowly shrinking vault.

"I believe he has commenced to realize that the mortal realm will increasingly present him with... That he finds himself encumbered there," said Moira, and wrapped her arms around her knees.

Aubrey gave her a sidelong glance. "And less elsewhere?"

She shrugged.

Into the silence of their suspended conversation came the sounds of movement beyond the hawthorn ring: the tread of creatures two-footed and four, and otherwise gaited. Rustle and shuffle, flutter and hop. Cloven air, flowing over and under wings both feathered and leathern. Splashes of assorted volume and rhythm. Rarely: a murmur, a trill or a sigh.

"One would hope," observed Rhys a considerable while later, apparently in reference to Aubrey's last question. Moira and the pooka looked at him. "We serve as fulcrum for the other worlds," he said quietly, although they needed no reminder.

After the vault overhead swung itself an all but imperceptible fraction farther upon its path, Moira said, "But he really understands quite little."

"At this point." Rhys got to his feet. "The ravens," he said to no one in particular. "After claiming Thought and Memory..."

Moira glanced up at him. "We cannot know. For that, we can only wait."

The smoky sphere wheeled along its track above them. Around them, the restless, assembled Elves, with infinitesimal but inexorable slowness, were obliged to approach the ring of trees and draw closer together on the gradually diminishing turf.

Tomas had hesitated before going back to Caraid's house that nestled among its herbs and flowers like a small ill-tamed animal in its burrow. Had hesitated all the more, perhaps, because Brendan urged him to return. But even if he hadn't needed to learn whatever Caraid could tell him of the Elves and the Sight, he could find no plausible pretext to stay away, and he didn't care to state difficult and complex truths before Brendan's guileless face.

And Tomas wanted to return.

When he appeared with Brendan, Caraid rose from the low table, her expression taut and removed. Wishing he'd followed his first instinct and taken himself down to the harbor, Tomas met her gaze. As you wish, he thought. As you wish.

Some tide within her turned at last; her eyes shifted from his to fix on a point in the empty air midway between them. Brendan had already shut and bolted the door, and gone to tend the fire that his sister had let all but gutter out.

"I would not--" began Tomas, his voice very soft, glancing at Brendan's oblivious back.

The Seer interrupted. "You are always welcome here," she said formally. "You have eaten? An infusion of mint, then."

Like a hurtled spear she darted past him to the garden. Brendan followed, after clapping Tomas on the back and wishing him well.

He looked around at the encircling house: the fire and the hides; the beams hung with ragged bundles of herbs; the walls bedecked with implements for cookery, sewing, gardening--and strife. He caught a green, sweet and slightly acid scent, just before Caraid returned alone. She was clutching an armful of fresh mint.

Whatever tenuous fretwork of reasons, impulses and indecision had netted Tomas back into this cottage, he was there now, feeling more precariously balanced on the pile of skins than he would have felt on a foundering deck. Purring, Finian regarded him with half-closed eyes from just within arm's reach. To Tomas's left sat Caraid, her hands curled loosely on her knees. The air was warm, and Tomas had pushed his sleeves above his elbows, but round her shoulders the Seer had draped a light cloak of Irish wool.

Fighting a twinge of nausea from the iron-taint, insistent in the closed space, Tomas glanced towards the door. If he proposed that they take what remained of the infusion out to the garden?

"Perhaps not just yet," said Caraid, noticing the direction of his gaze. "Brendan tells me you came across one of the Gentry in Faheys' wood. A great ugly fellow, hairy and brown, Brendan said he was. With a chest like a ploughhorse and frightfully scarred."

"No," said Tomas, staring. "That is, I didn't see him in the guise that Brendan did. The Elf was extremely tall, yes, but slender and fair, with green eyes. Blond and graceful and clear-spoken. Six fingers on each hand."

Caraid's eyes widened. "Oh, oh. Courteous, but jeering at you all the while?" Tomas nodded. That, explained Caraid with a shudder, was none other than Finvara, lord of the Irish Sidhe, to whose court she was brought when she first stumbled into Faerie.

Lord of the Irish Sidhe, as Rhys was lord of the Welsh... "What are the Elves, Caraid?"

Her brows lifted; her round blue eyes flew to his face. Not startled at his query, nor fearful, but puzzled.

As was Tomas. The question seemed to have taken root within him some time ago, to have sprouted, put forth branches and leafed out unrecognized till now, when it ripened and burst from him. He sat motionless, sensing the extent and weight of this questioning, the depths within him it had reached. He felt vast and heavy and encumbered.

"I do not know, Tomas, nor could any mortal. We can but guess."

"Guess, then," he said quietly.

She poured more of the minty brew into their mugs, then poked at the fire. Crossing to the door, which they had propped open with a footstool to let the crooked-eared cat pass as he pleased, Caraid stepped across the sill and gazed up at the sky.

Falling moonlight frosted her coarse abundant hair to rose-gold. It curled down well past her shoulders and over the dark woolen cloak that blended with the color of the night. For a moment she seemed to be a disembodied head of floating hair, freshly arranged with the jet comb that Tomas gave her. He thought of a ship's figurehead, or an image stamped upon a coin.

Caraid came back inside and tugged at the heavy wooden footstool, until the opened door wedged its makeshift prop more closely against the jamb. Finian lifted his head to watch, then settled into another feline knot at Tomas's feet.

Joining him, the Seer said: "There are so many legends. I have collected tales from wise men and women, and grandparents musing at hearthsides. And from travelers' gossip in alehouses and priests in their cups—and from watching the Gentry themselves."

She stretched her hands out towards the fire. "The old religion holds that at death, souls pass from one life to the next, from one physical envelope into another. But Christians believe that Elves have no souls. It's said they are immortal. I've never heard of one dying."

Remembering a conversation with Moira—"Do you know when

I will die, Tomas?"--he shook his head.

"Yet fewer of them appear to be abroad these days than in the past," Caraid continued. "Something seems to restrict their movements in Midgard and in Elfland both. But what could so impair the Sidhe? Iron afflicts them, but to that extent?" She gave Tomas a searching look. "What is it like, the iron-sick?"

"It differs. Nausea. Discomfort. My head spins. I can always smell the stuff, and there's pain if I touch it. A cold that burns, and weakness."

"In my house you feel--"

"Ill at ease," he muttered--then heard the full import of the phrase.

Caraid stood up, to pile all the utensils made of iron, and as many weapons as would fit, into two large wooden coffers. She banged their lids down with finality, and Tomas winced.

Returning, the Seer asked, "Better?"

"Ah, it could be, yes. I think perhaps it will," he said. If only all the reasons for his malaise could be put into those trunks.

"It's best not to have this sort of talk outside," she said, apology in her voice.

He hastened to agree, then asked, "Have you any notion, any at all, why iron disturbs them?"

She said, gazing steadily at the coffers: "I have often wondered. I think they may be an ancient race, once more numerous than men and women, a race of earth and tree and stone. Not Elementals. That is, not spirits of only one substance--fire, earth, air or water--but somehow mingling all of those. It would seem that iron is foreign to their natures, to their bodies. It poisons them. Their flesh is different."

Tomas was examining his hands, five-fingered hands that could play a flute, a harp, a lute and more. That could hold a horse's reins or the lines and oars of a ship. Hands that had touched an Elf Queen's hair--and buried an axe-blade in his brother's heart.

"Different," he murmured. "What else troubles them?"

"The Christian rite of exorcism. It's meant to banish evil spirits."

"Elves are not spirits." Of that, at least, he was certain.

Caraid shook her head. "The rite seems efficacious, nonetheless. A priest would say it's because Elves have no souls to save, and hence are damned by their own nature." She did not appear to accept this idea; her voice was neutral. Scratching the cat behind his ears, she watched the half-open door.

"But what is their nature?" Tomas asked.

207

Caraid and Finian both looked at him, the cat with a contented expression, the Seer with rising exasperation. "I mean," Tomas amended, "what, precisely, do Christians claim is in the nature of the Elves that damns them?"

Stroking the cat's uplifted chin, Caraid thought for a moment. "All I can do," she said with the air of someone concluding an argument with herself, "all I can do is relate to you the stories I've gathered over the years. What truth they may contain is beyond my ability to say." A glance of inquiry; did Tomas care to hear? He nodded. "Do you know of Adam and Eve, whom the priests say were the first man and woman?"

Tomas nodded again; his mother had spoken of them.

"Some hold that Adam had a wife before Eve. Lilith, her name was. And that for whatever reasons she and her union with Adam were neither one hallowed, and the Elves are their descendants. But others believe that the Elves are the children of Adam and Eve whom Eve hid from God, and so they have stayed hidden and unhallowed."

"In the North, the Elves are sometimes called the huldre-folk, the hidden people," Tomas said.

An owl called somewhere close by, its hoot loud and sudden in the hushed evening. Finian stood, tail twitching, then slipped out into the garden, black cat melting into a night no blacker than himself.

Caraid got up and closed the door. "Have you heard of Lucifer?" she asked. "The angel whom the Christians say revolted and fell, and became the devil?"

When Tomas nodded a third time, the Seer furrowed her brow. "Are there so many Christians in the North, Tomas, that you know all their beliefs?"

"My mother was one," he said briefly.

She flushed, then grew pale; her face sank into her hands. "Yes," she said, "I knew that. You are half Welsh, on your mother's side. I did know that."

"Caraid... Can you recall everything that happened while you were in Faerie?" He put a gentle hand on her slumped shoulders. No reaction.

"No," she said, her voice muffled. "I suspected there were clouded places in my memory. That was not to my liking."

"So you didn't care to think about what you might have forgotten," he finished for her.

Lifting her head to reveal a bloodless but dry-eyed face, the Seer said, "Yes. Do you believe you may also have forgotten—"

"I may have. I don't know." Tomas studied his hands again.

"Please, Caraid. Finish telling me about Lucifer."

Lucifer had led a horde of rebellious angels, or so the story went, some knowingly in revolt and others deceived by him. When God expelled the traitors from heaven, the misled plummeted down alongside the intentionally maleficent, some as far as Hell, but others only to the Earth. According to this legend, the Elves were those angels who fell more through gullibility than evil and remained trapped in the natural world.

Caraid knew still more tales. Some maintained that the Fair Folk were the unhallowed dead. The wise who lent credence to this theory cited, as proof, the number of hills and mounds inhabited by Elves. Or perhaps they merely kept watch over the dead. Another story held that the People of Peace were the original tribes of the Earth, driven back when others came, or the spirits of those earlier tribes.

"And that explanation makes the most sense to you," Tomas said, watching Caraid.

She shrugged. "Merely a guess, like all the tales." Her eyes flickered aside and down; she seemed about to speak but kneaded the back of her neck instead.

"You appear to be remembering a few more," said Tomas. When she didn't look at him, he asked, "There are others?"

"What?" She blinked, and he saw that she had been musing, rather than reluctant to talk. "Yes, a few. Perhaps the Elves were once gods. Are gods, gods who have dwindled."

"Dwindled? Why?"

"From unbelief," Caraid said carefully.

"Do you mean that without worshippers, there are no gods?" asked Tomas, frowning. "Or no gods without their faithful?"

She made a confused gesture. "I could not say. But a legend exists that the Elves once were gods, gods whose stature has lessened. You in the North, do you still sacrifice to them?"

"Less than before."

She nodded. "And as the Christ gains followers there, what will happen to the cult of Odin?"

Tomas's stomach heaved. The lining of his nose and throat grew dry and sour. "I don't know," he said abruptly. "Forgive me, please. I need some air." He fled into the garden. Behind him, Caraid's door swung shut against the night.

Outside it was cool and moist, and smelled of cattle, salt and herbs. Moving quietly, he strolled around the house several times before he stopped at the door and, stretching, gazed up at the night sky. Clouds thin as spiderwebs drifted overhead in a light breeze from the south-west, revealing a wealth of netted stars. Tomorrow should dawn clear with, no doubt, a fair wind for sailing to the North.

Something furred and supple brushed Tomas's shins; he bent to stroke the cat before ducking back through Caraid's doorway. Finian glided in after him.

The Seer had brewed a fresh infusion, and Tomas accepted a mug. "The iron-sick," he explained.

She nodded calmly.

"Another story?" asked Tomas, sipping his tea.

"If you like. You are not bored?"

He shook his head and smiled. "You forget. Stories are my stock-in-trade." And he wanted to keep her talking.

"Stories and songs," she said, giving him an odd smile in return. "Well. The Franks, and the peoples to the south of them, believe that the Fair Folk are in some wise like the Fates. The Fata or Fada, they call them. Or the Hada, or the Fees. It's said there were once just three of them--"

"Like the Nornir?" A chill fingered its way up Tomas's spine.

"Perhaps. They sometimes visit the Franks when a child is born, to offer gifts and foretell the infant's Fate. But how all of Faerie grew from those first three, if indeed it did, the tales do not recount."

Tomas hugged his knees. It seemed impossible that the Elves were Fates, like the Nornir. Odin Himself was subject to the Fates, while the Elves felt threatened by the movements of Odin's berserkers in Midgard.

Yet Moira had claimed that when she saw the Nornir weaving by the Saefren, she sensed they might lose their hold upon a thread-- Tomas's thread. She said that "Moira" meant Fate. "I am your Fate," she had told him.

"It feels so long ago," he muttered.

"That we were in Elfland?" Caraid sighed. "So it also seems to me. And how long ago to them, where Time is not?"

Where Time is not. Time was here, though, in this house, burning steadily down into ashes, like the hearthfire that overheated this small space.

Time and space.

Aubrey had detoured in and out of Faerie to get Linley to Chippenham before dawn, and Linley lost no mortal years during that journey.

"Time and space," Tomas muttered, not realizing that he spoke aloud until Caraid asked what he'd just said.

"Time and space," he repeated. "Only something I was

thinking. It felt important for a moment."

A scratching sound came from the door, and Tomas gave an involuntary start.

"It's Finian," Caraid murmured, and let the cat out again. Lingering in the doorway, she scanned the stars, then crossed to the pile of skins and stood looking down at Tomas. "It's late," she said gently. "Or early, depending how you see it. You should rest, Tomas. You'll have slow work finding a passage to Uppland if you go to the harbor exhausted."

Tomas glanced up at Caraid, wanting to talk, to hold her, to sleep till midwinter and wake to find he'd been dreaming. His eyes felt rough and dry, his throat seared, and his chest weighted down with small sharp stones. He took her hand.

"I'd like to stay," he began, his voice low and troubled, but she touched two fingers to his mouth to silence him, then sat down with her shoulder brushing his. She didn't move away when he reached for her. He kissed her temples and her eyelids, and laid his face against her lavender-scented hair.

"While you were gone with Brendan, I was thinking," she said softly. "Thinking that you might have left even if it weren't for Moira, and for Hel."

Much later, he asked why.

"Because you are a poet. And to be a poet, it is said, one needs a harp, and sorrow, and a wandering road."

CHAPTER FORTY: SUN-MONTH, 878 A.D.

Seated on a sturdy, battered sea chest full of costly walrus ivory, his feet braced against an identical chest in front of him, Tomas leaned into his rowing. The wooden oar-handle curved against his hardened palms; the blade dipped and pulled, dipped and pulled in rhythm with fifteen others. Bright square sail just lowered, sail-yard lashed into place, the Norse merchanter *Fjord-elk* moved cleanly through the indigo waters of Lake Malar, making for Birka's Kugghamm harbor.

The long voyage from Dubhlinn, while broken up with brief stops in the Sudreyar, Kaupang and Gotland, had been blessedly uneventful: no Rune readings, shipwrecks or draugs. Tomas was eager to see Birka.

Ottar, from the far northern stretches of Halogaland, stood at the bow and scanned the harbor for the best spot to run his vessel ashore. Most of the Frisian cogs already there were of deeper draught than the *Fjord-elk*, but the two harbors intended for smaller craft were already crowded. Ottar had been waved on to Kugghamm.

"Is the custom always so brisk here?" Tomas asked Einar, who manned the oar across from him.

"Nearly always," said Einar. "Even when most of the ships in Halogaland are laid in for the winter, there's still a great market for furs here. Pelts grow thickest in winter."

Without turning, Ottar said, "Mind you, that's if we can get underway before the ice does." He shaded his eyes with one hand and squinted at the men on the shore. "Bailiffs so soon? Good. Our wares are remembered. At least we'll be closer to town than the Frisians."

Adjusting course, the crew made straight for the two well-dressed men who signaled them from the shore.

"The bailiffs?" asked Tomas. "Why is that good?"

This time Ottar favored him with a shrewd look. The trader's narrow brown eyes glinted with impatience. "They're royal bailiffs. Birka law grants the King three days to buy whatever suits his taste before anyone else makes an offer. If he's eager enough to send men to look over the cargo so soon, other offers will follow."

"Salvik harbor might have had orders to watch for us," Einar commented, his voice low.

"No doubt. Hold your tongue before the bailiffs, Rhymer. And no questions at market. You'll not earn your passage by looking foolish."

No, Tomas would earn it with splinters and callouses, and by assisting at the *Fjord-elk*'s trade booths while her crew sampled Birka's

212

other wares. It might take time to raise the fare. Back in Dubhlinn, Ottar had demanded an exorbitant price, the entire contents of Ivar's purse. And shared labor on board—that, Tomas had expected. But Ottar required an additional fee, to be earned by minding a trader's stall at Birka, a richer market even than Dubhlinn, and more sophisticated.

Tomas held the flat of his oar against the current, helping to slow the ship so that she would glide ashore like a great wooden swan. No merchant, he. A poet, a sailor—a far traveler.

Still, he must hawk enough goods to pay Ottar and to arrange for a ferry ride up the waterways to Uppsala, to the temple and the grove. Or, failing that, he should earn at least enough to buy his way to the coastline east of the waterway, from where he could make his own way overland to Uppsala—with, he hoped, sufficient funds that he'd not starve before he arrived.

He lifted his oar clear of the bank; they ran ashore.

Birka market sprawled in gaudy confusion across the south-eastern part of town, not quite opposite Kugghamm harbor. Cradled by earth and stone ramparts broken by three gates, each with its wooden watchtower, a fortress topped the steep cliffs at this end of Birch Island. Between the fort and the town lay the garrison, hard by the noisy marketplace.

From one of the *Fjord-elk's* tented booths, Tomas squinted thoughtfully at the morning Sun above the eastern watchtower. He avoided the red and belligerent eye of an elegantly dressed but barefooted Dane who staggered among the booths. Clutching an exorbitantly expensive bottle of Frankish wine and muttering curses, the man almost tripped on the wooden planking that made a patchwork series of paths among the stalls.

Did the King place the market near the garrison to protect the foreign merchants or to control them? Probably both. In the rest of the North, one risked little by killing and robbing a man far from his home, who had no kin nearby to take his case to the law-courts or otherwise avenge him. Not so in Birka. Ottar had told Tomas of its strict new laws that shielded townsman and trader alike. Little wonder that custom thrived here.

The Dane having rounded a corner, Tomas looked about and breathed deeply, testing the air. Lake water, dead fish and latrines. Market smells: a tanning pit, leather scraps and sawdust. Chickens, goats and other livestock. Spices. Wine and ale. Various washed and unwashed bodies.

Tomas wrinkled his nose. There it was, the sour bite of iron,

213

clear at the other end of the fair. He'd passed that ominous booth far down the rows, and hidden his nausea while Ottar's men slowed to ogle the fine metalwork. There were Frankish swords with inlaid hilts and damascened blades, engraved with the smith's signature. Helmets and mailshirts. Spearheads, their shaft sockets decorated with traceries of silver heightened by black niello. Men thronged around the stall, some loud with inebriated praise, others silent, their faces pinched and covetous. Not a booth that Tomas would visit again.

Ottar did no traffic in weapons this voyage, but showed justifiable pride in his wares. Tomas had already completed several sales that morning. The King hadn't bought all of Ottar's fine walrus ivory, nor all the reindeer antlers and skins, nor the grey miniver fur. ("Not our best, but they crave furs here," Einar had said with a shrug.) The *Fjord-elk* sold ship's ropes of Finnish and Sami make, wrought from the hides of whales and seals. During their travels, the Halogalanders had picked up an impressive assortment of soapstone and whetstones from Kaupang and the Sudreyar. In Dubhlinn they'd bartered for Rhenish wine, glass and pottery, Irish and Saxon wool, fine jewelery and trinkets.

Tomas examined a box-shaped shawl buckle he particularly fancied, running his fingers across its gold and silver filigree. What would Ottar take back to the cold of Halogaland? Wheat and honey, wood and salt? Clay for metal casting? Perhaps some luxuries: silk, spices and fruit—or slaves?

Biting his lip, Tomas glanced down the winding rows of booths in the direction Ottar and his crew had gone. The slave market was that way, and so were the best wineshops.

To Tomas's right, a stout, mournful, one-legged man named Anskar sold great rounds of warm bread, skewers of hot sausages spiced with thyme and garlic, and ale brewed from bog-myrtle, apples and cranberries. Tomas sniffed the air more appreciatively. When Anskar had heard Tomas playing the flute before their booths opened, he'd hobbled over and insisted that Tomas accept a trencherful of breakfast. A music lover. That boded well for Tomas's plan to earn passage to the mainland by plying his skald's trade at Birka marketplace, once he'd discharged his debt to Ottar.

Ubbi, one of Ottar's crew, strolled by among the growing crowd. Casually, he glanced at the bare spots in their booth left by the most recent sales. He gave Tomas an approving grin and moved on without stopping; indeed, he hadn't so much as slackened his stride.

A subtle lot, these Halogalanders. None of Hrolf's bluster and frankness for them. They wanted no passer-by or other merchant to think they were watching Tomas, that he might be inexperienced and an easy mark.

Four women hovered near his booth, whispering and craning their necks at the prominent display of jewelery. They'd walked back and forth in front of him three times already. Birka folk, by their accents. Married, by the neatly tied kerchiefs that bound their hair. And wealthy, from the gold and silver rings festooning their bare white arms.

An occasional giggle reached Tomas's ears. One woman had round blue eyes—like Caraid's eyes. He shoved that galling thought from his mind and tried to look pleasant, approachable and inoffensive. He'd witnessed three brawls already this morning whose causes he never learned. They could have been anything: a combative drunk; a deceitful merchant; a jealous husband. It was all too easy to affront people when their customs were largely unknown.

There were plenty of foreigners to distract Tomas from the murmuring women. Olive-complected Saracens in loose flowing clothes conducted a brisk trade in silver, fruit, spices and jewels. Once the King's bailiffs trudged by, minding their step on the plankways and carrying a small squarish object made of intricately open-worked bronze. It had a domed top, four curving feet and a long protrusion from one side. Einar said it came from the Saracen lands, where he believed they made fires in it. A few tall slaves with strikingly dark shining skin were hustled past, shivering in the mild morning air. Tomas had even seen two small, silent, amber-faced men dressed in rich silks, with thick black hair and deep folds around their tilted eyes. They put him in mind of the wandering Finns of Halogaland. Ottar said they might be silk dealers from the remote East, but that he could scarcely credit it, since that land lay farther away than Bulgar and Itil, farther even than Chorezm.

Tomas sold a bundle of antlers to a Birka comb-maker who, without a word, paid the first price that Ottar had said to ask. The artisan walked away cradling the antlers as if they were glass, his expression dreamy and pleased. Perhaps Tomas could pay off his passage sooner than he'd thought.

He took his harp from under a table and began easing his fingers over the strings. "Play all you wish, if no one's at the booth," Einar had told him. "You play well, and the music will bring people back. But stop if someone looks over the wares."

Amid the jabber of strange tongues, the parade of goods and animals, women and soldiers and slaves, shipwrights and carpenters, moneyers and leatherworkers, Tomas's gaze kept straying to the stall on

215

his left. An old woman sat there, weaving baskets to sell.

Her booth displayed glass beads blown in Birka, bone skates, lathe-turned wooden bowls and assorted items worked in metal, amber, jet or bone. She was dressed in what Tomas now thought of as Birka-style, garments and ornaments from a variety of lands. Her sleeveless gown was made of lightweight wool, fastened at the shoulders with brooches of Saxon silver over a pleated petticoat of Frisian cloth. On her head she had knotted a gaudy silken kerchief from beneath which her silver-white hair fell half-way down her back. She wore an ancient cloak of what had once been very fine pale fur, clasped with a simple silver pin in front and thrown back over her shoulders. Weaving and sewing tools were fastened to her gown, and a small silk pouch hung at her waist.

There was movement at the right-hand side of Tomas's booth. He'd been so intent on the elderly peddler to his left that a small dainty woman had walked up without his noticing, and now stood sorting through a pile of fine silk headscarves. Nothing covered her unbound hair, which was dark brown, sleek and utterly straight. Her garments looked threadbare and old-fashioned, though quite clean. Still, there was something odd about her dress...

Tomas put down his harp. "Good day to you, my lady. How may I serve you?"

Her entire body went rigid; she clutched at the kerchiefs, then buried her hands in the cloth. Her head shot up. A pair of murky brown eyes flew to Tomas's face. Large, slanted, slightly protruding eyes; they were disarmingly pretty. Her lips were parted in surprise. Why had he startled her so?

Then he fully registered what he had only half-noticed before: the hem of the woman's gown was wet to the knees and her feet were bare. Following the direction of Tomas's glance, she squared her shoulders. Slowly and deliberately, she put down all but one of the scarves, her mud-colored eyes never leaving Tomas's face. And then he knew, even before she smoothed the pile of silken squares with one six-fingered hand.

She was a water-Elf, from Lake Malar, most likely. Not tall enough for a pooka, however, and Aubrey's human form had ten fingers rather than twelve. Besides, a pooka's clothing--when it wore any-- wouldn't drip with lake water: their shape-shifting was flawless.

Two young women charged up to the booth just then, giggling, their hair disheveled. They returned Tomas's greeting in well-bred breathless voices but almost crashed into the lake-Elf. Still staring at Tomas, she sidestepped the newcomers and boldly pocketed the kerchief she held.

The pair of women--they were hardly more than girls--didn't apologize. They were exclaiming over the jewelery. One spotted the headscarves and reached for them, her hand passing so close to the Elf that it all but touched the worn fabric of her skirt. She smiled ironically at Tomas and stepped back a pace. The small puddle of dark water where she stood was already seeping down between the planks.

That the lake-Elf was invisible to the girls didn't surprise Tomas; after all, the Chippenham brownie had been invisible to the Danes. Small wonder she'd been taken aback that Tomas saw her.

A red-faced matron materialized behind the youngsters. They turned, pleading and explaining, and pointed to various items on the table. The older woman shook her head. With a curt, suspicious nod at Tomas, she clamped a hand on the girls' elbows to march them away-- and would have collided with the lake-Elf, had she not dodged again.

"Well, well," said the Elf when the three women had gone. She pitched her words just above a whisper, and her voice had a trace of hoarseness. "How may you serve me, you ask? How beguiling. It's long since I've had such an offer from so comely a young man." Her manner was cool, but the long-lashed eyes fixed on Tomas were intensely curious.

He opened his mouth, but she held up a hand to silence him. "Call no attention to us, harper. Speak softly."

What to ask? It was doubtful that Moira had sent her, because of her surprise at being noticed. Still... "Where did you come from? Why are you here?" he asked in the quietest tone he could muster.

Her face went blank. After a moment she jerked her chin towards the waterfront. "From the lake. For my marketing." Surely you knew those things, her voice implied. "And for you, my heart, I've three questions. Whence came you, what brings you here, and how does it happen that you can see me?"

A glassblower slowed to admire some Rhenish pottery and ended by purchasing two pieces. During the transaction the lake-Elf strolled patiently around the booth. Tomas noticed her studying the harp and the flute under the table.

When the glassblower left, the Elf came to stand in front of Tomas. Her glance at him was expectant.

"I was born in Vestfold," he said. "I took passage from Dubhlinn to Birka with some traders; I'm on my way to Uppsala. And I have the Sight; I suppose that's how I can see you."

The lake-Elf folded her arms and regarded him.

Interpreting her expression as skepticism, he added, "I've

encountered your kind before."

She smiled suddenly. "That you have. They gave you the harp and the flute?"

"Yes," he said, with a twinge of something like hope. "Do you know them?"

The Elf's face twisted; she smoothed the damp hem of her skirt. "I? We of the lake fashion no such instruments."

She had not said no. Carefully, Tomas asked, "Might you have met those who do?"

"No." Her voice was stark. "In times past, we might have done. But your harp and flute were recently crafted. Midgard has changed," she said, as if that explained everything, then appeared exasperated at Tomas's puzzled frown. "All the worlds have changed, and now we find we cannot leave the lake for long," she said shortly. "You did not know?"

Tomas shook his head. So the lake-Elves' movements here were restricted, as were those of the Elves in Rhys and Moira's realm. There must be a connection.

After a moment, the Elf's lips formed a soundless word. From the bemused look on her face, the word was neither an oath nor an epithet, but a label. "Well," she said in a much milder tone. "You inquired how you might serve me, my heart, and I shall tell you. Make me a present of some kerchiefs, if you would be so kind, and as much of that bolt of fine cloth as you find yourself able to spare."

Too sudden a shift; Tomas's mouth opened and closed. The Elf gave him an expressionless stare, but he heard the thought behind it as clearly as if she had spoken. She would not beg--but fabric rotted all too fast at the bottom of Lake Malar.

He felt a pang of sympathy, abrupt and profound. Four-fifths of the cloth and all but three of the kerchiefs he gave her, and Ottar be damned.

The appealing brown eyes widened. Looking pensive and touched, the Elf folded the bundle into the smallest possible packet of fabric and tucked it into the front of her dress. Then, after a hasty glance at the neighboring booths, she darted around the table and gave Tomas a salty, lingering kiss on the mouth.

It was unexpected but pleasant; he suppressed a start of astonishment. Very pleasant indeed. As the Elf broke the embrace, her lips brushed his ear. "Good fortune go with you," she murmured, then slipped off into the crowd, leaving a trail of damp narrow footprints on the plankway.

Gazing after her, he realized what word she had mouthed but

not spoken a moment ago. The label was "Fool."

And if anyone had watched him converse with thin air, he'd doubtless been marked for another kind of fool. Tomas looked around at the booths nearest him, all ringed with customers. To his relief he saw no mocking or pitying stares.

Three Saracens converged on his stall and began arguing over the soapstone. He let them bicker; it helped raise the price. They left with one-fourth of the soapstone, but that made up for not even a third of the missing kerchiefs and cloth. He'd have some explaining to do.

Nevertheless, settled back with his harp, Tomas hoped that the custom would slow and allow him to think. Was he to see more and more creatures invisible to most mortal eyes, until he could no longer dissemble and really was judged mad? And what then?

His gaze wandered to the elderly woman in the booth to his left. Her knotted fingers working deftly among the reeds, she was weaving baskets again. What was it about her that kept drawing his attention? Not her clothes. In Birka, far stranger attire was commonplace.

Her face, then? In youth it must have been arresting rather than beautiful, and was arresting still. She had strong, hawk-like features, her cheekbones and jawline modeled into prominence by the stark touch of age. Her skin was fair, finely textured and well-seamed about the mouth and eyes. Perhaps that was it: her eyes. Even from this distance, Tomas could tell that they were dark blue, deep-set and clear, with none of the vagueness or fading that the years sometimes bring.

As if sensing his scrutiny, the woman's head turned towards him. Their eyes met. She didn't speak or nod, but gave him a long measuring glance, intelligent, gentle and grave. And calm.

That was it: her calm. How could anyone's face be so serene? The stillness of her features, the violet traceries of veins beneath her arched and hollowed eyelids, etched with lines, and the easy carriage of her head all drew one's gaze to her eyes. About the pupils their dark blue was flecked with gold, and they stood out startlingly against her silvered hair. Deep wells, those eyes, wells of tranquility, but alert and reflective. Tomas felt irresistibly pulled, yet knew she did none of the pulling. Everything about her exuded a sense of peace with herself and the world: the assured movements of her hands; the grace of her posture; even the folds of her clothes.

He was staring. There was no other word for it, and no excuse. He lowered his gaze to his harpstrings and felt his face growing warm.

219

"You play uncommonly well, both harp and flute," the old woman said amiably.

Tomas looked at her again. She was smiling. Warmth and humour glinted in her eyes without altering their calm in the slightest. Her voice and expression were--he groped for the right word--accepting. As if he were a friend of long standing. "Thank you," he said, set at ease, though he'd intended to apologize for staring.

"What is it that you wish to know?" she asked in the same comfortable tone as before.

He blinked, then said, feeling his way, "To know? About what?"

"Yourself," she said simply.

"Myself?"

Something was amusing her, but there was no mockery in her voice. "Yourself. Your life. Your Fate."

His Fate. He couldn't stifle a bitter laugh, but it soon died on his lips at the sight of those incredible, untroubled eyes. They did not change at all. He was too astonished even to feel ashamed of his outburst.

Someone tapped his shoulder. "Time to spell you," said Einar with a quizzical look. Still holding the harp, Tomas got to his feet.

"They call me Mother Aud," the old woman told him. She nodded affably to Einar who, after a small hesitation, gave her a nod in return. "Each market day I am here. My house is beyond the town towards Salvik harbor. I go there after market, if you want to know who in Birka has work for a skald."

Einar's brow cleared.

"My thanks, Mother Aud," said Tomas. "They call me the Rhymer." He stooped for his flute, bowed to Mother Aud and left for his scheduled rest time on the ship. His head felt full of mists, and his feet unmoored and weightless on the plankways.

When he returned for his next shift at the *Fjord-elk's* booth, Mother Aud was not there. A much younger, more garrulous woman tended the left-hand stall and laughed with her customers. Tomas would have liked to see Mother Aud again, although she unnerved him. He'd expected some questions about her from Einar, but the trader said nothing, as if the entire incident had slipped his mind.

When a client at the booth on the left inquired about Mother Aud's whereabouts, Tomas listened.

"She left not an hour ago. Off to her steading down Salvik way, I expect," the new vendor said cheerfully. She had a guileless friendly perspiring face, and a hearty voice that Tomas could hear without straining even while engaged in conversations with his own customers. "No, I don't know when she'll be back. Best go see her there, if you're troubled in mind."

"Good day to you," said a feminine voice near Tomas's elbow. Turning, he put down his flute and asked how he might be of service. The Birka woman with blue eyes like Caraid's smiled at him. Over her shoulder, he saw one of her friends buying bread and sausages from one-legged Anskar's booth.

The customer picked up Tomas's favorite item, the box-shaped, circular shawl buckle. Rich and formal, its top and sides were filigreed in gold and bound in strongly patterned silver. It was the only such piece on the table. The Birka woman held it up to her collarbone, then at arm's length, turning it this way and that to glint in the Sun. "Where is this from?"

Tomas had been well-primed about all of the goods, since formal and informal conversations on board the *Fjord-elk* frequently dwelt on the cargo. "Gotland, I'm told, my lady. We brought it here from Dubhlinn."

The friend joined them, a basket of sausages hanging from the crook of her elbow. Taking the offered piece of jewelery, she turned it over in both hands. Longing softened her brown eyes as she gave the buckle back to the first woman.

"Lovely, isn't it? You'll not find one like it in Birka." Tomas had been advised to keep up a stream of chatter with potential buyers.

Dimpling, the blue-eyed woman startled him with a flirtatious glance. "We've seen you look at it often enough. Not saving it for your sweetheart, are you?"

His throat felt as if he'd swallowed a thistle. "No, my lady."

Smiling, she reached for his hand and put the shawl buckle in his palm, prolonging the contact. The friend's eyes widened at such daring. Perilous: this could provoke a husband, start a fight. There could be fines for touching a woman one wasn't related to by blood or marriage. Tomas's hand jerked convulsively in hers, and the buckle thudded a couple of inches down onto the fabric-covered table.

Thanks be to Einar that the polishing rags were stored underneath. Murmuring an apology, Tomas took as long as he thought could seem reasonable to retrieve one.

The market had grown more crowded. Feet of every shape and size, wearing all styles of footgear, trudged by his booth--but one pair of elegant boots lined with seal fur stood planted a few yards away.

Ottar's boots. How long had he been there? Tomas

221

straightened up and scrubbed busily at the ornament. Squalls loomed in the captain's eyes.

The women didn't appear offended by Tomas's dive beneath the counter; their smiles were cordial. Breathing a little more easily, he put the buckle down.

Tapping it with one finger, the blue-eyed woman asked, "Is this gold and silver?"

"It is indeed, my lady."

Ottar had not moved. He appeared to be studying the bolt of cloth.

"Pure? Throughout?" asked the customer, an insinuating note in her voice.

Tomas met her gaze as briefly as possible. "The decorations are pure gold and silver. The framework is bronze."

She raised an arched eyebrow. "That's odd. Yesterday your captain assured me it was pure gold and silver throughout."

The thistly feeling in Tomas's throat turned to stinging nettles, then descended to his stomach. Fool. Pure throughout was how Ottar wanted all the jewelery represented, unless the thin coatings of precious metal were unmistakable. But this shawl buckle could have passed. Well, Tomas had known that avoiding the need to lie would be difficult at market, and that he'd no choice but to take his chances and trust his wits to turn the talk elsewhere.

Only seconds had elapsed since the blue-eyed woman spoke. Tomas cleared his throat. "I may not have been fully informed about all of our cargo." Undoubtedly not. "But the captain has."

Approaching, Ottar's glance at Tomas was volcanic. When he joined the women, however, his face was arranged in a trader's practiced smile. He touched Tomas's shoulder briefly. "This is Rhymer's first voyage with us," Ottar said, his voice indulgent, earnest, a little weary. "He's done well. Has good instincts for the work, and he'll gain the experience." He looked directly at each woman in turn, holding her eyes, letting something like appeal creep into his face. They smiled back at him, fascinated.

Ottar clapped Tomas on the back, aiming low, with more force than was necessary but not so much that the customers would notice. "Go take your shore leave, friend. You've earned it."

Grabbing his instruments and the leather wallet with his morning's sales, Tomas left precipitously for the ship. He heard Ottar say to the blue-eyed woman, "Now, you've got good instincts yourself, m'lady. Guessed this was pure yesterday, you did, and guessed rightly."

Tomas was halfway down the tented rows, hurrying past the

comb-maker and the water-seller. Holding his breath, he detoured to avoid the armorer's booth. When a beggar caught at his sleeve, he tossed the man some coins in mid-stride. Men scraped at upended keels in the shipyard, where the air was thick with fish-stench and circling gulls. After sprinting by the last wineshop before the harbor, Tomas padded up the gangplank of the *Fjord-elk*. A couple of the crew were snoring, sprawled on skins in the hold. No one stirred at his arrival.

Upon weighing the coins in the wallet, he almost awakened the sleepers with a gratified shout, but held it in to avoid questions and delays. His share this time, added to the rest of his wages, would finally pay for his passage. The captain had said more than he realized: Tomas had earned shore leave, although not enough for fare to the mainland.

Resolved to avoid any crew members after the scene he'd just caused, Tomas tied the fee for his passage into a strip of cloth. When he'd tucked the cloth into Ottar's bedroll—along with a wood chip carved with the T-Rune for Tomas, to show who'd left Ottar the money--he put the rest of the coins in his own Rune bag. Then he picked up his instruments and silently walked down the gangplank. Once ashore, he kept to the waterfront, intending to double back along the outskirts of town in the direction of Salvik harbor and Mother Aud's house.

223

CHAPTER FORTY-ONE: MOTHER AUD

Later, Tomas decided that the blue-eyed woman wasn't half-Sighted in the sense that Linley was, but that she must have possessed a trace of the Sight nonetheless. How else to account for the fact that she accosted Tomas again, at the first steps of the boggy track that led to Salvik harbor?

In as straight a line as the terrain allowed, a path ran through stands of birch and clumps of fragrant juniper from the edge of town to the harbor. Crew after crew of merchanters, ponies and slaves had carried cargo down the length of that trail, then clear across Birka to the market area on the opposite shore. No plankways began until the town proper. Prints left by heavily burdened feet and hooves combined with wheeltracks to score the beaten earth at the head of the path--not a place generally frequented by the well-to-do young matrons of Birka.

By ducking into the trees or around buildings at the outskirts of town, Tomas made his way there without being spotted by the two or three members of the *Fjord-elk*'s crew whom he passed. Wondering how close Mother Aud lived to the harbor, he detoured around the last smithy, stepped onto the potholed trail and stopped to redistribute his satchel's weight as evenly as possible.

Footsteps rushed up to him; a small hand clutched at his sleeve. "Wait, please, minstrel."

Tomas looked down at the kerchiefed woman who had tried to flirt with him earlier. Her eyes were bluer than ever.

If he'd seen the question coming, he might have had time to prepare a reply, but he mistook her intention. With a nervous glance about them for a husband or a brother, Tomas gently disengaged his arm and stepped away a few paces. "What brings you here, my lady? I am in some haste--"

She interrupted him, thrusting the shawl buckle under his nose and demanding, "Is it pure throughout, yes or no?"

"No--" he said instantly. His hand flew to his mouth as if to catch the word in mid-air. Too late. His head throbbed; he pressed his fingertips against the ridge of his eyebrows. The woman gazed up at him in triumph.

"Why have you come all the way here to ask me that?" His voice was flat, and all his carefully assumed merchanter's deference gone.

She bridled. "I didn't follow you, if that's what you mean. I was visiting my father. When you passed his smithy just now, I saw you go by."

"But why ask me, when the captain--"

"Him!" A scornful expression. "I knew he was lying." Her tone softened. "But I didn't think you were."

And to that, Tomas found he could make no reply whatsoever. His face must have changed, because a hint of alarm crept into her eyes. "I am in some haste to depart," he began, seeing an opportunity. Adding something about her health, the setting Sun and the proximity of her father for an escort back to town, he edged several feet down the trail, then turned and hurried away.

Standing doubtfully at the head of the path, she let him go. The shawl buckle gleamed in her hands.

Tomas was halfway to Mother Aud's house before he realized that by telling the truth about the piece of jewelery, he'd just given Ottar double cause for reprisals--and quite possibly ruined his own chances to sing undisturbed at the market for fare to the mainland. Curse this gift of true speech and its attendant complications.

The winding trail ran past the low hillocks of grave mounds. Tomas wasn't surprised at the sight of the howes, some new and piled high with raw earth, the older ones already grassy. The mounds felt peaceful, solemn and, for the most part, clear of any lingering presences.

He almost failed to see Mother Aud's small wattle-and-daub house. It was set back from the path and had a peaked, sharply sloping roof of thatch and a single wooden door. Overgrown junipers thrust thick stubby branches into Tomas's face as he approached. He stopped a few yards from the door.

The westering Sun fell on its rough-hewn weathered timbers, turning them the shade of honey. Ribbons of pale grey smoke twisted up from the roof to meet the darkening sky.

Why was he here?

Because Mother Aud might have some advice about who would pay for rhymes set to music, once the *Fjord-elk* sailed on. In the meantime, she lived out of sight and earshot of the market.

Because of her eyes and her voice, and her calm. Her unnerving, compelling calm. He had overheard other folk advised to seek her out, if they were troubled in mind. But could she actually tell him anything of himself, his life, his Fate? And would it be anything that he could not already have told her?

His satchel seemed, of a sudden, full of stones. Sliding his shoulders from its straps, Tomas cradled it in his arms and scowled unseeingly at Mother Aud's door.

Why was he here?

Because, finally, he could think of nowhere else on Birch Island to go.

When at last he made ready to knock, the door moved before his raised hand could begin its descent. Afraid he was gaping like an idiot, Tomas stood with his fist hovering in mid-air before Mother Aud's austerely smiling face.

"Enter, and welcome," she said, and swung the door open wide. Stooping to clear the jamb, Tomas passed within.

At first the interior of Mother Aud's home put Tomas in mind of Caraid's house in Dubhlinn. From the ceiling dangled bunches of drying greenery, strings of onions and fruit. Fresh plants, some chopped, lay beside a wooden cleaver at one end of a rugged table. In the central hearth a low fire burned, warming a soapstone kettle suspended from an old copper tripod.

But there were differences. Caraid lived in a comfortable jumble, as if her belongings were often rearranged by the random hand of a careless breeze. Mother Aud's orderly house was more sparsely furnished and somehow more restful. A loom and a spindle stood in one corner near some wooden chests and boxes. A bench was pulled up to the table, with more boxes serving as seats on the other side. Stoppered flasks of flawed Rhenish glass and other cracked oddments of crockery, all of which would have been costly if unblemished, gleamed in crowded ranks upon the shelves along one plank-lined wall. The glassware was full of berries, seeds, powders and dried plants. Sleeping niches, covered with furs, were built into the opposite wall. Clean straw covered the earthen floor, and three round loaves of bread sat cooling by the well-swept, stone-lined hearth.

Freshly baked bread, by the smell. Tomas's stomach contracted. He'd not eaten since morning, and the Sun was setting fast.

Mother Aud saw his glance at the loaves. "Come, share my evening meal."

In companionable silence, they ate a thick hearty stew served hot from the kettle with warm fresh bread. Tomas stretched his long legs, straightened his spine and felt his muscles slowly begin to relax. It was as if they released, little by little, the strain of his hurried walk here, the conversations with Ottar and the Birka woman, the hours in the traders' booth and the long watches at sea. When he let out a single deep sigh, grateful for the peace of this quiet room, Mother Aud gave him a smile but said nothing. And that suited Tomas admirably. Her calm was contagious.

When he declined a third helping of stew, Mother Aud carried their bowls outside in the twilight. She returned with an enormous beaker of ale, two mugs and a platter of dried apple slices. The room had grown darker, and Mother Aud took two soapstone bowls of tallow and lit their wicks. Tomas praised the meal—the first words either of them had spoken for nearly an hour.

She thanked him, then asked, "Have you ever kneaded bread dough?"

"No." He was puzzled, but too at ease to be startled. Any and all questions seemed askable and appropriate now, from the mild dweller in this mild room.

"I hadn't quite finished when you came," said Mother Aud, placing a wide-mouthed jug of flour on the table. She set an oblong cloth-covered wooden trough before Tomas, another before herself, and sat down again. Removing the cloth from each trencher, she revealed two mounds of sticky dough, which she liberally dusted with flour. She rubbed more flour into her palms and indicated that Tomas should do the same.

Like a ripple on the surface of deep water, a twinkle moved through her dark blue eyes with their odd central sunburst of amber. "It's thirsty work. We'll likely require lots of ale," she told him solemnly, and chuckled when he agreed.

Mother Aud kept their mugs full. Tomas found that he rather enjoyed kneading, decided he would like it with or without ale. It soothed him, somehow, the rhythmic pushes with the flat of his hands against the dough's increasing resiliency. "From your shoulders, not your elbows," was Mother Aud's only comment. She nodded approval when he got the motion right.

That batch done and the loaves set to rise, they began on another. Munching a piece of dried apple, Tomas was up to his elbows in flour when Mother Aud asked, "Did the merchanter captain miss what you gave to the lake-Elf?"

Tomas paused in his kneading. Mother Aud worked the dough with the swift efficient motions of long practice. In the muted illumination of the tallow lamps and the fire, her face was tranquil, its strong stark bones emphasized by the shifting light. She gave him a steady look, at once searching and patient.

"I think so. He was looking at the bolt of cloth. But I left before he could ask me about it." Somehow he was not surprised that Mother Aud had seen the lake-Elf.

"Will you be returning?"

That, of course, was the question. "Not to the ship. I've paid off my passage."

"But?" she prompted, pouring more ale.

"I still need to earn the fare to Uppsala."

"Ah." She studied his eyes. "But if the captain finds you singing in the market, you might be obliged to pay for his fabric, or be prosecuted for thieving?"

The last word made Tomas wince, but he nodded.

"There is something else, I think. Besides the cloth," she said, very gently.

He could think of no reason why Mother Aud should not know. Keeping his voice uninflected, he said, "I told a customer--the same customer, twice--that a shawl buckle was only coated with silver and gold, when the captain had said it was pure gold and silver throughout."

"And was it?"

"No. He was lying."

When Mother Aud laid a powdery hand on his arm, he stopped pounding his portion of dough. "Look at me, lad. Why didn't you lie, too?"

Before that shrewd compassionate gaze, Tomas felt his caution, his need for reserve, crumble away.

He told her everything. Of his childhood, marked by his mother's slavery and his own illegitimacy, by a domineering father and brothers with their passion for the arts of war. Of Tomas's own passion for and training in a different set of arts: music and rhyme. His days at court, and how his liaison with Sigrun had driven him aboard Olaf's ship.

And everything since the *Brilliant Dragon* ran aground on the banks of the Saefren. Tomas's flight from the slaughter and the Nornir-- to Moira. Aubrey and Elfland; Rhys and Caraid. Moira's gifts, tangible and intangible. Hel's pursuit, and Tomas's task. Alfred, Linley and the Saxons; Hrolf and the draug. The dolphin. Ivar's court--and how Olaf died. Caraid again, and Tomas's journey to Birka and to this house.

He even told Mother Aud his name.

It made for a lengthy recitation. Through it all, she sat motionless and listened, having released her grip on his arm and laid her flour-covered hands in her lap. Only the deepening of the lines in her forehead betrayed the extent of her concentration. A few times, when he told her of the Nornir, Moira's gifts and the ravens, or when he spoke of Linley or Caraid, there was an almost imperceptible flickering in Mother Aud's dark blue eyes. Otherwise, dispassionate and still, her gaze never wavered from him. Rarely had anyone listened to Tomas so closely.

"The Birka woman startled me, so I just blurted out that the buckle was coated, without stopping to think of ways round it," he finished.

"You have tried to lie, since the Elf Queen returned you to Midgard? Tried and failed?"

"Yes, to both."

She nodded slowly. No surprise showed in her hawk-like features, and no pity. Tomas returned the look of calm consideration that she gave him.

A log crackled; a spark flew out to flare and die on the stone hearth. Mother Aud got up to cover the last two loaves of bread with damp cloth and set them to rise. After she and Tomas washed and dried their hands, she retrieved her spindle from the corner, and they sat by the fire again.

This time he was more prepared when she asked, "What would you like to know?"

"About my Fate? So much that I can scarcely tell where to begin asking. Nor what you could answer."

"Nor I, until you ask." A smile creased her face. Her fingers, working the spindle, moved with assurance in the uneven light.

"The Elves," Tomas said, hesitating. "You saw the lake-Elf; you know something of them. Why does Moira want the ravens?"

"Thought and Memory," said Mother Aud softly, without slowing her hands. "Birds of the dead from the god of the dead, desired by an Elf Queen who cannot die. Some pattern, some riddle is at work here. For Odin is your god too."

Into Tomas's mind rose the images of a bloody town in Waleis and his headlong run to the Saefren. And the phantom of Olaf, looming above his own corpse in Ivar of Dubhlinn's hall. "Was my god," Tomas whispered.

Mother Aud gave him a keen glance. "God of poetry and magic."

He shrugged, not to gainsay her but to convey his confusion. An expression he couldn't interpret moved across her face and was gone.

"Ravens are birds of the dead," she said again. "They fly through the nine worlds and tell Odin what they see. She who calls herself Moira cannot die, nor can she fly through the nine worlds."

"No." He hunted for the exact phrase. "She said that their movements in Midgard were increasingly limited."

"Ah." Mother Aud's eyes were intent and very clear. Touching him like a current of balmy air, a profound sense of peace flowed from her, and some of the tension left his muscles. Yet it was not the sort of ease that leads to sleep. "And did she tell you why?"

Closing his eyes, Tomas concentrated. "Something about exorcisms hemming them in. And Odin's berserkers." He reached back in his memory for the rest of what he had heard. "And the two worlds drifting apart."

"Two worlds. Faerie the timeless, and mortal Midgard where the Elves are constrained. They require Odin's birds of death to--" Mother Aud grew quite still, then set the spindle on the floor. "A portion of it, at least, I begin to grasp. Elves cannot die. All of time lies before them, but they are limited in the world of form." She glanced at Tomas. When he nodded, she continued, "While mortals have only a limited time to live, but can go largely where they will in Midgard." Again she paused for his reaction.

"And?"

"And more than mortals, the ravens can roam at will through the world of form, to perceive places where Moira can no longer go. And, perhaps, be used to extend her influence there again. Who knows?"

It fit. It made sense. "That might be why she wants them," Tomas said slowly, frowning. So much remained a puzzle. "But why do exorcisms restrict the Elves? And why does the cult of Odin?"

After a long moment, Mother Aud said, "It could be a matter of beliefs. Beliefs have energy and power, and occupy space. Like names, after a fashion." She gave him a penetrating look. "The Nazarenes recognize no power but their own god, and as they spread through Midgard, the Elves find themselves constrained here. Perhaps Odin loses power as well, as the Nazarenes grow in numbers."

Pondering Mother Aud's idea about beliefs, Tomas scarcely heard her last two sentences. He decided she was probably right. After putting another log on the hearth, he stretched from head to toe and then asked, "But how could the Elves be constrained by Odin's followers? They recognize that Asgard has other gods. Some of them still sacrifice to the Elves."

"I could not say with any assurance. But you are not thinking, Tomas. One answer to that, you should know better than I." Her voice was gentle.

Tomas stared. She gazed back, her face tranquil.

No need for impatience; he was in no haste. Night had long since fallen, and the path to Birka town would be treacherous in the dark. Even in the light of day, a return to town would present its own hazards depending on Ottar's mood: a beating, a fine. Although Tomas had to earn passage to the mainland somehow.

"What do Odin's worshippers carry with them, berserker or no? And the raiders of the southern lands also?" asked Mother Aud.

He almost knew; he all but said it.

"What is there none of in this room, nor upon your person?" Something thudded insistently at the heavy-timbered door. It swung open; crisp night air streamed into the house. In the stillness of the room, the noise was loud and jarring.

Tomas had just enough time to notice how Mother Aud did not startle at the sound, before he spun on his heels and sank into a defensive stance. He smelled the acrid taint of iron--and something earthier.

He found himself face to face with a plump, shaggy goat.

The goat spared Tomas one brief indignant glare from her wild golden eyes, then trotted determinedly past him, making straight for the cloth-covered loaves on the hearth. A small iron bell at her throat jingled softly. Moving with surprising speed, Mother Aud seized the bread and put it on a shelf above the animal's reach. The goat bleated with irritation but accepted an apologetic scratch between the ears.

Tomas straightened up and started to laugh.

Mother Aud was chuckling. "Forgot Helga's supper, I did." She urged the goat towards the open door. "Sit you down again; I shan't be long."

"Iron," said Tomas when she returned. "The raiders carry iron. Why have you none here?" He gave her a quick assessing glance, and decided that she wasn't an Elf. Wise, yes; uncanny even, but human. Exactly why he was so certain he could not have explained, except perhaps that her eyes were too *present* for those of an Elf.

Mother Aud was smiling. "I have no Elf blood at all, Tomas. There is no iron here because it would discomfit the lake-Elves, who sometimes come calling."

"Does it discomfit you?" he asked, trying not to sound blunt.

"Not at all. I can perceive the Elves; I was born with the Sight." She shrugged. "I have little fear of them. Respect, yes--and sometimes pity." Her voice was very soft. "But they have worked no transformations on me, and given me no such gifts as they have given you. And I've not had your prolonged stay in Alfheim." Unexpectedly, she grinned. "Still, I am fond of my goat."

His mouth twitched, remembering his collusion in the theft from Ottar's booth. "The lake-Elves must pilfer a quantity of goods from the market."

"Over the years I expect they have," she agreed, studying him.

"What are you thinking?"

"That most mortals carry iron or have it about them in some form nowadays. Most mortals, not just warriors."

She looked faintly pleased with him, as if he had accomplished some minor feat of reasoning. "And all nine worlds are drifting further apart," she said, and added musingly, "'True speech and prophecy.' If you saw only one truth and only one world, Tomas, how could you move between them?"

She was right: it was one reason for that particular gift.

They regarded one another across the hearthfire. Tomas set down his refilled mug of ale untouched. Mother Aud's shadowy house was still and rather close, although less so since the recent influx of night air. Voices can carry farther than one might think, upon such air. Tomas looked at the door but made no move to open it.

A bitter taste filled his mouth. From the core of him rose the central question: what he most deeply wished to know about himself, his life, his Fate. "Why did Moira choose me for this deed?"

His gaze met and held that of Mother Aud. Winter-still she sat, her face absolutely tranquil, her dark blue eyes equally serene. In their depths he saw the fire reflected. At last she said, as one who states an obvious fact, "It suited you."

"Suited her, rather."

Mother Aud's voice was not unkind. "That remains to be seen. But it suited you. Or you were suited to it."

Biting back a more sarcastic retort, Tomas asked, "Then I was born to steal ravens from Odin?"

When she made no reply, he took a deep breath and asked humbly, "Would you please explain how it suited me?"

For the first time, her face changed. The creases between her grey-white eyebrows deepened. Tilting her head to one side, she gave him a long appraising look. He returned it as steadily as he could.

She wasn't doubtful, but she was weighing a decision. Some matter of judgment and not a trivial one, yet it didn't worry her. Her attitude reminded him of someone. And then he knew: his flute master, when Tomas played a more difficult piece than the teacher had thought he could handle. But Mother Aud's expression wasn't quite the same. There was assessment and a desire to guide, but no surprise, no doubt and no pride. It was a look one gives an equal, not a pupil.

Such a look, from such a woman, both perplexed and unnerved Tomas, but he didn't break the gaze. His hands started to tingle.

"It is my belief that without the Sight," began Mother Aud, "without an abundant measure of the Sight—though it may have been

232

dormant till then--you would not have perceived the Nornir in the sky above that village. Moira herself may have wanted to be seen, but I suspect she would not have made it easy. Your seeing her proved that you were well-fitted to her purposes."

The tingle in Tomas's hands moved up his arms and became almost an itch. From the center of his body, warmth crept outward along his limbs and met the tingling. The air around Mother Aud and himself took on a subtle golden tint.

"But the Nornir have no such purposes and no such designs to be seen."

"They don't want to be seen?" Tomas's heart thudded painfully, remembering the Nornir's bloody loom. Half the room glowed a pale saffron.

Mother Aud was shaking her head. "It is irrelevant to them. They don't experience desire as mortals do, nor as do the gods. The gods themselves are subject to the Nornir's weaving." She paused. "Yet you perceived them and, according to Moira, on a rare occasion when they wove awry."

He was still confused. "Then it's rare to see them? What does that mean?"

"I don't know." Almost-tangible, amber currents of air swirled dizzyingly around the two of them, but Mother Aud appeared not to notice. "You saw the Fates," she continued. "The Elf Queen said that a thread worked loose, and when she called, you came. She implied that you should have died by the river."

Tomas nodded bleakly.

"Of all the dying men and women I have nursed, not one has had a vision of the Nornir. And the dying have many a vision," she muttered. Tomas had the impression she was talking to herself. "Yet I think you could have perceived the Fates without Moira." After a protracted silence, she said, "Tomas. Did you see, actually see, a thread come loose from the loom?"

The air was raddled with ivory light that seemed, here and there, to be coalescing into streaks, while the warmth and tingling had subsided. "No," he said slowly. "No, I saw the Rune, Perthro, and the loom. And the Nornir. One of them quite clearly: Urd, she who spins the past. I don't remember more. I couldn't look for long."

"Ah." Mother Aud's expression was peculiar. "Then you must learn. Will yourself to look long and deeply at everything, until you perceive the core of it--and especially at yourself."

"What?"

"Why else are you a poet? Why else have the Sight? You are

foolish, in that you don't employ your gifts to the full."

Stung, Tomas started to reply, but she interrupted.

"You are no warrior; why agree to make songs about berserkers?" Her voice was low and incisive. "Why suspect nothing that Moira said, when you must have sensed layer upon layer of motives? Why not face Hel? She does not kill; she receives the dead, and you're a living man. Why leave Linley and Caraid?"

It was too much; she had gone too far. "I was compelled to find Thought and Memory!" he snapped.

"You do not look far enough beneath the surface of things," Mother Aud said calmly. "You do not ask the right questions."

"It came upon me, I tell you. It was my Fate!"

Leaning forward, Mother Aud reached for Tomas's hands. He was tempted to jerk them away, but the impulse seemed childish. Her grip was warm and firm, and he could feel the bones beneath her dry fragile skin. Pallid but distinct lines of energy now formed a kind of web throughout the house, with the two of them at its center. He'd seen such a web before, in Alfred of Wessex's tent.

"Look at me, Tomas," she said quietly. In that moment, she had the most compassionate eyes he had ever seen.

"Your own nature is your Fate," said Mother Aud.

CHAPTER FORTY-TWO: THE FARE TO THE MAINLAND

Tomas and Mother Aud spoke no more that evening, not from hostility or awkwardness, but because there seemed nothing more to say.

Although he expected to lie awake half the night, Tomas slept well. Wrapped in a fur on a sleeping-bench, he awakened early and blinked at the thin rays of morning light that streamed down through the smoke hole in the roof. The northern Sun had been up for hours. Except for a trim little ginger-colored cat he'd not seen before, Mother Aud's sleeping niche was empty. She hadn't mentioned going to market; perhaps she was tending her goat.

Tomas stepped outside and washed his face and hands with rain water from a well-caulked barrel near the door. It was cooler than the previous day. The sky was a brilliant cloudless blue, and there was only a light breeze. After carrying in some wood for the fire, he started looking for Mother Aud.

He found her in a small clearing directly behind the house. She waved to him; she was feeding the goat, an ugly rooster and three hens. The rooster flapped his wings and rushed to peck at Tomas's feet before she shooed the bird away.

After a breakfast of bread, goat cheese and dried apples, Tomas said, "I thank you for your kindness, Mother Aud, but I must continue on my errand."

"If you feel you must, you must," she said cheerfully, sweeping crumbs from under the table.

"After Ottar leaves, I can more easily sing in the marketplace, but I don't know when that will be. Until I can repay your hospitality, pray tell me how I might make myself useful here." He didn't understand why a flash of amusement crossed her face. "Your woodpile is low, and I can climb up to see if the roof wants mending." Then he smiled to show he was teasing. "Perhaps Helga's goatpen isn't quite sound?"

"Yes, to the roof and the woodpile," she said, smiling back at him. "And I've an old harp that I hope you can repair. But don't sing at the market. Ottar might have lodged a complaint, and he's many a friend here."

"I still need to raise the fare," Tomas began.

"The lake-Elves," Mother Aud told him, and chuckled at his expression. "No, not an underwater route to the mainland! But you did an Elf a good turn the other day." She picked up a birchwood walking stick. "Come with me." At the door, she paused and gave him a

235

thoughtful scrutiny. "You're not leaving yet, but bring your satchel."

Tomas followed Mother Aud down a twisting narrow path that started from the clearing behind her house. She refused his help and used the stick only twice, when stepping over fallen logs slippery with moss. The trail was drier than he'd expected, and burrs clung to his clothing. From the marshy smell in the air, he guessed that they were headed to the lake.

He was right. They soon came to a small deserted cove, where Birch Island twined its sandy arms about the shadowed blue-black water. It was very quiet and cool on the strand where the Sun had not yet reached.

The ground was damper here. Seating herself upon a stump, Mother Aud said, "Play something that might attract your lake-Elf friend. Best not to try a summoning unless you must."

A summoning, as Moira had summoned him? He started to suspect what Mother Aud had in mind, and he trusted her. So, tuning his harp, Tomas considered what sort of song would draw the Elf. Wishing he had Linley's lute, he dropped his voice into a lower register and sang:

"Pooka," they call me; my friends are few.
Maybe it's because of the murders I do.
Maybe it's the bones in the mud by the river.
Maybe it's the mark of Moira.

Rhymer, I'll bear you past Hel to Midgard.
It's the realm of the mortals, so best be on guard.
They're treach'rous; they're fragile; they're barely a snack.
Never, never trust one behind your back.

From the corner of his eye, Tomas saw Mother Aud's face display something not quite strong enough to be called surprise, followed by amused approval, before settling back to its habitual calm. Using his natural voice, he continued:

Pooka, tell me what the Elf Queen knows
What my chances are, do you suppose?
Am I a thief? More like a falling leaf,
And a hard wind blows...
Why am I chasing Odin's crows?

Before Tomas finished the last drawn-out syllable, he heard the

236

susurration of displaced water. The lake-Elf he'd seen at Birka market surfaced, sleeked her dripping hair back from her delicate face and waded ashore, making straight for him. Her expression was sterner than her slanting brown eyes.

"Ravens, not crows, Fool," she said, stopping two paces in front of him—disquietingly close. She exchanged nods with Mother Aud.

Apparently Tomas's shrug conveyed the humorous half-apology that he intended, because the Elf grinned. He hadn't noticed when she kissed him, but she had rather a lot of teeth. He was grateful for the distraction from the way her wet clothes clung to her body, although they seemed to be shedding water uncommonly fast.

"Skalds versify as they please," she said. "But why sing of pookas at Lake Malar? Moira is not our Queen."

"I know," he said shortly, and replaced his harp in the satchel.

Her fine brown eyebrows shot up. "And why sing of thievery, so close to Salvik harbor? You and I both have reason for such songs not to carry there."

With only a hazy idea what his reply would be, Tomas opened his mouth and heard himself say, "I hoped the tune might bring you. If you would be so kind as to assist me, I am in need of your aid."

The lake-Elf grew utterly still. She gave him an unreadable stare, glanced at Mother Aud, then back at Tomas. "Very well," she said quietly. "You've a claim upon it." Turning, she sat down on the strand by Mother Aud's stump and motioned for Tomas to join them. "What would you ask of me?" Her face was serious and composed.

"I haven't enough silver for the passage to the mainland," he explained, seated across from her. "But it would be wiser not to sing for it in the marketplace, and not to embark from Birka while the *Fjord-elk* is still here. Can you help me?"

The lake-Elf had plucked a blade of grass and was turning it about in her narrow six-fingered hands. Touching it to the tip of her chin, she said, "The *Fjord-elk* sails at first light tomorrow. A most profitable run, they say." She drew the blade of grass down Tomas's face and added sweetly, "Despite certain losses."

Tomas and Mother Aud both smiled.

"So all you require is some coins for your fare," said the Elf, rising nimbly to her feet. "I can't decide if I'm relieved or disappointed." She darted towards the lake. "Wait here."

In the arc of an astonishing leap, she tucked her head, brought her knees up to her chest, then kicked out strongly and dived into Lake Malar. Tomas let out a low whistle and walked to the water's edge to study the series of concentric rings that rippled out from where the lake had just closed over the Elf's bare pointed toes. When he glanced over his shoulder at Mother Aud, she was absorbed in rubbing sand from the end of her walking stick. Not the first time she'd seen this, then.

He went to sit with her again. "Will she be long?" he asked.

"I think not," said Mother Aud comfortably.

After five or six more minutes, at precisely the spot where she had dived, the lake-Elf surfaced. She swam a few powerful strokes, then waded the rest of the way ashore. Something large and bumpy was tied into the skirt of her dress. Through a rip in the faded shift she wore underneath, one of her knees and a few inches of thigh showed.

Sinking gracefully down on the strand beside Tomas, she busied herself loosening the wet knots. Her skirt was fastened around a kerchief, which in turn was twisted about something heavy. Hearing the clink of metal, Tomas wasn't surprised when the kerchief fell open to reveal a pile of coins.

What startled him was the amount of them. With the palm of one hand, the lake-Elf swept the coins into a gleaming swathe across the damp tattered hem of her dress. Gold winked among the coins, others of which were tarnished in varying degrees. Some were broken; some were whole, and several very old, and of mintage that Tomas had never seen.

He started to say that this was far more than necessary, but remembered that he still had to make his way from the coastline to Uppsala itself. "How can I thank you?" he asked, his voice low. "You are more than generous." Curiously, he picked up one ancient gold coin, imprinted with the badly worn image of a flower.

The Elf chuckled. "Perhaps I found your song to my liking." Then she shrugged and said dryly, "Time and travelers have been generous to the lake. We cannot spend it down below. And in Birka town, we're marked by these." She waggled her twelve fingers, re-knotted the coins in the kerchief and gave it to Tomas. "Well now, my heart. Am I discharged of my debt?" she asked, smiling, and stood up.

"Indeed, yes. How could you not be?" said Tomas, getting to his feet.

"Oh, in one way or three," she said cryptically. Standing on tiptoe, her hands on Tomas's shoulders, she gave him the kiss he had half-expected and this time cautiously returned.

"Farewell," she said, then dived into the lake without a backward glance.

CHAPTER FORTY-THREE: FAREWELL TO BIRKA

With an eye out for boats that might ferry cargo and passengers along the waterway to Uppsala, Tomas and Mother Aud strolled slowly through Kornhamm harbor. Although the wind was fair and the sunny morning a fine one for sailing, Tomas found it hard to attend to the search. He hated to leave Mother Aud.

After his talk with the lake-Elf, he'd spent the rest of the previous day restringing an ancient harp, cutting firewood and repairing Mother Aud's roof. The afternoon being warm, he'd tossed his straw-covered jerkin and boots down from the thatch and kept working. When he finished at sunset, he found his shirt washed and mended and his satchel, boots and belt cleaned and oiled. Mother Aud had even re-greased the wrappings of Tomas's instruments and found him a leather pouch for the lake-Elf's coins. They'd spent a peaceful evening together; he tuned her harp and played it while she worked at her weaving.

This morning, when they had almost reached the harbor, Mother Aud stopped, placed a hand on his arm and said quietly, "A word with you, Tomas. About your gifts."

He halted in mid-stride to gaze down at her. Her eyes were gentle but dispassionate and absolutely serious. Reaching up to clasp his shoulders, she told him, "Harper, poet, Seer: your truths are as valid as a warrior's. Only trust them, and they can carry you beyond time."

Then she turned her back to him, stepped off the path that wound through the island's juniper and birch, and onto the cleared area and wooden plankways of the northernmost harbor. Reading the finality in the set of her shoulders, Tomas realized she would say no more on that subject. Mutely, he had followed her to the waterfront.

Now, while they walked past a varying assortment of boats, she linked her left arm through Tomas's right and seemed to lean on him a little, though he knew she was spry enough scarcely to need the walking stick that she carried. He didn't mind. Glancing down at Mother Aud's bent kerchiefed head, he thought briefly of his own dead mother, who had been pliant and impressionable, so different from this strong, perceptive woman.

When someone gave his other arm an intimate squeeze, he looked down and saw the lake-Elf smiling at him. "All morning I've patrolled the harbor, my heart, and where were you?" She pointed to a broad-beamed, barge-like vessel, whose arguing crew was starting to untie its bowlines. "Yonder craft would ferry you up the waterway. Hoping for more passengers, they were, but gave it up just now. They're hauling lead; make haste!"

Having already contrived to hug the Elf and Mother Aud at the same time, Tomas was sprinting for the ship. "I cannot thank you enough," he called over his shoulder, then shouted and waved his arms to attract the crew's attention.

"Come aboard, then," yelled the scowling helmsman, a bony red-bearded Swede. Moving too fast to think, Tomas gathered himself and sprang from the jetty. With inches to spare, he cleared the low rail of the slowly moving boat. His satchel thumped against his back as he landed on the salt-weathered deck.

The helmsman's eyes widened, but he said only, "Whither bound, Leaper? If you haven't the silver, it's straight back ashore." The rowers held their blades flat against the lake water and waited.

"To Uppsala, or as near as you'll take me." From his pouch, he fished the largest silver coin he could find and gave it to the red-bearded man. "Will that suffice?" Some instinct told Tomas to glance towards the farthest boundary of the harbor--where he saw Ottar and the three largest members of his crew.

But the lake-Elf had said they were sailing at dawn. Tomas shaded his eyes for a better look. Still some distance away, pointing and shouting, Ottar and his Halogalanders began to run through the crowded harbor towards the slip that the Swedish ferry was now ponderously leaving.

The ferry captain saw only the coin in his hands. "Odd," he muttered. "Pure silver it looks, but I've never seen its like."

Tomas spotted the Elf dodging nimbly among livestock and sailors and slaves. Her eyes mischievous and intent, she raced barefooted towards Ottar and his crewmen, and her ragged clothing fluttered in her wake. Darting in front of Ottar--it seemed incredible that no one else saw her--she thrust one sleekly muscled leg into his path and tripped him.

Ottar fell heavily to the wooden plankway. Unable to check their pace with so little warning, the three burly traders crashed down on top of their captain in a pile of churning limbs. A few other passersby, including a bailiff, stumbled and fell with them. Off to one side now, atop a massive wooden post near the water's edge, the lake-Elf cackled and did an exultant little dance. Her dainty face looked more feral than Tomas would have believed possible, and he stifled a shudder.

Mother Aud waved to him from the shore. When Tomas waved back, the Elf blew him an ostentatious kiss.

A tap on Tomas's shoulder: the red-bearded Swede presented him with a handful of broken silver coins. "That settles our account for the trip. Unless you'd like it weighed?" His stare at Tomas was calculating and edged with suspicion, but not hostile. The crew looked attentive—and sullenly hopeful.

How much silver had changed hands, and who had profited? But Tomas declined to weigh what the Swede gave him, and put the coins in his pouch. The crew watched him, even those who were moving to put up a rather frayed sail, now that they'd cleared some of the Birch Island traffic.

Tomas unshouldered his satchel, tucked the smaller pouch into it and shrugged it onto his back again. Then he offered to help with the sail.

"No," said the helmsman, pointing to a seat on a nearby sea chest. "You're a paying passenger. Skald, are you? I saw a harp in your pack. My name's Yngvar."

"I'm called the Rhymer." Tomas remained standing. "Yes, I'm a skald."

"Playing at the festival at Uppsala? You've missed the beginning, but they're not done yet."

"What festival?" asked Tomas absently, shading his eyes to watch Mother Aud and the lake-Elf on Birka's receding shoreline. The Elf was still waving.

Yngvar exchanged glances with another man, a dark scar-faced Swede who was hovering nearby. "The nine-year rites. The sacrifices," Yngvar said loudly.

Tomas caught the consternation in the redhead's voice. Gods, the great festival at Uppsala. Now what had he done? Seven years lost in Faerie—yes, this year would be the ninth. "Of course," he said as easily as he could. "The sacrifices. You must pardon my not listening; I was thinking of something else."

"Left a maid behind in Birka, did you?" asked the scarred man after a moment, with an ugly quirk of his mouth.

Tomas gave him a quick glance. Best to fall in with whatever they were thinking. What to say that wouldn't be a lie? "You might put it that way." It wasn't difficult to grin; he imagined the lake-Elf's reaction. "Birka and elsewhere."

The two ferrymen studied him, their faces carefully blank, but he noticed the slight flickering of their eyes towards one another. Smiling, feigning confidence and good cheer, Tomas said, "It ill suits me to sit idle on board any ship. D'you need help with the baling?" An excellent chance they'd accept; this craft was old enough to require an inordinate amount of baling.

"Aye," said Yngvar at last. "You and Thorvald can take the first

241

watch."

Thorvald, a slight, stooped, balding Swede somewhat past middle age, got to his feet without a word. Tomas followed him amidships.

Standing in the hold, which reeked of dead fish, he handed a heavy bucket full of water up to Thorvald on deck, and waited while the smaller man emptied it over the side, then returned it to Tomas for refilling. He was grateful that Thorvald was silent. Baling was a lifelong habit, something that Tomas could do by reflex and still think furiously all the while.

Every nine years, the Svea people held a festival at Uppsala to honor all the gods. He had known that, as did all of the North and most travelers who spent any length of time there. But his voyage to Elfland had thrown off his reckoning, and his reluctance to leave Birka made him inattentive to what Yngvar was saying.

Tomas glanced towards the helm. One hand on the steerboard, the other at his side, Yngvar stood watching him. When the Swede caught Tomas's eye, he quickly looked away.

Damn the time lost in Faerie. His forgetting such a renowned and well-attended festival must seem unbelievable to these insular Swedish ferrymen. According to Ottar, they tolerated the foreigners at Birka with poor grace at best. Tomas had already roused their curiosity, if not their suspicion, by the strange silver coin that paid his fare.

A husky young billy goat bleated uneasily in the malodorous hold and pulled at his tether. Gnawing his lip, Tomas glanced from the goat to the crates of chickens nearby. Each had its rooster. There were sacrifices at this festival: nine males of every creature that could be found.

Including men.

Tales held that in the dim past, it was not unknown for the Svea people to sacrifice their own Kings. More recently, they'd offered up male prisoners of war. Or the poor, with no one to speak for them. Or slaves.

Or foreigners.

"Where do you hail from, Rhymer?" asked a voice above him.

Starting slightly, he looked up as the scar-faced man tapped Thorvald on the shoulder and took his place on deck. Handing his new baling partner the bucket, Tomas said, "From Vestfold."

"Then you've come a fair distance."

Tomas nodded.

Despite the ship's motion, the dark man balanced himself and handled the heavy buckets with ease. "First time in Uppland?" he asked.

Tomas nodded again, and jumped up on deck when the Swede finally declared that they'd baled enough for one watch.

He looked in surprise at how the choppy lake water streamed past the hull, and at the white frothy peaks that glinted in the Sun. They were making good time, with a stiff west wind that filled the aged sail. He'd noticed in the hold that the boat wasn't as heavily laden as he'd first thought, which was probably why they wanted passengers. Sighting over the bow, Tomas saw other boats moving along their general course. Festival traffic, headed for the mouth of the waterway, every bright woolen sail taut with the breeze.

The scar-faced Swede, still at Tomas's elbow, asked if he knew anyone in Uppland.

Gods, if he could only lie. This conversation kept establishing his lack of connections here. "Why, yes; I know Yngvar and the crew, and yourself," he said, laughing. "But you've not told me your name."

"Ketil," said the dark man, achieving a more civil tone than before. "Visiting someone, are you? At the festival?"

Why not come right out with the truth? Tomas grinned, then narrowed his eyes and lowered his voice dramatically. "Yes," he intoned. "The priests at the temple. And maybe all the gods in Asgard before I'm done."

He didn't have to force his laughter at Ketil's expression. The Swede appeared unable to decide whether Tomas was mocking him or merely touched in the head. From the curl of his lip, he didn't care for either alternative. At last he muttered, "I see."

Tomas chuckled again. He expected that Ketil would move on, but instead he turned and gazed over the bow towards the waterway. To walk away now might mar the impression that Tomas was trying to create, that of a carefree, eccentric, ingenuous young skald. A likeable fellow, who might well have friends here. Joining Ketil at the rail, he stood and watched the lake water streaming past the hull.

CHAPTER FORTY-FOUR: TIDINGS IN THE WATERWAY

Late that evening they reached the mouth of the waterway, where the land was lush and green. Apart from a boggy strip along the shoreline, the ground climbed steadily, and the air was more crisp. Thin scrubby birches soon mingled with pine, spruce, oak and alder. The sky was still lit by a northern summer Sun when Yngvar ran the ferry ashore.

Tomas helped carry cookware and skin bedrolls down the gangplank. Crayfish ribboned away from the aged hull; squirrels scolded vociferously from the treetops. The crew made camp that night in a clearing among the alders, near a tall narrow stone that marked the head of a wide and unusually level path. The stone was chiseled with precise, formal lines of Runes. Tomas lingered to study them.

"The King's roadway to Uppsala," Yngvar explained, coming up beside him.

"So I see," said Tomas, reading. "The water level fell, and traffic increased enough to warrant a road. Started some years ago. Is it finished?"

"Yes," said Yngvar after a moment. "You can read, then? Skalds can, I suppose." He turned on his heel and headed back to the ship.

The Swedes gathered fallen scrapwood, lit a fire, and made a bland and watery stew to accompany their dried fare. As the sunlight gradually faded, smoke rose in the distance from the hearths of steadings farther inland.

Yngvar didn't address Tomas again that evening, and the rest of the men spoke little even among themselves. The wind was nearly calm now, and the late-fallen night all but still. When Ljot, the youngest member of the crew, cleared his throat and asked Tomas to play for them, he was grateful for a chance to distract himself with music. Yngvar stirred, but no one objected.

Tomas played a few airs he'd learned from Linley and one remembered from Elfland. The ferrymen were silent, some dicing with gaming counters, others staring blankly into the shadow-drenched woods or down the King's roadway. Enjoying himself despite the lack of reactions, Tomas recited some poetry, then started to sing. When perhaps two hours had passed, the first man laid out his bedroll. Others soon followed his example.

The next day, they made an uneventful and lengthy passage; there was almost no wind. By the time Yngvar called a halt, the oars

244

had grown leaden and the water resistant. The ferrymen spent another night camped on the shore near a newer segment of the roadway. Here the woods grew thicker than before, the underwood more tangled, and the settlements lay farther from the thoroughfare.

Although largely ignored again during the day, Tomas was asked to play earlier that second evening. He devoted perhaps an hour to his flute, then set it aside for the harp. Without thinking, he launched into a song about Thor. He saw nods of approval, and hands fingering the hammer amulets worn by many of the crew. Remembering the festival sacrifices at Uppsala, Tomas decided to sing no more of the gods that night.

What to play instead? He let his hands wander the strings until a melody emerged. When scraps of lyrics came to him, he trusted that other words would follow, and began to sing:

Such a lovely lady,
sprung from mist beside me.
I have seen the Elven Queen
and held her against my body.
Long may we tarry
in the ferns and ivy.

Such a trembling mortal,
so young to be a poet.
I have seen the years between
Creation and the present.
Long will he tarry
in the Land of Faerie.

Oh, we're good together,
lying in the heather.
Joy flows; it goes
beyond the human measure.
To the land of Faerie,
beyond the realm of mem'ry...

His hands finished a series of notes; his voice trailed away. Tomas darted an encompassing glance at the crew. A few of them already slept, huddled deep within bedrolls pulled close to the fire, for the air was brisk. Other men stretched out on their backs, arms folded beneath their heads, and gazed at the night-laden sky. Some spoke softly to one another or watched Tomas's hands upon the harpstrings.

245

But three or four Swedes, Yngvar and Ketil among them, were staring fixedly at Tomas. He didn't think it was because of his last song, for he'd intercepted subtler versions of such looks on board ship.

Then he began to sense the intangible pressure of another intent gaze, coming from behind him and to his left, just beyond the clearing. One of the crew must be returning from the forest, after searching for moss to pillow his head, perhaps, or birds' eggs for breakfast. Tomas turned to see who was there.

He saw no one. The alders stood silent and empty, and there came no rustling from the underwood. Yet Tomas's left shoulder and the left side of his face felt warm from the unseen stare that he knew was focused on him from the trees.

Someone cleared his throat near Tomas's elbow. Ljot, the young crew member who'd first asked him to play, stood there looking cautious and hopeful. "Done for the night, Rhymer?"

"I believe I am. Or nearly so."

Ljot came closer, eyeing the harp and the flute. For a moment he made Tomas miss Linley. The tow-headed Swede had the same air of repressed eagerness, if none of Linley's poise. "I've not heard that last song before," Ljot ventured. "Did you write it yourself?"

Tomas said that he had.

"When?"

"Just now."

Ljot's eyes widened. Still sensing the observation from the woods, Tomas fought a temptation to go investigate. Yngvar sat within earshot, and Ljot showed no signs of leaving. "Do you play?" Tomas asked.

The young Swede's blush, faint but uniform, reached all the way to his ears. "A little. I'm still learning."

"So am I," said Tomas, smiling. "So are all skalds. As any honest one will tell you."

Yngvar gave Tomas a skeptical look. "Here's an honest one to teach you fiddling, perhaps." The ferry captain got up and walked off.

Someone called out, "I thought Ljot would sweet-talk the water-Elf for lessons." There were guffaws, and Ljot reddened again.

"Last trip he saw the fossegrimen, wasn't it?"

"No, the one before. Right here at Wolf Point."

"Till then he'd just heard it fiddling in midstream."

When Ljot made the crewmen no answer, their talk soon turned to other things. Tomas took a long time cleaning his flute, glad of an excuse to hide his face.

Fossegrimen were Norse water-Elves who were seen--when

246

they were seen—perched on rocks out in running water or lurking under bridges. Sometimes they frequented waterwheels or mills. Capricious, occasionally spiteful, fossegrimen were unsurpassed fiddlers. Legend held that if properly coaxed, they might give lessons, but that was a rare event.

Tomas would have wagered a great deal that a fossegrimen never taught his craft without some kind of recompense. Now he had a hunch about who was watching him from the woods. He could have pointed directly at the source of the unseen gaze, some fifty yards away. "You have seen a fossegrimen here?" he asked Ljot, his voice low and courteous.

After squinting judiciously at Tomas in the dim light, Ljot appeared to decide that the question was serious. "Only once," he said softly. "But I've heard it many a time."

"The others don't believe you?" Tomas jerked his chin in the direction of the crew. Those who remained awake were all dicing around the fire as it burned low in the evening air.

"They believe there's a fossegrimen here, all right. There always has been." Ljot's mouth twisted. "But none of them has ever seen him."

Tomas found himself looking at what he could see of Ljot's hands. Skin roughened from work and the Sun, they were scarred and grimy but strong, long-boned and supple. And half-clenched just now, as though Ljot expected Tomas not to believe him either. Were those a fiddler's callouses on the fingertips?

This could have been myself, thought Tomas, and not so long ago. He suppressed a sigh. "Then either none of them has the Sight—or the fossegrimen chooses not to be seen by them," he said quietly. Shouldering his satchel, he picked his way several yards farther from the fire and from the watcher in the woods. "Come sit with me a while," he said over his shoulder to Ljot. Unnecessarily, for the boy was following at Tomas's heels, his eyes wide with fascination and his mouth slightly open.

Had Tomas stared at Mother Aud that way? He managed not to wince. "Get your fiddle," he suggested, and sat down.

Nearly tripping over a root in his haste, Ljot ran to his bedroll and came back with an oblong bundle which he handed to Tomas. The fiddle was wrapped in a piece of brittle leather seamed with cracks, but when Tomas opened it, he discovered that the inner surface of the hide was clean and oiled. The instrument itself was old but well-made, and its neck and bow had no warps.

"I've not tuned it today," said Ljot, reaching for the fiddle.

247

Tomas gave it to him, then inquired bluntly, "Did you ask the fossegrimen for a lesson?" He could still feel the gaze from the trees but would speak with Ljot regardless.

"N-not yet."

"Don't."

Ljot looked up, his fingers busy at the strings, and an unspoken protest on his lips.

"I mean, not now. Not yet," said Tomas, afraid he sounded half-mad. "Wait till he offers to teach you."

"But would he offer?"

"Perhaps. If he were in your debt."

Ljot put the fiddle down, then took its leather wrappings and folded them carefully, oiled side in. His eyes, round and wary, never left Tomas, who cursed to himself. This exchange was not going well, when he'd merely wanted to help. He picked up the fiddle, which was now in perfect tune.

"Excellent!" he said, and was heartened to see Ljot's smile. "Here, play something. Good! Good...ah, that last measure dragged. You must attend to the beat."

So Ljot played, while Tomas encouraged him and played some as well. He found himself enjoying the lesson. Ljot's diffidence soon fled. With almost no training, the boy had a good ear, a deft touch, and didn't need to be told anything more than twice. When Tomas said so, Ljot thanked him, sounding pleased and surprised. His crooked teeth glinted as he put the fiddle down and flexed his hands.

After glancing over both shoulders, Ljot said softly, "A while ago, Rhymer. Did you mean that it's best not to make myself beholden to the fossegrimen?"

Sharp wits. "That," said Tomas approvingly, "is precisely what I meant. But if he should consider himself beholden to you somehow, that's when to ask him for lessons." Noting the sudden gleam in Ljot's eyes, Tomas added, "For just one lesson might be wisest--and I believe you're wiser than I."

Slowly, knitting his eyebrows, Ljot opened his mouth to ask why. Tomas pretended not to notice. Pointing at the bright dusting of stars overhead, he exclaimed at how late it had grown, and about how they should both get some sleep.

The next morning dawned clear and calm, and promised to be cooler than the day before. They hadn't much farther to travel. Wolf Point was only a short distance from where Yngvar wanted to unload his cargo, at the beginning of the section of road that led to Uppsala town some sixteen miles inland.

At first they thought to have no wind at all, so fair and still had the morning been. But not long after sunrise a few thin clouds appeared in the sky, as if blown there by the newly risen breeze. There was a moist piney scent to the air.

Standing calf-deep in the water off Wolf Point, Tomas scoured the last of the soapstone cookware. His satchel seemed heavier than marble, and he cursed himself for not leaving it on the bank beside his boots. The water was rapidly chilling his bare feet and shins.

What little sleep he'd gotten was racked with vivid dreams. Hel pursuing him with lumbering uneven steps. Himself running through a dark wood, with crashing in the underbrush and Rhys shouting nearby. And Moira, but Tomas couldn't tell if he was fleeing her, or she him. There was something important that she hadn't told him. Once he saw her and grabbed her arm, but when she turned, she had Hel's face.

There were other dreams. Linley at Chippenham fort at night, holding a lamp while Simon tended wounded men. Both brothers appeared tired and grim but unhurt, and some of the injured were well on the mend. Neither man said a word.

Somehow aware that he was dreaming and perhaps more than dreaming, Tomas tried to guide the images. Speak, he urged Linley silently. How is it with you? And with Alfred?

Shifting to give Simon better light, Linley looked up and wiped his grimy forehead with the back of his arm, but said nothing.

Speak, pleaded Tomas, but the scene at Chippenham was blurring.

Then he saw Caraid. Her back very straight, she sat before her own hearthfire and gazed unblinkingly at the flames. He thought she might be tranced. A somber-looking Brendan knelt beside her, holding her unresponsive hand. Tomas had roused himself from that dream, the last before dawn, by calling Caraid's name in a voice hoarse and muffled with sleep.

Now a heavy kettle slipped from his hands; they were slick with cooking grease. Before he could catch it, the kettle struck his bare cold foot. There was pain, sharp and intense, and a thin line of blood ribboned out into the water.

He cursed, the longest and most eloquent Welsh oaths that he knew. After retrieving the kettle, he examined his foot. The cut was superficial, but he'd have a thoroughly blackened bruise.

The shock and the pain seemed to have jarred something loose inside him, some stuck, resigned place. He muttered to himself in

Welsh. "Why continue this mad journey?"

Mother Aud had said that he didn't ask the right questions, nor look far enough beneath the surface of things, especially at himself. And that he should trust his gifts. But which ones?

"Why not stop here and take my chances?" he said between clenched teeth, lapsing back into Norse. "At Uppsala court, at least long enough to fatten my purse." He nested the pots inside one another, turned to wade ashore, still fuming--and saw the fossegrimen.

The water-Elf sat motionless on a large rock in midstream. His eyes flickered when they met Tomas's gaze. The fossegrimen carried the best fiddle that Tomas had ever seen, yet it was slung across the Elf's shoulder by an incongruously ancient strap of worn and faded cloth. His garments hung from his body in tatters. Something about the pattern of rips appeared deliberate... Tomas looked at the fiddle strap again.

It was braided. The fossegrimen had shredded his own clothing to make it. Still, the strap was so frayed that it seemed alarmingly close to giving way and dumping the fine instrument in the water.

The Elf was giving Tomas a calm, thorough appraisal. How long had the fossegrimen been there, and under what if any spell of concealment? When Tomas first waded into the water to scrub the cookware, there'd been no one on that boulder in midstream.

Tomas guessed that the Elf was of medium height and build, though it was difficult to tell, since he was seated. Extraordinarily thick and snarled hair, a shade or two lighter than the color of dry pine needles, hung halfway to his waist. With no trace of a beard or a moustache, his skin was fine-textured and pale. His high-bridged nose was large and beaky, and his mouth was full. The fossegrimen's deep-set, blue-green eyes were very mild and a trifle sad, but Tomas caught the glitter of a shrewd intelligence in their depths.

"Good morrow to you, skald," said the water-Elf in a rich, well-modulated baritone. He saluted Tomas with the fiddle bow. "Why not unburden yourself of that crockery? I shall wait."

Tomas stowed the pots high on the bank, gave his feet a cursory wipe with some leaves and pulled his boots on. When he faced the fossegrimen again, the Elf asked conversationally, "Why might you be advising your young acquaintance about the prospects of instruction with me?"

Still taking the Elf's measure, Tomas said nothing.

The fossegrimen appeared unperturbed. "You'd no wish to profit from your own lesson; you collected naught in return," he

250

continued. "Not that your advice and instruction were bad. Quite the contrary." The blue-green eyes locked with his. "What is your name?" asked the water-Elf, his voice very soft.

Tomas maintained an air of courteous detachment. "I'm called the Rhymer."

"But that is not your name," observed the fossegrimen, watching Tomas narrowly. "No more than mine is the Fiddler." His strong ivory teeth gleamed. "Well, Rhymer, my instrument could do with another strap. In trade for it, I offer some tidings you may find of interest."

What could this mean? Best to remain polite. "It's needed a strap for some time. Why have you not bought one?"

With an ironic smile, the water-Elf extended his arms towards Tomas and waved his long pale fingers--all twelve of them. "What mortal would sell one to me?"

Remembering the lake-Elf at Birka market, Tomas asked, "And you've not stolen a strap? You employ no spells of concealment or shape-shifting?"

For perhaps seven seconds the fossegrimen was utterly still. Then, using both hands, he pushed his tangled hair back from his eyes. "Spells of concealment. My, my. Tell me, have you been conversing with nisse?"

Tomas shrugged. "Brownies. Fenodyree. It amounts to the same thing."

"Ah." A wicked half-smile. "They might not agree."

"You yourself have no spells of concealment?" Tomas asked. He was weary of fencing. "The Birka Elves do." A hunch, based half on the lake-Elf's behavior and half on his own powers of discernment.

After a moment the fossegrimen frowned and looked away, then down at his hands. He turned them over and studied their palms. "Not strong enough," he murmured. "Uppsala town lies far inland. Too far from the water to ensure my acquiring a strap undetected." He sighed. "Not any more."

"Not since when?" Tomas prodded, with as much delicacy as he could muster.

The fossegrimen shook his unkempt head. "We do not measure time as mortals do. As I suspect you know." He shot Tomas an enigmatic blue-green stare. "A skillful shape-changer I'm not, but I've tidings of one. And my fiddle's in dire need of a strap. Your belt would do very well. Shall we trade?"

Why not? Tomas tugged his boots off, rolled up his trousers and waded out to the fossegrimen's rock.

The water was more shallow than he'd supposed, barely

reaching his knees, but it was chilly. Silently, Tomas untied his belt: a long strip of soft supple leather that Moira had given him. His clothes seemed looser of late, but he could manage with a length of mariner's rope, if need be. He handed the belt to the fossegrimen.

The Elf accepted it with a slight bow, ran his fingers along its length, then laid it across his knees. "Perfect," he said in his deep mellifluous voice. "I thank you, Rhymer."

At close range, the fossegrimen's eyes were remarkably clear and glittered with shifting turquoise lights. Tomas saw no hint of the melancholy he thought he'd glimpsed in them earlier. "Your tidings?" he asked.

The Elf was intent on untying the old strap from his fiddle, but the knots were waterlogged and swollen. "One moment, if you please," he said, abstracted.

Tomas took the stone knife from his Rune bag and handed it to him. The fossegrimen turned the viciously chiseled weapon in his hands, shot Tomas a wide-eyed stare, then started to cut through the strap. "I am most curious about how you acquired such a blade, my friend," he murmured, then added, "There is a pooka in the waterway. Quite near us."

His tone was appallingly casual. For a moment the words did not make sense. A pooka close by? Heavy and damp, the morning air pressed in at Tomas. Water swirled indifferently around his knees. His hands went as cold as his feet, and his ears began to ring.

"He is fatigued, as if he'd traveled a long distance in great haste." The fossegrimen spared Tomas another speculative glance. "Most uncommon, a Welsh pooka in these waters. So when you cursed in Welsh, and spoke of shape-shifters..." Shaking his head, he sliced through the last knot and returned the knife to Tomas, handle first.

"Rhymer! What ails you? Are you deaf?"

Tomas whirled and almost fell, but recovered his footing on the waterway's uneven bottom. He heard a brusque chuckle from the Elf.

The reloaded ferry had rounded the bend. It was bearing in their general direction, but avoiding the shallow water off Wolf Point where Tomas stood. Gods above, how long had he conversed with this creature? Shading his eyes, Tomas focused on Yngvar, who was shouting and gesticulating from the bow.

"--how long we've been calling, damn you? Babbling to yourself midstream! Get that cookware on board or rot where you are. For two moldy crayfish I'd drown you." His face and neck were flushed a deep red. Swearing, he pointed from Tomas to the pots on the bank.

The fossegrimen leapt to his feet, grinning, the fiddle now slung over his shoulder by Tomas's belt. Mimicking Yngvar's stance, he pointed at the captain and yelled, "You're mistaken about his parentage, and you've limited powers of expression!"

Yngvar didn't react, but Ljot, manning a pole amidships, glanced anxiously back and forth between the Elf and Tomas.

It happened very fast. Tomas saw churning foam beyond the ferry's stern, and caught one glimpse of a long grey horse's head beneath a sodden mane. "Aubrey!" he gasped. For an instant he felt a mad hope that Moira had sent a message, that she'd called off Tomas's errand--but then he saw the pooka's furious red-rimmed eyes and bared teeth.

"Tomas!" Aubrey bellowed. "Be off with you! Be on your way!"

"'Aubrey'? Hah! But *Tomas* is your name," said the fossegrimen from his rock.

The ferry bore alongside as close as it could come. Yngvar's lips were moving, but Tomas, staring at Aubrey in horrified fascination, was past hearing. Ljot twisted to look over the stern.

"Give him to me!" Aubrey shouted at the fossegrimen.

Squatting, the water-Elf grabbed Tomas's shoulders and heaved him onto the boulder; Tomas did his best to scramble up with the pull. "You trespass in my waters, Pooka," said the fossegrimen, his voice curt. He gave Tomas a shove towards the ferry and hissed, "Jump! You can clear the rail."

Howling in frustration, Aubrey surged toward them. The ship must be six yards away. Hopeless.

The pooka's neck snaked out; his ears went flat against his head. Ljot's pole fell from his nerveless hands into the waterway.

Digging his bare heels into the rock, Tomas sprang for the ferry. Astonished at the powerful bunch and release of his muscles, he just cleared the rail. Then his feet slipped; his head hit the sail-block. Stunned, Tomas slid to the deck.

Before he lost consciousness, there were voices.

"--see that leap? And not a berserk? He's either raving mad or jinxed. The festival be damned; he goes ashore." That was Yngvar.

Aubrey, out of breath, raged some distance away. The inflection kept rising, like angry questions.

The fossegrimen's rich, controlled baritone, a voice that carried well, answered coldly, "Because the Fool gave me his belt, and a trespasser gave me his name."

CHAPTER FORTY-FIVE: ON THE ROAD TO UPPSALA

Tomas put his hand to his head and touched the lump: tender and swollen, with probably more swelling to come, but there was no broken skin. He opened his eyes.

He must not have been unconscious for long. They were underway, and the Sun glinted off the chilly water at the same low early morning angle. The wooded shoreline resembled the land around Wolf Point.

Sitting on his heels near Tomas, Ljot held out a mug. Tomas blinked at it.

"It's ale," Ljot said loudly, then muttered, "You're not fit to be put ashore yet, but I don't know how long they'll delay."

Tomas sat up, took the mug and sipped, moving cautiously. There was no additional pain. But something was different—less weight on his back. He grabbed his shoulders where the satchel straps should have been.

"It's here. I took it when we stretched you out on deck." Ljot put the satchel in Tomas's lap. Above their heads, a debate was going on.

"Too crazed. It's not safe."

"But we agreed—"

"Not a berserk, after that jump? And if a priest got attacked?"

"He goes ashore. Now." Yngvar glared down at Tomas. "On your feet."

"I doubt he can stand yet. He's only just sat up," Ljot pointed out.

Directing his scowl at Ljot instead, the captain said, "We're late as it is." For a long moment he studied the Sun. "He's lost us enough time already. He goes ashore with the cargo." A cold glance at Ljot. "Take an oar. You're replacing that pole when we dock." Yngvar moved astern as someone vacated the nearest oar.

Ljot got to his feet. "That horse-creature's still nearby, I think," he murmured.

"Likely so," said Tomas. "But he's not apt to approach a busy port." He'd never known the pooka to disappear, only to shift shape. The harbor folk would try to catch a stray horse, and Aubrey's hulking human form with its tufted ears would alarm them. With good reason. "Keep away from him!"

From Ljot's expression, he would do just that. "Will he go after you when you leave the port?" he asked, turning towards the unmanned oar.

Tomas said, surprising himself, "He could weaken farther inland." Perhaps the fossegrimen had bartered more tidings than he knew.

The wedge-shaped harbor wasn't large, but it was busy and efficient. There were fewer booths than at Birka, one selling food, the others gear for shipping and carting. Sailors and thralls unloaded cargo to be examined by stony-faced bailiffs, before merchants or farmers received their share of the goods. Other men re-loaded the wares onto wide flat-bottomed wooden carts with low sides. What seemed an unnecessarily large number of the Svea King's soldiers kept a level eye on the proceedings.

As Yngvar headed the ferry in, several men waved and called to him, including more than one bailiff and a few soldiers. The rest of crew was silent, but Yngvar and Ketil shouted back: familiar, offhand greetings. Tomas was aware of curious glances in his direction. Once someone pointed at him, and Yngvar shook his head.

Pressed into unloading cargo, Ljot spared the time for a hurried good-bye, and mumbled something about looking for Tomas when he could.

They put Tomas ashore as he was, light-headed and troubled of mind, his satchel strapped to his back. He wore the clothing Moira had given him, his trousers still rolled to the knees from wading in the waterway. In his satchel, the dark green cape was neatly folded beside the leather purse of coins from Lake Malar. His Runes hung at his narrow waist by a length of rope that Ljot had cut from a spare coil of line. The Rune bag also held a stone knife, a sprig of mistletoe and a faded apple blossom.

Moving carefully, Tomas walked barefoot down the ferry's gangplank. Once ashore, he stood and gazed around at the waterfront. His pack was heavy. People turned to look at him as they passed, and a few soldiers were watching him. Yngvar was deep in conversation with one now. They weren't staring, but Tomas had armed observers. Virtually everyone but the slaves carried iron; he could smell it. On land its reek was worse than over water, and his stomach gave a small premonitory heave.

All the carts were trundling out through the harbor's single gate: the roadway must lie in that direction. Not good, to stay near Yngvar and so much iron. Nor so close to the waterway and the pooka.

Tomas picked his way across wooden planking that bristled with splinters, but his bootless feet seemed unharmed so far. Something felt wrong: it shouldn't be so difficult to think. He must be tired or

255

hungry. Or iron-sick. His head hurt. He trudged dispiritedly through the gate, left the planking and started up the roadway.

Stares from passing cart drivers. Could he buy a ride to Uppsala, he asked at random. The nearest carter, a dark-haired man with powerful arms and bad teeth, shook his head curtly and moved on.

But Tomas could pay. He'd prove it; he'd show a coin from the leather purse in his satchel. Shifting the weight of his pack while he groped inside it, he tripped and almost fell. The ground was potholed; he should have stopped walking while he fished for a coin. He found a likely one, large and not too tarnished. After a moment's thought, he put his Rune bag in the satchel for safekeeping.

Soon he came to a sharp bend where the road curved around a knot of ancient trees. Beyond them, the road straightened and continued past the bend. A short cut? Tomas stepped off the path and blundered through the underwood.

When he rejoined the roadway, slightly out of breath after a hike across brushy ground, he fell in beside a heavily-laden cart piled high with farming tools, soapstone cookware and wooden chests. Its driver, a thick-set man with sandy hair, held the reins of a deep-chested brown horse.

Beside the driver sat a little girl about five years old, as blonde as Ljot. She had a small feminine version of the man's freckled face, prominent hazel eyes and peaceful expression. The child spotted Tomas and waved, using her whole arm.

Chuckling, the farmer waved too. Then he looked more closely at Tomas, frowned, and clucked to the brown horse.

"Wait," said the girl, tugging the man's sleeve. "He's sick!"

The farmer gazed down at her. "Gudrun..."

"Please, Papa. He's sick like I was," the child said. Her lower lip quivered, and she hastily knuckled her chin.

His jaw set, her father guided the horse to the side of the road and drew rein. "You don't look well, friend," he said to Tomas. "Are you ill?"

Tomas tried to decide what to answer. The farmer climbed down from the cart.

"Where are your boots?" asked the little girl, blinking fiercely.

"They're back at Wolf Point." Tomas gave her a smile.

The farmer's calloused hand felt warm on his forehead. "You've no fever. I'd a sworn you did; you look that weak." He gave Tomas a long assessing stare, punctuated by one swift glance at his daughter.

"You can have my other shoes," she offered.

"That's kind of you. But I don't think they'd fit," Tomas said gravely.

His back to Gudrun, the farmer caught Tomas's eye and grinned. "Come up the waterway bound for Uppsala, did you?"

Tomas nodded.

"My name's Erik. Me'n Gudrun will give you a ride, if you like." Putting a hand under Tomas's elbow, the farmer steered him towards the cart.

A voice called in the distance. And that other sound, could it be running hooves? "I'd like that very much. I'm called the Rhymer. Allow me to pay--"

"Nonsense!" said Erik, pointing to a spot on the bench beside Gudrun. Tomas sat down gratefully. Gudrun peered from his filthy bare feet to hers, small and leather-shod, then shook her head.

Hoofbeats, most definitely.

"A skald?" asked Erik, and Tomas nodded again. "I thought as much. So's my wife's brother; I know a harp's shape when I see one. Get that pack off your shoulders, now. Put it in back." He shook the reins and the horse started moving.

Aubrey's exhausted voice called, "Fetch the ravens, mortal." A retching cough. "Do you want Hel to find you? Or me to reckon with?"

"You!" said a high piercing contemptuous voice not a yard behind Tomas's head. All the muscles of his back went taut. Warily, he turned to put the satchel on the cartload.

In a hollow between two wooden chests stood a nisse, his hands clenched. He wore a grey shirt and knee pants, a red vest, red leggings and sturdy wooden clogs. A long red woolen cap, pulled rakishly low and slantwise on his forehead, almost hid one matted eyebrow, while the cap's tip flopped down past his ears. The nisse's wiry grey hair and beard were as thick and glossy as the pelt of some small ferocious animal. Catching Tomas's gaze, he started violently. His eyes peered, black and truculent, from bony sockets above a flattened nose.

The nisse leaped atop the cartload and shook a small fist at the pooka's receding figure. "You to reckon with?" he shrieked. "So far from home? You're on dry land, Pooka. And my mortals have befriended this one." Aiming carefully, although Aubrey was well out of range, the small Elf spat an eloquent stream of saliva over the back of the cart.

Then he whirled, reached Tomas in one bound and grabbed his sleeve. Black eyes bore into his. "If you're under this family's protection, you're under mine. But let on you can see me and I'll toss

257

you in the waterway for the Pooka. Don't think I wouldn't. I've more'n enough bother already, with them moving house and all." He gave Tomas's shoulder an exasperated thump. "Now turn round and act right and quit worriting them."

Tomas drew a cautious breath and faced forward. Erik was rummaging under the seat, but Gudrun was studying Tomas's face. "What were you looking at?"

"I had to find a place for my satchel," he said after a moment. Clumsy, but the safest truth he could state on short notice, light-headed as he was.

Erik handed him a wineskin and a crusty hunk of brown bread. Tomas bit gratefully into the loaf. How long since he'd eaten?

"Wait!" said the nisse from close behind them. Tomas stiffened but didn't turn. "'Hel,' your stinking Pooka said? She'd be after you?" There followed a long ominous silence, as of one engaged in furious thought, punctuated by an occasional scuffling sound.

Whistling contentedly to himself, his face calm and ruminating, Erik gazed over the horse's back along the road ahead. He and Tomas passed the skin back and forth. The wine was surprisingly good, but it would be rude to ask how Erik came by such a luxury. The mild air smelled of berry blossoms and the track was beginning to climb. Yawning, Gudrun leaned against her father's side and closed her eyes.

Something narrow and pointy jabbed Tomas between his shoulder blades, and he couldn't completely stifle a start.

"You don't seem dead to me," the nisse muttered judiciously in Tomas's ear. "So Hel's after you for some other reason."

"No need to stay awake, Rhymer," said Erik. "Stretch out in back there. We've a long ride ahead."

"I think I will," Tomas agreed, climbing carefully over the bench and into the cartload of household goods. It would be easier to communicate with the nisse here. He wasn't sure he liked that.

"Hsst!" said the small Elf, beckoning Tomas to the very rear of the cart. He settled on his back next to the nisse, who sat cross-legged and studied him. "Why's Hel after a live man?"

"An Elf cheated her of my death," Tomas murmured.

The nisse scratched the bridge of his nose and made no reply. He was quiet for so long that Tomas had almost fallen asleep when the Elf produced a tiny malevolent cackle and said, "You think she wants a death, then. Yours, or would any corpse do?" He prodded Tomas in the ribs with one heavy wooden clog.

"I think it's mine," said Tomas, moving aside in distaste.

"You think it's yours," said the nisse, nodding, bright-eyed. "It's

258

as well that you do. I'd not care to endanger my mortals by your presence, should Herself not be choosy. What's your errand at Uppsala?"

Tomas kept his eyes closed. Would a Norse Elf suspect a threat in the journey to Asgard? Aubrey had just mentioned the ravens. But this Elf was a nisse and probably loyal to only one hearth. Still...

"Wake up!" Another dig in the ribs. "What's your errand at Uppsala?"

"What do you suppose? I'm a skald. I'd thought to recite there." Which was true.

"Ah. The festival. There'll be sacrifices," said the nisse meaningfully.

There was an increasingly tense silence. Feeling the Elf's gaze, Tomas opened his eyes. The nisse was scowling down at him, shaggy eyebrows drawn together.

"Well?" Tomas prompted.

"Sacrifices!" said the Elf, bristling with impatience.

Of course there would be sacrifices. What was he driving at?

"Deaths, witling! She was cheated of yours. I thought you intended to buy her one there." Eyes slitted, the nisse gave Tomas a measuring stare, somewhat impeded when the red cap slipped down towards his nose.

Buy Hel a death for his own? Tomas felt his mouth slowly open. He had never thought... But gods, a noose, a tree? Or an iron blade to rise and fall--

Nausea struck him in a sharp and unexpected wave. Tomas started to reach for the side of the cart, but the spasm passed as quickly as it came, leaving him dizzy. Lying back again, he shut his eyes.

"You'd have to sing a lot," remarked the ferret-like voice beside him. "It'd cost you dear."

Vile. Foul. If it would only go away.

"Huh!" snapped the Elf. "And you in the care of my mortals, and me merely pointing out choices!"

Tomas's heart gave a painful thud. Had he spoken aloud? He didn't think so, but he'd not felt another presence in his mind. He didn't know what to think. Swallowing hard, he sat up and looked at the nisse.

The Elf had withdrawn to the farthest corner of the cart and sat glaring at him. Tomas tried to say something, but the nisse held up a hand to silence him. After a pause, the Elf jerked his chin in Erik's direction and said, "While you're with them, I'm bound at least not to harm you. And I could choose to help. But I can't fathom you, and I

259

don't like it." He tugged irritably at his cap. "I don't think I like you. You've either far too much Sight or too little, and not learned to use whichever it is."

It was all true, and Tomas could think of no answer. They were both quiet for some time. The cart jolted over a series of ruts so deep that Tomas gripped the low side for support. Balanced easily on his grey-clad haunches, the nisse scratched the bridge of his nose and pondered. He glanced forward once or twice when Erik spoke encouragingly to the horse.

"I'll tell you one thing more, Rhymer, and one thing only," the Elf announced after perhaps half an hour had elapsed. "There's a smell of sacrifice about you. If you don't make one yourself, you'd best have a care."

A smell of sacrifice. Tomas thought of Moira, and of Hel. Linley. Caraid. He fought an involuntary burst of laughter, high and overwrought, and succeeded in choking most of it down.

"Hush!" said the Elf, black eyes cold and furious. Formally, he turned his back on Tomas and stared at the road behind them.

Tomas lay down again and, although he thought he couldn't, soon fell asleep from sheer exhaustion.

CHAPTER FORTY-SIX: ATHILS

There was a smell. Faint at first, it steadily crept into Tomas's dream.

In that dream he came alone to his father's farm at dusk and found the steading unnaturally quiet. With mounting concern he searched the empty house, deserted yard and silent cow byre. It smelled fetid and rank, unlike its habitually strong but still agreeable aromas of sun-warmed cattle, feed and manure. With the sudden realization that it was hog-slaughtering time, Tomas reluctantly started up the hill that led to the pens. On the ridge he stopped, gasping.

The pens were littered with corpses: cows, goats, hogs—and human bodies. Several slaves, their throats cut, lay heaped in a corner. Tomas's younger half-brother Bjorn slumped over a feed trough. Across the entrance to the nearest pen sprawled the body of Freydis, Bjorn's mother and Sigtrygg's latest wife. Over the corpse of Freydis stood Olaf, his own axe-blade buried in his chest as it had been in Dubhlinn, his eyes wide and staring straight at Tomas.

Then Tomas was sitting up in a strange cart, with chests and boxes wedged neatly around him. As he sucked in his breath for another scream, a nisse tugged at his sleeve and he remembered where he was. Erik finished reining in the brown horse, then jumped into the rear of the cart and gripped Tomas's shoulders. Swearing, the nisse backed away.

"There now, you're alright!" said Erik, letting go of Tomas. He mumbled an apology that the farmer brushed aside. "You were dreaming, Rhymer. Come join us up front."

They settled onto the bench. Erik took the reins back from Gudrun, who stared curiously at Tomas. "I have bad dreams sometimes, too. But I almost never yell," she told him.

"You're braver than I am," said Tomas, giving her hand an approving squeeze.

He studied the surrounding terrain. It was hilly, and the sun, much lower now, coaxed long violet shadows from the trees. The air was cooler, but the mild breeze full in his face didn't refresh him: it carried the smell of his dream. Ahead of them, three or four heavily-laden carts made slow progress while others rolled along in their wake. There was foot traffic too, mostly men, and a family or two.

Farther down the road, three mounds, like huge slumbering beasts, lifted their grass-covered backs towards the darkening sky. From this distance, each howe appeared the size of two or three great halls such as that of King Ivar of Dubhlinn. Their summits were roughly flattened but sunken in places, as though they'd collapsed at some time in the past.

What had Moira said? "Do not linger on the howes, the death mounds." Tomas examined them carefully but saw no one. The temple and the grove must lie beyond, with the sacrifices and the Well. As they drew closer, the mounds loomed large against the failing light. Gudrun wrinkled her nose and coughed.

"Stinks," said Erik in cheerful unconcern. "It'll stink worse before long, child."

He must realize what they were about to see. "What brings you to Uppsala?" asked Tomas.

Erik guided the horse through a series of potholes. "Gudrun, truth to tell. Rest of the family's already up on the summer farm. But she was taken ill and I stayed with her."

Gudrun, kneeling on the bench for a better look at the road behind them, hummed quietly to herself. Tomas decided that she was paying no attention to the conversation. "I hope she's recovered," he said.

"Oh, she has. Never better. We made a sacrifice to the Elves just before my wife left with the boys, and that broke her fever."

"Mind your tongue, Rhymer," said the nisse softly, standing behind Tomas.

Ignoring the tingling skin of his neck and shoulders, he asked Erik, "To the Elves?"

"Aye. And I vowed I'd make another one at the festival if Gudrun healed, before we went to the summer steading ourselves." The farmer gave him a friendly glance. "Where do you hail from, Rhymer? They don't offer to the Elves there?"

"From Vestfold. No, not so often these days."

A thin little mutter came from the back of the cart.

"Air's gone from bad to worse." Erik rubbed his nose. "They say we Upplanders make fewer sacrifices to the Elves than in my grandfather's time. I'd've preferred Thor, myself. But my wife's mother insisted on the huldrefolk. Says they're closer to us because they're of the earth, better for healing and luck and the crops and such." He snagged the wineskin from under the bench. When Tomas politely refused, Erik took a long swallow, then added, "I guess they don't see much sickness in Asgard at that."

They drew level with the first mound. It was colored a tender green by the young grass and dotted with a few random blossoms. Tomas absently counted them. He felt in no danger from the farmer, whose friendliness seemed genuine. But this talk of sacrificing to the

Elves... Why continue on this errand? What would happen if Tomas simply stopped?

The smell was growing worse; it made the threat of Hel seem more present than at any time since he'd left Faerie. Gudrun buried her face in her father's jerkin.

When they bumped to a halt, Tomas stood and sighted down the increasingly crowded trail. Other carts stopped to avoid running into one that had lost a wheel. Several men converged on the vehicle and, after some gesturing and debate, began to push it to the side of the road and retrieve its spilled cargo.

"I'd say they've got enough help," observed Erik, then leaned back and closed his eyes. Tomas sat down and glanced at the mound again.

A man stood at the bottom of its slope, quite close to the road and Erik's cart. A tall, powerfully built man, wrapped in a gilt-edged cape with a costly sword belted at his side. Through the rich fabric of his clothing, Tomas could see the flowers on the howe. The man was sunk in the mound almost to his knees. Pale light flickered up from the grass to dance around the outlines of his body.

He had been a King, and his body had been cremated in the howe. These things Tomas somehow knew, but no names. The insubstantial eyes that met his showed no malice, only detachment and something akin to fatigue. He marveled at how little fear he felt.

Still, a loud sawing sound to his left made him start up, only to sink down again when the nisse, like an oversized cat, landed with a thud on the back of the bench. "It's just the man snoring, Fool," the Elf said contemptuously. "Sit down and don't waken him. You've no call to fear the dead Kings; there's live men here who merit it more. Begging your pardon, Athils."

The man on the mound gave the faintest of shrugs. "Erik, Gudrun and the nisse, their errand is known to me," he said in what was once a deep voice. "But you who are called the Rhymer. What brings you past the place of my rest?"

"You know who I am," Tomas whispered, feeling more stupid than frightened.

"The dead know many things," replied the King. "Odin Himself once raised a sorceress from the dead to question her. Know now who I am, or was: King Athils, who died at a sacrificial feast here when my horse threw me."

"*I* did not raise—" said Tomas hastily. Carts were beginning to roll again; Erik sat up and shook the reins.

"No, you did not raise me. A ferment is centered here tonight,

263

from more than the festival and touching more than Midgard. It leaves me peaceless, and you I cannot see clearly. Why are you here?"

The question stung, echoing as it did Tomas's own. He turned to look at Athils and said, as the brown horse started forward, "That's what I myself would know—"

"Hold your tongue!" snapped the nisse.

"What's that?" asked Erik, twisting to glance over his shoulder. "Did they say something behind us?"

"No."

"Then who were you talking to?" asked Erik, chuckling.

Groping for words, Tomas said the first thing that he sensed would get by the constraints Moira had set on him. "No one who matters now."

"You must have fallen asleep again," said the farmer, unperturbed. "Quite a dreamer you are. First yelling, then talking."

"He was awake; I saw him," said Gudrun indignantly. "He got scared of the mound. Then he said, 'You know who I am,' and 'I did not raise,' and, um, 'That's what I myself would.' Then he looked like he said ouch, but no noise came out."

Erik blinked at Tomas, then began, slowly, to frown. The nisse let out an exasperated wail. Staring helplessly at the child, Tomas asked, "Are you sure you weren't dreaming?"

"I wasn't!" Gudrun burst into tears. "I wasn't even asleep. It smells bad here, Papa. Do we have to stay?" Sobbing, she hid her head in Erik's sleeve. Tomas couldn't make out her next words.

"I promised we would, Gudrun," said Erik, smoothing her hair. "Hush, now, I know you're no liar. Folk get confused when they're sleepy." The look he gave Tomas wasn't friendly. "Whyn't you crawl in the back and have a rest, hm?" he asked his daughter. "I'll put up the cover, do my errand and come right back."

Wiping her eyes, Gudrun climbed into the rear of the cart. She avoided looking at Tomas.

Erik gave him the reins. "Keep straight down the road," he said shortly, and followed Gudrun. Tomas heard him unrolling a bolt of cloth, which he tied to the sides of the cart to form a makeshift tent. After dropping from the rear of the cart to the road, he caught up with the plodding horse, climbed in and took the reins back from Tomas.

"She was a mighty sick girl not that long ago. You appear to have been ill yourself, but I don't care to see her upset," said the farmer.

Tomas apologized.

"Hold your peace." Erik cast him a wary sideways glance. "For all I know you're not sound and can't help it. But I'm letting you off just past the Well."

As they passed the third howe, the road rounded a curve and the Well came into view: a round squat lip of stone beneath an ash tree. The tree was smaller than Tomas expected. A wooden ladder led down into the Well, which marked the entrance to a grove of larger trees. Beyond them stood the temple, an open wooden rectangle about ten yards square, with a curved roof like the upended hull of a ship.

An astonishing number of people were milling around near the Well, through the grove and about the temple. Most held squares of cloth to their strained faces. Gods, the stench! The stolid brown horse threw up his head and sidestepped nervously, so that Erik grabbed at the reins.

Bodies hung from every tree in the grove. From the condition of the corpses, some had been there for days. Tomas identified rams, goats, roosters and pigs, before he shut his eyes to block out the sight of the flies and the circling crows, and reached for the side of the cart.

Erik shoved something into his hand: the wineskin. This time Tomas took a sizeable swallow, then forced himself to open his eyes and look again. "No human bodies," he said, relieved.

"There will be. Tonight's the last night," Erik said grimly. "Wish I'd got here the first."

On the last of the nine nights, they sacrificed men.

"Thank the gods I can make do with a rooster," muttered Erik. "And the sooner the better. Here's the Well, Rhymer. Out you go, and good luck to you."

Tomas thanked him, shouldered his satchel and climbed down from the bench. The nisse poked his head out from under the canopy. As he stepped away from the cart and followed a knot of people moving in the general direction of the temple, Tomas felt the little Elf's intent gaze at his back.

CHAPTER FORTY-SEVEN: A VISION

The sluggish breeze had died. Slaves lit the torches that stood atop tall staffs thrust into the ground beside the roadway. Greasy smoke, competing with the torchlight, soon filled the windless air and hovered in the treetops. Tomas tried not to jostle anyone as he wound his way among the throng, past the Well and into the grove. Iron, smoke and the stench all made him cough.

Partly to avoid the sight of the contents of the trees, and partly to avert unpleasant incidents with any passers-by liable to become belligerent, Tomas paid close attention to the people around him. Perhaps half of them were intoxicated, some quietly, others noisily, many staggering against their companions. A few richly dressed men and women, white and pinched about the eyes, attempted to block the smell from faces half-hidden by kerchiefs or hoods. Tomas saw farmers, merchants, sailors and craftsmen, but the majority of the crowd were soldiers or thralls.

Two or three times he passed other skalds; they carried cloth-covered instruments. Somewhere someone was beating a drum. A fat-faced pale man, garments immaculate, white hands heavy with rings, went by arm in arm with the bailiff whom Tomas had last seen with Yngvar and Ketil. The bailiff gave Tomas a hard stare as they passed.

The sloping temple roof was closer now; he'd almost crossed the grove. Once he got through this last clump of festival-goers, there was a break in the throng from where he could probably see the whole building free and clear.

Someone fell heavily against him then stumbled down onto the ground, so that Tomas was hard put not to lose his own balance. With an apology he crashed into a third man, who stank of vomit and ale. Regaining his balance, Tomas blocked with an elbow and ducked to avoid a wild punch at his eyes.

Reflex made him blink. When he opened his eyes and straightened up, looking warily for his drunken assailant, no one was there.

No one at all. Every last one of the people had vanished and with them the noise, the grove and the smell. Tomas stood alone on thick untrodden grass, not the deeply scored and slippery ground of mere seconds before.

A bird called. Turning, he saw that all the trees that had lined the roadway were gone too, except the ash tree that flanked the vanished Well. That tree was taller now.

For reasons he could not have explained, he was reluctant to move with any speed. He glanced carefully in all directions. Where the temple had been stood a much larger, towering structure, with oddly shaped staves jutting out from a roof now peaked and angular. He stared in disbelief at the cross of the Nazarene that crowned the building. Was he still in Uppsala? Forgetting his caution, he whirled to look behind him for the howes.

The three mounds were there, but taller, rounder, greener—and not empty.

Athils, his expression somber and alert, stood at the foot of the howe where he'd been before. Two blurred figures kept watch on the summits of the other mounds. From all the howes, Tomas heard the faint mumbling of voices.

Was he dead, then? Need he go on?

He glanced down at his body, felt of his arms. Living flesh. Tentatively, he waved at Athils. When the King waved back and seemed about to speak, Tomas took a step in that direction.

Something hard and solid slammed into his back. Felled to his knees, he threw out his hands for support. His head began a fierce pounding ache as his palms dug two furrows in muddy ground, then caught and held.

Soft muddy ground? Not the lush grass of a moment ago?

A sharp blow to his ribs: the kick of a booted foot. Tomas covered his head with his arms. A second kick. He opened his eyes.

He was kneeling on the bare trampled earth of Uppsala's grove.

The air was full of streaky light; it mottled the trousers and leggings that crowded around him. To his relief, all the styles of clothing were familiar. A roaring in his ears came and went.

"--won't fight. I told you he's fey." Was that Ketil?

"--purse full of coins." Another man, behind Tomas.

A woman shouted, "Stop!"

Laughter. More spectators elbowed closer.

"Get him to the priests," hissed a cold refined voice.

Someone wrenched at Tomas's satchel. The harp, the flute! And Moira's greenery.

He let the tugging at his pack, the fumbling at its straps, help boost him to his feet. Half-crouching, he shoved suddenly backward with the pull, and felt the startled man behind him start to topple.

Tomas rammed the top of his throbbing head into his attacker's chin and struck out at the man's inner elbows. Grunting, the man let go of the satchel and fell heavily to the ground, his arms flung wide.

It was Ketil. With a metallic waterfall of clinks, coins sailed from Tomas's open purse that the ferryman still clutched in one hand.

People began struggling in the mud for the lake-Elf's scattered treasure. At the next man's furious charge from the right, Tomas spun, ducked, and sliced out with a foot. His fist caught the falling man-- Yngvar--square on the chin. There was a muffled cracking sound and a groan.

The throng shuffled in a peculiar cursing dance, the ones closest to Tomas pressing back in alarm, while those behind them tried to push forward for the coins. Ketil remained on his back, panting, the breath knocked out of him.

Using his elbows for leverage, Yngvar sat up slowly and clutched at his face. "I think my jaw's broken," he muttered.

"Godhi!" a woman called imperiously. "Godhi!" She stood near Tomas, inside the ragged circle of onlookers who were doing their best to back away from him. Why was she summoning a priest? But she might want a judge instead: a godhi was both. Straightening his pack on his shoulders, Tomas gave the woman a quick scrutiny.

She wore a lightweight cloak sewn from fine pale fabric and clasped at the throat with a brooch of twisted silver. The cloak's hood was pushed back, its hem set with sullen red stones. White streaked her plaited blonde hair, but she stood tall and straight at the edge of the restless crowd, as one who will not move before a time of her own choosing. A small bag of well-tanned leather hung at her waist. Runes, no doubt. A Seer, then, or a priestess. Or both.

Tomas met her eyes. Her expression was proud, yet her gaze flickered away, then slowly back again. She set her mouth in a hard line, but not before Tomas had read the trouble in her face.

She possessed a touch of the Sight, less than Linley had, but enough to recognize--and fear--how much more it was possible to command. She also had a triple measure of ambition. And she knew that Tomas had just experienced a vision far beyond her powers.

Yngvar and Ketil, now on their feet, started drifting away. "Stay where you are," said the woman, a fine edge of contempt in her voice. "They attacked and robbed an unarmed man, godhi, before these witnesses."

This last was addressed to a white-faced corpulent man. Tomas had seen him earlier in the company of the bailiff who knew Ketil and Yngvar. People stepped back in haste to let the priest go by. Silently, he came and stood beside the Seer.

The godhi had the eyes of an insect, small and black, with an unnaturally reflective sheen. His gaze fell on Tomas, Yngvar and Ketil in turn, resting for a long moment on Tomas's purse in Ketil's hand.

"He's mad, your worship," said Ketil uneasily. "He stole these coins from our ship. We'd got them in trade."

"So we thought we'd settle it ourselves," Yngvar put in, holding his jaw.

"You're lying!" said Tomas. Rage flooded him. His breathing grew shallow; he clenched his fists. Ketil and Yngvar both took a step backward. Tomas's head had never stopped hurting, and now blotches of color began to stain the air around people's shoulders. Not a good sign. If he could just keep the vision from going any further... He dug his fingernails into his palms.

The cloaked woman had looked intently at each speaker. She focused on Tomas, her eyes widening.

"For an unarmed man, he defended himself quite adequately," observed the godhi in a voice like stones dropping into a pool. Black, dark red and oily yellow churned around his head.

"He's crazy; just look at him."

"Might be a berserk."

The priest asked Tomas, "Did you steal this money from them?"

"No!" His head was pounding. Ketil and Yngvar were wreathed in reddish brown.

"Where did you get it?"

His mouth opened; he heard himself say, "It came from Lake Malar."

Hoots from the listeners. The Seer's eyebrows shot up.

"And you earned it in trade?" the godhi asked the ferrymen, who nodded. "Show it to me."

Ketil detoured around Tomas and offered the bag.

"These coins are quite old," said the priest, turning them avidly in his pudgy hands. "This one I've never seen before. Nor this." He studied the three men and the Seer. "It seems we've something to settle here. The coins will remain in my custody for now. Come to the law hall two mornings hence; I've other work tonight."

"They attacked and robbed an unarmed man during the festival," the Seer protested.

The godhi contemplated her; his expression was neutral. "Take that charge to the law hall. You summoned me; he's in your custody till then. Be sure he brings the fee."

"Fee!" Tomas snapped. "But you have all my money."

"A pauper, at the festival--" Ketil said quickly, and subsided when the priest glanced at him.

Tomas could not prevent his explosion. "You'll decide in their favor. With no one to speak for a penniless man, I'm to be killed," he shouted at the godhi, then wheeled on Ketil and Yngvar. "He told you to rob me; he needed a sacrifice. But he lied when he promised you the purse. He'll claim it's his fee!"

Yngvar and Ketil gaped at him, their complexions the color of pack-ice. Tomas would have known he had spoken the truth even without their reaction, but with it, everyone else knew as well. The crowd was absolutely silent; no one moved.

A coin slipped from Ketil's sleeve and thudded to the ground. Wetting his lips, the ferryman looked nervously at the priest.

The godhi's formal mask was gone. Sallow color flamed in his cheeks, and his gaze at Tomas was vicious.

Tomas stared back, flexing his hands. Tremors of rage shot along his arms and legs.

Then the Seer was gripping his elbow. "Two mornings hence, at the law hall," she said coldly to the priest, and began ushering Tomas away. People melted aside to let them pass. She held herself straight and assured, moving with grace so that the cloak flowed regally in her wake. "Say nothing," she muttered to Tomas, her face impassive. But purple colored the air all around her, purple increasingly streaked with grey, and Tomas knew how deeply she was frightened.

CHAPTER FORTY-EIGHT: IN THE TEMPLE AT UPPSALA

His head still pounding, Tomas let the Seer guide him where she would. Egg-sized specks, opaque and colorless, throbbed before his eyes as if keeping time with the pain in his skull. As they hurried through the festival-goers, the Seer trailed a hazy cloud of grey and purple air. Perhaps colors wafted from Tomas as well.

Without warning, the heads of three passers-by blurred, then turned to skulls. Torchlight glanced off naked bone and rows of teeth that clenched on emptiness. So real did the vision seem that Tomas flinched as his path took him by each set of blackened eye sockets.

The Seer tightened her clasp on his elbow. "What is it?" she breathed.

"There's three will be dead before morning," he muttered, and felt her shudder.

"Try to hide your reactions," she said tersely. "Please."

A wise suggestion: they'd attracted plenty of notice already. Tomas concentrated on looking at no one; he stared down at his unshod feet instead. They crossed beaten earth, followed by grass. Then wooden planks—an illusion. When his toes passed right through the wood, he faltered a pace or two, and the Seer let out a tiny exasperated cry.

Bare earth again. Before his eyes the opaque specks grew larger; in his path, figures dissolved and re-formed, to melt again slowly. The iron-smell came in gusts, making his stomach churn. But the strong impersonal grip on his arm was constant. The Seer kept her chin lifted and her gaze straight ahead, not reacting to any of the phenomena that plagued Tomas—even when they passed the screaming from the Well.

Then a set of solid cross-beams loomed above his head; beneath his feet was the reassuring thud of wood: boards that did not dissolve. Squinting, Tomas tried to will away the specks before his eyes. His vision remained capricious, but he and the Seer were definitely within the temple now. It was crowded and unnaturally silent but for the bleating of animals. Their faces mottled by the torchlight that blazed upon all sides, people stood in whispering, fidgeting rows and waited to speak with the godhis near the statues.

There were three statues, each half again the height of a man. Eyesight impeded by wavering spots and streaks of color, Tomas could only focus on the image of Freyr before him. Very old it was, cut from wood dark and crumbling with age, and much of its detail was worn away. The god sat naked and cross-legged, his hands curled about the root of an erect and oversized phallus.

271

From her knees, the Seer tugged at Tomas's elbow. "Kneel. Make an offering or recite," she hissed.

He dropped to his knees beside her, staring up at the statue of Freyr. God of fertility, brother to Freyja. Moira said that Freyr had once spent much time with the Elves. Tomas still carried an apple blossom meant for Freyr--not for a wooden image. That flower he could not offer.

Now every last tint of the rainbow was reflected in the shimmering air. Something about the carved features of the god, spare and elegant despite their age, reminded him of Rhys. Half-dazed, Tomas rose to his feet. Taking up his harp, he sang all the lyrics that came to him, though they were meant for more than one voice.

> I am the King,
> and I rule a fading kingdom.
> When winter turns to spring,
> Faerie is the fulcrum.
> Shall I reveal my heart?
> Rely on the saddening part.
> I am so afraid
> to see the world fade.
>
> Faerie is the balance
> in centuries dark and brighter.
> And we still have a chance:
> Meet Tomas the Rhymer.
>
> You bring this mortal man.
> He sings; he has a harp in his hands,
> too young to be afraid
> to see the world fade.
>
> My world is fading.
> My world is fading;
> I see it fading.
> I am so afraid
> to see the world fade.

When Tomas finished, a hush fell on the temple's other voices. A baby whimpered and was quickly stilled, and feet scuffled here and there. The overwhelming sensation was that of a damp and penetrating chill, far too cold for this summer evening. Was that something hexagonal and patterned, like a snowflake, in the opacity that clotted the air? Shivering, Tomas noticed how many people drew their cloaks about themselves.

The Seer had gone so white that the immaterial purple stain about her head seemed black in contrast. Slowly, she got to her feet, eyes flickering towards a small commotion in the throng. "Come with me. Now," she murmured.

Too late. "No!" said a strained voice on their left, not addressing the Seer. "Leave him be. He's touched by the god."

A man slipped easily through the unresisting crowd and approached them. Younger than Tomas, he was dressed in the robes of a godhi, their as yet unwashed cloth still heavy and stiff with newness. He wore his light brown hair braided tightly back from his round high forehead. He stopped in front of Tomas, who stood at least half a foot taller. The godhi's eyes were a pale and watery blue, slightly protruding, and wide with anxiety.

Was that one of Yngvar's crew behind the young priest? Tomas shook his head to clear it. The extraneous colors remained, but the specks dwindled.

"Of what world's fading do you sing, to bring such cold into the hall of the gods?" asked the godhi, his voice formal but not altogether level.

"Cold?" exclaimed a voice in the crowd.

"It's gone now," someone else said.

The priest's mouth tightened. So not everyone had felt the chill.

Tomas understood the godhi's question: three years' winter, the Fimbulvetr, would precede Ragnarok—the battle and fall of the Aesir. "I was not singing of the Fimbulvetr," he said quietly.

The godhi's pale blue gaze shifted to the Seer.

She said, "He is under my protection until the law-court two days hence." She placed a faint emphasis on the word 'my.' "I was escorting him from the temple, Arnulf. Have we leave to go?"

Arnulf's eyes narrowed. He gave Tomas and the woman five seconds' scrutiny and a polite shrug. "No need to ask my leave, Seer."

She inclined her head, then swept past him with Tomas in tow. The crowd parted to let them through.

Tomas glanced back over one shoulder. It was indeed one of Yngvar's crew he had seen, now gesticulating at Arnulf who stood thoughtfully watching their departure.

Night had nearly fallen outside; a few crisp stars winked overhead. After the sour, close atmosphere in the temple, Tomas took

273

appreciative gulps of fresh air even with the stench from the grove. The Seer urged him through the trees. Just beyond the howes, she steered him off the roadway and into a maze of tents and wagons pitched at random in the woods.

It was almost a small village. The sight of Athils on the mound must have distracted Tomas from noticing the encampment earlier. They passed cookfires, dodged dogs and goats, and stepped over drunks. At one point three men chased a fourth across their path, all breathing in spent gasps, and startling a solitary chicken from its roost in a tree. Scraps of music competed for Tomas's attention, and he twisted to look over his shoulder for the players.

"Come!" The Seer tugged him into a tent some distance from the others. When he barked his shins on something solid and rounded in the dark, he let out a curse.

"Be seated. I'll light a lamp," said the Seer.

When the wick flared, Tomas saw that he had almost fallen over her soapstone kettle and cold hearthfire. He sat back with a sigh. Lit from below, the face of the woman seated across from him was lengthened and eerie with flickering shadows. He suspected he looked much the same to her.

"Are you hungry?" she asked, her voice formal.

Tomas nodded.

The Seer waited in impatient silence while he devoured half a loaf of day-old bread and a small bowl of tepid stew. Then, brushing aside his thanks, she leaned forward and asked intently, "What was revealed to you? What do you know?"

He took a swallow of excellent ale, and another. It was full-bodied and strong. "I don't understand."

"Before those men attacked you, you had a vision. I saw the look on your face; I was watching you. What did you see?"

"I saw no one." At her irritated gesture, he said in a rush, "No, wait, it was just that. No one was about, and there wasn't any grove. Only the howes, and one tree where the Well was. And a Nazarene temple."

She stared. "How do you know? What did it look like?"

"A wooden building much larger than ours. All angles, with staves sticking out. And a cross-Rune on the roof."

"Gods," she said softly. After a moment, she reached into the darkness behind her head and cast a handful of dried herbs onto the burning lamp. There was a sizzle, then a flare, and the air turned pungent.

"And on the way to the temple a while ago?" asked the Seer,

refilling Tomas's mug.

This time he knew what she meant. "Three passers-by had skulls instead of heads."

"Ah. And in the temple itself?" she pressed.

"Colors. Shifting shapes. No more than that."

Even in this weak light, he could see the woman's scowl. "But the cold when you sang--"

"That I cannot fathom," he said flatly.

Her hand shot out and gripped his wrist. "Then how did you know the first godhi was lying? And come out of trance to stop an attack? You've been touched by Odin."

"I've been left by Odin, for leaving Him! How else could she bind me to her?" Tomas snapped. He was standing. He didn't remember getting up.

The Seer sat rubbing her hand. Her glance at him was deceptively calm; he sensed her excitement. "So your gifts come from a woman? Who is she?" When Tomas said nothing, she persisted, "What is the exact nature of your gifts?"

Why not answer? "True speech and prophecy. And you'd not want them," he told her wearily and sat down again.

Her posture grew rigid; her gaze became icy. "You judge me incapable of wielding such powers? Think again."

"You don't understand," said Tomas, reaching for his ale. "It's not just discernment of truths and not just the Sight. I cannot lie, even when my life's at risk." He stopped, thinking of Linley's concern for Alfred--and of Caraid. "Not when the truth is full of wounds. Would you want that?" he finished dully.

"Where did you come by such gifts? Are mortals capable of that?" she demanded. The avid look she trained on him with slitted eyes left him speechless. "Well? Answer me!"

He stared. She stared back, greedily.

Tomas started to laugh; the Seer's lip curled with distaste. "Where did I come by them? The Queen of Elfland."

At last the Seer was surprised. Catching herself, she closed her gaping mouth, but promptly opened it again.

"Queen of the part closest to Waleis. Not Alfheim," Tomas said, anticipating her question. "And I don't know if mortals are capable of it." Rocking with laughter, he clutched at his sides. "Do I appear to be handling it well?"

"Gods above, to give such gifts to a fool," she muttered. "Put down that mug and listen to me! How did you find this Elf Queen?"

"She found me."

"Idiot! Is that what she said? They don't lie, but Elves don't tell the truth straight and entire. You have to take it sideways or backwards, somehow. Tell me everything she told you. Every word."

The dim stuffy tent, the colored specks, the flame-lit, angry face across from Tomas, all performed one last drunken twirl around his head. Suddenly, coldly jarred into sobriety, he felt as if a horse had kicked him.

Sideways or backwards. He set down his half-empty mug and rose to his feet.

"Stop! Where are you going?" cried the Seer, as he ducked through the tent flap into the night.

"Where she told me not to go. Sideways and backwards, to speak with the dead."

CHAPTER FORTY-NINE: THE DEAD KNOW MANY THINGS

At the foot of the howe where he had seen Athils, once lord of the Svea people, Tomas searched his memory for all of Moira's instructions about the passage to Asgard. Had Moira told him half-truths, sideways and backwards truths, about just how dangerous it was to defy her and abandon her errand? Perhaps if he followed those counsels "backwards and sideways," his quest might end here at Uppsala—and without the threat of Hel's pursuit.

His mouth was dry; his heart leapt crazily in his ribcage. A more rational corner of his mind judged that possibility a dangerous and slim one at best. But the proud Seer's unthinking words had given Tomas the most hope he'd felt yet, and to that hope he fiercely clung.

The Seer seemed equally determined to cling to Tomas. When she asked to come with him, he could think of no reason to refuse. Since Moira had told him to be alone when making the Runic passes to unveil the Asgard bridge, it might even be wise to keep the Seer with him for as long as she could stomach his company.

She did not relish it at the moment. The night sky glittered with stars, and the summer air was cooler, if still mild. Even the smell was less, since the wind's direction had changed at dusk. But the Seer hugged her elbows to her sides and clenched her jaw as if fighting a winter storm. She had ceased all conversation when it became clear that Tomas was leading them to the howes, and her eyes flickered uneasily in each direction.

"Do not linger on the howes, the burial mounds," Moira had said—while Athils knew who Tomas was. Since Odin Himself had once raised a dead sorceress to question her, there could be a reason, some unstated sideways truth, that Moira had told Tomas not to linger at the mounds. Perhaps she didn't wish him to speak with Athils.

Despite Athils's claim that the ferment centered at Uppsala left him peaceless, there was no sign of him now. His howe lay untrodden and quiet beneath the stars, which shed the only illumination upon the new grass of late spring. It was the dark of the Moon, and the torches were too far away to give light here.

Tomas breathed deeply of the still black air. Did he dare to raise the dead, assuming he could guess how it was done? Odin had compelled that sorceress with Runes, no doubt, but Odin was a god. The Rune-master, who had suffered on the world-tree to win the Runes, and taught their lore to mortals.

Not all that lore, Tomas suspected.

Perhaps the King stood invisibly before him and the Seer even now. "Athils," said Tomas in a courteous voice, aiming his words at the empty air about a man's height above the howe. "May I request an audience with you?"

No answer came from the mound.

The knees of the woman beside Tomas sagged abruptly; she clutched his arm with a frozen hand. "Are you summoning him?"

"I don't know. I hope I won't be obliged to."

Her face was grey and tight. "Then what--"

"He was here before. Today. I saw him twice. I want to talk with him again."

"But he is *dead!*" The Seer swayed against Tomas, then sat down suddenly and hard. One foot struck the mound; she yanked it back against her body.

"I know he's dead! That's why I must speak with him!"

Her breathing quick and ragged, she gazed up at Tomas and struggled to master her fear. Fear of Athils, not Tomas. She was fighting panic in order to stay and learn. Tomas didn't like the Seer; he could tell that she didn't like him. But he respected her determination.

He thought of all the tales he'd heard of vengeful spirits. Ivar of Dubhlinn's men had taken Olaf's body from the King's longhouse by knocking a hole in the wall, to prevent Olaf's angry ghost from finding its way back through the door to haunt them.

"Listen to me, Seer," said Tomas gently, seating himself in front of her--right on the grass-covered howe, but he didn't care about that. Carefully, he took her cold hands. "King Athils was not murdered. He died at a festival here when his horse threw him; I cannot say how many years ago. But you had nothing to do with it. He would bear you no grudge."

Their eyes met. The Seer compressed her lips, nodded, and removed her hands from his, politely but hastily. Her color was better, or she was blushing. To give her time to collect herself, Tomas got up and strolled around the howe.

Athils, once King of the Svea people, stood on the other side of his burial mound. His pale head was tilted towards the stars that shone dimly through his body, and his large square hands were relaxed at his sides. "Ah, there you are, Rhymer," he said without turning. "You've come."

Tomas stopped in his tracks. "'There I am'? Gods above, did you summon me?"

"No." Athils faced him. "No more than you summoned me. But I was expecting you. Twice, you had seen me. Do you not know how often such things work in threes?"

"I do now," Tomas said heavily. "It becomes clearer just how much I do not know."

"The beginning of wisdom," observed the King; his voice was tranquil. "Your companion seeks you."

With uneven steps, the Seer edged up to Tomas. "You are speaking with him now?"

Tomas nodded. "What do you perceive?"

"Nothing." A small shrug. "Better for me, perhaps, at least this time. Does my presence here disturb you?"

Athils shook his head.

"No, Seer. Stay as long as you wish," Tomas told her. Knotting her fists, she stood and gazed unseeingly towards the King.

"Why are you here?" Athils inquired for the second time.

"On this mound? Or at Uppsala?"

"Both," said the King--which made the third time.

So Tomas told him, not the entire story, not baring his heart as he had to Mother Aud. He related his vision of the Nornir, his encounter with Moira, and the nature of her gifts and of the quest forced upon him by the threat of Hel.

The abbreviated tale was still long in the telling. Through it all, Athils studied the sky, his expression never changing. The Seer gasped once or twice, but otherwise listened to Tomas in open-mouthed silence. Finally she sat down--not on the howe--propped her chin on her fists and stared at him. Her face had gone the color of a week-old snowdrift, and a tic came and went beneath her right eye.

When Tomas finished speaking, Athils lifted his head to track a shooting star across the night, then asked, "Now, why are you on this mound?"

"Since the Elf Queen didn't want me to tarry here, I thought you might be able to tell me if I could stop."

Athils regarded him steadily.

"Not go to Asgard. Not steal the ravens. Just stop," said Tomas, waving a hand in the air.

"Yes. You could," said the king, and returned his gaze to the sky.

"But would Hel--what would happen if I stopped here?"

Silence.

"Can you tell me? Will you?"

Athils murmured, "The dead know many things. Not everything." Tomas thought he might actually have sighed. "The ferment here continues, and intensifies. In more worlds than one. You are far from being at the center of that ferment. And yet, Rhymer, you are one of its centers. That in itself does not compel me...but you have seen me thrice. While three times I have questioned you. And you have asked--" He shook his head. "There is much to consider."

In the ensuing silence, Tomas felt as if his bones had melted away. He dropped down beside the Seer and put his face in his clammy hands. After a few minutes, he was startled by the Seer's swift inquiring tap on his shoulder. "Only fatigue," he muttered. "We are not done yet."

After what seemed so long a time that Tomas wondered why the summer sky refused to lighten, Athils said, "Rhymer."

The Seer sat bolt upright as Tomas stood and faced the King. His body was more transparent than before, and his eyes brighter, though more distant and unfocused.

"You possess the perception of truths," Athils intoned. His voice sounded hollow and farther away.

A reply seemed expected, so Tomas said, "I do."

"Go perceive your own reflection in the Well," said the King, lifting his shadowy face to the heavens. "Go now." With a rippling blur, he disappeared.

Would the grove and the temple vanish again too? Tomas whirled to stare down the road towards the Well, but nothing had changed. Scattered carts rolled along and the torches burned as before.

"I heard a man speaking!" the Seer whispered, her mouth round with astonishment. "But I could not understand the words."

"I could," said Tomas quietly. "I must go to the Well."

CHAPTER FIFTY: THE WELL

Tomas accepted the Seer's offer to accompany him to the Well. They picked their silent way through moisture-laden grass from Athils's mound to the road, where the traffic had dwindled to a solitary cart near the temple farther ahead. Once an owl soared out of the trees and across their path. The road was poor and the Seer tripped over more than one pothole, but refused Tomas's outstretched hand with a grim shake of her head.

When they drew level with the second and third howes, Tomas studied them as best he could in the dim light. He saw no shadowy figures on either mound. His vision seemed clearer than it had for hours: no specks, no blurred forms or colors staining the night. He felt alert and calm, his weariness gone for the moment.

After they passed the third mound, the Seer heaved a small sigh of released tension. She twitched her shoulders, straightened her robes and touched the bag of Runes that hung from her belt. Reaching the lighted area, they fell in with other festival-goers, mostly men, either drunkenly boisterous or mute and brooding. Apart from some curious stares no one bothered them, while quite a few people detoured around Tomas.

When they neared the grove, chanting floated towards them through the trees. The Seer stopped to indicate a footpath that bore off to the right. "It's shorter that way. And farther from the temple," she said, eyes darting towards the singers and back to Tomas. "Do you want this cloth for your face? There's no route to the Well that doesn't go by some sacrifices."

Tomas tied the offered scarf over his mouth and nose. It smelt strongly of garlic but did little to block the other odors.

With half her face hidden by her own kerchief, the Seer looked haughtier and more mysterious than before. "Should we be stopped, let me speak for us," she said warningly.

They continued down the right-hand trail, mercifully less well-lit than the main thoroughfare. Tomas avoided looking directly at the carcasses suspended from the trees, but it was impossible not to see some of them. Stained hind legs, bloated bellies: a goat, a ram, another goat.

Tomas shut his eyes as they passed the headless corpse of a pig by the side of the path. "No men?" he whispered.

The Seer, lost in her own thoughts, gave a start at the sound of his voice. "By the temple. Later tonight," she said brusquely, with a jerk of her chin in the direction of the chanting.

281

It couldn't be much later. The trees made it difficult to tell, but through their branches Tomas thought he saw the first subtle hints of charcoal that signalled the early Northern dawn.

Then they came to the entrance of the grove, and the Well. It lay in a clearing lined with burning torches thrust into the trampled ground. Round and wide and low, the Well was made of weathered, well-fitted stones. From the rim emerged the twin bars of a wooden ladder, like petrified fingers pointing at the single ash tree that grew close by. Except for Tomas and the Seer, the clearing was empty.

"Where is everyone?" Tomas asked.

The Seer shrugged. "At the temple? They'll return, but we can't know when."

She had asked him nothing of his reasons for coming to the Well. "Thank you for guiding me here," Tomas said. Taking the nearest torch from its holder, he started towards the waiting mouth of stone. "I'm going to look at the water."

"Look at it?" she repeated, startled out of her discretion. "I thought you would ask something."

Offerings were made here, in prayer and supplication. The ladder facilitated the retrieval of the offerings that floated, which indicated refusal of the querent's request. Only when the Well wholly swallowed the sacrifice had the gods granted their assent.

"I am, I suppose," Tomas told the Seer, and approached the Well before he could change his mind.

Blessedly empty, the dark water was less malodorous than he'd feared, and utterly still. Tomas had swung his legs over the rim, perched on the lip of the Well, and set both bare feet on the rungs of the ladder before the full import of his act struck him. Almost dropping his torch, he made a successful grab for it with his free hand and even maintained his balance. Behind him he heard the Seer gasp.

"Perceive your reflection in the Well," Athils had said. Would Tomas see the truth about his quest or about himself? Or both?

But a reflection reverses the image. Should he take the dead King's words backwards and sideways too?

Tomas stared up through the branches of the ash tree. "Stand alone between the tree and the Well, at the dark of the Moon," Moira had told him. It was the dark of the Moon now: one of her conditions, at least, that he could not alter if he went on to Asgard.

One hand on the ladder, Tomas descended it with his back to the rungs, taking care not to snag himself with his satchel. When his feet were just above the water, he gazed downward, the torch held low.

Encircled by stones surprisingly innocent of moss, the water looked oily, black and slick. It would probably feel resinous on the skin, not that he intended to touch it. He waited for the Well to still from the inevitable jarring he'd given the ladder.

The fire-tipped column that burned above his hand was already mirrored in the water below his feet. Soon the last of the ripples died away, and he saw his reflection clearly.

Having last directly observed it in Vestfold and indirectly at Ivar's court in Dubhlinn, the image that confronted Tomas was a shock. His features looked no older than when he'd shipped out on the *Brilliant Dragon*, although he was considerably leaner, almost scrawny now for his height. But there was a supple wiriness to this lanky barefooted figure who balanced easily on a waterlogged ladder while holding a sputtering torch. There was a powerful grace he'd never believed himself to possess. He thought of lynxes, of wolves--and of Elves.

"Gods above," he muttered, peering at the face in the water.

After all that had happened since Waleis, he'd expected the wild head of blond hair, streaked even lighter now from weeks in the open, as well as the untrimmed beard and sun-weathered skin. What startled him were his eyes, no longer those of the skald who had joined his half-brother's crew. Now far too old for his haggard face, they glittered with a stunned intensity. Tomas had seen such eyes in men who wandered snow-blind into ice-bound halls, struggling to focus on what was before them and desperately conjuring images that weren't there--all from the mind's need to make sense of what lies within its realm of vision.

Little wonder that Ottar's and Yngvar's men had called Tomas fey, and so many festival-goers given him a wide berth.

Once he looked deeper than the shock in his expression, bruises were evident, not of the body, but the spirit.

This, he already knew. This he did not need to see. "You do not ask the right questions," Mother Aud had told him. What then did he need to see?

Tomas withdrew his attention from the heft of the torch in one hand and the curve of the ladder's wooden shaft in the other, until those sensations melted away and the arches of his bare feet grew numbed to the rung beneath them. He would not feel, would not think, would listen only to his breathing. Staring at his reflection in the Well, he ignored the image's sharp-edged clarity and its liquid sheen. With fierce concentration he looked straight into the mirrored eyes. Grey as harpstrings, grey as sorrow, they returned his gaze.

Slowly and carefully, Tomas shaped a question in his mind, then aimed it at those deep-set eyes with all the force he could muster:

'What will befall me, should my wandering road stop here?'

Abruptly the water shattered like icicles, and with it his reflected face. He clutched at the ladder; the torch wavered in his shaking hand. He could scarcely breathe. Shifting his feet against the bite of the wood, he felt them prickle and throb with returning blood. He climbed a couple of rungs, then looked back down at the Well.

Although still troubled with sluggish ripples, the water had calmed enough for another image to appear: a tree by the temple. Beneath its branches stood the white-faced priest who'd taken Tomas's coins. The godhi held an oiled ceremonial rope in his fleshy hands. A knot of struggling men scuffled their way towards him, dragging someone who fought with all the abandoned savagery of terror, but who was outnumbered and exhausted. Who was to be sacrificed, hung from the tree. A tall, lean young man, his dark green clothing half-torn from his body, his white-blond hair matted with blood.

Fool. The victim was Tomas himself.

As he cursed his tranced slowness of wit, he heard shouting, then the Seer's aborted scream.

He scrambled up the ladder until his head just cleared the lip of the Well. Yngvar's men and a score of others were in the clearing. All of them looked fighting-drunk, glaring sullenly left and right, their faces greasy and blotched with rage. Ketil held the Seer's arm twisted behind her back at a vicious angle, and his bleeding hand was clamped over her mouth.

Wild with fear for the Seer, Tomas ducked back down the ladder before the men spotted him. He stopped on the last rung above the water.

"--couldn't a gone far--"

"Take your hands off her! It's the skald that we want!" Ketil snarled.

Rape was not their object, then; Tomas expelled a sigh of relief. He alone was their target, as he should have known. That left only one way of escape.

To Asgard.

"Search the woods!" Yngvar ordered. "Now!"

Tomas dropped his torch in the Well. Fulfilling one of Moira's conditions, he wet his hands to the wrists in the oily water--perhaps that was essential for the crossing. Everything was a gamble now; he could not know. Perhaps it was also necessary to stand under the ash tree. Too late for that: it was only a matter of time before they'd think to look in the Well.

Balancing on the ladder, Tomas fanned out his fingers and

began the series of Runic passes that Moira had taught him. His open palms felt slick with perspiration and tingled with each sweeping gesture. The clearing's torches and the slowly approaching dawn gave some illumination; he glimpsed the motion of his arms reflected in the dark liquid at his feet. But had it been pitch-dark, he could have seen the Runes that he sketched in the air. Each line glowed with an eerie phosphorescence of its own, shining in the water below and glancing off the moist inner surface of the Well, where the stones sweated in the damp.

By the time Yngvar thrust his head over the rim, Tomas had drawn the last pass. The Swedish ferry captain's shout of triumph changed to a guttural yelp of fear when he saw the intricately netted luminescence that issued from Tomas's hands. When both the radiating web of light and the skald first turned all the colors of the rainbow, then completely disappeared, Yngvar sat down and howled so bleakly that his men, who had seen nothing, feared for his reason.

CHAPTER FIFTY-ONE: ASGARD

Pain stabbed his skull. When nausea followed, Tomas lost all sense of balance. He spun weightless in a thick grey mist, but there was no sensation of falling. There was no sensation of anything at all. He saw nothing, heard nothing, felt nothing.

He must be dying: the passage had failed. This must be why Caraid could see no farther than the grove. When would Hel appear to claim him, if she could claim someone who'd left no corpse?

Then, with a resonant thud, he landed on something hard and unyielding.

Shocked to feel the aching length of his body again, Tomas lay on his stomach for a moment with his eyes closed before he sat up and flexed his arms and legs. He'd have bruises, but nothing was broken. Incredibly, the satchel was still strapped to his back.

Before him lay a green and empty field. Prime farmland, without a boulder in sight, though he spotted several patches of dead grass. Beyond the meadow a fine stretch of woods, firs and hardwood both, reached up into the gentle lines of hillier terrain. Overhead, the windless air was the violet-blue of wine grapes, paling to aquamarine near the horizon.

Tomas frowned. Skies of that rare tint were usually clear as glass--but this one was mottled at random with clumps of grey clouds like so many filthy sheep. Still, wherever he was, it wasn't Hel's strand of corpses. Then he glanced downward and gasped in amazement.

He was sitting on a hard, slightly sloping surface that glittered with bands of color. It was formed by imprisoned particles of some sparkling variegated substance, and it leveled off in the meadow grass before him. It was Bifrost, the rainbow bridge. He was in Asgard.

Asgard, at last. He could scarcely compass it. With extreme caution Tomas rose to his feet, then turned his head, inch by inch, to peer over both shoulders. On either side of the immense and gaudy arc on which he'd landed, two identical arcs stretched away into hazy nothingness. More nothingness lay between all three sections of the bridge. Off into the blue-domed haze curved the meadow's vast circular rim, as precise and sharp as if edged with a monstrous sword.

Vertigo threatened; he swayed where he stood. The meadow looked safer, so he turned and started forward. As his bare foot came down upon the rainbow bridge, it echoed. Loudly.

Tomas's startled leap produced more echoes which rolled and rumbled off into the distance. So did each step he took to reach the turf. With a grimace he sank down onto the lush grass: he'd just announced his arrival in Asgard.

Clutching his head in his hands, he waited for this new world to stop spinning.

The dizziness hadn't completely passed when someone gave his satchel a few inquisitive pats. "Yes, indeed: a skald. I thought as much," said an amiable tenor voice. "Congratulations on your passage to Asgard alive. Who are you, mortal, and what brings you to this bower?" The last words were dark with sarcasm.

Tomas opened his eyes. Squatting on his heels less than a yard away was a slightly-built young man whose crest of thick curly hair was an improbable shade of ruddy ginger. No, not a young man, despite his lineless skin, so pale that all its color appeared sapped by the flaming hair. The redhead's age was indeterminate and variable in the same way as that of the Elves. It was impossible to meet his narrowed eyes for very long; they burned with a wild and malevolent hazel intelligence like evil spirits trapped in amber.

Tomas could not quite suppress a shudder. He recognized this being. The son of two frost giants, foster-brother to Odin. The Father of Lies. "Loki," he said involuntarily.

"I've been called worse," Loki allowed. "And what might they call you?"

"The Rhymer." Tomas was relieved not to be asked, in so many words, for his name. Concealment would be difficult; his ideas were trailing off in all directions as if pulled apart by inquisitive fingers. Between Loki and himself the air felt charged with erratic currents.

Reveal your errand to Loki only if you must, Moira had said. Tomas's errand. To steal the ravens. To act like one of Odin's slain warriors, obtain a key and—

Slain warriors.

"How did you know I am alive?" he whispered.

"The feet of the dead make no sound upon that bridge," said Loki, raising his burnished eyebrows. "And you're not a god. I'm well acquainted with that lot." His mouth contorted in a sneer.

Tomas winced and looked away. Had he given offense? His mouth dry, he glanced hastily back at Loki.

The redhead's faintly amused scrutiny, unhurried and invasive, took Tomas in from head to toe. Disoriented, he started to fidget, then forced himself to hold still.

"You rather put me in mind of an Elf, but they no longer come here." A hard-edged glitter crept into Loki's eyes. "What are you planning to do in Asgard?"

287

Caught off guard, Tomas felt himself gaping.

"Come, now! You can tell me!" said Loki in conspiratorial tones. He leaned forward, hazel eyes boring into Tomas's, and tapped him on one bare foot. The long flexible fingers were so unnaturally hot that Tomas flinched. "No mortal would come all the way to Asgard without some great deed plotted out. And you a skald! You must have a whole saga in mind." Loki chuckled, a series of sharp yelping sounds. Beneath them were the unmistakable notes of mania, corrosive and rising.

Tomas ached to leap to his feet and run, but sensed how unwise any sudden move might be. Besides, it was so difficult to focus his mind that he wasn't certain how well his legs would respond. Managing a thick swallow, he thought: this must be how a bird feels when a snake fascinates it.

"Frightened?" asked Loki, his voice soft and intimate, almost a croon. Without warning, it roughened. "Then you've better sense than most of the Aesir. We've not lost all our power—" His mouth snapped shut; his eyes flared. "State your errand here, mortal," he said coldly. His hand shot out and clamped on Tomas's wrist.

In desperation he said, "I must steal something," and closed his eyes. It was over. He could not refuse to answer questions to Loki's satisfaction, because he might go mad if forced to endure that searing fierce grip for very long.

But Loki said nothing. Slowly and experimentally, Tomas attempted to tug his arm away. When it was released without a struggle, he looked warily at Loki.

Staring straight at Tomas but not seeing him, Loki was rigid and motionless as granite. Fire still smoldered in the unblinking amber eyes, but their attention was turned inward. For a few dazed seconds, Tomas sat and rubbed his wrist. Perhaps because he was now free of Loki's notice, some of his confusion evaporated, and he got up and started to back away as silently as he could.

He'd not gone two paces when Loki leapt to his feet and grabbed Tomas's elbow. "Stay and speak further with me. We've something in common, friend Thief." Loki's bemusement had vanished, and his face was alight with malice.

"Very well," said Tomas in a dull voice. "Just let go of me, please."

"What delicate sensibilities for a robber," said Loki dryly, but he released Tomas's arm. "When I might be offering advice or assistance! At the risk of having my greater experience scorned, I shall ask: what do you purpose to steal?" Rubbing his palms together, he

288

assumed an injured, patient expression.

But the redhead's eyes were hungry and calculating. Loki was muting his viciousness, temporarily and for his own ends.

Moira had said, "He is a trickster, inclined towards chaos, not order. Yet he may assist you. For his Fate is to help bring down the Aesir and the Vanir both, and he may regard a meeting with you as a step along that path."

The mistletoe's time had come. "Before I answer, I must show you something," Tomas said quietly.

CHAPTER FIFTY-TWO: A BARGAIN

Tomas slipped out of his satchel straps. Refusing Loki's outstretched hand, a mute offer to hold the pack, Tomas cradled it in his arms and seated himself on the thick grass. Loki dropped down eagerly beside him. The redhead's mobile face was sharp with curiosity, and he hummed beneath his breath.

One by one Tomas undid the satchel's fastenings. Unable to find the mistletoe right away, he lifted out the harp and the flute. When he began to open the instruments' inner wrappings to look for the plant, Loki gave him an easy tap on the wrist. "May I?"

Tomas nodded. Loki's hands, nimble and strong, made short work of a maze of knots. He lifted the harp free and held it up admiringly. Against the enamel-blue sky of Asgard, the polished wood shone mellow and sleek, although Tomas's two burned fingerprints stood out sharply.

When Loki touched his own thumb to the burned spots, his eyes narrowed. "Lovely," he murmured, setting the harp down on its coverings. With the same swift dexterity, he uncovered the flute and took his time examining it. Sighting down its length, he said, "Elvish make, both of them." He raised the flute and blew a complicated trill. Too breathy, but powerful. At the thought of that searing touch upon his flute, Tomas stifled a grimace.

"Celtic Elves," Loki pronounced, an assessing look on his face. "That explains one thing. I knew you weren't full-blooded Norse."

Tomas was too startled to comment. Loki shot him a measuring glance, pursed his lips, then started to grin. "Too square in the face, and your eyes aren't set right," he said airily, using the flute to point at the features in question. He appeared pleased with himself. "Who gave you these?"

Keeping his voice neutral, Tomas said, "Moira, Queen of Elfland."

From the redhead's chuckle, he might have detested Moira or loved her passionately, might have left her an hour ago or never have met her. The only certainty was that he knew whom Tomas meant.

Hugging the flute to his chest, setting one hand on the harp, Loki said maliciously, "Moira, Queen of Elfland. And now you're giving them to me?"

"No!" Tomas grabbed up the harp, reached for the flute.

"Temper," said Loki, smiling--but he handed Tomas the instrument. "Not put your little treasures to full use yet, eh?"

Groping in his pack for the mistletoe, Tomas didn't answer.

290

Loki uttered a delicate snort and leaned back on his elbows. When Tomas found the small cutting at last and glanced up at the redhead, Loki was watching him.

"What are you showing me, then?" asked Loki, smothering an ostentatious yawn.

"This." Tomas set the scrap of mistletoe midway between them. What reaction he'd expected he didn't quite know, but not this slow quizzical lift of Loki's eyebrows as he sat up and studied the withered greenery. "All of it?" he asked politely. "Dead leaves, dried berries and kindling-stems--all for me?"

"Perhaps. But not just yet."

"Why, I don't know how to thank you," murmured Loki, not lifting his eyes from the plant. His face cool and guarded, he tapped one forefinger against his knee.

Now what? Tomas stifled a frown.

"Might you care to tell me what this is?"

"Mistletoe," said Tomas, taken aback.

Loki slanted a burning amber glance at him from half-closed eyes. "I am well aware that it's mistletoe. And a sorry specimen at that. But why are you showing it to me?"

Tomas shuddered. To bring down the Norse gods...

"Take your time, friend Thief," said Loki, inching closer. "It must be portentous to have brought you here alive."

Tomas set his fingertips on the mistletoe, ready to retrieve it if need be. A corner of Loki's mouth twitched.

"I must ask some assistance from you, Loki. In return I offer you this plant."

"A bargain? How appetizing. Tell me more."

"I need you to bring me the key to the chamber where Odin's ravens, Thought and Memory, are kept."

"Why? You look able-bodied enough to me," Loki said with an insinuating smile.

Tomas didn't care for the way Loki was eyeing him. "Because the key is made of iron. And kept near Valholl, where there are weapons--"

"And you're susceptible to the iron-sick. Aren't you?" Loki interrupted. His voice was very soft.

Meeting that intrusive gaze, Tomas nodded curtly.

"Poor delicate creature," said Loki, shaking his head. "What else am I to do for you? Hypothetically, of course."

"Let me into the chamber with the ravens."

"Whatever do you propose to do there?"

Tomas braced himself. "Steal them."

"Steal Thought and Memory?"

When Tomas nodded again, Loki gave him a prolonged and enigmatic scrutiny. "Why?"

"For Moira."

"What does she want with them?"

Damn her gifts of true speech and prophecy; Tomas had no choice but to explain. "Odin's followers and the Christians restrict the Elves' movements in Midgard somehow," he said wearily. "Elfland is weaker."

Loki raised his eyebrows again.

"Moira wants a bargaining chip, something of Odin's. To force an alliance, perhaps. Maybe to drive his cultists from the part of Midgard closest to her." Tomas pushed a strand of snarled blond hair out of his face. "Perhaps to learn something from Thought and Memory themselves. I don't understand all of it."

"You don't, do you?" Loki's tone was mild, but he studied Tomas closely. When Tomas shook his head, Loki compressed his lips and glanced at the mistletoe. "So I open the chamber and you take the ravens and leave, I presume. That's all you'd require of me, before making me a gift of this twig?"

"Ah, no." Wrapping his arms around his knees, Tomas hunted for words. "Your daughter, Hel..."

At Loki's scowl, the air between them thickened with tension, and Tomas struggled to retain his train of thought. "She's pursuing me," he said flatly, his chest tightening. "Can you call her off?"

The pale narrow face went cold and still for so long that Tomas began to fear he would get no answer. But how would he obtain the key if he got up and walked away--and would Loki let him?

At last the hazel eyes darted from side to side, then settled on the mistletoe. "Why is she hounding you?"

Tomas described the loose-working thread on the Nornir's loom, and how Moira had called to him by the Saefren. "Hel was cheated of a death," he finished tonelessly. "She desires one."

Loki was nodding. "So that's how Moira constrained you to her--at least in part. How else?"

Exhausted and despondent, Tomas gazed down at his hands.

"You swore an oath? Elves do seem fond of them."

"Two oaths," Tomas muttered. "One to her. And one by the Magician's oath with Fate, that I would bring her the ravens." He glanced at Loki. "Will you help me?"

A thin-lipped, insidious smile. "Why should I?"

292

"Moira gave me the mistletoe in case I came across you here in Asgard."

Loki folded his arms and waited.

"She said--" Tomas remembered Moira's every word to him, but which should he repeat? "She said, 'Remind him that mistletoe is sacred to us, to the old beliefs, and to the ancient rituals.'"

The redhead was giving him an unblinking stare of concentration.

"She said, 'Inform Loki that this plant the Norse gods may overlook only to their peril, and that a day may come when he deems this knowledge useful.'"

"Indeed," said Loki after half a minute. "What else did she say about me?"

When Tomas hesitated, the redhead caught his wrist in a grip that felt capable of raising blisters on the skin. "What else?"

"Let go of me!" Tomas failed to wrench his arm away.

"Not before I've heard the rest," Loki hissed.

Tomas shut his eyes. "She said: 'Loki misses little of what happens in the nine worlds, in Asgard most of all. Should the Father of Lies approach you, take heed: he is a trickster, inclined towards chaos, not order. Reveal your errand to him only if you must; he may or may not assist you. Yet I doubt he would betray you. For Loki's Fate is to help topple the gods, the Aesir and the Vanir both, and he might regard an encounter with you as a step along that path.'" Grimacing, he opened his eyes. "That's all she said of you. I swear it."

The fierce amber gaze was unnervingly close. "How do I know you're telling the truth?"

Tomas laughed, harder and harder, until he was shaking as if he were feverish. At first Loki looked incredulous. Then his face contracted in a snarl as he clamped down viciously on Tomas's wrist.

Perhaps his bones would break as well as burn. "Because I can't do otherwise," he gasped. "She gave me true speech and prophecy. I cannot lie."

Eyes veiled and slitted, Loki sat back and released Tomas's arm.

Try as he would, it was some time before Tomas could force himself to stop laughing, even when, to his surprise, Loki began to laugh with him. Were the notes of mania audible in one or both of their voices?

"I like it well," Loki announced when they grew calmer. His glance at Tomas was wicked with collusion. "The Father of Lies and a teller of truths. And both of us thieves. More akin than one might

293

think, we two."

Tomas stared at him.

"That stung?" asked Loki sweetly. "For shame. You'll hurt my feelings."

"Then you'll help me?"

A self-satisfied nod. "I will indeed." Loki's perfect white teeth gleamed. "Not that you know if I'm speaking the truth." He chortled at Tomas's expression. "But I shall assist you regardless. To help topple the gods is my Fate, remember? Like yours."

"*Mine?* My errand is for the Elves--"

Loki's mouth twisted. "Fool. Did she drain your Norse blood while she beguiled you?"

Tomas's spine went rigid, but he said nothing. Too dangerous to provoke this red-haired being--even when he was provoking Tomas. Especially then, perhaps. He set his jaw.

Acrimony filled Loki's gaze. "The god Balder dreams of death and his passage into Hel's hands in Niflheim. Balder's demise will precede Ragnarok--our destruction. Had you forgotten, skald?"

Tomas shook his head.

"The goddess Frigg obtained from every animal, plant and substance their promises not to harm her son Balder." Loki pointed at the sloping green hills across the field. "The gods throw sticks and stones at Balder now, for sport. Nothing hurts him; all falls harmlessly aside. While I have been asking myself if some creature, stone or plant, however small, escaped Frigg's notice." A sarcastic smile. "My daughter Hel will gladly relinquish her claim on you, Rhymer. You're sending Balder in your stead."

A flash of the Sight: a tiny whittled twig of mistletoe piercing the eye of Balder, the mildest of the gods. Balder felled to the ground-- With a cry, Tomas threw himself on the mistletoe.

So did Loki. Their hands met and clasped upon the sprig of faded green.

A deafening boom split the air above their heads.

So loud it was that Tomas gasped at the pain that stabbed his ears. He expected lightning, but there wasn't any. Instead, the grassy surface of the meadow beneath him heaved and buckled and heaved again. Tomas grabbed Loki's wrist to keep from being hurled onto his face, and felt his own forearm gripped in turn.

They clutched the mistletoe between them, and Loki's touch burned as before. More booms came, from underground this time, followed by a sonorous grating wrench. Not even the *Pride of Skiringssal* breaking up on a reef in the Irish Sea had sounded like this. There was no splintering of wood in this sound: it was vaster, slower, like a cavernous groan from the frost giants from whose body Midgard had first been fashioned.

The earth shifted again, trembled once more and was still.

An unnatural silence descended. Tomas released Loki's arm and relaxed his grip on the mistletoe. Loki did the same. When the plant fell to the ground between them, a few dried berries came loose and rolled away to lodge in freshly exposed soil.

Tomas straightened up and looked at the fractured terrain all around. It was like the aftermath of an earthquake, or the damage of a hundred winters heaving the earth at once. The meadow had been carved into several ragged layers, dotted by enormous boulders and crossed by a random network of gaping fissures. Great shelves of raw earth overlapped one another, uprooted trees lay prone and broken along the ridge, and the sky was full of ominous grey clouds. A hard wind sprang to life in the colder air.

Ginger hair whipped by the breeze, Loki rose slowly to his feet, shielded his eyes with one long hand and sighted down the devastated plain of Asgard. To Tomas's horror, the redhead began to smile, and smiled more widely with each scar that he observed upon the landscape. When he stooped to pocket the mistletoe, Tomas got to his feet and edged a few yards away. Glancing over his shoulder at the rainbow bridge, he sucked in his breath.

Bifrost was a fraying ribbon of its former self, seamed and cracked with nothingness between its broken strips of color. Smoke roiled in the air about the gaps that marred its curving length. It was still passable, but passable to where?

Loki turned to follow the direction of Tomas's gaze. For a long moment neither of them spoke. Then Loki said, "We'd best speed you on your errand, Thief, if you intend to leave the way you came." His tone was light, but his face was a blackly triumphant mask of exultation.

"What happened?" Tomas asked, shivering from the increasing chill.

A high-pitched, spiteful chuckle. "We had a meeting of the minds, you and I. Or hands, as it were, upon the weapon you and Moira gave me."

"You're lying!"

Loki doubled over with laughter. "But you aren't, Rhymer. That's just it." Tears of mirth spilled from his eyes. "It seems Asgard is crumbling too. Of course it is; we're linked to Elfland." Gasping, he sat down hard upon the tumbled earth. "The best part is that Moira must have known." He peered gleefully up at Tomas. "I wonder how the other worlds fared when we met, brother of mine?"

A salvo of booms echoed from beyond the ridge. Red and orange swirled in the air between Tomas and Loki; orange and red swirled in Tomas's brain. He remembered Olaf's corpse in Ivar of Dubhlinn's hall, with Olaf's own axe-blade buried in its chest, while from its mouth a slushy wavering form—

"I'm not your brother!" Tomas shouted. "My brother is dead!" It was the Sight, only the Sight. Not Olaf's ghost, not here. "Get up! You have the mistletoe; I've done my part. Get up and help me!"

Loki bounded to his feet. "With pleasure! Whose doom shall we be now, my twin?" He flung an arm around Tomas's shoulders.

Tomas backed away, flexing the tension from his arms and unclenching his hands. Never had he so ached to strike someone. Melted colors still stained the air. "You act from choice," he snapped. "I am constrained to act."

"How, constrained?" Eyes blazing like a funeral ship, Loki moved towards him.

"By my own loose thread that Moira caught! By a Magician's oath with Fate!"

Loki grabbed Tomas's shoulders. "Do you think I don't obey the constraints of my own Fate?"

His breath coming in short hard gasps, his skin burning in Loki's grip, Tomas knotted his fists.

"You don't understand your own nature yet; you're still a Fool." An ogre's smile; a cannibal's. Loki yanked him closer, until the molten eyes were inches away and Tomas felt the hot dry breath upon his face. He braced himself as best he could. The fear and rage were galvanizing: his head grew icy-clear, and the spiraling reds and oranges faded from his vision. He knew better than to pull away, but all his muscles tensed.

"Maybe the ravens will help a Magician unborn, and maybe not," Loki crooned. His fingers twitched convulsively on Tomas's shoulders. "It's difficult to know, with one more inclined towards chaos than order." He licked his lips. "Are you wondering what I mean?"

Tomas nodded once. The wind was picking up.

Loki's grin was more of a snarl. "In that at least, we are alike, friend Thief. Could Moira make the Nornir spin amiss? She is as subject to the Fates as are we all. Did you believe that the Nornir did not *intend* to drop your thread?" He shook Tomas and hissed, "Do you think there's naught but order in the universe? You Fool!" Releasing Tomas with a shove, Loki wheeled and set off towards the ridge. "Make haste," he said without turning. "We go to steal your key."

CHAPTER FIFTY-THREE: THE CHAMBER WITH THE RAVENS

Beneath a slowly darkening sky, Tomas followed Loki across the broken plain. The ground was treacherous. Dirt clods rolled unexpectedly underfoot; the rocks were slippery, and many of the newly heaved embankments, taller than a man, required thought and assistance to climb. Neither Tomas nor Loki spoke. Tomas winced inwardly each time he accepted a boost or felt obliged to offer one, because he knew, from tales he had heard since childhood, that Loki could shape-shift into a form that would have no trouble with this terrain. Loki had spent time as a horse, a bird, a woman.

Perhaps some of Loki's reasons for maintaining his own shape now were to discomfit Tomas with their occasional physical contact and with the contrast in their levels of exertion. His hands clasped behind his back, the agile redhead strolled along at an easy clip. Before they reached the ridge, Tomas was panting, but Loki whistled to himself as they crested it. When they stopped at last, Tomas was glad of the chance to get his second wind.

"Valholl," said Loki, pointing. "And Yggdrasil, where your key is hung."

Below them stretched another grassy field, not so damaged as the one they'd just crossed, but whose surface was also marred by long uneven fissures. Even from this distance, Tomas caught the reek of iron from Valholl. His stomach knotted; sweat broke out on his forehead. The leaden sky had grown no darker for some time, yet the air was progressively colder. Apart from some deer and a goat grazing near Valholl, the traumatized plain was deserted. "Where is everyone?" Tomas asked, shivering.

Loki shrugged. "Wondering what's come to pass. In their own halls with their own folk. Or asking the Nornir at the Well of Urd, perhaps."

Valholl was the largest hall Tomas had ever seen. Much larger than he'd imagined, though he'd known it had hundreds of doors--he'd often sung of them. Its keel-shaped roof, curved and sloping, was covered with shields. Some were so old that particles crumbled from them as he watched, some new and round and rimmed with shining iron, and the rest of all ages in between. Spearpoints bristled from the edges of the roof that overhung the breast-plated walls. Within were Odin's warrior-dead, those slain in battle.

Was Olaf there? Would his death be accounted one in battle?

"You've gone paler than the Moon," said Loki softly. "From more than the iron-sick, I surmise. Most intriguing. Best look at

297

Yggdrasil instead."

There were other roofs, other halls, farther down the splintered fields of Asgard, but Tomas shifted his gaze to the immense ash tree that towered near Valholl. Yggdrasil: axle-tree of the nine worlds, vast and immeasurably ancient.

One root sank down to Hel's dominion, Niflheim, a second to Jotunheim of the frost giants, and the third root ran its gnarled way through Asgard. Scattered sections of the trunk looked dark with rot. It was said that an eagle perched in Yggdrasil's branches, and that a squirrel darted up and down the tree between the eagle and a serpent which gnawed the root in Niflheim below. Tomas squinted but could make out neither eagle nor squirrel, only the deer that grazed on what leaves still clung to the tree. He stared uneasily at Yggdrasil's visible root. The Well of Urd was located nearby.

"Can you come with me?" Loki asked, waving a hand at the giant ash.

Nausea lapped at Tomas's midsection. "I thought that you would fetch the key?"

"I will. But you might attract attention wandering alone. Skalds usually search for me or Freyja when they first arrive. Not for Odin, not so soon."

"Would someone who saw me know I am alive?"

"Freyr would." Loki made a fastidious gesture of distaste. "That's his domain, life and its increase. It would never occur to the others to suppose that you were anything but dead." He grinned. "You're in my company, though, so none of them will come close enough to tell if you're mortal, Elf or beast. Let's be off. I'll stay as far from Valholl as I can."

With Tomas at his heels, Loki picked his way nimbly down the ridge, then headed towards Yggdrasil in a ground-eating lope. Tomas labored not to lag too far behind. As they neared the hall, the iron-stench assailed him, coating his nose, his throat, his lungs. His empty stomach heaved, and he started coughing as he ran.

Loki slowed his pace and fell into step beside Tomas. "Tell me, has the iron-sick always taken you so hard?" he asked solicitously.

Tomas shook his head. His eyes were streaming. "Only since Elfland," he muttered.

Matching Tomas stride for stride, Loki cast him an appraising glance. "Perhaps, were you to think of other things," he suggested, grabbing Tomas's elbow long enough to steer him around a ditch. "If you even *believed*, I might go so far as to say, that you would not be overwhelmed to this degree... If you were distracted--"

298

Caraid had offered similar advice about blocking unwelcome visions. But the iron-sick was different. Physical. "How could I be distracted?" asked Tomas bitterly.

"Like this!" Loki lunged at Tomas and wrestled him to the ground.

No, by all the gods. Not these fiery hands and twisting arms. The hazel eyes were mad and staring, their pupils smoldering black with intent. A searing touch grazed Tomas's thigh.

He drove his fist into smooth white skin and solid bone, by the more yielding flesh of the nose.

One hand to his face, Loki let go, rolled away and got to his feet.

So did Tomas, crouching low, gathered and balanced and cold with rage. Ready to hit Loki again, past caring if he died for it.

A bruise flowering darkly beneath one incandescent eye, Loki gave him a demented smile. "Quite a punch, friend. You made your point. Did I make mine?"

"What do you mean?" Tomas maintained his coiled position.

But Loki stood easily, arms relaxed at his sides. There was no anger in his face, only a frenzied sort of mirth. "How do you feel? Other than violent, that is."

Tomas straightened up, flexing his hands. The iron-sick--

And when he remembered it, the malaise came back. But not before he remembered it, and with less than half its previous intensity. Astonished, he let out his breath.

Loki made a sound somewhere between cackling and the hiccups. "Not going to thank me? I forgive you. A gentle spirit, mine." Clutching at his ginger hair, he sank down on the grass and sputtered with laughter. "Pay me no mind," he gasped. "We'll be on our way again momentarily."

Tomas turned his back and stalked off towards Yggdrasil. After he'd taken a dozen steps, Loki, still giggling, bounded to his side. Staring straight ahead, Tomas walked faster.

"Long life and good health to you," said Loki, and clapped him on the shoulder. Then he set a blistering pace in the direction of the giant ash tree. Tomas ran after him.

When they saw Loki and Tomas approaching, the deer moved off to the other side of the enormous trunk. Two halls the size of Ivar of Dubhlinn's could have fit beneath Yggdrasil's branches. Even half-stripped of their yellow-green leaves, they cast considerable shade on the scuffed earth below, which was bare except for drifts of slender, winged ash fruit.

There was still no sign of the eagle, nor of Ratatosk the squirrel. A shimmering almost-haze hovered in the spreading tree limbs and an infinitesimal quiver moved through their tips, although the wind had died.

Loki slowed to a walk as they neared Yggdrasil. Just before the sweep of the outermost branches, he stopped. His face was reflective, and the fresh bruise startlingly dark against his pale skin. Faint pink tinted his cheekbones, but otherwise he showed no sign of the race they had just run.

Panting, Tomas stumbled to a halt. He didn't know if his legs or his lungs hurt more. Perhaps it wasn't wise to breathe so deeply of this air: there was too much power around this tree. It made him dizzy. Ancient, inhuman and utterly impersonal, it emanated from the rot-infested trunk, poured from the branches overhead and, like so many fanned and pointing fingers, streamed from each separate twig. What manner of animal would graze upon these leaves or gnaw that thick furrowed bark? Let the deer stay on the other side of the tree; he didn't care to see one at close range. He sniffed the air: a sharp, green, woody scent. And an undernote, fetid and musty.

Something that he could only describe as *movement* was occurring here, movement that he did not see, but sensed. Layers of motility all about and above the tree and deep in the earth beneath it. Vast ponderous spiraling motions, complex and intertwined, revolved around more than one center. And the centers themselves were in motion--

He was swaying on his feet when Loki caught his elbow. For once the scorching touch was welcome: it anchored Tomas upon this seed-strewn soil.

Shaking his head to clear it, he pulled his arm away. "I'm quite well," he told Loki, clipping the words.

The redhead's grin was wide and intimate. "How comforting." He seemed entirely undisturbed by the uncanny atmosphere around Yggdrasil. Pointing at the turf that encircled the expanse of bare ground beneath the tree, he asked, "Care to sit and fume while I fetch your key?"

As Tomas settled down on the grass, its rich green blades interspersed with shriveled brown, Loki leaped to catch a sturdy branch. He swung himself onto it and got to his feet with effortless grace. Amber eyes gleamed down at Tomas. "I haven't any idea how long your bit of burglary will take." Making almost no noise, he confidently began to scale the enormous tree.

Tomas soon lost track of Loki's ascent. An occasional leaf

floated down, but no more than had before. Shivering, Tomas blew on his fingers to warm them. He rubbed his scarred bare feet; their skin was thick with callouses and full of blisters old and new. He got up and stamped, then walked twice around the tree before remembering Moira's dark green cape in his satchel. He wrapped himself in it and sat down again.

Loki might find it amusing to return with the wrong key, or without one.

He might not return at all.

He could transform himself into a bird and fly away. Warn Odin. Warn the ravens.

There was nothing Tomas could do to prevent these possibilities. He had no control over Loki at all. He could only wait, and hope that Loki would climb down from Yggdrasil with the right key.

Tomas's muscles twitched with nerves and his head was throbbing. How long had it been since he'd slept? In the farmer's cart? He was too tense to fall asleep now, but he might as well try to rest while he could. He stretched out on the grass, pillowed his head in his arms and surprised himself with a prolonged and gaping yawn. He closed his eyes.

Heaving himself upright, Tomas cuffed Loki's hand from his face. The air was sour with iron.

He blinked at the redhead who balanced on his heels a few feet away. Loki was toying with a large ornate key on a leather thong looped carelessly around one grimy index finger. A few ash leaves were tangled in his hair.

"Sleeping!" he said reproachfully. "While I labor in your service. I even missed you." He spun the key in a whistling arc about his head, and Tomas ducked. "Come, let's find the raven coop." Looking expectant, he pocketed the key and stood.

Tomas got up slowly. "Where is it?"

Loki had already turned his back to Yggdrasil and the ridge they'd crossed earlier, and started down the field. "Near Odin's high seat." He glanced over his shoulder. "Don't trouble yourself; Odin's not there."

"Good," muttered Tomas, brushing dead grass from his cape.

"Present company suffices, eh? I'm flattered." Loki's voice suddenly turned flat. "The whole lot's probably off holding Balder's hand and whining about why the ground trembled." With a scowl, he tapped the pocket that held the mistletoe.

Tomas wrinkled his nose at the scent of the key, but the iron-sick was manageable if he didn't dwell on it. Still, he wouldn't care to touch the stuff bare-handed—which meant he needed Loki. Tomas's throat constricted with loathing.

I wish I'd hit him harder, he thought bitterly. Best not to dwell on that idea either.

An increasing number of cracks and fissures blocked their path, some so wide that he and Loki had to jump them. Smoke rose thinly from two or three of these miniature canyons. Loki pursed his lips at the sight and lingered to study the gaps, but made no comment. Fighting a lunatic urge to shove Loki into one of the chasms, Tomas moved several yards away each time the redhead paused.

They were nearing another of Odin's halls, Valaskjalf, not nearly so large as Valholl, but thatched in silver that flashed and glittered even beneath these somber skies. Tomas eyed the hall with growing reluctance. It was not a simple rectangle like Valholl; various rooms had been built on at odd angles, and several outbuildings clustered nearby. In Valaskjalf was Odin's high seat, Hlidskjalf, from where he and Frigg could survey the nine worlds.

Somewhere in or near that hall was the chamber with the ravens.

Thought and Memory. What would happen when Tomas brought them to Moira? Perhaps she would take back her gifts of true speech and prophecy, heightened Sight, and all the changes that came with them... But his transformation might well be permanent.

"Second thoughts?" murmured Loki.

Tomas shook his head.

"Excellent. I would have kept the mistletoe regardless." Loki's voice was cool. He pointed at the smallest outbuilding, which would have made an impressive home in Birka or Dubhlinn. Roofed in ordinary thatch, it lay farthest from the main hall and closest to Tomas and Loki. "There," said Loki as they approached. "The ravens are inside."

They stopped a few yards from the timbered door, which sported a large square iron lock. Loki produced the key from his pocket and put his hands on his hips. "Shall I unbolt the door and be done with it?"

The moment had come. Tomas was vaguely surprised at how calm he felt. Numb, perhaps, instead of calm. Meeting Loki's eyes, he nodded.

Loki inserted the massive key; it turned soundlessly in the lock. The redhead didn't open the door. Standing motionless, one hand still on the key, he studied Tomas. Loki's face was demure but his eyes shone with suppressed excitement, and his supple fingers twitched. Why the pause? Tomas gave Loki a wary look, and found himself balancing his weight as if he expected another attack. But he felt no warning twinge of the Sight. He felt nothing at all. "You have been a help to me, Loki," he said at last, forcing the words.

Loki's half-anticipated outburst came so suddenly that Tomas might as well have been completely unprepared.

"I have, at that!" Shrieking with glee, Loki flung the door open and shoved Tomas into the hall.

He stumbled, recovered his footing. The air was full of cawing. Feathers, black and glossy, whipped past his eyes and got in his nose. Sneezing, he protected his head as best he could. Loki's retreating howls of laughter were still quite close.

In case the startled birds took a notion to peck, Tomas shielded his eyes before he glanced around the hall. "Gods above," he said despairingly. "A thousand ravens!"

CHAPTER FIFTY-FOUR: THOUGHT AND MEMORY

The place was fitted with perches, great posts joined by crossbeams at various heights. Ravens preferred to nest in trees or around cliffs, and within this hall every effort had been made to accomodate their tastes. Moss, probably intended to line nests, was piled in the center of the floor. Tomas saw none of the hoods or jesses used with tamed birds, however, while the many small openings cut into the walls allowed the ravens free passage. The door and key, it seemed, were meant only to keep beings in human form outside. Carved wooden benches stood here and there, but otherwise the hall was set aside for the birds.

They were calmer now, returning to their nests and perches, and fluttering in and out through the slitted windows. Their earlier commotion apparently came more from Tomas's sudden unexpected entrance than from fear of him, or perhaps Loki's presence had disturbed them. Several of the dark shining birds winged in lazy circles before Tomas or flapped down onto the straw or the perches nearest him. They regarded him with inquisitive black eyes and sidled on their scaly, strong-clawed feet. Expecting food, probably. Ravens would eat almost anything, but he had nothing to give them.

"Sorry," he said, spreading his empty hands. "I'm hungry myself, friends."

The guttural cawing didn't sound angry. Studying their shaggy throats and heavy prominent bills, Tomas was thankful that not a single bird had made a dart for his eyes. No one must rob these nests of their spotted eggs, then. Not even Loki.

Loki be damned. Tomas had traded the mistletoe for nothing but an iron key.

That was something, however. It was why he was in this hall.

Brushing a drift of feathers from a bench chosen at random, he sat down. "Which of you are Thought and Memory?" he asked in a loud clear voice, feeling ridiculous—all the more so when no answer came. Black plumage glinting almost purple in the light from the windows, many of the nearest ravens had already flown away.

Section by section, Tomas began to scrutinize the entire flock. He took his time, getting up and moving to different vantage points. Sometimes he spoke.

The place was well-tended. Someone must sweep the droppings out fairly often, and the rows of windows made for good air circulation. The bird-smell was pungent, warm and moist, but neither overpowering nor unpleasant. He discovered more benches pushed against the walls and a waist-high pile of twigs beyond the moss. None of the birds spared him an extra glance. Not one of them appeared to be anything more than a common raven.

Glumly, he took a seat on the nearest bench. Perhaps Thought and Memory were still flying over Midgard and hadn't yet returned to tell Odin what they had seen this day. Would the god bring the ravens here, or would they return here of their own accord? They weren't caged, unless Odin kept the cage with Him.

They weren't caged despite what Moira had said: that Thought and Memory flew back to their cage each night.

Frowning, Tomas knuckled his chin. Sassy black birds swooped and gamboled through every window, chattering, mock-fighting and tumbling in mid-air. By no stretch of the imagination or bending of the truth could this place be called a cage.

Yet Elves did not lie.

Loki, however, most certainly did, and might have escorted Tomas to the wrong hall.

Perhaps Moira was unaware there was no cage. There could have been one before.

What else did she not know? That Balder's premonitory nightmares had already begun, and how soon the nihilistic Loki might contrive to have Balder killed with Moira's mistletoe? Balder's death was the long-foretold catalyst that would unleash Ragnarok, the destruction of the Aesir.

That a great colony of ravens nested here, and Tomas had no way to identify the two she wanted? Nor, supposing he found them, to persuade them to accompany him anywhere at all?

After sitting for some time with his head in his hands and the hood of the dark green cape drawn over his face, Tomas got up and stretched. He removed the cape, folded it and tucked it into his satchel. Then he took out his harp and sat down to play. There was little else to do, and he sought the eased spirit that music could give him.

Gods, he had needed this, the flow of music from head to hands, soothing him, stilling his thoughts. On and on he played, the notes drawing him in. Airs heard in Elfland or Dubhlinn; songs learned in Wessex; tunes he began to compose then and there. Patterning of notes to weave sounds in the air, and to measure Time by sound. Time well-measured, and never better spent than in this fashion. Before long he caught himself smiling. He closed his eyes, dissolved into the harpstrings.

A melody much to his liking eventually appeared. Wishing for

Linley's lute and voice, Tomas sang:

> And so it seems my road stops here:
> I'm lost within this hall of birds,
> though Thought and Memory may appear,
> and Truth will speak in all my words.
>
> Commanded by an Elven Queen,
> a Magician's oath with Fate,
> given music, Truth and Sight,
> I came to Asgard's gate.
> I came to Asgard's gate.
>
> Not more and not less than a Fool,
> picked by the Sisters at their loom
> to crush Asgard and Elfland both?
> Between three worlds I've carried doom.
>
> A thousand memories in this hall,
> each blacker than the ravens' wings.
> A thousand thoughts that turn and twist
> away from what the morrow brings,
> away from what the morrow brings.
>
> Which bird is Memory, which is Thought,
> I cannot tell; I'm not so wise.
> I know too little of the Truth;
> I have believed too many lies.

Without singing, Tomas played the tune a second time and a third. The melody needn't be changed. The words would require more work, but he could neglect his flute no longer. He stretched, shook out his hands and reached for the harp's wrappings.

Two ravens, perched on a bench at right angles to his own, were watching him closely. They hadn't been there when Tomas started playing. Average in size, neither sleek with youth nor feeble with age, the birds were in no way remarkable.

Until Tomas saw their eyes.

The harp cover fell forgotten from his hands, yet he wasn't afraid. Aubrey, while in horse-shape, did not have such eyes as these. Shining and black, a raven's eyes could look sharp and wary, even mischievous—but nothing like this. By comparison, the expression in the eyes of most men and women resembled that of beasts.

The ravens' eyes were conscious.

Conscious, ancient and dispassionate. The glance of both birds held intelligence, deep and subtle but far from identical. The mentality of one raven was logical, swift and observant. No less lucid, the other was more reflective, attuned to something beyond the present moment and the immediate surroundings. That mind was partly turned within, more convoluted than the first.

At first these perceptions came through Tomas's Sight: an undeniable and immediate awareness, tangible as a sound or a scent. Then, as he gazed at the ravens, something changed. There was a delicate probing at his mind, not like Moira's deft and confident insinuation of herself into his thoughts, but not tentative either. Were it a physical touch, it might have been produced by a finger just grazing the right-hand side of his forehead, near the hairline.

Not an invasion. A request.

Tomas stared into two sets of uncanny black eyes. He felt slightly disoriented, but the sensation was not unpleasant and produced no anxiety. In the air around the pair of birds, he saw none of the immaterial colors that he'd learned to associate with strong emotions. Nonetheless he sensed a certain uneasiness in the ravens. Tremors from the shifting earth of Asgard must have reached here, even without the keen hearing of most birds.

These were no ordinary birds. They were asking for admittance to Tomas's mind.

But Loki was a shape-shifter. So, for that matter, was Odin. If there were some way to ascertain the identity of these two ravens...

Tomas had true speech. He would attempt to name the birds. If he failed, he was wrong. And quite likely in danger from whomever the birds truly were.

Prepared to leap to his feet, Tomas sat on the very edge of the bench. "You are Thought," he said softly to the raven with the more restless mind, and to the other, "You are Memory."

The names, easily spoken, rang out in the airy hall. From both birds flowed silent agreement and receptiveness. And something more, that had the nature of both an offer and a question.

Names have power.

Awed, but accepting the trust that he felt, he said, "I am Tomas the Rhymer."

When he opened his awareness to the ravens, a tugging, an invitation, heated the skin of his brow and tingled his scalp. The birds wanted the communication to flow in both directions.

He met their brilliant dark eyes. Centering his attention in his forehead, Tomas reached out along an invisible line between himself and the ravens.

And found refusal halfway, like a wall of solid air. He stopped, puzzled. Thought and Memory held his gaze, then slowly and deliberately shut their eyes before the pulling came again.

This time Tomas shut his eyes as well, and encountered no barrier.

The first thing he noticed was the disappearance of his sense of smell. The musty odor of the hall, the sweat and dirt stains on his clothes, even the freshness of the air filtering in through the high windows, all evaporated. The taste of his own mouth went flat. But the slightest movement of every blade of straw upon the floor and in each nest rang in Tomas's ears, with the exaggerated rustling of feathers all about. Vastly louder, the flock's cawing was almost meaningful. If he listened long enough...

A picture leapt into focus in Tomas's mind: himself, playing the harp within this hall. Accurate in every detail, the scene showed the smallest of rips in his jerkin, his filthy and calloused bare feet, down to the bemused sideways tilt of his unkempt head. But the image was small, seen from above, with each separate motion of his hands upon the harpstrings not so much slowed as profoundly *noticed*.

It was how the ravens had first seen him.

With that realization, something shifted in Tomas's midsection. It was an increasing tautness rather than nausea. Lyrics echoed in his skull: 'Though Thought and Memory may appear, and truth will speak in all my words.'

He had continued to see the picture of himself within the hall. Now, as if in answer to the phrases in his mind, Thought and Memory flew into the image, and the sensation in Tomas's belly took on a more urgent note.

It was a question. Why was Tomas here, and why had he summoned the ravens with his song?

He concentrated on projecting a carefully worded message that he'd intended no summoning, though he'd wanted to find Thought and Memory.

Nothing happened, and the urgency remained. Of course: the ravens didn't communicate in words.

How did one experience *seeking*, within the body?

As an alertness akin to hunger. A restless darting tension behind the eyes. A pull in every direction at once.

Tomas sent that quality of visceral awareness to the birds, with

308

a picture of himself shading his eyes to gaze into the distance. Next he tried an experiment; after forming an image of himself calling the ravens, he immediately blotted it out and aimed a wave of head-shaking denial at them.

Relieved comprehension flooded him in return, followed by inquiry: a quivering in his stomach. He hadn't summoned the birds, then, but why was he seeking them?

From the *Brilliant Dragon* departing Vestfold to Tomas's arrival at the ravens' hall in Asgard, he pictured his quest in a series of carefully constructed images. He included every person he'd met: mortal, Elf or other. And each place, within or between each world, and all of the events that happened there—or seemed to happen.

He left out nothing, conveyed no partial truths. And was so far from experiencing any fear that he did not even question that he felt none. Throughout the process, the birds' attentive concentration enfolded him like warm air.

When he finished, he cleared his mind's eye and waited. For several minutes, no pictures or emotions came. Sensing that his communication with the ravens wasn't over, Tomas was patient. The vividness and power of the image that finally appeared nearly caused him to leap from the bench.

It was Odin.

The stony-faced god was wrapped in an indigo cloak. His old broad-brimmed hat did not quite conceal His solitary narrowed eye, fierce and arrogant, the blue-purple color of ice in the twilight. Scars puckered His hollow eye socket; He stared grimly straight ahead. In one hand He held a spear, in the other an empty iron cage. It fell from Odin's grasp as Tomas watched.

The ravens' refusal and negation rose within him, tightening the muscles of his jaw. Thought and Memory were denying any claim the god once had upon them. They no longer cast their lot with Odin.

When the vision faded, Tomas leaned bonelessly forward until his head rested on his knees. His eyes were still shut, his breathing ragged with shock. The Age was shifting indeed.

An unexpected flash of agreement came from the birds, with a quick view of the devastated earth of Asgard. Again Tomas felt their uneasiness.

And his own. The dizziness gone, he straightened up but kept his eyes closed. No sooner had he regained an upright position than an overwhelming torrent of images poured into his mind.

First he saw himself--with Thought and Memory on his shoulders. He reeled in disbelief: he wasn't a god.

Agreement from the ravens, but the vision stayed. Behind it grew a complex and many-layered picture with a curving line down its center.

The nine worlds, joined by Yggdrasil.

Tomas recognized Asgard and Vanaheim, homes of the Aesir and the Vanir. Alfheim, and Svartalfheim where the dark Elves lived. Jotunheim of the giants. Nidavellir, realm of the dwarves. The land of fire, Muspellheim. And Hel's dominion, Niflheim, from which he averted his attention. All the worlds looked blurred and nebulous in varying degrees, and were gradually floating away from each other and from Yggdrasil.

All but Midgard, the Middle Realm.

The superimposed picture of Tomas and the ravens moved from Asgard to Midgard to Alfheim–Elfland--and hovered briefly over Elfland before going to the rest of the nine worlds in turn. With the image's motion came a query that Tomas was slow to comprehend.

After an instant, the picture of himself moved from Asgard to Midgard, where it stopped. A tightness in his midsection, the questioning grew until he began to perspire.

The birds wanted to leave Asgard with Tomas. If he'd understood them correctly, they believed that he could travel with them between the worlds.

At their wave of assent, he sent them a despairing set of pictures. He could not do as Thought and Memory wished. Neither a god nor such a being as themselves, he didn't know how to travel between the worlds. He could only employ the Elf Queen's Runic passes to take the ravens to Uppsala. Moira had transformed Tomas's Sight and given him true speech, but he wasn't an Elf. He was wholly mortal.

Disagreement struck him hard in the temples; they stung as if hit by hot pebbles. He rubbed his head, then twined his hands in his hair. What, precisely, were the birds denying? He tried to deepen his shallow breathing. He wasn't an Elf; of that he was certain.

Accord from the ravens.

He was wholly mortal.

Negation, swift and vehement.

Partly mortal, then? Did he have Elf blood?

Thought and Memory's agreement exploded in Tomas's mind, then shook his body in a small series of tremors. "*What?*" His eyes flew open; he rose in stupefaction from the bench. He'd gone mad. He was dreaming.

The ravens flew to perch on his shoulders; two sets of claws

310

dug into his jerkin. He was awake and the birds were alive, or if not alive as mortals are, were most definitely solid. Their plumage gave off a warm feathery scent.

Tomas picked up the harp cover, twisted it in his hands. Mindlessly, he wrapped it about the harp and put the instrument back in the satchel. "I have Elf blood?" he whispered, still standing. "But I'm half Norse and half Welsh." Sigtrygg was wholly Norse, beyond a doubt. But Tomas's mother...

Thought and Memory understood his astonishment, if not his words. The strong claws flexed and shifted their grip. An image came, this time with Tomas's eyes wide open, of himself seated calmly on the bench. Overlaid on the airy hall, the vision had a horribly disorienting effect.

The birds wanted him to sit down. His head spinning, Tomas sat. He closed his eyes.

An insistent tingle at the base of his skull almost made him bolt up again, not so much from the sensation but from what he perceived was its intent. The tingling carried an application for admittance to a different part of his awareness, a part about which he felt strangely vulnerable--his memory.

But he'd come this far with the ravens, and his Sight had given him every indication that he should trust them. Slowly, he forced himself to relax and to focus his mind.

Tomas had just grown big enough to scramble onto the tallest sleeping bench without a boost, and was so proud of this new accomplishment that he spent as much time there as possible. One summer morning, he found his uncle Anselm's knife upon that bench.

The weapon was attached to Anselm's belt, tossed onto his tunic when he stepped outside for a wash. Short and wooden-handled, the knife was clean and sharp. Tomas drew it curiously from its leather sheath and touched the flat of the shining blade. He dropped it immediately and started to sniffle.

Hearing him, his mother came to his side. "Did you cut yourself?" she asked in the Welsh that she and Tomas spoke when Sigtrygg wasn't present.

"No." Tomas gave his eyes a hasty wipe. "But the knife hurt my hand. It's colder than snow and it smells bad."

His mother shot him an intent look as she resheathed the blade. "Best not to touch things that don't belong to you. Especially weapons. When you're older--" She glanced at the open door to the yard. "Tomas, when you're older, you'll learn to use a knife. And a sword, and spears and axes too."

"They all stink." He thrust out his chin. "This one was little, so I thought it wouldn't. But it did, and it hurt my hand."

"Hush. Come with me." She hurried him outdoors. After crossing the sunny yard and waving to Anselm, they made for the cow byre, empty but for a dozing cat and her kittens. The cattle were all turned out to graze. Inside, the byre was shadowy and cool, and smelled faintly of fresh milk.

Tomas's mother dropped to her knees beside him in the clean straw. "When I was a little girl, iron pained me the same way, but I learned not to let it. And so must you. You'll be obliged to handle iron far more than I do."

He had never seen her look so serious. "Why does it hurt us?"

"You must not ask me that. I don't know." Her eyes filled with tears. "I don't want to know. It's wrong to ask."

"But why?" he persisted, disturbed that she would cry.

She gave him a crushing hug. "Jesus says we shouldn't ask about such things, Tomas. Please."

Jesus and Odin. He would never understand.

"When you touch iron, you must think of something else. Or ask Jesus not to let it hurt you. Here, hold this." She reached for a cowbell. "Tell me when it doesn't trouble you any more. I know you can do it. I did, and I think it bothered me more than it does you."

"Why?"

"Don't ask me that!" She pressed the cowbell into his hand.

He soon learned not to let iron pain him--his mother gave him no peace until he did. But he never cared to handle that particular metal. More and more he turned from the weapons training that obsessed his father and brothers, and at which Tomas was mediocre at best, to throw himself into music and rhyme. For which, all his teachers agreed, he showed decided gifts.

It was largely because of those gifts that Sigtrygg, ambitious to have a court poet in the family, eventually declared his Welsh concubine's son a free man.

Tomas needed air. The drafty hall of black birds was a shock after his vivid recollection of the dim byre that smelled of warm sweaty cows. And his long-dead mother's pale tired face, no older than Tomas was now, her grey eyes wide with strain, insisting that he learn to control the iron-sick...

Standing, he wiped his clammy palms on his trousers. The

312

ravens still perched on his shoulders, Memory on the left and Thought on the right. Picking up his satchel, Tomas carried it to the door.

He stepped outside into starry darkness, alive with bitter but sporadic gusts of wind. Night fell in Asgard, then. The Sun and Moon must rise and set here much as they did in Midgard, unlike in Faerie.

He had Elf blood.

CHAPTER FIFTY-FIVE: TO MOVE BETWEEN THE WORLDS

Numbly, wanting to put distance between himself and the ravens' hall, Tomas headed across the broken fields of Asgard towards the rise he had crossed with Loki. After perhaps thirty paces, a prolonged splintering noise ripped the air at Tomas's back. He spun, and on his shoulders Thought and Memory flapped their wings to keep their balance.

The near corner of the ravens' hall had collapsed, its timbers cracked and fallen to the ground. Dust rose from the crumbling thatch, with minute particles of straw, ghostly specks beneath the stars. Birds shot from the windows and through the raw-edged wound at the near end of the building. Cawing, they arrowed in all directions, like black salt poured into the blacker sky. Another section of the roof gave way with a great tearing sound and sagged slowly earthward as Tomas watched.

The two ravens with him dug their claws into his jerkin with such convulsive strength that he flinched in surprise. He was even more startled by a vivid image of Odin's stark, dour face, His glacial eye warily darting from side to side. Odin was kneeling by the side of a prone fair-haired figure who must be Balder. A cluster of concerned faces surrounded the two gods.

Apparently the opening of Tomas's memory to the ravens had created a deeper and more fluid bond with them than he'd realized till now. His stomach knotted in response to their anxiety. They were urging him to get as far from the birds' hall as possible, for Odin had sensed a disturbance there.

Shrugging his arms through the straps of his pack, Tomas hurried on his way. The ragged empty terrain made him feel dangerously exposed. When he finally reached what was left of the once-thick stand of woods atop the ridge, he slipped into the welcome concealment of the trees.

Leaf mold, spongy and damp, muffled his passage through the underwood. He picked his way through fallen branches, acquiring scratches on his arms and hands in the process. His five-fingered hands. Had there been six...

How many other signs of his heritage had his mother taught him to forget? How much Elf ancestry did she possess, and how much did he? He pushed some twisted vines out of his face and kept moving.

He was no more than one-quarter Elf, assuming that his mother was at most half. But enough of that alien current flowed in Tomas's blood to account for the return of the iron-sick and for his steadily blood to account for the return of the iron-sick and for his steadily increasing Sight. As well as for the changes in how his body looked and moved since his voyage to Faerie.

Enough to explain why he'd seen the Nornir at their loom, and why he was suited to Moira's task. "Your Welsh blood is attuned to us," she had said. Did she realize that Elf stock mingled with the Welsh? Hard to imagine she would not have seen it. But Moira had her limits. She and Aubrey were startled at how quickly and to what degree the gifts of true speech and prophecy had augmented Tomas's Sight. Moira seemed unlikely to send someone with Elf blood to steal an iron key. Probably she had not known, though he could see arguments for both sides of that question.

He emerged from the last stand of trees on the ridge. The night was exceptionally clear, and the fitful wind kept any clouds away. From long habit, Tomas glanced up at the stars.

Puzzled, he craned his neck and stared overhead while he started down the other side of the slope. The sky was glittering, sprinkled with light. But this was not the summer night all sailors knew. Unable even to locate Odin's Wain, Tomas shivered as he walked. Where was Asgard drifting, that the very stars were strange? Would Elfland's fading harm him too?

An image of his own healthy unscarred body flashed through his mind. With the mental picture came a distinct impression that the deterioration of Faerie would not harm him physically.

That, he fully understood, recalling his reflection in Uppsala's Well—not all wounds are visible. But did that mean he was immortal?

At the ravens' negation, Tomas let out his breath. He could not have said why he felt so relieved. Shaking his head, he reached the blistered surface of the meadow and continued towards the rainbow bridge.

The tumbled embankments that he couldn't circle were much easier to climb, since the ground was no longer treacherously soft. He thought of Yggdrasil's rotted bark, and his vision of the nine worlds drifting apart. With each step he took away from the birds' hall, he sensed less tension in the ravens, but he knew they shared his desire to leave Asgard as quickly as possible.

He would not bring them to Moira at Uppsala. He had no wish to do so--and Thought and Memory were a power unto themselves now, not for anyone's giving or taking. Even if that were possible, Moira herself might have trouble meeting Tomas near the temple. The Elves would probably experience increasing difficulty in passing between the worlds. Particularly to Midgard, where belief turned from them.

But Tomas was neither wholly Elf nor wholly human, and he saw more worlds and truths than one. That might be why the ravens had chosen to come with him, at least for now.

Their prompt assent warmed him. He nodded acceptingly; they were welcome to accompany him wherever they pleased. Then he smiled, amused at himself. Were they not welcome, he had no notion how to dismiss them.

Recognizing the glimmer of the rainbow bridge reflected in the sky not far ahead, Tomas cast another curious glance at the unfamiliar heavens as he hurried on.

Faerie had no stars at all.

Did Moira know that Asgard's Fate was tied to that of Elfland? And that Tomas's meeting with Loki would-- He wasn't sure exactly what their encounter had done, but something had changed besides the upheaval of these fields he was now crossing. Loki had said that Moira must have known. Known what?

Tomas came to the circular edge of the meadow, and Bifrost, the rainbow bridge--or its remains. It was as though a sash of solid multicolored light had been cut at random, to stretch away in a truncated arc across the heavens. Plumes of smoke drifted in the spaces between the sections of the bridge and wafted along the meadow's sharply defined rim.

The disquieting thing was how the dome of stars ended as well, just above that curving perimeter. The earth and sky of Asgard were enfolded in a sphere of blackness, opaque and soft, pierced only by the remnants of the rainbow bridge. Even the wind slowed and died at the meadow's edge.

Tomas seated himself on a large flat-topped rock near the frayed beginnings of the bridge. Fluttering from his shoulder, Thought landed on the nearest variegated chunk that sloped onto the grass. Black head tilted, the raven studied the span of the bridge.

Where did it lead, he asked the birds.

Where did Tomas wish to go?

A good question, one he'd pondered all the way here. Not back to Uppsala and the godhi's sacrificial rope, although he sensed that it would now be far easier to evade such an attack. Memory's claws shifted their hold upon his jerkin.

Standing, Tomas began to pace. If he could ask Moira some questions, and watch her reaction when he did not present her with a pair of caged ravens. Could look straight into her eyes, and...

Look her in the eyes.

But not at Uppsala. And not in Faerie either, not in Moira's realm. If it were difficult for her to come to Midgard now, there might be some point in between--

Hecate's crossroads.

As he formed an image for the ravens, Thought flew back to Tomas's right shoulder. His link with the birds had improved, but he wanted to be absolutely sure they understood.

Carefully, he added himself and Moira to his mental picture of the crossroads, and concentrated on his desire to speak with her there. Then he aimed a question at the ravens: was such a meeting possible?

Agreement, prompt and unambiguous.

Eyeing the segmented bridge across the soft black void, Tomas tightened his satchel straps and flexed his hands. The ravens thought he could move between the worlds, and he believed them. Beliefs had power. But how did one begin such a journey?

He shifted uneasily where he stood. The sudden flapping of Thought's wings, beating the right side of Tomas's head, took him completely by surprise. Jerking his head to the left, he tried to duck out from under Thought's grip on his shoulder. But the raven clung to Tomas's shirt and uttered a single loud caw in his ear. When he got a brief but terrifying impresssion of Odin's enraged face, Tomas understood that the god had just realized that Thought and Memory intended to leave Asgard--and with whom.

From Loki's scornful howls of laughter, echoing in Tomas's mind, it was only too clear how Odin had come by that news. But Odin's single eye was rolling wildly; He did not know where the ravens were. Not yet.

Tomas had very little time to learn to travel between the worlds.

Mother Aud had said that he did not look far enough beneath the surface of things, nor ask the right questions. "Will yourself to look long and deeply at everything, until you perceive the core of it. And especially at yourself," she had told him.

At himself? He was a skald, his flute and harp of Elvish make. And a far traveler. He had Elf blood, true speech and the Sight: he saw more than one truth.

The only route he could attempt might be madness, pure and simple, but the mustering of all his Sight presented him with no other path. He would bend that Sight to the perception of Hecate's crossroads: the truth of it. And, he hoped, of its location in both Time and Space, or beyond them. And not least within himself, though that was something he didn't entirely comprehend.

The air between himself and the rainbow bridge began to swirl and glow. Phosphorescence eddied about his head and coalesced into a pearly gleaming fog. So thick it was that he lost sight of Bifrost and the lightless void it spanned. He couldn't even see the meadow at his feet.

But he could feel his body, lean and tense, the wiry strength and the weariness in all his limbs, and the ravens' spasmodic grip upon his shoulders. Shutting his eyes, he visualized the crossroads.

He remembered the place well, with its three glittering lanes. Where the tracks met was a statue carved of pale stone. A woman with three faces. Each face bore an imprint of the waxing, full or waning Moon: maiden, woman, crone. He knew those faces; he had met them. All but one, perhaps, or a certain aspect of one.

The roads were not precisely as Moira had described them. They didn't lead to Hel, Elfland and the realm of the Nazarene god. But Tomas sensed that the lanes were somehow connected to Hecate's three faces, and to three other beings.

Urd, Verdandi and Skuld. That-which-has-become, that-which-is-becoming, that-which-shall-become. The Nornir.

Past, present and future. Outside Tomas, and within him.

He had arrived.

Tomas blinked at the statue of Hecate and the empty platter at her feet. The mist of Asgard was gone. He stood in front of the mature woman's face; the full Moon's image gleamed from her untroubled brow.

To his surprise the journey had given him no disorientation, no discomfort at all. Thought and Memory perched calmly on his shoulders: a good sign. Stretching, Tomas looked curiously about the crossroads.

Three hard and well-packed lanes still met here, but they were trackless and empty. He saw no bramble-covered road, no wide and easy passage, no Elf hall crowning hills of green. Except for the ravens and the statue, he was alone.

Furrowing his brow, he considered the plate at Hecate's feet. Then, following an impulse he only half understood, he took the faded apple blossom from his satchel and set it on the platter.

"Moira," he said softly but clearly. "Tomas the Rhymer wishes to speak with you at Hecate's crossroads."

CHAPTER FIFTY-SIX: AT THE CROSSROADS AGAIN

Sighting down each lane in turn, Tomas half-expected to see Moira walking along one of them. She might materialize a few feet from him instead. Aubrey might bear her to the crossroads in horse-shape, perhaps, or Rhys accompany her here.

Tomas weighed the last two possibilities; it might be wise to fear them more than he did. The threat of Hel was gone, but the pooka and the Elf King could be perilous in different ways.

While Moira represented dangers of her own.

Still, so much had changed. The ravens dozed upon Tomas's shoulders. Willing himself to relax, he sat down and settled into a long reflective wait. He didn't feel particularly patient, but he was calm.

He was gazing at the statue and debating whether to play his flute, when he heard Moira's resonant briny voice, soft with fatigue.

"Tomas the Rhymer."

His chest tightened. Rising, he turned and faced her.

She wore her travel-stained, dark green trousers and tunic. Glossy black hair spilled down her back. Her face was the bloodless shade of newly carved ivory, with the hollows at cheekbone and temple somewhat deeper now and the wide coral mouth compressed the slightest bit. Tension showed in the set of her pointed chin, and where the exquisite sweep of a not-quite-human jawline curved into her delicate throat. But her carriage was still poised and graceful, and her head held high.

The huge grey eyes, deeply shadowed, widened as they took in Tomas and the ravens. He would not have thought it possible for her to grow more pale, yet she did. "Elf blood," she whispered, pressing a narrow hand to her lips.

"You didn't know," he said, feeling a vague unfocused sadness. And some mistrust, but there was little heat in that, and little fear.

It was not a question, but she shook her head. "That explains much," she murmured.

"There was a whole flock of ravens in Asgard," Tomas said without inflection. "Did you know that?"

She shook her head again, staring at Thought and Memory. "But I came to fear something of the sort, when the drifting grew worse." Her voice was so low that Tomas scarcely caught the words.

"Elfland's drifting or that of Asgard?" he asked. "They are linked."

Moira's nod was bitter. Then, holding Memory's gaze, the Elf

319

Queen stood motionless. A blunt but respectful inquiry moved through her grey eyes, followed by wistfulness and a passionate regret. Next there was a spasm of pain, intense and hopeless and laced with fatigue. Before the depth and ancientness of that pain, Tomas took an involuntary step backwards.

As he did, Moira's eyes turned flat and stark. The glance she gave Tomas was cool and shuttered, full of self-protective reserve. It was the look of a dice player who'd thrown and lost a final, mighty and ill-calculated toss--and house, ship and lands in the bargain.

"You gave Loki the mistletoe?" she asked tonelessly.

"I traded it. For the key to the ravens' hall."

"How did you find Thought and Memory?"

"They weren't there at first. I was playing your harp--" Moira stirred but said nothing, so Tomas continued, "When I looked up, they had come."

An unfocused and unseeing stare. "We are undone. And so much of that can be traced to my own hand."

It was past time for Tomas's questions. "Moira?"

With a small start, she looked at him. Her shuttered expression was back.

Remembering something Loki told him, Tomas said quietly, "The Nornir intended to drop my thread."

Moira's eyes flickered, then returned to his face. Nodding, she pushed a hand through her heavy black hair. "The Fool has become a Magician, it would seem."

Perhaps. He didn't feel like a Magician now, though he might be less of a fool. "And Hel? She could have picked up that thread?"

"That was one of your futures."

Loki had asked if Tomas thought there was nothing but order in the universe, and had called him a fool... "And you, Moira?"

Another shifting of her eyes. "I took your thread, but only briefly. One might rather say that the two skeins ran together." Glancing down at her worn green tunic, she smoothed it with her fingers. "But your thread has passed from my hands or those of Hel and into your own, Tomas." She studied the ravens. "Tell me, what will you do? Where will you go when you leave here?"

Tomas had intended to ask if the gift of true speech would remain with him--but he knew, with growing certainty, that it would. Nor did he care. True speech would still cause him some uncomfortable moments in Midgard, no doubt. But he would no longer travel there as a hunted and bewildered fugitive.

He recognized the possibilities and limitations inherent to his

320

gifts--and to his nature, which was his Fate.

Moira was watching him. He considered carefully but found no reason to hide his plans, such as they were. "First to Birka, I think. Then Dubhlinn."

She nodded slowly.

"And Wessex, perhaps. After that, I don't know." He paused. "It might be hard to stay in any one place in Midgard for long."

Her smile was ironic with comprehension. "True speech is not the gentlest gift. Nor is the Sight."

"You told me I would find that mortals loved truth less than Elves."

"We do not always love it." Her mouth twisted. After raking her hands through her hair, she gave him a milder look. "And the other worlds, Tomas, will you go there?"

"Perhaps. Should I have reason to."

"And Elfland?"

The hint of warmth in Moira's voice, the gentler expression in her face, alarmed him. "I don't know," he said cautiously. "The time lost there can be troublesome in Midgard."

There was appraisal in the Elf Queen's eyes, along with something not so hard-edged, almost mellow. In a mortal, Tomas might have called it friendliness. A shiver ran up his spine. But he felt no glimmering of the Sight, and the ravens were quiet on his shoulders.

"You will visit Midgard less," he said at random, and Moira agreed. He hesitated. "How is it in Elfland now?"

"We are constrained," she told him bleakly. "Our realm is shrinking as we move farther from the other worlds. Some of us have elected to remain in Midgard, but most will go among mortals less often."

"What will become of you?" he asked, unable to imagine that she would choose to dwell in Midgard.

Another measuring glance. "The Elves? Or myself?"

"Both."

"We will change," said Moira. "Not die. We are immortal. We have no souls as humans know them, to move from one mortal body to the next with no memory of that passage."

Chilled and fascinated, Tomas was puzzled by Moira's attitude. It was neither condescending nor acrimonious. The subject was distressing to her, but she wanted him to understand.

"In Midgard, Elves are creatures of the natural world, the elements. Wood and water, wind and stone." She gave him a faint smile. "And more besides. Some of us will consciously assume those forms. And live apart, rather than live in Faerie as it will become."

He wet his lips, repelled, yet with some dim corner of his mind intrigued. His own Elf blood, perhaps. To pass into the Earth... "Can you change back again?"

"Yes. If one so desires, or is called. One's mind alters somewhat, you see."

"Moira, do you plan to--"

"Live apart? Not yet, if ever I do."

As she gazed at him, Tomas felt the Elf's ambivalence and grief, mingled with that strange new desire for comprehension. And other layers of motive that he could sense but not quite perceive, not even when he bent all his Sight to the task.

After a long moment of mutual scrutiny, for his reasons and for hers, Moira held out her hand to him.

Tomas stared. What was this? With a whir of black wings, both ravens left his shoulders and flew down to the surface of one of the glittering lanes.

She took a step towards him, and another. No longer remote, her grey eyes were tender. Vulnerable rather than seductive, as they had been in Waleis. Conciliatory. Open.

Between shock and amazement, Tomas didn't move. Moira came to him, looked him full in the face. Her expression was tentative and yielding.

She slipped her arms around his neck. He stood like a stone as the Elf buried her supple hands in his tangled blond hair.

Her touch was as warm as he remembered. Warmer. Inhaling, he caught a scent of briar roses, rich and dizzying, that he remembered too. The slanting grey eyes that had haunted him were very close. Shadowed with fatigue and endurance, they searched his expression, but Moira made no attempt to reach into Tomas's mind. He sensed respect in that granting of privacy--or a desire for privacy of her own.

Her lips parted. Tomas knew how soft and pliant they were, how they tasted, their lingering and articulate pressure on his skin. He was trembling even before Moira leaned the length of her body against him. Astonished beyond reason, he felt her draw his head down to her upturned face.

"No, Moira," he said very gently, and gently removed her arms from around his neck. He released her wrists; he stepped away. And thought of saying he'd not be deceived the same way twice. Of saying harsher words than that, despite knowing that Moira had been as constrained, in her own way, as she in turn had constrained him.

Still, while feeling the presence of secrets he couldn't fully discern, he realized that it would not have been quite the same. Her motivation must differ now; her earlier goal had failed and was lost. And while there was not equality between them, their roles had shifted. No, Moira's second invitation came from something closer to her core. If she had approached me so to begin with, thought Tomas dully, and shoved the thought aside.

Had she approached him with no secondary motives and no secrets now, as transparent as fresh water, he still would have refused. He didn't trust her. Too much pain lay in the way.

Moira stood and gazed at him. Her expression was absolutely neutral, her hands relaxed at her sides. She looked more lifeless than the statue of Hecate that Tomas had put between them.

The silence lengthened as they faced each other. Apologies were not at issue--unless, perhaps, Moira made them to him. And that, Tomas knew, she would not do.

"I am leaving now," he told her in courteous tones, having said all he wanted to say.

Her nod was formal.

Thought and Memory settled back onto Tomas's shoulders before he resumed his wandering road.

EPILOGUE

Moira watched as Tomas began his departure from Hecate's crossroads. Closing his eyes, he turned his attention inward and to his next destination: Birka, most probably.

Flanked by a raven on either shoulder, Tomas's gaunt sun-browned face took on a bemused expression that showed his Elf blood even more clearly. Moira wasn't surprised that Tomas no longer needed Runic passes to move from world to world; most adepts could quickly dispense with such gestures. Still, when Tomas vanished, it was with a hint of mortal clumsiness: a quirkish little rippling of the air around his tall thin body.

Moira smiled a bit. Still a novice at this method of travel, was Tomas. But that would change. Magicians soon learned their artfully patterned way through Space and Time, and this particular Magician, though newly come to self-awareness, could already manipulate the energies with far more skill than most. And with Thought and Memory accompanying him... Moira shook her head. Before long, Tomas would disappear as easily as a good intention.

Perhaps she should have told him that she was carrying their child.

She could have given him those tidings a few moments ago. But first it had seemed important to weigh his disposition towards her, because it might bear upon the manner and localities in which their offspring would be raised. She wanted to determine Tomas the Rhymer's attitude towards herself alone: Moira, Queen of Elfland that was, and of whatever it might yet become. Not his disposition towards the Elf woman whom he'd gotten with child.

In that Moira had sensed no hatred for her, Tomas's attitude did not displease her.

She had not foreseen this pregnancy. At times the Sight obstructed as much as it revealed, particularly where the individual Seer was concerned--and the patterning of Tomas's thread would never be orderly, nor easy to predict.

That thread had run together with her own.

Unlike Tomas, any children of theirs would grow up aware of the two currents in their blood. Moira wished it so. She felt confident that when she told Tomas, who had spent virtually all of his life in ignorance of his own heritage, he would second that wish. Tell him she would, eventually. In Midgard or in Elfland, their paths would cross again.

She went to stand before the statue of Hecate.

Maiden, mother, crone.

Absently, Moira gazed up into the face of the woman who wore the full Moon of the Mother on her forehead. More than half Elf this infant would be, yet mortal. But until Moira gave birth, that mixed lineage was all that she could foretell of their child's nature--and its Fate.

GLOSSARY

Aesir: one of the two types of Norse gods; by the Viking Age, thought to be higher in rank and power than the Vanir or fertility gods

Alfheim: Norse realm of the light Elves

Alfred the Great: c. 848-899; king of the West Saxons or Wessex, from 871-c. 899

Ansuz: Rune of Omens and Messages, Loki's Rune

Asgard: Norse realm of the gods called the Aesir

Athils: said by Norse saga writers to have been a sixth-century king of the Svea people in what is now Sweden

aurar: a Norse unit of money. Eight aurar made up one mark.

Balder: the mildest Norse god, whose foretold death signals the beginning of Ragnarok

Berkana: the Birch Goddess, Rune of Growth and Rebirth, Rune of the Mother

berserkers: piratical worshippers of Odin to whom the god granted violent and fearless trances

Bifrost: the rainbow bridge connecting Asgard to other realms

Birka: c. 800-1000 A.D., a Norse trading town on the island of Bjorko or Birch Island, in Lake Malar in what is now Sweden

Blessed of the Mothers: a Welsh name for the Elves

Brisingamen: the love goddess Freyja's golden necklace

clinker-built hull: a ship's hull with overlapping planks, making a boat light, flexible and leaky

draug: an evil Norse sea spirit who appeared to sailors in danger

Ehwaz: the Horse-Rune, Rune of Movement and Cooperation

Éire: Ireland

Elementals: spirits composed of only one Element: fire, earth, air or water

Fair Folk: British Isles name for the Elves

Fehu: Rune of Possessions and Nourishment

fenodyree: a Welsh brownie, a small house-Elf

fossegrimen: a Norse water-Elf who plays the fiddle near rivers and mills

Fimbulvetr: the three years' winter that will precede Ragnarok, the battle and fall of the Aesir

Freyja: Norse goddess of love, beauty and fertility. Half the warriors slain in battle are hers, and half are Odin's.

Freyr: Norse god of fertility and harvests, Freyja's brother

Frigg: Odin's wife, said to be perhaps the wisest of the Aesir

gentry: an Irish name for the Elves

godhi: a Norse priest or judge

grave mounds: The Norse often buried royalty in mounds, sometimes in ships

hafvilla: condition of a Norse ship fogged in and lost at sea

Hagalaz: the Hail-Rune, Rune of Disruption and Irresistible Forces

Hecate: Greek or Thracian goddess of triple aspect--Maiden, Mother, Crone--who rules crossroads, turning points, magic, night, the dark, and women's mysteries

Heimdall: the watchman of the Norse gods

Hel: daughter of Loki and a troll, the Norse goddess of the dead in Niflheim. The dead not taken by Odin or Freyja belong to Hel.

Hlidskjalf: Odin's high seat from which he surveys all nine realms

huldre-folk: Norse term for the Elves; literally, the Hidden People

Isa: the Ice-Rune, Rune of Waiting

Ivar the Boneless: a fabled and dreaded Viking Age pirate captain

Ivar of Dubhlinn: a Norse king of Dubhlinn during the Viking Age. Brother of Olaf the White, Ivar first ruled Limerick and took over the governing of Dubhlinn in 870 when Olaf was recalled to what would become Norway.

Jotunheim: Norse realm of the giants

Kenaz: Rune of Opening, Ingenuity and Fire

knorr: a Norse merchanter ship, broader than the dragon-craft, with a taller mast

Laguz: Rune of Water, Release and the Sea

Lake Malar: a nearly land-locked lake in what is now Sweden

land-spirits: each land was thought by the Norse to have indigenous spirits, Elves and Elementals

Lode Star: the Pole star

Loki: a fiery Norse demigod, a trickster whose Fate was to bring down the gods

mark: a Norse unit of money. One mark weighed eight aurar.

Memory: one of Odin's ravens

Midgard: the Middle Realm, Norse realm of the mortals

Mjollnir: Hammer of Thor, the Norse thunder-god, much favored by working people

Moors: generic and loosely applied Viking Age term for the inhabitants of Spain and North Africa

Muspellsheim: Norse realm of elemental fire

Nauthiz: Rune of Constraint, Necessity and the Forging of Character

Nidavellir: Norse realm of the dwarves

Niflheim: misty realm of the dead who were neither Odin's, slain in battle, nor claimed by Freyja

Nornir: the three Norse Fates, the sisters Urd, Verdandi and Skuld, or Fate, Being and Necessity. They rule the past, present and future, and even the Aesir are subject to them.

Odin: the chief Norse god, of war, magic, poetry and the dead, favored by aristocrats, warriors, skalds and those who attempt to wield magic

Odin's Wain: Norse name for the Big Dipper

People of Peace: British Isles name for the Elves

Perthro: Rune of the Web of Fate

pooka: a shape-shifting Welsh water-Elf who often appears as a horse

Ragnarok: the destruction of the Norse gods and their realms, Asgard and Vanaheim

Raido: Rune of Journeys, Rune of Method

Ratatosk: a squirrel that runs up and down the world axle-tree, Yggdrasil

Runes: both an alphabet and an oracle, each Rune standing for a letter and a specific divinatory meaning

Saefren: now the Severn river between England and Wales

Sami: the nomadic Lapplanders' name for themselves

Sessrumnir: the goddess Freyja's hall in Asgard, where Her subjects among the slain dwelt with Her

Sidhe: an Irish name for the Elves

skald: a Norse bard, a poet and a musician

Skuld: the third Norse Fate, who rules the Future or Necessity

sounding-lead: a length of line with a weight, used to check water depth

Sowing-Tide: a Norse month in the spring, when crops were planted

steerboard: an oar attached to the right-hand side of Norse boats as both rudder and tiller, from which our nautical term "starboard" derives.

Sun-Month: a Norse month in midsummer

sunstone: a transparent piece of feldspar, held up to the open sky by Norse sailors to locate the Sun in cloudy weather

Svartalfheim: Norse realm of the dark Elves, who seem to have been synonymous with the dwarves

Svea: Norse name for the people who gave their name to modern Sweden

Thing: a Norse local assembly of government where the laws were recited and cases heard.

Thor: Norse god of thunder and strength, much admired by the common people

Thought: one of Odin's ravens

thrall: a slave or largely indentured servant

Tuatha de Danaan: an Irish name for the Elves

Tylwyth Teg: a Welsh name for the Elves

Uppland: part of what is now Sweden

Uppsala: an Uppland town with a temple to the Norse gods, where their worship probably lasted into the late eleventh century

Urd: the first of the Norse Fates, who rules Fate and the past

Valaskjalf: another of Odin's halls.

Valholl: Old Norse term for Valhalla, Odin's hall of warrior dead in Asgard

Vanaheim: Norse realm of the gods called the Vanir

Vanir: one of the two types of Norse gods, gods of fertility, the sea and the winds

Verdandi: the second of the Norse Fates, who rules Being and the present

Vestfold: a kingdom in ninth-century southern Norway

Waleis: what is now modern Wales

Wessex: what is now southwest England, mostly Wiltshire, Somerset and Hampshire.

Yggdrasil: the world axle-tree that connects the nine worlds of Norse cosmology

THE ORIGINAL LEGEND OF THOMAS THE RHYMER

The original legend contains no blending of Norse and Celtic traditions, as in my novel. Four British manuscripts dating from the fourteenth to the sixteenth centuries record the tale, though it may be far older. A fifth text lists only prophecies attributed to Thomas. The manuscripts are now in the Lincoln Cathedral library, the Cambridge University library and the British Museum. Damaged by fire, rain-water, poor re-copying and sheer age, the manuscripts tell the story of one Thomas of Erceldoune--now Earlstoun--in the Scots border country.

The legend has been re-worked by many folklorists, including the novelist Sir Walter Scott, who composed a ballad about Thomas. In fact, Scott grew so enamored of the tale that he bought land near Earlston, where he landscaped a "Rhymer's Glen." The modern folk group Steeleye Span has recorded their version of Scott's ballad.

In the original texts, Thomas is lying on Huntlie Bank, when a beautiful woman rides by on a grey horse. He meets her at the Eildon Tree, kneels, and asks if she's the Queen of Heaven (an ancient name for the Goddess).

Her answer, taken from the manuscripts, as is the rest of the material in quotation marks, gives the sense of the old tale:

"Thomas, let such words be! For Queen of Heaven I am not; I took never so high degree. I am of another country."

Thomas says, "Lovely lady, as thou art wise, give me leave to lie thee by."

The Elf Queen warns Thomas that the act will mar her beauty but, smitten, he plights his troth, "whether thou wilt to Heaven or Hell."

"And, as the story telleth right,
Seven times by her he lay.
She said, "Mortal man, thou likes thy play.
What bride in bower could deal with thee?
Thou marrest me here this long day,
I pray thee, Thomas, let me be!"

She takes Thomas to Faerie, saying, "Take thy leave of Sun and Moon, and all the leaves that grow on trees. This twelvemonth shalt thou with me go, and middle Earth thou shalt not see."

"This deed will work me woe," says Thomas, "for my soul follows where my body fares."

For three days, they ride "through water to the knee." The Elf Queen shows Thomas three roads: to Heaven, Hell and her own country. She forbids him to speak to anyone but her during his stay, or her lord will know that Thomas is her lover. Lest her lord suspect something, her beauty had to vanish during the journey but now reappears.

During his time in Faerie, Thomas mingles with Elf lords and ladies, hears music, attends banquets and dances, but speaks only to the Queen. After what seems merely days yet is actually several years, the Queen says she must return Thomas to middle Earth, because a fiend of Hell is coming to claim its regular sacrifice from Elfland. Since Thomas is "a fair man and gentle," he would probably be chosen by the fiend.

Thomas objects, but the Queen takes him back to the Eildon Tree. He asks for "some token, that I may say I spoke with thee."

"To harp or carp, Thomas, take thy choice with thee," she says, apparently offering him the choice of excelling in music or in voice.

He chooses voice, "for tongue is chief of minstrelsy."

Whereupon she informs him, "Tongue is thing that fast will bind. If thou will speak, or tales tell, Thomas, thou shalt never lie."

Beware those ambiguous Elfin gifts!

Thomas requests some predictions about events in the border country and discovers that because of his true speech, he can prophesy on his own. He weeps at the thought that the Elf Queen is leaving him forever. The manuscripts are muddled at this point, but she seems to promise to meet him at the Eildon tree whenever she can. "I shall reckon (or, "I shall know you") wherever I (thou) go, to hear the price of courtesy."

The Eildon Tree was probably a huge thorn tree, named for the Eildon Hills near Melrose. "The Rhymer's Thorn" was blown down in a nineteenth century gale, but the Eildon Stone marks the location. Two fields close by could be Huntlie Brae or Bank. From the east end of Huntlie Brae, one sees the road and the hill as far as the Eildon Stone and the site of the tree. Earlston legend claims a "Rhymer's Tower," now in ruins at the west end of town. In 1294, nine and a half acres of "Rhymer's Lands" were given to Trinity College Church in Edinburgh.

True Thomas is supposed, subsequently, to have often met the Elf Queen and traveled back and forth to Faerie. He advised sovereigns in both worlds, because the gift of true speech rendered him so wise. Years after his initial return from Elfland, it is said, a hart and a hind were seen fearlessly wandering the streets of Earlston. Thomas followed them into the forest and was not seen again.

--Jodie Forrest
Chapel Hill, NC
Midsummer, 1995

333

Dragonship

IF YOU'VE ENJOYED *THE RHYMER AND THE RAVENS*...

* Look for the sequel, *The Elves' Prophecy*, coming soon from Seven Paws Press!

* Jodie Forrest's husband, Steven Forrest, wrote a rock opera based on *The Rhymer and the Ravens*. Jodie, Steven, and their band, Dragonship, are performing the show. Interested? Send a self-addressed stamped envelope to Seven Paws Press for details. **Or look for Seven Paws Press and Alpha Lyra Consulting on the World Wide Web:**
http://www.intrex.net/alyra7paws
email: alyra@intrex.net

* Jodie and Steven are professional astrological consultants and writers. For a catalogue about the Forrests' astrological work, send $1.00 (credited towards your first order) to:
Alpha Lyra Consulting, POB 2345, Chapel Hill, NC 27515 USA.
Or see our Web pages, address above.

* **To order additional copies of *The Rhymer and the Ravens*,** call, send, or FAX your name, address, phone number and payment (check, money order, or V/MC number with expiration date) to:
Seven Paws Press
POB 2345, Chapel Hill, NC 27515 USA
919-929-4287; fax 919-929-7092

$13.95 per copy, plus 6% tax for NC residents. $18.75 in Canada.
No COD orders. US postage paid courtesy of Seven Paws Press.
Canada/Mexico surface rate postage: $2.50 per book.
Other foreign surface rate postage: $5.00 per book
Foreign air mail book rate postage: $8.50 per book

Dealer and distributor inquiries welcome.